AMERICAN SUBVERSIVE

A NOVEL

DAVID GOODWILLIE

Scribner

New York London Toronto Sydney

Simon & Schuster, Inc.
1230 Avenue of the Americas
New York, NY 10020

First Scribner hardcover edition April 2010

SCRIBNER and design are registered trademarks of The Gale Group, Inc.,
used under license by Simon & Schuster, Inc., the publisher of this work.

For information about special discounts for bulk purchases, please contact
Simon & Schuster Special Sales at 1-866-506-1949
or business@simonandschuster.com.

The Simon & Schuster Speakers Bureau can bring authors to your
live event. For more information or to book an event contact
the Simon & Schuster Speakers Bureau at 1-866-248-3049 or
visit our website at www.simonspeakers.com.

Designed by Carla Jayne Jones

Manufactured in the United States of America

3   5   7   9   10   8   6   4

Library of Congress Control Number: 2009042233

ISBN 978-1-4391-5705-3
ISBN 978-1-4391-6992-6 (ebook)

For my brother, Douglas

Let me say, at the risk of seeming ridiculous,
that a true revolutionary is guided by great feelings of love.

—Che Guevara

Americans learn only from catastrophe
and not from experience.

—Theodore Roosevelt

I AM IN HIDING, SOMEPLACE COLD. SOMEPLACE THEY WON'T FIND ME, OR *haven't yet. Weeks have passed, weeks spent watching weather through windows, flash storms, incessant rains. And now the first snow. It fell in the night, six inches or more, and with dawn came the groaning plows down in the valley—the digging out before the long settling in. The hillsides are barren, the foliage all fallen away, leaving only the trees themselves, shivering and vulnerable. I can see most of the driveway through the bare branches, a half mile of unpaved switchbacks winding through the fields, before the final run-out to the county road. To civilization, if that's what you'd call it. That's what I called it for a long time, or would have if I'd ever thought like that. About America, I mean.*

The house isn't so bad. It's a retrofitted barn with two low-ceilinged bedrooms upstairs, and down here, a central space for eating, working, living. Plenty of furniture, too, a jumble of cast-off antiques and yard-sale specials, amassed slowly over the years—spared, salvaged, saved. A running theme, perhaps. There is no romance in going underground, in becoming anonymous, stateless, tended to by strangers who come and go in shadows. I have no TV, no phone, no computer or Internet. They're serious about communication, or the necessary lack of it, because you never know who could be listening in. The best I can do is a small radio and days-old newspapers, which my handlers bring on their twice-weekly vis-

its. Tuesdays and Fridays at dusk. They flash their high beams at the bottom of the driveway and again closer to the house. Otherwise I split. That's the plan.

I don't know the history of the place, but I imagine it's been used like this for a while—as a hideout, a safe house, a place to regroup and then move on. Everything here is transitory, cheap, easily left behind. Even the few decorations—the model ship above the fireplace, the sun-faded posters advertising Pan Am 747s and British Rail routes to Scotland— speak to travel, to escape. But there's nowhere to go, not right now, and so I sit here at this timeworn desk, keyed up on coffee and cigarettes, searching for a voice, a way into the story. I want to remember what my life was like before. Sounds stupid, I realize. I lived it, so how hard can it be to put into words? Well, I've tried:

> My name is Aidan Cole. For three years I wrote and edited a popular New York–based blog called Roorback.com. Defined literally, a roorback is a "defamatory falsehood published for political effect," but I wanted the grand old word to stand for all the defamations and falsehoods published and proffered in our irreverent media age. Indeed, my blog was a wryly cynical and slightly subversive examination of the fourth estate's daily lies and blunderings, a kind of meta-media—

Oh, you know all that already, and you know much of what's to follow as well. The public facts are all too familiar. But the truth . . . the truth has remained elusive.

Even now, it's hard to accept—to really comprehend—what has happened. Maybe putting it down on paper will help. Somewhere out there—and I wish I knew where—Paige Roderick is doing the same, using words to explain her actions. Our actions. That's the promise we made on our last night together: to write our stories as best we understood them. Perhaps these accounts will aid our defense if we get caught, or enlighten others if we get killed. That was Paige's original intent, after all—to hijack people's scant attentions and warn them of the world to come. Maybe, months or years from now, hidden behind foolproof identities or living safely on foreign soil, we'll combine the two tales, then post it all online or publish it as a memoir, a kind of warning shot across the

American bow. And why not? We're a decade into the century of the self, the age of endless explanation, where every life demands a public forum, every face a shot at fame. More likely, though, these pages will never find an audience. Our tenuous situations will change, or certain memories will prove too much to revisit day after day. And maybe that's for the best. Still, we must try, while we have time and truth on our side. We're far from innocent. But we're hardly guilty as charged.

AIDAN

· · · ● ● ● ● ● ● · · ● ●

TO THINK THIS ALL STARTED AT MY GIRLFRIEND'S PARTY, LESS THAN THREE
months ago. I say *girlfriend*, but Cressida preferred lover. *Girlfriend*
meant something different in her native London, she always told me,
but I think she just liked the mystery, the vague open-endedness of her
favored term. That and it read better. Cressida Kent, in case you're not
from New York (and believe me, there's no reason you should be), was a
metro reporter and monthly "relationships columnist" for the *New York
Times,* the latest—and most accomplished—in a long line of shameless
girls-about-town who documented the romantic possibilities of the
city after dark. She lived with two other women in their early thirties
(a reality-TV producer and a senior editor at *Glamour*), in a converted
warehouse on Gansevoort Street, smack in the middle of the Meatpacking District. They were of a type, the three roommates—assiduous,
attractive, and unmarried—and judging by the crowd that night, they
seemed to know every young media professional still lucky enough to
be employed after two long years of recessionary layoffs.

It was the last Wednesday in August. Almost four days had passed
since the explosion, but its effects were still evident in every corner of
the room. New York, despite the faded memory of 9/11, had never really
been a city of bombs. So many countries were represented by its consul-
ates and realized in its boroughs that I'd always believed there was a kind

of unstated agreement to fight the terror wars elsewhere, in distant gulfs and deserts. But those assumptions had just changed overnight, and quickly, the nine years since 2001 seemed nothing more than time to catch our breath.

Cressida's large, exposed-brick loft was full of wrinkled shirts and wearied brows, tired but exhilarated men and women still seeking answers to the most basic journalistic questions—the *who, how,* and *why* of the act itself. The story of the year was up for grabs, and every able reporter in the city was chasing it. Hence the scattered cliques, pockets of people in corners, horse-trading gossip, running rumors on margin. Still, the party wasn't all business, because terrorism, in the end, is personal (just as politics is local). It starts with the one, with private fears and anxieties and an inevitable looking inward, until we each lift our heads and find one other. It was the first night people had ventured back out, and the feeling that we'd once again dodged some kind of bullet—or bomb—hovered over the proceedings like so much cigarette smoke. The collective relief was palpable.

Our hosts hadn't held back: two male models poured liquor from behind a fully stocked bar; moonlighting actresses slithered through the crowd carrying trays of dumplings and miniature spring rolls; in a corner near the kitchen a voluptuous woman in a flowing ensemble read tarot cards to a captivated audience; and toward the back of the space, beyond the dining-room-cum-dance-floor, stood a dead-eyed DJ in a black-and-white-striped bodysuit, spinning seventies glam rock sprinkled with new wave. The party was loud and crowded, and that was the point: to get people out of their offices and away from their iPhones, their BlackBerrys, their laptops. If only for a night. It was almost 1 a.m. and I'd spent the last half hour inching through the high-ceilinged room, hugging friends and sparring with acquaintances. For these were the very people I chronicled. I was trying to find Cressida and had come within sight of her more than once, but every time we made eye contact, she shook her head and turned away. You see, I hadn't actually been invited. We'd been fighting since her last column appeared, the week before, but still, I hoped my surprise appearance, coupled with the larger events of the moment, might bring her to the bargaining table. If not the bedroom.

Then I saw Touché. He was talking to the DJ as he flipped through her milk crate of LPs. She stood behind the turntables expressionless, pretending not to listen, but her headphones were down around her neck, leaving her ears vulnerable to that purring South American accent. She was all black bangs and colored tattoos—not Touché's normal quarry, but my friend was nothing if not adaptable—and she was trying so hard to remain aloof. Indeed, her tortured disdain for her surroundings was a thing to behold, all these young professionals in their boutique clothes and jangling accessories, blurring after a while into the same self-important person—Exhibit A being this suave Latin guy flipping through her records, far too well dressed and classically handsome for her taste, but still, there was something about him. I watched her glance his way, once and then again. And then I knew she had no chance. Julian Touché was tall and dark, with smooth hair and flawless skin, but his eyes were what did it. They were charcoal colored, but when they fell on someone (and they always fell, moving down from some higher place), they became at that moment the brightest in any room. He could look a woman dead on and she'd forget what she was saying. It was a talent we, his friends, had noticed early on, and Christ, how it worked: send Touché to break the ice and everyone was in for a memorable night. And yet, something about his rakishness was completely sincere. He never tried too hard; with his looks, background, and bank account he didn't have to. He was the kind of person you just wanted to be around because there was always a chance something extraordinary would happen. I watched him pick out a record, then lean in close to give it to her. He whispered something in her ear, and that's all it took: she fell out of character. She bit her lip, grabbed his forearm, and giggled. Suddenly she was just another jaded hipster who knew too much about music.

She was examining the album in her hands when Touché looked up and saw me. A grin spread across his face, a grin that reached back past our recent months of silence to the luminous years that had come before. He gave the DJ what looked like a kiss on the neck, then turned and came striding toward me. When he put his arms out to greet me, I got that same old feeling—that I was in the glowing center of it all.

"Too long," he said. We hugged, then he stepped back to take my measure.

"You're the one who disappeared."

"Ah, Aidan, I'm not so hard to find."

A new song came on, some nineties Brit-pop number, Pulp or James or Blur—I always got them confused—and Touché turned and gave the DJ a small wave.

"You picked this?" I asked.

"Yes."

"Who sings it?"

"I have no idea. But she has to like it. They're her records, no?" He laughed, then looked at the empty drink in my hand. "That won't do. I'll be right back." Before I could answer, he disappeared into the crowd in front of the bar.

He was always disappearing. Sometimes it was minutes, often it was months. As it happened, I hadn't seen him since before Memorial Day, when he flew down to Venezuela to spend a few weeks with his family. He did it every year, except this time he didn't come back. Or maybe he did and never told me, which was entirely possible: Julian Touché's life was defined by ambiguity. Part of it was the money, of course; money can make anyone mysterious. But Touché seemed to thrive on vagueness. We could pick right back up where we left off, as if the last three months had never happened, and as long as I didn't ask questions, as long as he was ultimately calling the shots, everything would be fine.

We met in the fall of 2002, a few weeks into our first semester at NYU's graduate school of journalism. It was the night the clocks changed, and I was at a bar on the Bowery with a girl I sat next to in Politics and the Press. When the conversation dried up, she used the extra hour as an excuse to head home to get some work done. This was some years ago, when the Bowery at 2 a.m.—or 3—was still a shadowy obstacle course for a woman dressed like she meant it, and so I said I'd walk her back to campus. On Mercer Street, we fell in with a group of fellow journalism students heading to a party. When my date heard the host's name, she suddenly got her second wind.

Their destination was a stately Washington Square apartment building with a uniformed doorman and a spacious lobby that had us talking under our breath out of respect for the marble. The doorman didn't ask whom we were visiting. He just looked at the girls with a smile, then followed us into the elevator, pulled the cross-hatched gate closed, and up we went. All the way to the top. There was no exterior hallway; the doors opened right into the apartment. It was a small detail at the time, but one I still remember these many years later. How real wealth is so often measured by absence. The apartment was a maze of frayed and well-worn rooms filled with cracked-leather armchairs and antique armoires, a collage of old-world styles and colors, the accumulation of generations— generations of Touchés, as it turned out. I walked down a corridor lined with sconces and into a living room the size of a small Broad-way stage. Other halls wandered off toward distant bedrooms, but everything happened in that central room. I perched on an arm-rest and watched pretty people come and go, the party continually refreshing itself like a stylish European airport bar as small waves of new arrivals appeared (after last call at the bars) to replace the not-so-early departures.

I met the man himself in the kitchen. He'd just finished pouring shots for a semifamous actor and his friends, and when he saw me, he simply walked up and introduced himself. He didn't ask who I was or how I'd gotten there; for that matter, no one did. Just find-ing the place meant I belonged. He looked familiar, and for good reason. We weren't in any classes together, but we knew some of the same people, had noticed the same girls. We talked awhile, and when he was finally called into other conversations, I wandered back to the living room, with its period furniture and peeling wallpaper. A painter's easel near the windows held a half-finished watercolor (Mrs. Touché's sometimes hobby, I later learned). In a nearby corner rested a stand-up globe, its faded sepia surface hinting at the hard-won boundaries of earlier empires. But Touché the younger had made his mark as well, and the room now tee-tered between generations: nude Nan Goldin photographs beside nude Picasso prints; a flat-screen TV wedged between century-old French windows; and behind the globe a complex stereo system, its lights and buttons blinking down upon the dusty earth like alien crafts in formation.

When I finally left, around 5 a.m., I did so with the impression that Julian Touché and I had, well, hit it off—a rare thing for two straight men in New York—though I couldn't for the life of me remember what we'd discussed. In the weeks that followed I tried to piece together my new friend's background. Everyone at school claimed to know something about him. His father, Santo, was a successful businessman-turned-politician from one of Venezuela's oldest families. Mary, his exquisite mother, was an American heiress, a descendant of Du Ponts. From here, we moved toward conjecture. It was said that Santo Touché played a large role in the palace coup that had just that year brought down the socialist regime of Hugo Chávez. But in the power vacuum that followed, Chávez was sucked back into office, and Santo and dozens of other aristocratic revolutionaries were forced to flee with their families to the relative safety of distant provinces. Some, citing Julian's extended absences, believed my new friend had played a significant part in these proceedings. Others thought him nothing more than a generous playboy living high off his two noble bloodlines—the New York apartment, a summer house on Fishers Island, a chalet in Courchevel—while his father moved among hidden estates in the foothills of the Orinoco River.

This was my introduction to the legend. And there was so much more. I heard—and would soon become part of—stories that became almost mythical in the retelling, but I'll spare you the specifics. It is enough to say that Julian Touché enjoyed excesses of every kind, traveled in circles I'd only glimpsed, and all the while stage-managed the many facets of his life so carefully that after many years of camaraderie, even close friends never quite knew where they stood within his wide and graceful orbit.

It was late now. Cressida's party was getting sloppy. Touché had returned with our drinks and was nodding toward the dance floor.

"Look," he said.

The lights were low. The DJ had hit her stride, and the crowd was responding—a mass of drunken, gyrating bodies trying to ward off impending middle age. And now I saw her, our dear hostess, shimmering in the middle of it all. She was being spun around by a fleshy editor from the *Post*, and as the song ended and their bodies came together, he suddenly dipped her one last time, pausing momentarily as her hair scraped the floor. Cressida came up laughing, grabbed the low-cut front of her top, and gave him a hug. A few nearby couples clapped.

"She knows you're watching," Touché said, taking a sip of his drink. "So much fun, relationships."

"If that's what you'd call it."

"Let me guess. You're fighting about her latest column."

"Have you read it?"

"I read them all," my friend said, trying, and failing, to stifle a smile. "Dissecting the details of your hapless love life is one of my life's great pleasures."

"So you'd be pissed off, too."

"I wouldn't be involved with a dating columnist in the first place. Even the lovely Cressida. What did you expect?"

"She swore she'd never write about us."

"Aidan, come on. I think deep down you like what she does, the power of her pen, so to speak. Of course, the power of *your* pen seems more the issue these days."

"Fuck off."

"Ah, yes . . ."

We'd gravitated to the two large, south-facing windows, open wide to the breezy night, and were looking out across the balconies and rooftops of downtown Manhattan. Below us the bruised and cobbled streets of the old West Side sagged uncomfortably under the weight of discovery. Once a host to blood-spattered union men and long-limbed transvestites, the Meatpacking District was now a vulgar orgy of development, the titivated epicenter of New York's grotesque and tragically hip. Even Touché, who was unbothered by things that drove most people to distraction, muttered as he gazed down on the midnight hordes stampeding past in denim and heels and highlights. Had these people been impacted by the bombing four nights before? Or had the news already been forgotten, brushed aside in favor of the more digestible, the more personally affecting, the more assuredly insignificant? I'm sorry if I seem bitter. You see, I know the answer.

The bomb went off on the deserted fifteenth floor of 660 Madison Avenue at 3:45 a.m., on Sunday, August 22 (almost three months ago exactly). The building, as you know, houses Barneys, and as New York awoke that rainy morning to the searing image of a burning office tower, it was easy to believe the worst. Television: I remember so clearly that shaky helicopter camera panning in on the blast site. The hole was two stories high and almost as wide, and through the smoke I could just make out the hollow offices inside. It was all so familiar: the dead cell phones, the buzzing fear, the desperate need for information, and something else . . . an odd sort of pride. We were a city again, united through tragedy despite our countless divisions. But New York—or at least Manhattan—also presented a unique problem of geography. I was making coffee in my West Village studio, a short block from the Hudson, when I turned on the TV and saw the news. Instinctively, I went to the window and looked out at the sliver of visible river, wondering, if it came to that, how the hell I'd get across. It was something all of us on that overcrowded island had secretly pondered, because there was always the chance that more might come.

But more didn't come. The morning progressed apace. The mayor delivered a few steely-eyed assurances, then left the airwaves to the talking heads, the experts of our age, already spilling over with speculation. It was the beginning of a new battle; it was the end of an old war. It was us; it was them. For a while it was even spontaneous combustion—a kind of manhole explosion in the air. At some point a broader target was identified: consumerism. Could there be a better symbol of flawed Western values than Barneys, that most famous of high-end department stores? The war of civilizations had reached America's upper classes—our preening, clucking socialites—and there'd be no ignoring it now. This, then, became the story, until late morning, when a fellow blogger, a guy I vaguely knew, wrote in a post that he'd recently been to Barneys with his girlfriend, and from what he remembered, the store didn't go up fifteen floors.

In the days that followed, the hole in the building became a voyeuristic extravaganza. I took the E-train uptown to see for myself, and there it was, a giant black cavity, taunting the city with the expanding mystery of its origins. Yet Touché and I had yet to mention the event. That's what friendship with him was like. A bomb, quite literally, goes off, shakes the foundation of our urban lives, and he's making eyes at a DJ across a hazy room.

"She's good," he said, as some synthesized Joy Division knock-off crescendoed through the loft. Or maybe it *was* Joy Division.

"So what have you been up to?" I asked.

"Taking flying lessons."

"Really? You're becoming a pilot?"

"I already am. I got my license last month."

"Why?"

"Ah, Aidan, it's what we do. We children of the wealthy are doomed by the long shadows of our forefathers to lives of insignificance. And so we learn to pass the time with material pleasures, embrace the hobbies of our birthright—boats and planes, horses and golf. How else to forget the failures of our class?"

"Oh."

"*I'm kidding,*" Touché said, laughing. "A joke, you know? Maybe not so funny. My father flew when he was younger. And my uncles. And I thought if I learned, it might . . . it might help back home."

I didn't push him further; Touché was always guarded about the situation in Venezuela. But even the silence worked in his favor, fueling rumors of his secret second life. Legends grow from a lack of information.

He sipped his drink and looked at me.

"What?" I said.

"Why don't you ever ask me about it?"

"Venezuela? Because you'd never answer."

"You know what I think?" said Touché. "I think sometimes you . . . how do I put this . . . you buy too fully into the American narrative. And when opposing ideas are introduced, foreign ideas, you can't accept them as potentially valid."

"What are you talking about?"

"Oh, forget it. We don't have to get into this."

"Into what?" I said.

"A real conversation."

"Do you think I'm not capable?"

"I think you're not willing," he replied. "And why should you be? You've found a place for yourself, a certain niche, even if it's . . . again let me say this right . . . not *undeserved* but perhaps a bit *inconsequential*."

"Are you talking about my life or yours?"

"Ah, yes. Maybe both. Maybe everyone's." He looked out over the party again. "The busy lives of the eternally hip."

"Sounds like a book title."

"Except the eternally hip never get around to writing books."

"Just blogs?"

"That's not what I meant," Touché said.

"It is what you meant."

"I'm talking about me. What my life's been like for too long. But you. You have, what, thirty thousand people who read what you write every day?"

"More like fifty."

"Fine. An impressive following. But you can get that many people to go watch a preacher, or professional wrestling."

"What's your point?"

"That it doesn't matter. That we focus too much on statistics. On small details. Americans sit too close to the television." Touché laughed. "I'm sorry. I'm getting wrapped up in everything that's happened this week, and we're here to have—"

"You boys should always greet the hostess when you come to a party," said a voice behind us. We both turned. Cressida was standing there, flush from the dance floor. Her auburn bangs were matted to her forehead, and her halter top clung like a wet stamp to her pale, freckled frame. Cressida wasn't traditionally beautiful—her lips were too thin, her breasts got lost in bras—but with her curious eyes, her small button nose, and her almost perfect English ass, she could be quite stunning in specific moments.

"A vision," said Touché, kissing her theatrically on both cheeks.

"And you must meet my friend Aidan. He was just asking about you." But Cressida wasn't playing along, so Touché held up his empty cup. "I'll let the two of you get *reacquainted*," he announced, and with that he drifted off in the general direction of the dance floor.

"He's such an asshole," I said.

"You love him." Cressida was looking straight at me—questioning, considering, accusing, all at once. Then she blinked. "What's wrong with you? You've been glaring at me all night. You can't come over and say hello?"

"Not if you can't invite me in the first place. It's so great to find out about your girlfriend's party from someone else."

She rolled her eyes, a habit I hated (although when I'd said as much, months before, she replied that eye-rolling was what I did for a living, one blog post at a time). Someone called her name, and she looked up and blew a kiss to a departing couple. When she turned back around, her smile had evaporated. "Aidan, can we try not to ruin the night? It's been a hard enough week already. It's all hands on deck at the paper. Dozens of reporters, hundreds of leads . . . all leading nowhere. I've been at the office late every night. I must look a right mess."

"You haven't called once."

"There hasn't been time."

"There's always time. You said it yourself in one of your fine columns on commitment."

"Stop it." She moved closer, clasping her arms loosely around my waist. Then she looked at me again. This time the bravado was gone, and I could see how exhausted, how fetchingly vulnerable she was under that dusting of freckles and makeup.

"I'm sorry," I whispered, through strands of damp hair, and I was, though for what, exactly, I wasn't sure. Fighting, I guess. Stubbornness. Selfishness. Hell, when aren't we sorry?

I don't want to make this sound overly dramatic. This was hardly the height of romance. We were just two people on the fringes of a party, made small by sound and circumstance, but—and I keep thinking cinematically as I recall that night—if the camera had panned in close, it would have caught something genuine. Though I wouldn't call it love. We were too far along for that.

"Stop looking at me," she said.

"But you look nice."

"*Nice?*"

"Yes. Nice. Sexy. Beauti—"

"We need to talk."

"I know."

She cleared her throat and gazed outside. "What do you want?"

It was the worst kind of question, and it grew in the silence that followed. There were a thousand answers—all correct, but none quite right.

"I want to have dinner tomorrow night," I said.

She looked surprised. "Okay, fine, but I have to work late again."

"What exactly do they have you doing?"

"I don't know. Chasing scraps. Not even scraps. The metro desk is a mob scene, which means I probably won't have to write a column this month."

"Oh, too bad," I said, but she ignored the comment.

"There's just so little information, something has to break. I mean, how can someone *succeed* at—that's not the right word—but you know what I'm trying to say. How can a person plant a bomb, completely undetected, inside a well-secured office building in the middle of Manhattan? Do you know how many security cameras there are on Madison Avenue?"

"We're still in the early days," I said.

"But there's been nothing. And not a peep from the FBI either. Oh, listen to us, prattling on like everyone else. We throw a party to give people a few hours of fun, and look, we're all still working."

The room came back to us then, puncturing the moment, what was left of it. Cressida suddenly seemed unfamiliar, like someone I knew only casually. People were hovering nearby, waiting to talk to her, to say hello or good-bye. She had to go. We kissed, lingering for a moment, but no longer.

"Okay, tomorrow night then," she said, and waded back into the scrum.

I made my way to the bar and ordered a beer. The party had peaked and was coming down the other side. It was a weeknight after all, and we weren't so young anymore. Early thirties, midthirties, a few even older. We had entered the second stage of city living. These days we checked our watches, wary of the critical difference between one and three in the morning. These days we agreed with each other more than we used to, if only to avoid awkwardness or argument. And these days we betrayed one another, too. With women, with men, with work. Our close friends—from childhood, from college, from those first anxious years in New York—had moved away or melted into marriage. Our new friends were hungrier, more successful, a bit ruthless. We'd all been here a long time now.

I was drunk and floating, group to group, like everyone else. No one cared at this hour about listening. The music was still loud. People were making out. I walked to the bathroom but the line was too long. Where once we laid our drugs out on coffee tables, now we sniffled and fidgeted as we waited to do them alone. Why hadn't Cressida asked me to stay the night? Maybe she'd tried and I'd missed the signal. No, there had been no signal. I looked across the room at the DJ. She was doing a shot with another girl. Had Touché gone home? Maybe I should go home. Cut the proverbial losses.

Then I saw my boss, Derrick Franklin. He was holding court near the front door. I turned back toward the bar, but it was too late. I'd been spotted. Derrick waved me over with a sly grin, followed by an aside to his older male companions. They laughed, too readily. Money people, I thought.

"Aidan, you're out late," he said, making a big deal of looking at his watch. "Collecting material, I hope."

Derrick found this sort of thing amusing. I—and the rest of his blogging empire—found it exasperating. But he signed the paychecks, so I stood there and endured fifteen torturous minutes of Roorback anecdotes and Cressida jokes—all of them at my expense. When the talk finally shifted to weightier matters, I excused myself and ducked into Cressida's empty bedroom. My phone had been buzzing all night with e-mails, so I shut the door and turned on her computer.

Blogging was a business, at least for me, and I was contractually obligated to produce at least a dozen well-researched posts a day, the first by 8:30 a.m. For this I received a modest salary and health insurance, but the real benefits weren't so quantifiable. If Roorback wasn't New York's most popular blog strictly by numbers, it was certainly one of its most essential; the people who read it were the city's new bourgeois, the complex circuitry of the information age (and I, a kind of hidden conductor). Because of Roorback I now had access to a New York I'd only read about before. Touché's New York. Cressida's New York. A New York of public names, private clubs, and the kind of parties that made the papers. It's funny: you search forever for success, and then, as soon as you stop trying so hard, you wake up one morning and suddenly you're somebody. Of course, you also remain the person you were, and for me that meant in debt. I was thirty-three years old, had $35,000 in unpaid student loans, and $1,200 in my checking account. In life's slower moments—on subways or in bed—these facts momentarily caught up with me, until I got to where I was going or fell safely asleep. I'd convinced myself that living paycheck to paycheck was some kind of martyr's life, the only true way to experience New York as a young man. Implicit in that lie, of course, was the assumption that my situation was temporary, that being mildly impoverished was only a phase. Except the phase had settled in, become steadfast, enduring.

Cressida's laptop was coming to life. Lights and beeps, a soft whir. I looked around the room. She'd been here three years, and still it felt only half lived-in. The walls were bare. Her books were stacked in a corner on the floor. She'd made an effort to clean up, but that meant lumping clothes into piles, kicking shoes under the bed. Only her desk was neat, a few folders to one side of the computer, a collection of recent clips on the other. I picked up the one on top, her latest column, and skimmed it, my eyes landing hard on the all-too-familiar sentences.

> Something has come between us, and it's never been more evident than in the moments before sleep. Once, these were ours, together, but now the literary has replaced the libidinal, and the stuff of rainy weekend mornings—books and lazy crosswords—has become the focus of our bedroom nights. "What's wrong with me, Jack?" That's what I want to scream as I lie there beside him, feigning interest in some

magazine of my own, but really reading the same page over and over again, like an obsessive child, unable to concentrate on anything—

I couldn't go on. When friends asked, Cressida and I were quick to throw up a smoke screen, tell them her columns were an amalgamation, a compilation, even a fabrication, but no one really believed us. "Jack" was no work of fiction. The bitch.

Outside the door, the party was dying. The DJ's turntable classics had been replaced by someone's iPod, and songs kept getting cut off halfway through. I clicked my way online. I'd learned early on that late-night blogging was a fast road to trouble. Beware the drunken slur, the 3 a.m. slander; it was advice I adhered to closely. But blogging was an addiction, the Internet a drug. There was always an in-box to sift through, comments to read, links to follow. But that night the online traffic was lighter than usual. In the drawn-out aftermath of a major story, the rest of the world had gone quiet. News was still being made, of course, but the press wasn't paying attention. The limelight could only shine so much, even in this day and age, and just then there was only the bombing. That left the rest of us—we cynics, humorists, and online opiners—feeling ignored and slightly worthless.

The Roorback in-box contained just four e-mails—a celebrity sighting (James Franco outside Cafe Gitane), a publicist hawking a new chick-lit book, and some (potentially libelous) gossip from *Vanity Fair*. Nothing I could use the next day. I clicked open the last one. The subject line was blank, as was the body of the e-mail. But an image was attached, and as Cressida's laptop labored to open it, I heard a banging behind me, followed by laughter. "Just turn the knob," said a girl's muffled voice, then the door opened and two bodies came stumbling into the room. The DJ regained her balance, took a few running steps, and jumped onto the bed. Touché began to chase after her, then stopped. He opened his mouth to speak, but no words came out. He wasn't looking at me, he was looking past me, at the screen. I turned back around just as the picture finished loading. You remember it: the now iconic shot of a young woman with long, dark hair striding purposefully across Madison Avenue, the red Barneys awnings visible in the blurry background. She wore a knee-length skirt, tasteful sleeveless top, and oversize sunglasses that covered much of her face. Her head was turned to the side, toward the camera, and she seemed in a hurry, like a European beauty hastening past a group of lecherous men.

"Who the fuck is that?" Touché asked, from over my right shoulder. But something else had my attention. The words below the photograph:

This is Paige Roderick. She's the one responsible.

PAIGE

· · · ● ● ● ● ● · · ●

KNOW YOUR SURROUNDINGS: MEMORIZE THE ROOM, THE PEOPLE, THE EXITS. A run-down truck stop on an old tobacco highway. Long-haulers eating breakfasts in corners. A church group in the gift shop. Old couples shuffling arm in arm toward the restrooms, then breaking off at the last moment—to HIS, to HERS. Vans of Girl Scouts and Little Leaguers: kids in uniforms, pleading and tugging, hungry for food, starving for attention. That had been me once, but a long time ago. I was their opposite now. A person trying to fade away, climb into a car and disappear completely. I was sitting at a table near the window, newspaper spread before me, pretending to read. No eye contact, no conversations. In my excitement I'd arrived too early (despite biking the route twice the week before, nine miles of hills through a Smoky Mountain dawn), and after dumping the bike out back, had no choice but to buy a cup of coffee and settle in. It was the longest hour of my life. I got up and walked to the bathroom, fighting the urge to glance in the mirror, take one last look. Would I have recognized myself? The faded jeans, the loose peasant top, the old running shoes. My hair tied in a simple ponytail, no makeup. But I didn't look. What was the point? I went back out and sat down. Know your surroundings? It wasn't difficult. Everything was so familiar. The hard part was realizing I might never see any of it again.

At 9:04 a.m. a gray Toyota Corolla slid into a parking space beside the picnic table farthest from the entrance. I got up, went outside, and walked casually across the bustling lot. Keith was behind the wheel; next to him sat a wiry girl with dirty-blond hair. I climbed in behind her and pulled the door shut. Then the locks clicked. It's a sound I still hear these many months later. The sound of leaving one life for another.

Keith turned to back out and caught my eye. It was only a second, but it was enough. No one said a word. We edged past minivans, mud-splattered pickups, and on the far side of the rest stop, the big rigs, parked diagonally like giant dominoes suspended in midfall. For several minutes we drove in silence. Up front, they peered into mirrors and sneaked looks at passing cars. Keith changed lanes a lot, slowed down and sped up, never too fast. The inside of the car was spotless, no maps or magazines. A single blue duffel bag inscribed with the words TEXAS IS GOD'S COUNTRY lay on the seat beside me. I didn't touch it.

This went on awhile, the silence. Maybe ten minutes. Had I done something wrong? Keith and the girl were fidgety but focused. They'd traveled a long way already. They'd come up out of the South and the plan was to keep going. Where, I had no idea. That was the toughest part in the beginning, the lack of information. I knew not to ask questions, not to speak at all. But I knew something else, too, knew it as soon as I sat down. That this felt right. These two people, this car, it was where I wanted to be, *needed* to be. The thought soothed me as we drove east, past towns I knew well, then not so well, then not at all. The sun was high now, the fog had lifted, and as the minutes passed, so did the memories, as if taking a victory lap before disappearing forever—school dances in Dellwood, family camping trips on Fontana Lake, and out of nowhere, little Danny Ingram, a childhood crush whose house I'd biked past hours earlier. How many times I'd written that name in the margins of my sixth-grade notebooks, how many crayon-drawn love notes I'd taped to the inside of my locker—

We're clear, Keith said.

I jumped in my seat, startled.

You're sure? the girl asked.

Yes.

They both exhaled at once. The girl rolled her head around, stretched her neck. The tension evaporated, the car lost weight.

Sorry, Keith said, addressing me in the mirror. That's always the most dangerous part.

We had some trouble a few days ago, the girl began. We stopped for gas and a car started following—

Paige, this is Lindsay, Keith said. Lindsay, Paige.

Oh, I'm so sorry, said Lindsay, turning fully around. She smiled, then put a hand on my knee and squeezed. It's really nice to meet you.

You, too.

And don't worry, you were perfect back there, she continued.

I don't think she *was* worried, Keith said.

Of course not, Lindsay replied. I didn't mean it that way. Her eyes darted around, looking for a soft landing, and settled on the bag beside me. Oh, that's for you, some clothes and stuff. Keith guessed your size.

Thanks.

I unzipped it. The contents had been stuffed inside haphazardly, clearly all bought at once, probably in a hurry. A few plain T-shirts and tank tops, a pair of cutoff Levi's, a zip-front windbreaker, knee-length skirt, blue drawstring sweatpants, flip-flops, and a pair of open-toed mules I could tell were too small. At the bottom was a plastic bag with some basics: underwear, socks, black tights. I held each item up, like a Christmas gift from a distant relative, then folded it neatly and moved on to the next.

There wasn't much of a selection, Lindsay said. But, you know, it's not like we'll be out on the town that often.

Right, I said, and laughed nervously.

Lindsay played with the radio until she found a static-free station—a breathy teenager singing of love. I tried to ignore the music and forget the clothes, their awful anonymity. Everything would be fine. I'd made this choice carefully, thought it through for weeks. But that doesn't make it any easier in the moment. The moment your history disappears, all you've known cast aside for all you don't.

Ten miles short of Asheville, Keith pulled off I-40 and headed east toward the Blue Ridge Parkway. We were driving through the backcountry now, no one in front, no one behind. I thought of rolling down the window, breathing in the Appalachian pine. But I didn't know the rules yet, and I didn't want to ask permission. I could wait. I had been waiting. From the radio came another ode to youth and lust. Lindsay started humming along. Suddenly, without a word, his eyes never leaving the road, Keith reached down and tuned in a country station. The old stuff. Kris Kristofferson drinking a beer for breakfast, and one more for dessert.

Lindsay went silent. I stayed quiet, too. But I knew all the words.

His full name—or at least the one he went by—was Keith Sutter. I knew him mostly by reputation, though we'd met once before, late one night last spring, in a dimly lit apartment in Raleigh. Keith had showed up there to recruit me, though I was far too occupied by the illicit particulars of my new life to realize it at first. It was a life that had risen from the black depths of grief following my brother Bobby's death, and while its day-to-day requirements partially tempered my despair, the void was still vast, and I would come to see Keith as a worthy surrogate. And my only chance for vengeance.

But let me start at the beginning, or the end—Bobby's funeral, a year ago yesterday. Having endured the twenty-four longest hours of my life—unbearable hours I cannot revisit, even now—I flew home to Maggie Valley foolishly determined to pull myself, and everyone else, together. And for a few days—consumed by the hushed and morbid business of the funeral itself—my parents and I managed to scrape along intact. The agony came afterward, when the people we cared about were still lingering around the house, bringing us food and magazines and books about bouncing back. What we really wanted, of course, was to be left alone. We needed time. I called the think tank where I worked in D.C. and told them I'd be gone a few more weeks. Each day, each hour, became a marathon of emotion punctuated by free-flowing tears and drawn-out embraces, by muted dinners and sleepless bodies shuffling across late-night floors. I was worried about my mother. She was taking it worst. For days she cooked and cleaned with a singular ferocity, then switched gears, loaded up on pills and pushed the world away. I talked to my father when I could, when he could, in the morning mostly, before the hours of memories had a chance to pile up. He'd been a soldier, like Bobby, and I thought he might have answers, some kind of explanation. He tried his best, but there are no answers when a soldier dies. Only questions. Only blame.

Weeks passed, then one night my parents accepted an invitation to a dinner party down the street. My mother did her hair, put on a dress, and, taking my father's hand, followed him out the front door. From my childhood bedroom window I watched them stroll down the driveway. They looked tall and determined. *Now*, I thought. I can go back to my life. People do recover. A faint light comes on somewhere in the darkness of despair and instinctively we move toward it. We move *forward*. Of course, *I* hadn't moved forward. In taking care of my parents, I'd shut myself down, become a professional support system, a body to lean on, talk to, cry with. My mourning would take place over many months and years. I knew this, even then—though I couldn't know the form it would take. Bobby's death would haunt my solitude, test my sanity, drive away those I loved. Because my older brother—my *only* brother—was everything to me. And as hard as I would try, I just couldn't accept what had happened to him.

The next day I told my parents it was time. I had to get back to D.C., just as they had to get back to their lives, piece together some semblance of normality. I found a flight and packed my bags. My father insisted on driving me to the airport, so I hugged my mother good-bye, then hurried out to the garage where he was waiting in the car.

Mom seems much better, I said, reaching for my seat belt. When he didn't answer, I looked over. He was staring straight ahead, tears streaming down his face.

Dad, I said, putting my hand on his cheek.

But he didn't move.

Dad, it'll be okay.

But even as I said it, I knew it wouldn't be. That was the hardest moment of all, the two of us just sitting there. The breath had been knocked out of me, and the life would be next. What was I doing? There was nothing I cared about in Washington anymore. I'd just be running away from myself. From my parents. From my brother. The only way to survive overwhelming grief, to emerge on some theoretical other side, was to face it head-on. I couldn't leave. And I didn't want to. I kissed my father on the forehead, then opened the car door and took my bags back inside.

Old routines. Nothing maudlin. We didn't set a place for Bobby at the table or leave his old bedroom untouched. Just small comforts. A way to get through time intact. Another month passed. Back in D.C., my sublet ran out and my leave of absence at the institute ended. My boss e-mailed several times but I didn't respond, and a week later he wrote to say I'd been let go. I was almost relieved.

I began taking walks, to the edge of the backyard and beyond, into woods at once remote and intensely familiar. In autumn Maggie Valley, North Carolina, became the most beautiful place on earth, the leaves bursting into color overnight, like fireworks exploding across the sky. In the forest it was my brother and I again, playing cowboys and Indians, our faces painted, feathers in our hair. We carried child-size hickory longbows, fashioning quivers from rawhide sacks, arrows from the branches of elms. Bobby spent hours whittling each one down until it flew straight and true. Or hikes we took along old homestead trails, Bobby naming all the animals we saw. Once, he tiptoed up to a deer and stroked its head so softly it didn't even flinch. We spent our childhoods back there, in the hills behind our modest ranch-style house, hills and then mountains that ran hundreds of miles in every direction. The Great Smoky Mountains National Park, the jewel of the Appalachians, a world unto itself. It was a place you were born to, rooted to—a place you could never leave behind. Our lives came flooding back, one year after the next, until the memories became too recent, and I pictured my brother as I'd last seen him, the morning he deployed, surrounded by his friends from Appalachian State. Just twenty-nine and with so much life to live.

They all came to the funeral, of course, caravanned down from Boone to say good-bye. At the service they stood off to the side, but still no one could miss them. Their pain was so raw that for several minutes I was too overcome to focus on anything the minister was saying. Afterward, Carter, Bobby's old roommate and best friend, came over and we hugged, long and hard, wiping tears away with our sleeves.

You should come up and see us for a weekend while you're still home, he said.

I told him I'd try, then turned to greet the next tortured face.

● ● ●

Carter Gattling was from Black Mountain, not far from Maggie Valley, and he shared my brother's love of the outdoors. They had both majored in Sustainable Development, and after graduation Carter put his studies into practice. He bought a patch of forest in the middle of nowhere and joined the small community of back-to-the-landers who called the wilderness around Boone home. A few weeks after that scene in the garage, I took him up on his offer. It was late November by then, and the air was ripe with the smell of burning leaves. I met Carter and his girlfriend, Jodie, at a bar near campus, and for a long, idyllic afternoon we drank cold draft beer and shared stories about Bobby, stories I'd heard before or hadn't, it didn't matter, all of them were wonderful. I'd spent a lot of time around Carter over the years, but always with my brother, the result being that while Carter and I knew the facts of each other's lives, we didn't *really* know each other. We realized this right away and were embarrassed by it. To compensate, we moved quickly to stress our more flawed natures, if only to make Bobby seem more perfect. We unburdened ourselves in the comfort of loose acquaintance, laughing and crying and then laughing again. Everything I'd stored up, all I couldn't show, couldn't say, back home.

They asked me to stay the night. There was a party in the high country. Good people, friends of Bobby's. I said I couldn't, that I had to get back to Maggie Valley, but even as I spoke I pictured my parents in their half-lit living room, silently staring at the TV screen, *through* the TV screen, through the Saturday-night movie, through even their own reflections, their eyes drawn to the images, the color and light, but unable to follow story lines or process plots. I called them on my cell phone, told them not to wait up.

Two hours later I was sitting at the edge of a lake watching a blazing sun sink below a cloudless green horizon. It was a pageant of perfect color. The lake caught the waning light and held it for a time, dead still, and the fifteen or twenty of us assembled on the small, rocky beach watched with reverence until the last glow vanished beneath the surface. We were in the mountains, a few miles from Silverstone, but we could have been the only humans on earth. Nothing man-made marred the landscape—no boats on the water, no electrical towers in the hills—and I knew that wasn't a coincidence. Bobby's friends were called back-to-the-landers because there was cachet to the term, but really they were Luddites, smart kids who'd grown up near nature and felt an attachment to it that trumped all else. They weren't starry-eyed hippies. They held down jobs as geologists, engineers, park rangers, community planners. Most owned land and paid taxes, had young families, and drove hybrid cars. In other words, they lived, however tenuously, within our fragile system. Still, they rejected its creature comforts in favor of organic farming, renewable energy—*sustainable living*. These weekend get-togethers, it was clear, were their chance to talk shop, and as we settled in around the campfire, I listened trans-fixed as Carter and his friends began discussing agronomic breeding, gyroscopic precession, photovoltaic incentives. . . . It was another lan-guage altogether, strange and scientific, the language of pioneers and homesteaders stuck in the wrong age—the modern one—and perhaps it was the glow of the embers, or the flawless starry night, but every-one suddenly looked so beautiful, so wonderfully alive.

It was Jodie who brought up my brother. I'd been introduced to everyone by then, seen the smiles turn, the expressions fleck with sadness, pure and haunting. These were people like me, people who'd spent the last month trying to come to terms with the world they inhabited, a place of gorgeous sunsets and godless deaths, and you just couldn't think about it too much—about how it happened and who was responsible—without losing your mind. *And now here was his sister.* Jodie cleared the air gracefully and without artifice. She just said how much Bobby would have wanted to be here, at this moment, with the fire, the lake, the company. That was all. No piling on. Peo-ple nodded and raised their drinks. I could have stayed right there forever.

Tight joints and cheap red wine. Carter was talking about a coun-try separating from the natural world. His voice gave way to a chorus of others, a conversation expanding ever outward. At some point I realized Carter and Jodie were gone. Several people were gone. Turned in maybe. Pleasantly stoned, I got up, dusted myself off, and stumbled toward the small cluster of tents in the grass above the beach. The moon shone as the sun had earlier, illuminating the lake like a dream.

I found the tent Carter had set up for me and began unzipping things—flaps and folds, a sleeping bag. The ground was hard and cold, but tonight it felt like home. I lay there, between water and woods, and experienced that rare sensation of coming down just right. Glowing contentment, perfect languor.

The voices must have woken me, but the flashlights are what I saw. Beams dancing in the darkness.

Is Paige asleep? I heard Carter whisper.

I think so, Jodie answered. She wasn't up by the fire.

More footsteps, people bunking down. I peered through a flap and there was Carter's foot, inches from my face. He was searching through a backpack.

I'm awake, I whispered.

Carter jumped, startled, then quickly regained his composure.

I'm sorry, he said. We didn't mean to be so loud.

What time is it?

Late.

Where were you guys?

A meeting, Carter said, his voice low and earnest. Behind him, I could make out Jodie's silhouette. She was brushing her teeth at the water's edge.

Do you usually hold meetings in the middle of the night?

Pretty much every week, he answered. Five or six of us. Kind of a core group.

A core group of what?

Do you really want to know?

Well, I'm up now.

Carter tilted his head and regarded me curiously, as if silently debating something.

What is it? I asked.

Nothing. It's just . . .

I kept my eyes on him. He sighed.

Okay, come with me.

I slipped my sneakers on and followed him back to the fire. The clearing was deserted, the flames reduced to thin wisps of smoke. We sat on the ground, our backs against a log.

You cold? he asked.

I was, but told him I was fine. He picked up a stick and started poking at the ashes. I watched him and waited.

So, he said. I'm not sure how to say this. But in terms of activism or advocacy—Carter patted himself down, searching for a cigarette he didn't have—well, some of us are more *involved* than others.

In what?

In trying to change things. His eyes narrowed. He was concentrating on the end of the stick in his hand. He swallowed and continued. Living off the grid is one thing, he said, but it's mostly a defensive measure. You don't like your neighbors or your church or your government, so you pick up your ball and go play by yourself. And that's fine. Actually, it's admirable. But there's a more *offensive* approach as well.

Like protests?

Like *action*.

My eyes were adjusting to the darkness. I could make out rock formations across the lake, trees behind the trees that surrounded the clearing. Distance and depth and it felt like I'd traveled a great distance to get there. Carter was watching me; I could feel the weight of his gaze. Then he tossed his stick in the remains of the fire and looked up at the brilliant sky.

When I was a kid, he said, we had a telescope on our porch. I used to spend hours looking for the American flag on the surface of the moon. And after a while, I always convinced myself I'd found it. I guess I just wanted to believe in my country.

I think there are six of them, I said, smiling.

Six what? Carter asked.

American flags on the moon. One for each Apollo landing.

Really? How'd you know that?

I read too much.

Carter looked almost sheepish. What I was trying to say, he continued, is that I've never lost that feeling, that naïve patriotism, even with all that's happened in America. *Especially* with all that's happened.

Are you telling me this because of Bobby?

I'm telling you because you asked.

And if I asked you to keep talking?

I'd say I would have guessed as much.

● ● ·

Naïveté. Carter used the word that night in the woods, and it still hovers over me these many months later. How a girl like me could fall so quickly, so deeply, into a world like that. Let me say, first, that the transformation occurred in stages, one leading rationally to the next. At least it seemed rational at the time. And perhaps that's an answer right there. *At the time.* Because I was drowning, even before Bobby was killed. My many personal failings, at work and in love, in New York and then D.C., had led to a loss of . . . not *hope*, per se, but *anticipation*. At twenty-eight, my life had simply stopped getting better, had reached a plateau in a windowless K Street office, in a crumbling basement apartment off Dupont Circle. The air around me no longer circulated, and I'd retreated inside myself. Was I depressed? I suppose, though I'd never have admitted it at the time (and even now I struggle with the idea of that clinical diagnosis, *any* clinical diagnosis). My problem was one familiar to political idealists and aid workers everywhere. I was beginning, through countless cycles of hope and disappointment, to understand the bitter truth of governmental stagnation. Policy was achieved solely through great power, progress by something more like accident. And when you've fallen for all the youthful clichés about making a difference, when you've tailored your life around them, hitting that impenetrable wall of reality is devastating. For things were only getting worse. The global economy was in shambles, the developing world falling out of reach. I was falling out of reach. I was losing myself.

And then I lost my brother.

When Bobby died, I went from feeling helpless to feeling nothing. I left my life in Washington behind and began operating in a far less definable space. Outwardly, I poured my energies into taking care of my parents. Christmas was coming and they'd thrown themselves into the season with all the vigor of true believers, zealots on a mission to prove that enough tinsel and lights and wrapping paper could conceal their suffering forever. I couldn't blame them, but I couldn't watch them either. The house I'd grown up in had changed overnight. The seventies motif, once homey and eclectic, suddenly seemed worn down and badly dated—the carpets clashed, the furniture bled. At some point the numbness began to wear off, and what replaced it was quiet anger, then seething rage. Nights of not even trying to sleep. Days of wondering why. Why him? Why me? Was this how America paid people back? My insides churned to the point of physical sickness, and as the new year approached and my parents began a slow and somber recovery, I realized I had to leave. But I had nowhere to go, nowhere I *wanted* to go. The East Coast—New York then D.C.—had failed me, or I, unprepared and ill-equipped, had failed it. San Francisco loomed, of course—as it always had for searchers and misfits like me—but it was really just a name, an aging idea, the place where you ended up when you could run no farther. But run I had to, somewhere. Anywhere.

Carter must have guessed my mind-set that night by the fire. He must have known I'd say yes.

With my parents' blessing (they were thrilled to see me getting out of the house, even if they didn't know exactly why), I started driving to Boone once or twice a week. Carter's little cabal had almost a dozen members, and we met in private homes or designated places in the hills. Someone usually brought wine, but it was never a party. Too much was at stake. The group's goal was to bring environmental offenders to the public's attention. They attended protests—from local boycotts to national marches—and wrote opinion pieces, but that, I soon learned, was a benign front, a public face for friends and family. Because their real talent was civil disobedience and minor subversion: vandalism, sabotage, agitation, sedition. They disrupted press conferences, leaked stolen company documents, and tagged physical structures with wanton artistry. Their targets were lumber companies, chemical factories, and biotech start-ups. Small-town mills and national food conglomerates. Anyone and everyone who treated the world as a waste site.

I was indoctrinated slowly. I cooked meals, painted signs, and handed out flyers at rallies. The tasks were small but exhilarating, for we were confronting the world ad hoc, on the fly. And the results were right there in front of us—on local newscasts, in the morning papers. My former employer—a leading environmental-policy institute—spent tens of thousands of man-hours a year accomplishing not nearly as much. At least in terms of visible progress.

Bobby's death afforded me a certain status among Carter's friends, a kind of inherited trust (that also served to dissuade romantic inclinations). In this tightest of groups, I was suddenly everyone's sister. Still, I couldn't shake the feeling that I'd snuck in through a side door. I had no credentials, warranted no respect, so I set out to earn these things. I raised my hand when others didn't—to buy supplies, to research targets. January passed, then February. I told my parents I'd found a part-time job with a small environmental group (which was more or less true) and soon thereafter moved into a crash pad outside Boone (though I still came home most weekends). Everything seemed temporary, but I didn't mind. I threw myself into my new life, buoyed not just by the physical excitement of our days, but by talks that lasted all night, discussions and debates, rants and lectures, about how the country had stalled out, and how it might get up and running again.

I began to take a more central role in the Actions. I snuck around warehouses and drove getaway cars. I enjoyed the planning stages—I could lose myself in details and forget my larger life for a while—but carrying out the plans was the real thrill. I didn't care about consequences and quickly realized I had no fear of authority. We saw ourselves as charismatic rebels—striking back at a faceless oppressor—and if such aggressive, offensive-minded thoughts were unfamiliar to me, they were also not entirely unpleasant.

At a meeting one night in late February, Carter pulled me aside and asked if I'd like to be the point person for an Action being planned outside Keyser, West Virginia. One hundred and fifty acres of first-growth forest along the Savage River had been cleared to make room for a new paper mill, and the double-barreled assault on the environment was too much to ignore. I jumped at the chance. The Action was already in motion, and I quickly caught myself up on its particulars. The factory's building permit had been approved by the state in a backroom deal typical of controversial projects. There had been no community hearings. The public, Carter said, was barely aware of the factory at all, and it was up to us to change that.

The plan was to build a massive bonfire in front of the unfinished building. Once lit, the flames would leap into the midnight sky, illuminating a message scrawled above the entranceway in giant red letters: PAPER BURNS WELL. GET OUT! We'd alert the press beforehand, so they'd be there to witness the whole gorgeous scene. Would we ultimately stop construction? Probably not. But if the arson was reported in the news, people would become aware of the factory's existence, and, well, at some point citizens needed to take responsibility for their own communities.

I would spray-paint the wall while Carter built and lit the fire. Jodie would be watching from an idling car, and when she gave the signal (via walkie-talkie), a fourth member of the team would call the local newspapers and TV stations from a nearby pay phone. Timing was essential: we wanted the press (and police) to arrive while the flames were at their height; at the same time, we had to be long gone. So we planned meticulously. We cased the construction site, in daylight and darkness. Carter practiced building fires in clearings, adjusting the tinder ingredients (reams of paper, wood, and a healthy dose of lighter fluid) until the flames leaped and danced and threatened to ignite the world.

Finally, one rainy afternoon in early March, we packed up a car, changed its plates, and drove north.

I don't know if these pages will ever see the light of day, or even, as I delve deeper into all that's happened, if they should. There are practical concerns, people still out there—friends. So I'll protect them here by changing names (Carter's and Jodie's, for instance), and when it serves to, leaving out the inner machinations of our Actions. Mostly, though, I have nothing to hide and nothing to lose, and what I'm relating here is as true as memory will allow.

I remember clearly what it felt like to sneak across that construction site under cover of night. I was dressed all in black and wore gloves and a ski mask. It had been raining on and off for several hours and the air still hung heavy, fog enshrouding the far-off streetlights. The grounds were deserted. The wall up ahead was blank and beckoning. I located the ladder we'd snuck in the day before and got to work, spraying haphazardly. The paint looked like blood, and I guess it was supposed to. I could hear Carter behind me in the darkness, wrestling with wood, tearing open packages of paper. A block away, phone calls were being made. I peered at my watch: two more minutes. Paint was everywhere. It started drizzling again. I moved the ladder along the factory wall, once, then again, as the giant words crept into being.

When I was finished, I whistled into the night—it was the signal to light the fire—then jumped down, grabbed the ladder, and placed it, for aesthetic purposes, back where I'd found it. I threw the paint cans into a pile of nearby debris and started jogging back toward the car. I glanced in the direction of Carter's fire. There should have been flames by now, but I saw nothing. Was it blocked out by machinery? Was my timing off? I looked at my watch again. I had just enough time to get across the site and duck through the hole we'd cut in the fence. But something wasn't right; I could sense it. I was now fifty or sixty yards from where the flames should have been—but still weren't. And there was no sign of Carter either. We'd have company soon, news trucks and squad cars. We'd been told to keep to the plan no matter what, but I stopped in my tracks, then ran back the way I'd just come, through the rain and the night, until I could make out a figure hunched over a hulking pile of wood wrapped in soggy paper. Carter was cursing quietly, urgently.

Hey, I hissed.

He turned around, the look on his face wild, desperate. *What the fuck are you doing?* he demanded. You should be back in the car.

Yeah, with you, I said. What's wrong?

What do you think's wrong? *The rain!* I can't get the damn thing to stay lit!

Where's the lighter fluid?

I've been using it!

Here, I'll pour. You trail behind me with the flame. It'll still catch underneath.

He threw me the can of fluid. It was almost empty. I stepped up to the tepee-shaped pile and pushed aside the outermost layer of paper and wood. It wasn't dry underneath, but it wasn't soaked either, so I started spilling a trail of liquid into the depths of the sticks and stakes and kindling. Beside me, Carter leaned in and pulled the trigger of his industrial-size lighter, concentrating the flame precisely where I was pouring. A sudden flash of fire jolted us both, then died down before finally sustaining itself. We did the same thing on the other side—though I'm not sure we had to, as the flames were already spreading—until the container was empty. I threw it on the fire, grabbed Carter by the wrist, and we started running. I don't know who heard the sirens first, but we slowed down a moment, before speeding back up, before sprinting, through the rain, past piles of steel beams, around cranes as high as clouds, and I felt it then, the unburdening, the sudden freedom of the anticitizen, the cool blackness of an illicit world—open and immediate and malleable for the first time. We didn't turn around until we were in the car, driving back past the half-finished factory. The fire was magnificent now, an inferno mocking the constructions of man. And behind it the massive red words flickered in eerie shadows like a warning cry, like a reason to live. We turned onto the main road and saw the first police car twenty seconds later. In the backseat we ducked down and giggled as it hurtled past us at a hundred miles an hour.

I was treated like a star after that, and it felt as if there were no turning back. In the countless retellings, Carter exaggerated my role until it sounded like I'd saved his life when all I'd really done was help light the fire. Still, what a fire it was! The arson led off the local newscasts, but we didn't rest on our laurels. By the time the West Virginia attorney general's office announced an investigation into the factory's permits, we'd already moved on to other states, other Actions. *Stages, each leading naturally to the next.* I learned how to pick locks, how to hot-wire cars. I was told to stop attending public protests (they didn't want me photographed or arrested). And soon, I was being introduced to a new group of people, solemn men and women who carried themselves with the confidence of bigger battles fought and won. They appeared late at night and peppered me with questions. They were looking for reasons to reject me, and when none surfaced, they changed their tone and invited me in. This was the realm of professional radicals—eco-warriors and anticapitalists. Within weeks, my old friends—the regional activists like Carter and Jodie—fell away. Hobbyists, my new comrades called them.

If we had a physical presence, a de facto headquarters, it was the dimly lit basement apartment we rented with cash in a run-down section of Raleigh. We started using it for meetings in late March, when the days were still short and the streets mostly empty. It was there, late one night, that I first met Keith Sutter. A housing subdivision was being laid out on contested Native American land in the Ozarks, and a few of us stood huddled over a table, staring at a set of project plans we'd found online. Those nights, when our chosen target was still at a distance, when the factory or the warehouse or the gated community was still an abstract concept, lines on a blueprint, those nights were my favorites. The event was still before us, and the potential destruction, the victims, the *consequences,* were far off and always negligible.

Destruction, victims, *violence:* it seems an indelicate way to introduce Keith because, until that point, physical aggression had not factored into anyone's planning. Our Actions were pointedly small and precisely planned and never involved weapons of any kind—guns or explosives. Violence of that nature was so far from our thinking that it never even came up. That's not to say we weren't aware of other groups out there—other *people*—that went to such extremes. We were always hearing stories, and most of them, sooner or later, included the name Keith Sutter.

The rumor had been going around for days: that he was in the Carolinas. It was passed along in self-congratulatory whispers, as if his mere proximity were a validation of all our work. His physical appearance was a well-kept secret, so when he finally showed up, we didn't even realize it was him. He walked into the apartment with another man, and they milled around in the kitchen awhile. We were aware of them, as we stood over the table, but only in the dimmest sense (activist-types were always coming and going in the background of our lives, hovering on the edges of low-lit rooms at odd hours). If you weren't directly involved in an Action, then, for reasons of both security and plausible deniability, you steered clear of the talk surrounding it. So the two men kept their distance until we'd stashed away our maps and notes and dispersed. I walked over to get a beer, and that's when one of them put his hand out and said hello. It was that simple.

Did I know he was there to see me? I had an idea. Without trying to sound vain, I was aware of my growing status within the group. I was one of only a few women in our ranks, and I came without questions or complications—unless you count motive. But everyone had motives, whether made public or kept private, and mine were more than justifiable. What set me apart was my willingness to act on them physically. To take surveillance photos in the black of night. To trespass with wire cutters and spray paint. To press forward where others held back.

I followed Keith out to a small patio area, and we sat down on two foldout chairs. Before us lay a narrow back alley that led off into the darkness. That's why they'd rented the place, I realized: the escape route. The multiple-exit rule. All of this I registered in an instant. How my mind was changing.

He didn't talk about himself; he didn't have to. Instead, Keith asked about my past—Maggie Valley and UNC, New York and Washington. I answered his questions. I had nothing to hide. He didn't mention Bobby, but I could tell he knew the story. He seemed to know everything I was saying. Which is when he told me why he'd come.

He was going to blow up a coal mine in eastern Kentucky.

Using explosives? I asked.

Yes, using explosives. It's in Pike County. A slope mine owned by Tarver Coal and Energy. They're responsible for twelve miner deaths in just the last two years. To say nothing of their aboveground offenses—the air pollution, contaminated streams, the cancer clusters. In *kids,* no less. Blue baby syndrome, ever heard of that?

Yes, I said, and waited for him to continue. I had also heard of Tarver Coal, and I knew what a slope mine was, and how it differed from a drift mine and a shaft mine. I knew, in fact, that over three hundred coal mines existed in Kentucky, and could even name most of the counties they were in. Why? Because I was a child of Appalachia. I'd grown up around coal, had friends and uncles and even a grandfather who had at one time or another worked underground. It was an awful business, dirty in every conceivable way, but *blowing something up* . . .

Keith leaned forward, resting his forearms on his knees, and explained his plan in a voice so low I had to strain to hear it. He would use nitroamine combined with mineral oil to set off a controlled, delayed-fuse explosion that would cave in not only the shaft, but the entire length of the mine. Why was he telling me this? And why in such detail? Because he was daring me to stop him. Daring me to stand up and walk back inside. It was a test. If I stayed silent, I'd become complicit. And then I'd be with him.

So I said, You shouldn't do it.

Really? Okay, then . . . Keith scratched the back of his neck, as if disappointment had suddenly made his skin itch. What's the problem? he asked. The method? Bombs are no different from anything else, really. They just let us play in a larger arena. The rules are still the same, chief among them being *no human casualties*. But I understand. What I'm talking about . . . it's not entered into lightly. Now, it goes without saying, you can't discuss a word of this with anyone, including—

Keith, I said. What I mean is . . . there's a better target.

Excuse me?

Than the Tarver mine.

He looked directly at me for the first time, as if he'd only now decided to grant me total access. It was a neat trick, emerging from imaginary shadows, and it worked. I stumbled for a moment. It's not that he was physically overpowering; on the contrary, he was on the slight side. He had a close-cropped beard, and his face was hard and tan and a bit worn by the elements. His lips were permanently chapped, like a mountain climber's, but he still looked young, taut. His eyes were green and watery and somehow optimistic. In another world I'd have found him handsome. In this one I found him *strong*.

He was waiting for me to continue. So I did. If you're going after a mine, it should be aboveground, I said. A mountaintop mine. They're the worst. The mining companies don't even bother to drill down. They just remove the mountain itself, layer by layer, and dump the toxic excess—it's called coal slurry—into huge black ponds that they dam up and leave there until the protective layering leaks or bursts. And they leave what's left of the mountain, too, except it's not a mountain anymore. It's just a bald plateau. And your beleaguered miners? You don't have to worry about them because they'll have been replaced by bulldozers and bombs. Ammonium nitrate and diesel fuel, I believe, but that's your department. It shouldn't be hard to find out what they use. Just drive up to West Virginia and stick your head out the window. You'll hear the blasts.

Keith leaned back, a trace of a grin on his face.

That's very interesting, he said. But tell me, why blow up a mine that's already been blown up? Who would notice, or care? The object of every Action should be visibility, generating attention. A cave-in serves that purpose. It'll shine a spotlight onto a gloomy little corner of America, at least temporarily. And that's all we can ask for.

Keith was humoring me, but I didn't mind. I'd just been showing off, pretending this talk of bombs had no effect on me. Because it did. Still, he'd raised the stakes and I hadn't flinched. I went inside and (ignoring the curious looks) got us two more beers. We talked a while longer, about other stuff, music and books and places we'd been, and if you'd missed round one, you'd have thought it was the most normal conversation in the world. Hell, it could have been a date.

Finally, he stood up and dusted off his jeans. I need to get going, he said. Probably been here too long already.

Well, it was a pleasure to—

Do you want to come work with us? With me? This coming summer?

It was, I knew by then, what he'd come here to do. Recruit me. And before I knew what I was doing, or why, I said: Yes, I'd like that very much.

AIDAN

· · · ● ● ● ● ● ● · · ● ●

WE STARED AT THE SCREEN IN DUMB SILENCE. IT'S NOT THAT WE BELIEVED the woman in the photograph was involved in the bombing (we never *believed* in anything, which, as I write now, seems as good a generational epigraph as any); it's just that she was mesmerizing, even slightly out of focus. Hell, it was late: we were all out of focus.

"She looks like that actress with the great tits," Touché said, from over my shoulder. "I met her once at a party in Silver Lake. I think she lives in Brooklyn now."

"You can't even see her tits," I said, squinting at the screen.

"But her face, her hair."

"Are you guys looking at porn?" the DJ asked from across the room.

We weren't sure what we were looking at. Paige Roderick—or whoever she was—had been captured in transit, and the blurriness dulled her features, made them difficult to pin down, hidden as they were behind the sunglasses. Still, the image suggested real beauty; her jawline, her nose, these things came through. It could have been an outtake from a photo shoot.

"Who sends you this kind of shit?" Touché asked.

"Who doesn't? You should see my in-box. Every publicist in the city e-mails me about their clients—new restaurants, movies, books, bands, you name it. But fake photographs of glammed-up terrorists? That's something new."

"Juuulian," the DJ purred. She was lounging on the bed, flipping idly through an art book.

"Why don't I let you two—"

"Ah, Aidan, yes, perhaps . . ."

I signed out of my e-mail account, slapped Touché on the back, and made my exit. Out in the main room, the bar was being dismantled, and the last of the stragglers—including, apparently, Derrick Franklin and Cressida—had moved on to an after-hours club on Chrystie Street. I stepped across the room and through the front door.

It was after 3 a.m., and the Meatpacking District was tucking itself in for the night. I wandered south down narrow, tree-lined blocks, in no particular hurry to get home. A lifetime in New York and still I found myself happening upon streets I'd never heard of before. Downing. Dominick. Collister. King. There was even a Gay Street— crooked and colorful—right in the middle of all the action. I lived on one of these hidden estuaries myself, a dark, vice-filled alley named Weehawken Street. It existed for only a block, between Christopher and West Tenth, just off the West Side Highway. While gentrification threatened from all directions, it never quite reached little Weehawken Street. But everything else did: hookers from the Carousel Club; dealers from the piers; gangbangers from the PATH station; and beefy drunks from the nearby leather bars. I had three locks on my door. And they took forever to figure out when I was wasted.

I woke to a vibrating phone and the smell of stagnant river water. Outside, the sun was already high in the sky, and the thin slice of the Hudson visible from my fifth-floor window had been disconcertingly replaced by a white building, sparkling and enormous. And then it moved! It wasn't a building, but a *cruise ship*, sliding slowly out to sea.

The phone buzzed again. I knew it was Derrick without even looking, and I knew what he was calling about. It was midmorning, and I should have started posting almost two hours ago. Still, I let it go to voicemail and focused instead on ingesting Advil and coffee. I was in the shower when I remembered the girl on the screen. Now, in the daylight, in the cramped but familiar confines of my apartment, the episode hardly seemed real. I toweled off and walked over to my computer.

Two clicks and there she was, right where I'd left her. Who was she? I threw on a pair of boxers and sat down. *This is Paige Roderick. She's the one responsible.* Here was the Internet in all its worthless glory. A pretty face captured at the right—or wrong—time and place, then twisted to fit some idiot's idea of a sinister joke. Such is the currency of our voyeuristic age. The sender's address was EmpiresFall@gmail.com. A bit heavy-handed, but a nice touch. Whoever sent it must have figured a legitimate news organization wouldn't fall for a prank like this, but what about a hungover blogger looking to generate page-views to get his boss off his back? I could already see the headline: BARNEYS INTRODUCES THE NEW FACE OF TERROR.

I checked my competitors, but there were no posts about a Paige Roderick. Google revealed a handful of women who shared the name— a librarian in Barstow, a city-records clerk in Cedar Rapids, and a girls' summer-camp archery champion in Boone, North Carolina—but none appeared to be moonlighting anarchists. I kept going—Facebook, Flickr, Twitter, YouTube, a few online directories—but the woman in the photo, whoever she was, didn't materialize. So I decided to post the thing. Why not? I'd put it in context, give my readers a taste of the absurdity I dealt with daily. She'd certainly arouse commenter interest. But what if she aroused other interest, from people not known for their taste in irony—the cops, say, or the FBI? That's the last thing I needed. And so I reconsidered. Here's another generational epigraph: *The potential hassle outweighed the benefits.* Paige remained where I'd found her. In my in-box.

Where was I? I wasn't anywhere. No ideas, nothing to follow up on. I scanned the online news sites, but I was hours too late. They'd all been read and digested, considered and critiqued, then vomited back up by people like me. Desperate, I turned to the gossip blogs. They were always good in a pinch. I drummed up a few snide headlines, some pithy one-liners, then linked to the more outrageous items. Nonoriginal original content: the secret to blogging longevity. Unfortunately, the secret was not lost on Derrick Franklin. Which reminded me. I checked my voice mail and there he was, launching into his familiar diatribe about audience retention, click-through rates, expectancy levels—all that technical crap that had made him rich. I pressed ERASE when he started in on my nocturnal habits—the hypocrite—and sat down to work.

Blogging was like any other addiction: I couldn't get away from it, and I couldn't get enough. I talked in paragraphs; I thought in punch lines. I was always *on,* playing the person in life that I was on-screen, and it was tiring and draining and I never wanted it to end. Luckily, it never did. Five days a week I ticked off my dozen posts—rain or shine, drunk or sober—with notebook hash marks, a latter-day Edmond Dantès passing the time before his escape from prison. Except I had nowhere to go. I'd been institutionalized, and the real world was now a far scarier place than the blogosphere. Out there, I was like everyone else. Online, I was royalty, and Roorback, a never-ending roast—a grand exercise in mocking what we love. At least that was the party line. And people did ask at parties. They asked how I lived with myself, smiling as they did so, lest I take offense.

Thank God for the reliable fallbacks, the ongoing train wrecks that saved the slow news days. Chief among these was the oft-rumored demise of the *New York Times.* Print media had been ailing for years, of course, but the recession was threatening to finish the job, leaving midsize cities without newspapers, and Middle America without beauty magazines. Now the *Times* was in real trouble. How much, no one knew exactly, but it sure was fun to speculate. And it pissed the hell out of Cressida, who saw my posts about her employer as retaliation for her monthly dating columns. But that was just it! What the hell was the *Times* doing with a dating columnist? This was the paper of record, not the paper of romance, and yet there they were, like everyone else, dumbing down their content for some focus-grouped, survey-driven, perfectly average American reader who didn't exist. To Cressida's credit, the column was just a sideline. She'd been reporting hard news all along and had recently asked the editors if she could give up her columnist duties altogether. They had begged her not to, then offered her a raise.

I wrote a paragraph detailing a rumor I'd heard (at the party) about a fresh round of editorial layoffs. The newsroom was getting smaller, foreign bureaus were closing. Journalism as we knew it was done. Let someone else argue that we needed reporters now more than ever. As markets swooned and countries bled. That wasn't my job. I kept the political and economic commentary to a bare minimum. I kept everything to a bare minimum.

I posted the item and tried to build on the momentum. But inspiration was tough to come by. I'd like to blame the hangover, but I'd functioned fine on worse. The truth is I couldn't stop thinking about Paige Roderick. Was it the photograph itself? Or the bizarre context surrounding it? I worked into the late afternoon, and then, my quota almost met, wrote the e-mail that had been forming in my head for the last several hours:

> To: EmpiresFall@gmail.com
> From: RoarHere@Roorback.com
> Subject: Barneys
> Thanks for the photo. How was the shopping?

I pressed SEND and moved on. Another hour of work. A drink or two. Then a party in Alphabet City.

Days in the country move slowly. I watch sunsets, notice subtle changes, the cycles that become seasons. And I take things a step further, because there's time now. I guess I'm learning to be alone. Perhaps the writing helps, reassembling my life a chapter at a time. I'd planned to fully introduce myself by including a few of the more intriguing items I've posted over the years (my handlers even printed them out for me), but Roorback seems so sadly pointless now. I think I better give you the story straight.

I grew up on the Upper West Side. It was still a liberal neighborhood then, and my parents fit the stereotype. They met the day Armstrong walked on the moon, at a "landing party" in New Haven (where they were both spending the summer before their junior year at Yale). Susan Hamlin was a young activist, involved with antiwar groups; William Cole was open-minded. They spent the next two years together, thoroughly immersed in the issues of the age (and with the pictures to prove it). They were liberal but they weren't lost, and when graduation came, they did the practical thing—got married and moved to New York. My mother went to work for various homeless and affordable-housing groups. My father, squirmish in suits but not lacking ambition, fell into advertising (does anyone ever *choose* it?). It was a compromise, a steady paycheck in a creative field. As it turned out, his timing was perfect. The seventies were the golden age of brand building, when a single catchy tagline—Bounty's *The Quicker Picker-Upper*; AmEx's *Don't Leave Home Without It*; Volkswagen's *Think Small*—could build a company and make a career. My father helped come up with all of those or, as my mother explained when I asked her years later, was at least present at their creations.

"They'd go to the '21' Club for three-hour lunches," she said, "and then stumble back to the office hopelessly drunk but with America's next great jingle scribbled on a wet cocktail napkin stuffed in someone's pocket. The Absolut vodka concept—you know, the one with the bottle—well, your father made me run to the dry cleaner one morning to save those sketches. He'd forgotten about them. I got there just in time."

Absolut was his crowning achievement. One afternoon, in 1980, an art director at his agency drew a bottle backlit with a halo. Below it he wrote, *Absolut: The Perfect Vodka*. He showed it to my father, who nonchalantly crossed out the tagline and replaced it with *Absolut Perfection*. And that was that. Thirty years and eight hundred ads later, it's become the most successful alcohol campaign in history.

I was three when he wrote those words, and they came to define my urban childhood. My parents believed in the city, even then, *especially* then, when so many didn't. I went to public schools, had friends who lived in Harlem, Brooklyn, Queens. I spent untold hours with my mother in church basements and community centers, listening as she preached and pleaded and organized. Occasionally, she'd run into people from her past, college activists who'd stayed involved. Then there'd be hugs and coffee, maybe dinner if my father was working late. He'd been hired by one of his clients by then, the renegade creative director turned corporate branding executive. This was Reagan's America now, clean and sober, rounded at the jagged edges. The bums in the park outside our apartment on Seventy-third Street and Riverside began disappearing. And so did what was inside. The overstuffed couches of my youth gave way to chairs no one could sit in. The once homey kitchen was redone with marble countertops and track lighting. The bookshelves were jettisoned for a Basquiat that later turned out to be fake.

They started fighting when I was in eighth grade. My mother was hoping I'd apply to Stuyvesant, that most famous of public high schools, nurturer of New York's best and brightest. For a certain type of parent, Stuyvesant represented an educational ideal, proof of what was possible in the beleaguered souls of American cities. I doubt I'd have got in—I was an indifferent student—but we'd never know for sure because one morning, at our speckled breakfast table, my father announced I'd be attending Dalton, the rich boy's school on the East Side. It was a place of patches and pledges and codes, a well-endowed testament to conformity of every kind. I remember vividly the look on my mother's face that morning, a sad mix of defiance and inevitability. As if it were the very moment she'd been dreading. We were never the same after that.

I spent four years riding the crosstown bus, did an academically necessary PG year at St. Andrew's in Scotland, then skied away another four at Middlebury. A decade of youthful exuberance pointed in the wrong direction, years that had their moments but never found a groove. A raison d'être. A thousand parties, five thousand, and the only one that mattered was the one I'd missed in New York. The one that had made everyone else rich. I graduated from college two months after the Internet bubble burst and arrived back to a city in flux. But the biggest changes had occurred closer to home. Or what was left of it.

The apartment on Riverside Drive was for sale. Or maybe it had already been sold, I can't remember. My parents had separated and then divorced while I'd been in Vermont. My father—the guilty party—had packed up and relocated to Connecticut, where he'd commenced a series of short, inelegant relationships that eventually led to wedded bliss with Julie, a former cocktail waitress a year older than me (and with three kids of her own). My mother, meanwhile, had gamely soldiered on in New York, until the city became too much for her, the memories and all that. During my senior year she moved upstate. With no family apartment to crash-land in after graduation, I sublet a small room in a friend's loft just west of McCarren Park, in a then desolate stretch of Williamsburg, Brooklyn. From there I began a cheerless trek through one failing dot-com after another. What I remember from the year 2000 is the paperwork: endless options grants and health-care plans, Cobra applications and unemployment forms. I gave up after the third company went under.

What to do? I'd majored in English—a fact I kept returning to as if it carried some secret inevitability—and had always been open to writing, in that I could string sentences together and didn't feel terribly put out doing it. So I found a bartending job on Bedford Avenue and weighed my literary options. This was the great age of freelancing, outsourcing, contract work, and no profession lent itself to the time as much as journalism. But I knew people traveling that rutted road—pitching articles, sending out stories on spec, *building clips*. They'd show up at the bar, proudly waving around their latest piece—a D-list celebrity Q-and-A, a back-of-the-book band review, a restaurant profile in an airline magazine—and I'd pour them a drink on the house and try to muster some enthusiasm. But it was just so much work for so little reward. The cover letters, the rejections, the research, the writing, the editing, the mailbox-checking, the disappointment, the depression, the drinking. And I could drink just fine without the rest of it. I did my best to commiserate, but the unhappy endings took their toll. You can start with all the good intentions you want, but soon enough they'll drown in a pool of other people's failures. The idea of writing was losing its luster. Paying dues suddenly felt like an old-fashioned concept. Hadn't the Internet promised to speed everything up, hustle us along to our true destinies?

I fell in with a dodgy crowd of young Brooklynites: art handlers, line cooks, waiters, and actresses—always actresses—everywhere I went. We became nocturnal creatures, midnight poseurs, thrift-shop dynamos: thin-waisted and scraggly. Oh, life was heavy out there in the borough, laden with all the irony of the age. We lived on the cheap, carping like victims, carrying on like addicts. In the aftermath of the tech bust, *money,* like *Manhattan,* became a tainted word. Yet we cared a great deal about appearances, how far we could take our various guises, the many versions of ourselves. The truth, of course, is that we could never get anywhere. We were too sneering and self-aware, too busy mocking the earnest, the successful, anyone we didn't know. We all get lost in little worlds, but they usually have a point—money, maybe, or love. But not us. Never has absolutely nothing been done with more style and determination than in early twenty-first-century Williamsburg, Brooklyn.

Then came 9/11. I was still half-asleep when I heard the news on the radio, but I jumped up, grabbed my roommate's bike, and took off toward Brooklyn Heights. The streets were full of people hurrying every which way, some going home, some to the waterfront. TVs glowed urgently through ground-floor windows. All the taxis had disappeared. One of the bartenders I worked with lived in a tall building near the promenade. We'd partied on her roof before, a bunch of us gazing at the lights of Manhattan as we drank from bottles of wine we'd smuggled out at closing time. And that's where I found her that Tuesday morning, up there with dozens of others, staring out across the East River at a scene we'd never fathomed. A few people were taking pictures, but there wasn't much talking. That would come later, and last for months. At some point the wind stiffened, and with it came that awful burning smell. Most everyone went back downstairs, but some of us stayed. We stayed and watched the towers fall. We stayed and watched streams of men and women course across the Brooklyn Bridge. We stayed and picked through flying papers—business cards, tax forms, résumés—shreds of people's lives, former lives. No longer strangers, we stayed on the roof and held each other, wondering how the world would change.

We all remember what happened next, the days of mourning, not only for the lost, but for our newly vulnerable selves. As the rest of America found solace in blind patriotism, we New Yorkers, momentarily sincere, gazed inward. It was time to revisit the past— old girlfriends, shelved plans. For me that meant journalism. The world, through loss, had suddenly become a fascinating place, acerbically intriguing, almost open-ended. Who wouldn't want to play a role in the remodeling? That winter, I applied to Columbia and NYU. Uptown and down, I could have gone either way, but only NYU said yes. I took out a student loan (my father had retired from financing my education), picked up more shifts at the bar, and spent the months before grad school lost in a haze of hipster nights.

At NYU, I enrolled in classes with glamorous-sounding names— International Reporting, Politics and the Press, Investigative Techniques. It should have been a thrilling time. On the far side of the globe, reporters were camping out with rebels and embedding themselves in Humvees. The present—right then!—was teeming with journalistic opportunities, but the lectures and textbooks watered down any sense of adventure. Other people's stories, other people's wars. Terrorists, generals, presidents: they all blurred together in an endless time line of privileged impropriety. And the reporters, they were just middlemen, information runners, bending the news to their personal beliefs. I don't know, I just wasn't getting the bug. These, remember, were the days leading up to Iraq, and at NYU—and everywhere else in New York—you were either against the war or you were an idiot. There was never room for debate, and that bothered me. It's not that I was a Republican. Far from it. The GOP, with its religious posturing and bullshit moral high-ground, was dangerously out of touch. At least they stood for something, though. The Democrats lived for polls. They ran scared, and voted that way, too.

Was I disillusioned with the system or just lazy? Sitting in the back of class one day, I listened to a former UN diplomat compare Guantánamo to the Gulag, and I realized I was a million miles from either place, from decisions that mattered, events of consequence. I'd grown up with parents who'd once believed change was possible, if only in increments, small measures and token gestures. But the increments never added up. The sixties drifted further into the past, its idealism became the material of memoir—*this is what we did before we grew up*. My father gave in. My mother became irrelevant. What was the lesson in all this? That you couldn't shape the world in your image. And it was a waste of time to try. Life would roll along as scheduled, and all a journalist could do was shine a weak light on the passing trains. I guess my problem—or as I saw it then, my saving grace—was that I didn't think American life in 2003 was so bad. Just look at us, I thought. We were still the most profitable nation in the world, our major cities thriving, our suburbs reaching out like tendrils across a shining landscape of middle-class satisfaction. Sure, there were problems, but I took a long view of history. American prosperity encouraged us to disengage, to stop caring. And so I did.

I dropped out of school before my second year started and, after several months back behind the bar, found a job in advertising. Grow up around an adman and you can't help but read taglines, watch commercials, believe in brands. But the business had changed. Gone were the martini lunches and Madison Avenue addresses. Advertising had been hijacked by the Internet and all that came with it—e-commerce specialists, Web-marketing gurus, and inked-up graphic designers—an army of dot-com holdovers still speaking that confident language of the future. I wrote banner ads. During the boom they'd been a source of revenue on thousands of business plans, except no one ever clicked on them. But it all comes back around if you wait long enough, and when a leaner, smarter Internet emerged, banner ads found their place. Everything found its place. The boys at Google made us think again of possibilities. This time it wasn't all about money. Sure, the staples were still there—e-mail, porn, shopping, stock-trading—but what had finally won the day was content, the scope and speed of available information. Online, people could write anything they wanted. And soon enough they did.

Derrick Franklin—the man on my answering machine, the voice in my head—was the first to make blogging a viable business. After taking a security-software company public in the midnineties, he moved from Redwood City to New York City and reinvented himself as a new-economy philosopher. He'd earned a cult following by getting out before anyone else had gotten in. I used to see him, bald and sharp-jawed, on CNN, casually explaining the future to those of us who couldn't yet see it. Of course, it was impossible to be wrong during the boom, but even afterward, Derrick stuck to his vision of a converging world. One day, he mentioned blogs—their importance, their possibilities. Millions—no *billions*—of people would soon be reading these things, and not just occasionally, but continuously—people with specific interests, people who could be marketed to. He looked squarely into the camera and said the numbers were too good to ignore. And he meant it. A few months later, before anyone else knew what was happening, he'd convinced a dozen of New York's best online writers to come work for him. It was a simple idea: they'd provide the content, he'd provide the site, the paycheck, the health care . . . and the ads, banner ads, the old business model given new life.

Wino, Drummergrrrl, Cindy from BodyPolitic, Rob from LESismore, Sophie from SophiesChoice. I'd read their posts all day, then see them out at night, clustered in corners, shy but secure in their status as the new arbiters of everything. People whispered about them the way our parents must have whispered about Warhol's superstars—with the seething jealousy we save for those who've bucked the system. But had they bucked the system, or did they just understand it better? Derrick's bloggers lived in an impending world, somewhere ahead of the rest of us, posting what we hadn't yet heard, didn't yet know. It was a tricky game, with the race to be first tempered by the risk of being wrong. But on the Internet, speed trumped truth, and sensation always won.

Soon Derrick's bloggers were being read by tens of thousands each day. They stepped out from their dark corners and began hosting readings, appearing on gossip shows, lunching at Michael's. They got book deals and started rock labels. They sat down with Charlie Rose. By 2005, blogs were breaking more hard news than the networks and serving up more cultural commentary than the print magazines. They'd become commodities. They'd become legitimate. Derrick had been proven right faster than even he'd foreseen.

One hungover morning at the agency, I saw an ad I'd written (promoting an animated-fish movie) cycling through the top of the restaurant blog, SophiesChoice. I sat there staring at my lame sea-pun tagline and suddenly had an epiphany. *A media blog.* Derrick Franklin didn't have one. He had the gossip hound, the arts critic, the nightlife guide, the technology guru, the political hack, the porn purveyor, but nothing dedicated to journalism. Or the lack of it. So why not me? I was as unqualified and disillusioned as anyone else. I'd take on the vaunted press, all those bombastic newspapers and formulaic magazines, the whimpering network newscasts and deafening cable shout-fests. The pomposity, hypocrisy, and self-aggrandizement: I'd call it all for what it was.

I practiced for months, regurgitating the news of the day in a series of thoughtful diatribes and funny manifestos. I honed a voice over endless hours of agency time, but my bosses never noticed. I'd been working there three years by then, a lifetime in the ad world, and people left me alone. I was a "creative," after all.

And then it all came together, like nothing else in my life ever had. I found Derrick Franklin's e-mail and sent him my blog in beta. Two days later we met at a coffee shop in Tribeca. We shook hands and sat down with our lattes. He spoke slowly. Precision, I thought. Then: money. That was it: money must be soothing.

He asked about journalism school, why I never finished.

"I'm not that earnest," I said.

"A real New Yorker."

"Born and raised."

"Well, there is a certain swagger to your bitching," he continued. "And it's something I've been thinking about, this whole *New York Observer,* meta-media thing—reporting on reporters, creating news from news . . ."

On and on he went, this modern-day seer, until he arrived at what I'd been hoping for: an offer. It wasn't much—$3,500 a month to start— but I'd be operating under his corporate umbrella, which meant free publicity and libel protection—two things a blogger should never take lightly. We stood up and shook hands. I'd been out of college almost six years. Maybe the Internet would save me after all.

The e-mail arrived at 5:42 p.m., just as I was posting my last item of the day.

> To: RoarHere@Roorback.com
> From: EmpiresFall@gmail.com
> Subject: Barneys
> The shopping wasn't so good. The blowout sale was on the wrong floor.
> P.S. This is your chance.

Who was this? Some kind of practical joker, obviously. But what was the joke? *This is your chance.* To do what? Post Paige Roderick's photograph? Why not just do it themselves? Why choose me?

But the other part is what got my attention. *The shopping wasn't so good. The blowout sale was on the wrong floor.* The intended target of the attack had become a subject of increasingly wild speculation in the four days since the explosion. With the exception of Barneys, 660 Madison Avenue was a typical Midtown office tower populated by dozens of companies, from financial firms to fashion designers. The northeast side of the fifteenth floor, where the bomb actually went off, was the New York headquarters of the dressmaker Claudio Valencia, and for most of that first hectic day the scorched fabrics and blown-apart mannequins that littered the surrounding blocks had everyone thinking his atelier was part of Barneys (which, in fact, topped off on ten). When the smoke subsided and the police and press finally got their facts straight, Valencia became a wanted man. Two days passed before he emerged, on Ibiza, teary-eyed and spaced-out on pills. Turns out he and his all-male entourage had been there for weeks, "seeking inspiration" for his next clothing line. Ah, worlds colliding. The ensuing press conference made for riveting television as Valencia, dressed all in white, broke down completely in front of cameras while U.S. Special Forces stood in the background, bewildered expressions on their hard faces. Clearly, the man knew nothing.

So the trail went cold. No one claimed responsibility, though several Muslim groups were immediately suspected. Local imams were rounded up and questioned. Pundits appeared on TV, blaming various Al Qaeda–trained offshoots. But even the experts weren't particularly impassioned. Something didn't feel right. Bin Laden's boys didn't usually bother with haute couture.

The day of Cressida's party, a *Times* editorial raised the possibility of a botched job; the bomb, they posited, might have been meant for someone or somewhere else. But that's as far as it went. The argument was rooted more in frustration than fact.

The blowout sale was on the wrong floor.

I stared at the e-mail, remembering something a techie friend had told me when I first started Roorback: *Be careful what you write, because a record of every word you type and every site you visit is being stored not only on your laptop hard drive, but in a massive mail server somewhere in Virginia.* He also said there were ways to trace e-mails to their sources. A second language existed behind the first—IP addresses and proxy servers, subnetworks and geocoded metadata. It all sounded complicated. And frightening. Anyway, I'd never sought out someone's online identity, and I wasn't going to now.

But the hook was in. I was curious. I called Cressida at the *Times*, and she answered on the first ring, hurriedly spitting out her name as if angry at its length.

"It's me," I said.

"Aidan, I don't have time for—"

"I need your help."

"Can't it wait till dinner? We are still having dinner tonight, right?"

"It's about the bombing. I might be onto something."

"You?" she cried. "How could *you* be onto anything? What, did one of your readers confess?"

"Come on, I'm serious. I'll fill you in later. Right now I need you to do a background check on someone."

"What the hell has gotten into you? Does this have to do with Touché?"

"Cressida . . ." She didn't answer, which I took as a sign of intrigue (she *was* a reporter, after all). "Please," I said.

"Fine, give me the name."

This I wasn't ready for. And I did something I still can't quite believe.

"It's actually a few names. Easton St. Claire, Paige Roderick, and Kimball LeRoux." I spelled them out.

"Are these real? They look fake. Did you just—"

"Come on, stop."

"Okay, okay," she said. "I'll see what comes up."

"Thank you. How's Malatesta at nine thirty?"

"Do you promise you'll explain this when I get there?"

"Yes."

"All right. I'll see you then, love."

The line went dead, but her last word hung in the air. As if it didn't belong.

PAIGE

· · • • • • • • · · •

Pennsylvania. Keith stayed in the car while Lindsay and I paid cash for two rooms. She snores, Lindsay told the young man behind the desk, motioning at me for effect. He smiled faintly, nervously, then printed out the paperwork. Lindsay signed it using a false name. We were ready with a backstory—two tired girls driving to a friend's wedding—but he never asked. How difficult it might have been. How easy it was. Details were everything, and Lindsay, I was learning, was a pro.

The rooms were next to each other on the ground floor. We parked a few doors away, then slipped inside—Keith into one, Lindsay and I into the other. I turned on the TV while she took a shower, but when I saw American soldiers on CNN, I turned it off. The news never changed. Lindsay was still wrapped in a towel when someone knocked on the door. Three raps, then two, then one.

It's Keith, she said.

Should I get it? I asked, glancing at her outfit, but Lindsay was already moving across the room. Her hair wet, her body glistening from moisturizer, she peered through the peephole, opened the door a crack, then turned and sauntered nonchalantly back to the bathroom. Keith stepped inside.

Are you two okay sleeping together? he asked.

Sure, I said.

And you're holding up well?

So far.

Good.

When Lindsay reemerged, she was wearing a small T-shirt and striped underwear. Unhurriedly, she bent down and picked up the jeans she'd left strewn on the floor, then slipped them on and joined me on the bed.

We should talk logistics, Keith said. There's a house waiting for us in Vermont. I'm told it's very private and set back from the road. It'll be our base of operations for now. Paige, you'll start building your new identity. Lindsay and I already have ours.

They get them from death records and obituaries, Lindsay explained. Children who died in infancy. Once they've found a baby that's suitable—someone who's the same age, sex, and ethnicity as you—they send away for a copy of the birth certificate and the rest is easy—Social Security card, driver's license, passport, you name it.

I already knew all this, but said nothing. What I didn't know was who *they* were.

In any case, Keith said, we can keep using our real names in private. At least until the first Action.

The word rolled off his tongue casually, but its effect was immediate. A chill shot through me. Lindsay pulled her hair back. And there we sat, still as stones, while the details of our fugitive lives were laid before us. Keith and I would work in and around the house, researching, planning, and—here Keith paused, searching, I suppose, for the perfect turn of phrase—*assembling,* he said. Lindsay would be our eyes and ears. Using her new alias, she'd get a job at a local store or restaurant and watch for anything suspicious. She'd even have her own car, gassed up and waiting in the driveway.

Next came the rules, many of which I already lived by. No cell phones (except Keith's, for emergencies), no e-mail, no unnecessary contact or budding friendships. It was about blending in. Becoming nobody. There would be code words and rendezvous points. Keith would teach us how to hide our tracks—roam the Web anonymously, wipe down a house, vary our routes and routines. Lindsay and I were completely clean, Keith said, and as far as he knew, he was, too. There'd been no one on his tail for quite some time. Still, from this moment on, we'd be living underground. Leaving our given lives for invented ones. Within a country but without it.

Clearly, he had been saving this speech, because Lindsay was hearing it for the first time as well. Perhaps it was his way of saying we'd be on equal footing from now on. She may have had more experience with this kind of life, but when it came to what lay ahead, she knew what I knew, nothing more.

But what about the past? Well, I didn't have to wait long. Keith said his piece, hugged us both good-night, then retreated to his room. I'm sure he was exhausted—he'd driven for hours—but he was also aware of boundaries and bonds, and Lindsay and I needed to create our own.

At first, we circled each other politely. In the bathroom, I washed my face and brushed my teeth. When I emerged, the TV was back on and Lindsay was flipping restlessly through the channels. I lay on top of the sheets and closed my eyes.

I've always been able to stay quiet for long periods. My brother used to say it was because I was comfortable in my own skin. I suppose that's true. Because it wasn't shyness or nerves; I just never craved attention. Not until my freshman year at UNC did I realize how self-conscious my silences could make other people. The fleshy-cheeked girls from vast Southern families, the perpetually stoned boys in their cargo shorts and fraying ball caps. All they did was talk and talk, incessantly self-absorbed and completely unaware of it. When I didn't add my voice to their booming chorus, I was labeled mysterious, a challenge, above it all. And so I gave in. I started dressing like everyone else. I drank at house parties, cheered at basketball games, even joined a sorority. Except nothing ever fit right. I could never quite get there—wherever there was. Instead, I existed on the outskirts, a girl once removed. Outwardly, I remained placid and unruffled. Inside, I clawed desperately at the air as I fell toward the dark and hollow center of conformity.

I say this because Lindsay was starting to fidget. My silence was wearing on her. She dug into her bag and produced a pack of Parliaments. Mind if I smoke? she asked.

Go ahead.

She walked to the front of the room and opened the curtain partway. A streetlamp cast dull yellow light over the car-lined blacktop. Lindsay cracked the window and looked around for an ashtray, settling for a plastic water cup on the bedside table.

Keith speaks really highly of you, she said.

I sat up. He's only met me once, I responded. But that's nice to hear. I've heard a lot about him.

Like what?

Nothing that concrete, I guess. Just his reputation.

This was the answer she was looking for, and she came over and settled down at the foot of the bed.

Well, I'll tell you if you want to know, she said. About me and Keith, I mean.

Okay.

And so she did. Armed with her cigarettes and her past, she told me their entire history. Or her version of it. Enough to let me know there *had* been a history. *Me and Keith . . .*

They had met at the WTO protests in Seattle. Keith Sutter was an ELF organizer; Lindsay Hardt was a student activist at a local community college. In 1999, the Earth Liberation Front was the most radical environmental activist group in the country. They tinkered with explosives, but arson was their real calling card. Economic sabotage. Working in small cells with little central coordination, they burned down everything from SUV dealerships to freshly painted housing developments, but their most famous action was the 1998 torching of five buildings and four chairlifts in Vail, Colorado, in response to the resort's impending expansion. The brazen and clandestine nature of the group gave them allure, and more than a little media attention. They even had a press office that released statements and conducted anonymous interviews. Keith Sutter was that press office. He was also heavily involved in the Actions themselves.

The ELF was one of dozens of radical groups that descended upon the dreary streets of Seattle that November weekend—tens of thousands of angry bodies seeking a common outlet. Lindsay said it was bound to get violent, the law of large numbers, of mob mentality, of sneering chaos, coming to the fore. It was supposed to be an antiglobalization protest, but that was just a catchphrase for the many ills of a changing world, and the varied agendas of its fuming revolutionaries—anarchists and punks, communists and labor leaders, crusaders and criminals. And the issues they advocated read like a dossier of the downtrodden and left-behind: racism, poverty, prison abuse, nuclear disarmament; the evils of science, energy, religion, property, capitalism, imperialism, free trade; the raping of Africa, Tibet, the earth. This was the throng that amassed and then combusted in a smoke-filled cauldron of clubs and tear gas and rubber bullets. Black-clad anticonsumerists smashed Starbucks windows; nihilist skinheads looted department stores; and through three breathtaking nights, the world watched transfixed as the young crusaders shut down the trade meetings and battled with beleaguered cops for control of an American city.

If it sounds like I'm adding personal commentary here, well, I am. Because I was one of those watching. From my sorority-house bedroom in Chapel Hill, I gazed at the images pulsing through my roommate's TV and wondered what it all meant. I was a sophomore, majoring in Political Science, and fully enveloped in the puerile routines of college life—the safe majority, a world that made sense. In 1999, the country was fueled up and running strong. UNC's job fairs were like high school proms, the fresh-faced dot-coms showing off their slender silhouettes while America's corporate giants, the companies our fathers had entrusted their working lives to, sulked in the corner like wallflowers. Ours was a land of opportunity, of jobs and growth and freedom, and so the searing images from Seattle were completely incongruous. What was happening out there? All those people. That naked rage. As my so-called sisters flirted and fucked in the rooms down the hall, I stared at the screen and felt the first pangs of recognition, a kind of longing to be in a place that made less sense. Or more. That somewhere in this country of plenty, people (like Keith and Lindsay) were charging at lines of armed men, rocks against guns, dreams against grenades.

Lindsay lit another cigarette and let her damp hair back down. She was a mesmeric wisp of a girl, pale and hipless, completely self-contained. Her face was flawless—the smooth skin, the button nose, high cheekbones, accentuated chin. And her eyes, freed for the first time from her ubiquitous aviators, were a raw and piercing blue. Everything about her was a bit raw, a bit piercing, as if a sculptor had spent years shaping her into his masterpiece, only to forget some final coat of polish.

Picture it, she said, licking her lips. All these cops, rows and rows of them, suddenly raising their shields and marching in lockstep toward us. It had been a standoff until then. We'd been blocking the key inter-sections; they'd been protecting the convention center. And that was fine with us. I mean, what were we going to do? Throw rocks at a huge building? Unfortunately, they finally figured out the delegates couldn't get to the meeting with all the roads cut off. Which is when they got serious.

Were you part of a group? I asked.

Lindsay offered me a drag. I took one.

I was in the Black Bloc, she said. A bunch of us up from Eugene. We looked so scary, dressed head to toe in black, our faces covered with bandannas, but really we were a bunch of Goths and neo-hippies. We were nineteen and twenty. Half of us were only there to cut classes.

I remember on TV, I said, that huge white banner hanging from a crane. The one with arrows pointing in opposite directions. WTO one way, DEMOCRACY the other.

The Direct Action Network did that. They were older, more organized. We were . . . oh, God, we were just kids standing in the cold trying to find some food. That's the real reason we smashed up those coffee shops: we were hungry. No one thought it would escalate. That the cops would start moving again. We were on the corner of Sixth and Union, and it was daylight, and overcast, and there were camera-men in the crowd and helicopters above us. We'd been out there since five a.m., and still there was this vitality to everything. We were all part of different groups, but it didn't matter. When a uniformed force is amassed against you, it's amazing how quickly defiance becomes a common cause. Earlier, we'd been chanting and singing, and a few of the protesters still had bullhorns. When the cops started toward us, I remember hearing this voice rising above all the noise, saying, *Hold your ground, hold your ground.* And the voice was so calm, so natural. I was close to the front, maybe the second or third row, and when the shields went up, we started throwing things. Rocks, batteries, anything hard. Not that it mattered, we couldn't hurt them. It all just glanced off their protection. The cops kept coming. And still that voice: *We're Americans! We have rights! We have rights!* Then they gassed us. We smelled it before we felt it, before the burning. I didn't know what it was and kept my eyes uncovered too long. A few people tried to pick up the smoking canisters and throw them right back, the way you can with grenades if you're quick enough. But none of us were quick enough. And anyway the cops were wearing helmets. They started moving faster, relentlessly forward, their sticks out, splitting us up, driving us back. By then I couldn't see, could barely even open my eyes. The whole world was going dark, and I just looked at the ground and tried to follow other people's feet, the direction they were running. And then the voice was saying, *Don't panic! It's only tear gas! Cover your eyes and noses!* I'd lost my friends, or anyway, I couldn't see them, so I moved toward the voice. It was like the one thing that made sense.

I was sitting up in the bed, perfectly still. All of this. She was such a frail girl.

It was Keith, she continued. The voice of reason in all that madness. I ran right into him while people were getting clubbed everywhere around us. They go for the back of your legs, you know. It's what they're trained to do. So you just wilt right there in front of them, get kicked and crushed and trampled. They were coming after him specifically, but he had friends surrounding him, protecting him, and the cops couldn't get close. When he saw me, he grabbed my waist and half-carried me through the crowd. He had dropped the bullhorn, but by then it didn't matter. There was no chance for order anymore, not with the sirens and the screaming and the hovering helicopters.

We regrouped in an alley a couple blocks north of the fighting. Someone made a call, and soon we were in a car, a half dozen of us piled on top of each other as Keith directed the driver through the wild streets. We ended up at a house on the edge of a boho neighborhood called Capitol Hill. It was like a temporary command station, with posters and protective gear everywhere. They had gas masks in the living room. People were shouting into cell phones, getting updates on the carnage a mile away. Everything was still blurry, but Keith was forcing my eyes open, squeezing drops into them. They stung so much. And my nose was running. And my skin. Have you ever been gassed?

No, I said.

Well, you're lucky. It's effective. Anyway, Keith and I were pretty much inseparable the rest of that week. And after. But that's not the point of the story. . . .

But that was the point of the story. Or one of them. Lindsay was laying out her credentials as an extremist, and, in that shrewd way familiar only to women, laying out her ground rules as well. Keith was hers, or anyway, not mine. That this had all gone down more than a decade ago wasn't important. She was in love with him. I'd realized that right away and accepted it as part of the arrangement. It wasn't new love, of course. There was nothing overtly passionate or physical about it—not that I'd seen. No, they'd probably known each other on and off for years, had lived and slept together in any number of incarnations that were now a part of history. Episodes from other adventures.

It all came down to this: I trusted Keith. And if he, in turn, trusted Lindsay, then I did, too. The man was that magnetic. The more he kept his distance, the more I wanted to know him. It's an amazing thing to hear a person spoken of in such reverence, and then you meet him and he's twice as impressive as you imagined. The business of extremism was, like all others, a business of people, and Keith was someone to go to war with. There was that past, sure—he'd managed to thrive as a leading radical for years without getting caught—but it was more than the résumé. He inspired loyalty. And faith. Now there's a word I use with trepidation. Yet he brought it out in me. I felt secure around him, even then, especially then, in those first days, as I was being whisked off to help commit some treason yet unknown. He was incredibly careful and quietly confident, and it wasn't hard to imagine it all might somehow work out. And to think I'd been handpicked over any number of capable and committed activists in dripping basements and seaside bungalows and everywhere else where people have come up against a wall in their lives and decided to smash through it.·

Lindsay and I said our good-nights, and I turned out the bedside lamp. Two weeks after I met Keith, that fateful night in Raleigh, I had read about the Pike County coal mine collapse in the *Washington Post*. It had happened in the dead of night, and although there'd been no deaths or injuries, the governor of Kentucky had immediately ordered OMSL inspectors to fan out across the state and reevaluate mining safety procedures. Tarver Coal was taken to task. Their track record was trotted out in the press, and the company's financials were scrutinized and found lacking. Tarver was levied with fines as its stock plummeted and its CFO resigned. Against this hardship, they announced the closing of two of their least profitable mining operations. Throughout the ordeal, Tarver's CEO had insisted the collapse was triggered by a small explosive device, but when investigators eventually verified his claim, it hardly mattered. The damage had been done.

Could it really be so easy? Could targeted violence truly work? I lay awake in that motel room for a long time, as Lindsay slept peacefully beside me, curled up like a question mark. We'd just traveled for nine hours through five states, and still I kept coming back to the same moment. We were crossing into West Virginia on Route 161 when Keith lowered his window and stuck his head out.

What are you doing? Lindsay asked.

Listening for the blasts, he said, catching my eye in the rearview mirror.

I smiled. That he'd remembered.

AIDAN

· · · ● ● ● ● ● ● ● · · ●

FROM A WELL-POSITIONED SEAT AT A CHARMING SIDEWALK TABLE, I WATCHED as Cressida came striding across Washington Street, her high heels negotiating the cobblestones with practiced assurance. I'd been waiting more than half an hour—and had already polished off a carafe of red wine—but I didn't really care. We embraced, awkwardly, and Cressida began a complex untangling of wires and straps—from headphones, a purse, and various bags—that quickly came to involve diners at the tightly spaced neighboring tables. Finally, she fell into her chair, bumping the table just as I was filling her glass. The wine spilled. "Fuck," she said, grabbing her napkin, then mine, as the red pool started to spread. "Sorry I'm late." It was her standard entrance, perfected over time by actually being late, to everything, always.

It was rarely just the two of us anymore, and we weren't sure where to begin. We were always at parties or large dinners. The things other couples did—movies, walks, brunch—we never quite got around to. We were busy, knew people, *had lives*, and quiet moments had never been part of them. That is, until now. For life's natural pauses, the gaps in conversation, had begun to widen. We were great around others, but got moody, fell silent, around each other. Tinkering with cell phones, text messages, later plans, we pretended not to notice what was becoming painfully clear: that we'd run out of things to say to one another. But didn't that happen to everyone? The vacant stares, the unintentional tuning out . . . these, I told myself, were symptoms of nothing more than time gone by. Besides, Cressida could never be quiet for long.

"So I have something for you," she said, when we were finally organized. She pulled an oversize envelope from one of her bags. "Here's the deal: I'll give you everything I've got, but you have to tell me what this is about."

"It's probably nothing," I said. "Just some weird e-mails I've been getting."

"About the bombing?"

"I guess, yeah."

"What exactly did the e-mails say?" she asked.

"Why? Did you dig something up?" It was possible, which is the reason I'd asked her in the first place. As a staff reporter, Cressida had access to dozens of information-gathering programs and websites, and she knew how to use them.

"Maybe," she said coolly.

This is what we *were* good at—pushing buttons, testing boundaries, baiting each other. I reached into my pocket and produced a copy of the second message from EmpiresFall (though I'd been careful to erase the sender's address). Cressida read it out loud: " 'Subject: Barneys. The shopping wasn't so good. The blowout sale was on the wrong floor. P.S. This is your chance.' " She frowned. "What the hell does that mean?"

"I have no idea. And the other e-mails are just as cryptic. Except one of them mentioned the three names I gave you."

"Why would they e-mail Roorback?"

"Exactly. It's ridiculous, but I wanted to get your thoughts just in case."

"Did they claim responsibility? Send photographs? Anything else at all?"

"No," I said.

The waiter came and we ordered more napkins, wine, and finally, food. He didn't write anything down. When he was gone, Cressida opened the envelope and pulled out three file folders.

"Okay, then," she said, lowering her voice. "Let's start with Easton St. Claire. He's the easiest because he doesn't exist. I checked everywhere. He sounds made up and he is made up." She handed me the folder labeled ST. CLAIRE. In it were three pages of search requests. I tried to look engrossed as I thumbed through them. "Next is Paige Roderick, who does appear to be real, inasmuch as there are humans who exist with that name, but . . . oh, *come on.*"

"What?"

"I know what you're up to."

"No you don't."

"You're wasting my time with these two phony names so I don't figure out who you're really after."

"And who would that be?"

"Kimball LeRoux."

Kimball LeRoux? I thought I'd made the name up on the spot, but maybe I'd lifted it from somewhere. It did sound familiar, now that she'd said it out loud.

"Let me ask you something," Cressida said. "Is this your way of getting back at me for the column?"

"No. But if you want to think so, fine. It's probably what we should be talking about anyway. I just thought we could work together for once, focus on something other than our fucked-up relationship."

"Really? Is that what it is?"

"That's not what I meant," I said.

"It's exactly what you meant."

And so we sat there in silence. When the food came, we ate in silence. Malatesta was the kind of inexpensive trattoria you might find on any corner in Florence or Milan, but for whatever reason was rare in New York. Candlelight set the mood, and a beautiful staff sustained it. At nearby tables, people laughed and carried on in foreign tongues. I wondered what we must look like to them, jaws clenched, poking at pasta. A friend of Cressida's appeared, and we smiled our way through pleasantries and the vague promise of future drinks. Finally, no doubt getting the hint, she blew us kisses and walked away.

"Look at us," Cressida said. "We're becoming one of *those* couples."

"Apparently."

She peered up at me then, shifting her eyes without moving her head. "I'm sorry," she said softly. "But I just want you to be honest with me."

"There's nothing to lie about."

"But if there *were,* then you *would*? Is that what you're saying? That's just—"

"No!"

"—perfect! Look, let's just get through the rest of this, okay?" She reached into the envelope, pulled out the two remaining folders, and slid them across the table. As casually as I could, I opened the one labeled RODERICK. "As you can see," Cressida continued, "there are lots of Paige Rodericks, but none of them strike me as terrorists."

The familiar list included a few new additions. I read through their brief bios, but they were all too young or too old. The last three pages were a compilation of photos from a high-tech *Times* image search. Cressida started talking about Kimball LeRoux as I quickly scanned the rows of anonymous Paige Rodericks, plucked at random from the American landscape like—

There she was!

Did Cressida see my eyes widen? For a fleeting moment she might have, before I recovered, before I narrowed them again and ground my teeth to conceal my astonishment. It was a small photograph, and I tried to look closer without raising suspicion. Paige Roderick! *My* Paige Roderick! Same face, same dark hair, but now she was wearing a cocktail dress and had her arm around an Ivy League type in a coat and tie. They looked like a well-heeled young couple dutifully posing at someone else's wedding. There was a tiny caption, but I couldn't read it without attracting Cressida's attention.

I picked up the third folder and tried to appear interested. Kimball LeRoux, Cressida was explaining, was a middle-aged blogger from the Gulf Coast who'd made a name for himself several years back by exposing various governmental lapses during Hurricane Katrina. He'd broken into the national consciousness for a few news cycles and hung on as long as he could—expanding his blog and writing opinion pieces—before fading back into American oblivion.

That's where the name must have come from.

"—I mean it must be him," Cressida was saying excitedly, as I flipped through the file, a man's life laid bare in a dozen scattered pages.

"I'm sure whoever sent the e-mail was just *pretending* to be LeRoux," I said.

"But why? Look at some of the antigovernment stuff he's written. Don't you think we should follow up?"

"On what? There's nothing here. Half the country hates the government. It doesn't mean they're blowing up buildings."

"I can see why you didn't become a fucking journalist," Cressida said. "Do you know what your problem is? Or one of them, at least? A complete lack of curiosity. You spend your life waiting for people to make mistakes, and then you publicize them. And when, God forbid, something interesting comes your way, a story you could actually chase down, you let it pass right by. Look! We have his address, his phone number! Don't you think it's worth fifteen minutes?"

Here it was: all the ardor and zeal that had first attracted me to Cressida. We'd been introduced almost a year ago, at one of Derrick Franklin's dinner parties. He'd seated us beside each other in the hope that she might fall for my slight charms and write about Roorback. But she hated blogs, she told me, before the appetizers had even arrived, and hours later, when we'd jousted for long enough and she'd decided I'd do (at least for the evening), it was too late: the veneer of objectivity was gone. The sex was fine that first night, but what got me was the morning after. While most girls would have scurried around collecting clothing, mumbling excuses, Cressida lay clear-eyed and comfortable in my barely unpacked room on Weehawken Street (I'd relocated from Brooklyn the week before), the creeping sun revealing in her eyes a measured calm, as if we'd done this a hundred times before. I kissed her neck and she moved in close.

"What's your name again?" she whispered. I laughed, thinking she was kidding, and laughed harder when I realized she wasn't.

It was a marathon weekend, a whirlwind of comings and goings, sex and sushi, galleries, cocktails, a concert, and late Sunday night, when we finally said good-bye, we were on the phone within the hour, talking quickly, slowly, softly, about how easy everything suddenly felt.

I don't think it was love, even in those first beaming months. We were both too experienced for anything so unambiguous. But the physical attraction was real. And we liked each other's stories. She'd clambered her way up from a local newspaper in the British Midlands to the rollicking Fleet Street tabloids, where she spent her late twenties chasing celebrities through hotel lobbies. She had a disarming way of getting people to talk. David Beckham, Kate Moss, Prince Harry—they'd all spoken into Cressida's tape recorder and regretted it the next morning. By this time, she'd become a name herself, a sought-after entity on both sides of the Atlantic. She was approached by a half dozen stateside gossip pages and celebrity magazines, but she'd grown tired of chronicling the detritus of fame. She was after something else, and only the rebranded-for-the-masses *Times* could offer it: a job reporting real news, with a saucy column on the side.

Now she stared me down above the rim of her wineglass, challenging me as she challenged everyone whose lies or lapses might slow her own progress. She wasn't telling me anything new. I was aware of my faults and had tailored my life so as not to magnify them. And in New York you almost could. But the world eventually catches up, confronts you, offers up a choice. I could have come clean then, saved myself in her eyes. Because I *was* chasing the story. I was doing exactly the thing she accused me of never doing—being the *very person* she was begging me to be—and yet I couldn't let her know it. Not yet.

Cressida was stuffing the LEROUX folder into her bag. "If you won't do anything about him, then I will," she said, standing up in front of her half-eaten pasta. She paused, as if to say something else, then shook her head, kissed me quickly on the cheek, and strode out as she'd strode in, her heels hitting the sidewalk with rhythmic determination.

She'd left the other two folders on the table.

I paid the check, grabbed them both, and hurried the few blocks home. Cressida and I had fought enough to become masters at making up, so it seemed strange that we hadn't even tried. It had been like a business dinner, two wary competitors discussing a potential merger, tentatively trading information before deciding against the idea and quickly going separate ways. But I couldn't blame her. She was one thing before the other—I'd always known that—and now she was heading home with a folder of information she thought might lead somewhere. What should I have expected?

That's why the text she sent me as I walked up my dark stairwell took me by surprise. *You used to make me laugh,* it said.

● ● ·

Three stubborn locks later I was sitting in my living room—my *only* room—spreading the RODERICK folder out across the coffee table. I peered down at the image I'd spotted earlier. It was Paige, *that* Paige, I was positive. She was wearing what looked like a vintage dress, bare-shouldered and tight through her torso. I squinted at the tiny caption: *Brendan Carlyle and Paige Roderick enjoy the smooth sounds of Ernie Lombardi's Jazz Quartet at last Saturday's Fishers Island Club Gala.* That was it—no date, no context.

None of this felt right. Over the course of the day Paige Roderick had evolved in my mind, become someone obscene and extraordinary—a bomb-building revolutionary mocking the poisoned culture that consumed the rest of us. But now here she was, just another girl in a fancy dress, advancing effortlessly down the primrose path of blue-blooded courtship. I peered again at the photograph, at the faded face, the impassive eyes. They looked distant, empty. She wasn't smiling or posing, but she was hardly defiant. I reminded myself that photographs were only captive instants—the briefest flickers of history—and they lied just as people lied. But they told great truths as well.

She existed, though, and wasn't that something? A kind of journalistic progress? But toward what? At NYU, I'd heard well-known reporters talk about an indefinable force that propelled them through investigations, one improbable lead to the next. At the time, I'd scoffed at such self-important nonsense, but there I was, staring again at the photograph as I considered the progression of events, and there *was* a logical rhythm to it. Questions were supposed to come before answers, frustration before understanding.

Then I was looking for my cell phone. I had my next move.

Touché answered on the fourth ring. "You don't sound good," I told him.

"That fucking DJ. We were up until dawn. Lord knows what I told her. Hasn't she learned never to listen to a Latin man after two in the morning?"

"The girl last night. She's real."

"Very much so."

"And I have a picture of her on Fishers Island."

"No, she lives in Brooklyn somewhere. Red Hook, I think."

"She does? How do you know?"

"Because she told me," Touché said.

"What the fuck are you talking about?"

"What are *you* talking about?"

"Paige Roderick."

"That wasn't her name."

"Not the DJ!"

"Oh. Who then?"

"You don't remember? The e-mail I opened in Cressida's room?" There was silence on the other end. "You thought she looked like Jennifer Connelly."

"Ah, yes! I almost forgot. I *did* forget. The beautiful mad bomber. So she did it? You caught her? And here I thought we'd wasted the evening chasing—"

"I'm being serious. I just saw her in another photograph. She was with some preppy guy at a ritzy dinner-dance on Fishers Island."

"Fishers Island?"

"That's what I'm saying! I think it was the golf club your parents belong to."

"What was her date's name?"

"Brendan Carlyle. Do you know him?"

"I know his sister," said Touché. "Brendan was a bit younger. Banker, maybe."

"He looks like a banker."

"When was it taken, the photo?"

"There isn't a date."

"And you're sure it's her?"

"Positive."

"Well, then, there's only one thing to do."

"What's that?" I asked.

"Are you free this weekend?"

PAIGE

· · · ● ● ● ● ● ● · · ● ●

THE HOUSE WAS A SLANT-ROOFED SALTBOX BUILT IN THE 1960S WHEN THE nearby ski resorts were still in vogue, and it bore the effects of hard weather, the cedar sides beginning to rot, the roof speckled with replacement shingles. The ground floor was separated into living and dining areas by a pretty stone fireplace, and an adjacent staircase led up to three small bedrooms tucked into the roof like a crawl space. It was nice enough, though all personal flourishes or effects, anything that might hint at the owner's tastes or identity, had been stamped out by years of renters up from New York and Boston.

What the house did have was privacy—thickets of dense foliage that protected us from the road and the vacation houses on either side. It was early summer and the ground was a mud-caked sponge. Nearby streams flowed fast with mountain runoff, and the nights were still cold enough to make me miss the South. The few locals we came across seemed dazed and half-asleep. It was the low season.

The location was convenient; the garage was a necessity. It stood alone, a dilapidated concrete structure fifty yards from the house. When we pulled open the paneled, two-car door on our first morning in residence, we were greeted with great piles of rusted tools and rotting furniture—lawn mowers and Weedwackers, a stained rug, a cushionless couch. Keith waded bravely in, past decades of castoffs—

vintage bicycles, a dollhouse, telemark skis, parts of a Ping-Pong table.

Old *National Geographics* if anyone wants them, he said, pointing at a stack of discolored magazines. He disappeared behind an overturned canoe.

What a fucking mess, Lindsay said, backing out.

Yes, but the walls, came Keith's voice, from within. Look how thick they are.

Someone else had seen how thick the walls were. Someone else had been here before us, scouting out prospects, dreaming of possibilities, and this sad house, this sleepy valley, had been chosen over dozens of other houses and valleys across New England. But these were things left unspoken—names I couldn't know, faces I shouldn't see. Uncertainty was part of the program.

And what a well-oiled program it was. Our first week up North fell quickly into place. Lindsay found a job in town while Keith and I busied ourselves at the house. We embedded the dedicated Wi-Fi with digital inhibitors and mounted a counterbug on the phone line in case we got calls. We walked the property, scouting escape routes, peeking through neighbors' windows. No one was around. Still, Keith didn't like surprises.

Finally, we tackled the garage. We spent two days moving junk to the basement, sweeping and cleaning, mounting tables and hanging lights, until the space was as spotless as a laboratory. Which was exactly what it would become.

They used to build bombs in basements, Keith said. We'd just finished and were standing near the open door admiring our handiwork. But garages are better. Any stand-alone structure. The Weathermen found that out too late. You know about the town-house explosion in New York?

On Eleventh Street, I said, near Fifth Avenue. I walked past it once. They rebuilt the house, but you can still tell. It looks different, much newer than the others.

Yeah, well, those guys made a lot of mistakes, he said. But still, they were on the right track. Speeches don't spotlight the world's problems. You need to be louder.

With that, Keith turned to sort through a box of tools he'd bought a few towns away. I went inside to make dinner.

● ● ·

Though I didn't know it then, that brief conversation would be one of the only times we discussed the devices that would soon define our lives. Keith—and, to a lesser extent, Lindsay—just seemed so *at ease* with the idea of explosives—wires and caps, plastics and springs, batteries and detonators. The cold components of violence. I was living, I realize now, in a kind of peer-pressurized bubble, where the increasing irrationality of my existence was tempered by the ostensible sanity of everyone around me. I went with the flow of things, dispassionately, as if removing myself from emotion might justify my actions, make them easier to perform, and digest. It had worked in the aftermath of Bobby's death, after all. Is it spilling into these words, the icy objectivity, the obsessive detachment, of those early days? Perhaps it's for the best, because that's how I felt (that's how the entire house felt). If Keith and Lindsay were comfortable with this life, then I would be, too. Questions still plagued me, of course, not because they had no answers, but because they were never posed. It was as if challenging each other, probing beneath the surface of our surreal reality, into ethics, say, and responsibility, had been deemed unnecessary, irrelevant. Keith was right: bombs *had* worked before. In this country, in every country. They had worked until they hadn't (morally, at least), and it was up to us to recognize that line and not cross it. To me, it fell before the word *casualties,* and as long as that remained clear, I would let the rising wave of adrenaline take me where it would. I was buoyed by belief and a sense of creeping destiny. I needed to prove myself. See something through. For once.

Anyway, Keith was a realist. He wasn't interested in the tired rhetoric of radicals past—class warfare, overthrowing governments—but rather, in highlighting specific evils. Making progress in dramatic increments. America, he argued, had long ago moved past the potential for mass revolt. Change would now come from working *with* the system, manipulating its weaker components, burrowing into its cracks and fissures. He was talking about exploiting the media—its hunger for high drama, its appetite for fear. And that's exactly what he—what *we*—would provide.

What were those evils? They were legion of course. Every night we talked about the latest front-page horrors—wars of religion, cultures of corruption, an economy on life support. Record-setting temperatures in Anchorage. Kidnappings in the Middle East. Never-ending nuclear threats. The young Obama administration, once a source of so much hope, had moved to the center, as they all do. And that left the idealists—America's true patriots—on the outside looking in, or worse, looking away, in disgust. But our developing platform went well beyond party politics, left-wing or—certainly—right. Politics should grow from people, and people just weren't engaged. They didn't understand. And that's where we came in. Keith believed the ills of the country, of mankind, could be traced to one word: *energy*. And America's energy policy is what he intended to change.

Our days took on a regimented form. The three of us met every morning over coffee, then went our separate ways. Lindsay drove to work. Keith went to the garage or made a supply run (which, I assumed, included some form of contact with our mysterious backers). I sat down at the computer. My job was research and logistics—identifying potential targets and then systematically eliminating them until we were left with a logical short list. For hours every afternoon I searched the darker corners of the Web, seeking fragility in a country built on strength. At night we assembled for dinner and talked through the day—or Lindsay talked and we listened. At some point we drifted to the couches, read newspapers, played cards or Scrabble. This was important to Keith, the veneer of normalcy, the idea that our lives were like everyone else's—work and leisure, wake and sleep. We grew close, bonded by the weight of circumstance. We needed to control as much of our reality as we could, keep luck and surprise from our lives, and this meant open communication. Small sleights and recriminations were immediately addressed or forgotten. There were no drugs, not much alcohol. We became hyperaware of our moods and steered clear of conflict. That we were three in number was no accident. The history of groups—of *cells*—like ours was rife with threesomes. We were small enough to keep secrets, large enough to hold debates. But we were hardly a democracy. We talked, then Keith made a decision and we moved on. Yet, each of us felt integral to the success, the very existence, of the group.

If we were never quite friends in the traditional sense, that was fine, too. Even preferred. My relationship with Lindsay was especially vulnerable, for it was unnatural. If we'd met one night at a party, been introduced as friends of friends, we'd no doubt have smiled, then quickly turned our backs and wandered off—not out of malice but lack of interest. Maybe we'd have pegged each other as types—she, the knee-jerk objector, malleable and easily manipulated; me, a threat, quiet and a bit haughty. But in that house we quickly reached a level of accommodation, understanding, respect. Keith was careful not to upset the balance by introducing—or reintroducing—sexual feeling or desire. If Lindsay took issue with the two of us home together day after day, she didn't mention it. Likewise, I put their history where it belonged—behind us.

Our routine held for three weeks, then broke. It was lunchtime on a sunny weekday afternoon. Lindsay was at work and I was online. I didn't hear the front door open, or any footsteps, just Keith's voice:

Care to join me for a drive?

I jumped in my chair.

Of course, I said, trying quickly to recover. But even as I said the words, I knew it would be anything but a leisurely drive. Why? Because a fundamental rule of the house was that someone would always be there, to ward off hunters or hikers or mailmen or worse. In other words, he needed me. I turned the laptop off and walked out to the car.

Keith locked the front door, the sliding deck door, double-checked the garage door, then scanned the woods around the property. Satisfied, he climbed behind the wheel and we started north. He drove slowly, cautiously, like a driving instructor with a new student, and it took almost an hour to get to the highway. Where were we going? Keith didn't say. But I'd gotten used to his reticence, had even come to admire it. I thought I understood where it was coming from.

We tried the radio and eventually found a news station—a report on the latest round of violence in Palestine. Keith turned it up. I gazed out the window.

You should listen, he said.

Why? It's been the same story all my life.

A great story, Keith said. The ultimate story.

Israel and Palestine? The whole thing's unbearable.

On the contrary, it's what we're all about. It's our proof.

I turned and looked at him. It was an odd statement. Plenty of activists I knew—including several Jews—supported Palestine. Ours was a business of underdogs, of contrarians, and Palestine fit the bill. But ancient religious struggles weren't Keith's forte. He was solidly a man of his time.

Proof of what? I asked.

That this works. Small acts. Targeted violence.

Terrorism, I said.

That's a trumped-up word and you know it, he said, waving his hand dismissively. If the Palestinians had sat around waiting for a dip-lomatic solution, they'd have no land left. *There is no leverage without violence or the threat of it.* It's the ultimate fact of world affairs. Look at Pakistan. They have the bomb. If they didn't, we'd have been in there a decade ago. Iran. Syria. North Korea. They get nukes, they're players; without them, only actors. Look at Iraq— Sorry . . .

It's fine, I said, though it wasn't. I suddenly felt hot. Self-conscious. Angry.

Well, you know what I'm trying to—

Sure.

The towns gave way to farmland, rolling fields of heather and hay, then forest, thick and green. We had the interstate almost to ourselves. At one point I held the wheel while Keith unfolded a map and studied it. I glanced down and saw handwritten directions scrawled along the white borders.

We're close, he said.

Ten minutes later we pulled off the highway and followed a back-country road deep into the middle of nowhere. Deer grazed along the shoulders, unafraid, oblivious.

The turn's coming up, Keith said. There should be a sign.

Saying what?

No trespassing.

We pulled up beside a gap in the trees, which, upon closer inspection, revealed two overgrown tire tracks heading into the brush—the beginnings of a rudimentary path.

No sign, I said.

But this has to be it. Keith looked up and down the main road and, seeing no one, turned onto the trail. It was slow going. Tall grass had grown up between the tracks, hiding rocks and ruts that slowed us to a crawl.

No one's been up here in a while, Keith said.

Is that good or bad?

Don't know.

We pressed on. The road became an incline, then a hill. Twice we got stuck and had to back our way down to attack the offending ditch at speed. The third time it happened, Keith stopped the car and cut the engine.

Too bumpy, he said.

We can make it farther.

I'm worried about the way back down.

What do you mean? I asked.

But he was already out of the car and opening the trunk. He rooted around awhile before emerging with a large flashlight and bolt cutters.

We can walk from here, he said, slamming the trunk shut. Shouldn't be far.

It had been a warm, muggy day back in semicivilization, but in the woods, under a canopy of leaves, it was dusky and cool and the ground crackled underfoot. We hiked uphill, maybe two hundred yards, then came upon a single, heavy chain drooping across the path. Signs were attached to the wooden support stakes on either side.

Government Property
No Trespassing
Violators Will Be Prosecuted

But another sign had Keith's attention:

Land Monitored by State Police
Department of Transportation
Department of Homeland Security

Keith shook his head. Fucking idiots. What kid wouldn't trespass after reading that?

By the looks of it, though, we were the first. The faint tire tracks ended and the forest closed in around us. We proceeded in single file, Keith's shoulders brushing past branches that kept springing back and hitting me so that I had to walk with my arms up, like a boxer. In time, the land leveled out into a plateau of sorts. Keith stopped. He was staring at a large concrete structure in the middle of a clearing. Behind it, the trail ended and the land rose up sharply, becoming a steep, mountainous rock face.

This is it, he said.

It looks like a fallout shelter.

It's a storage facility for the road crews.

The only entrance was a massive door adorned with more warnings and related consequences. Keith handed me the flashlight and I pointed it at the padlock. It was thick and shiny, seemingly impenetrable.

Over here with the light, Keith said.

He was pointing not at the lock but the ring that secured it to the building. It was older, weaker.

Figures, Keith said. They attach a brand-new titanium lock to a worthless rusted loop plate. Christ, look at it, I think it's the original.

He clamped the bolt cutters onto the ring and went to work, marshaling his full strength upon the weather-beaten mounting. It didn't take long. It snapped without warning, throwing Keith to the ground. He grinned as he got up and dusted himself off.

Together, we pulled open the heavy door. The hinges groaned as it gave, and light crept inside, revealing parts of two yellow snowplows and dozens of giant bags of road salt, piled almost to the ceiling.

We came all this way for road salt? I said.

Wait.

Keith flipped a light switch but nothing happened, so I handed him the flashlight and he disappeared between one of the plows and a collection of interstate exit signs stacked against a side wall. Behind me, the wind had picked up and the trees rustled ominously. I thought about the car. Were the windows up? And would we be able to navigate those rutted dirt tracks if it started storming?

Keith, I said into the darkness, why don't I run down and check on—

Aha! I heard him exclaim. I *knew* it was here! Paige, come on back.

He shone the flashlight in my direction, and I weaved through the obstacle course. Keith was kneeling beside a stack of wooden crates lined up against the rear wall.

Look, he said, pointing the beam directly onto one of them. I bent down to read the stamp on the side:

DANGER
HIGH EXPLOSIVES – TOVAL
Keep Away from All Metal,
Flammable or Corrosive Substances
Do Not Store Near Caps or Primers
Property of U.S. Govt.

What's Toval? I asked.

A nitro-compound manufactured in gel form, then packed in dynamite sticks.

Let me guess: they use it to blast through rock when they're building roads.

You got it, Keith said. It can't be detonated by heat, so it's safer than regular dynamite. Of course, you can't exactly toss the stuff around either.

And they just keep it up here in the middle of nowhere?

They keep it in a few places. This was the easiest to get into. And the most remote. They won't notice it's missing until they come for the salt in December.

So what do we do? Just carry all these cases out of here, stick them in the trunk, and go home?

Pretty much, Keith said. Except two should be enough.

We have room for more.

Keith chuckled. We won't need more.

So we got to work. Toval was a stable explosive, but an explosive nonetheless (puncturing the dynamite shell could set it off), and we slipped our hands beneath the first crate extremely carefully. It was much heavier than I'd anticipated, and I started putting it back down to get a better grip.

Don't, Keith said sharply. We work in unison. Warn me before you make any sudden moves. There can be no tilt, do you understand?

Yes, I said, struggling to wedge my fingers farther underneath.

We shuffled forward a few feet at a time, feeling for each step, and when we finally made it outside, we placed the crate down delicately on level ground and rested. Keith squinted at the sky. He was sweating. My arms hurt. And still the hard work lay ahead. It took twenty minutes and several breaks to reach the car. Already exhausted, I leaned against a door and waited for Keith to open the trunk, but he wanted to keep going, all the way to the main road. Better that than driving the dynamite over all the ruts and bumps. It was late afternoon now, and a breeze had picked up. It felt as if we were the only people for miles, and maybe we were.

It was another fifteen minutes to the bottom of the hill, where we stashed the case in deep brush, and hurried back up to do it all again. The sky was darkening. When we left the storage building for the last time, Keith tried to replace the lock's mounting to something approaching its original state, but it was beyond repair. Employing a rhythmic system of stops and starts, we shuffled down the hill. Eventually, we reached the road, and I stayed with the crates as Keith jogged back up to get the car.

I waited, hidden behind thick roadside trees, my eyes fixed on our ill-gotten gains, as thunder clapped above me. When Keith lumbered to a halt in the wheezing Toyota, we placed the first crate carefully in the trunk, but it was too tall and the top wouldn't close, so the dynamite came inside with us. We secured the crates to the backseat with the only things we had: bungee cords and blankets.

I told them we needed a station wagon, Keith muttered, as he put the car in DRIVE.

It was the last thing he said for an hour. The skies opened up before we made it to the highway, and he gave his attention completely over to the task at hand. I turned around every few minutes to check on our cargo, resting innocuously on the cushioned seats. It could have been anything under those blankets. But it wasn't anything. It was high explosives, a fact I thought might lend our journey a certain intimacy—a shared acknowledgment of our feat, our felony. But Keith stared straight ahead, his green eyes fixed on the wet road, the close distance, the near future—no mirrors, no looking back. They were the eyes of a true believer, I realized then, and for a moment they scared me more than anything else in the car.

AIDAN

· · ● ● ● ● ● ● · · ● ●

THE CAB RIDE TO THE ESSEX COUNTY AIRPORT IN NEW JERSEY WAS A NIGHT-mare. Touché, who was already there, had made it sound like nothing, a quick twenty-minute jaunt, fifty bucks tops. But as we inched west on Route 3, twenty minutes became forty, then sixty. It was a hot, muggy day, and the cabbie took the Friday-morning traffic personally, muttering in some Middle Eastern tongue with every roadway slowdown. Somewhere past the Meadowlands, his frustration boiled over and he glared at me in the rearview mirror, his cursing—if that's what it was—becoming more pointed. I opened the *Times* and tried to ignore him.

Almost a week had passed with no major developments, and the bombing had been relegated to page A17. According to the article, an Al Qaeda splinter group had taken credit for the blast on their website, and though an FBI source questioned the group's credibility, the larger implication was clear: the culprits were Islamic. A few days ago, I'd have glanced at the piece without raising an eyebrow. But now . . . I put the paper down. Reading in traffic was making me queasy. And the meter was climbing—soaring!—toward triple digits. I lowered the window and turned my head into the breeze. Except there was no breeze. We weren't moving.

Touché's idea was simple enough: fly up to Fishers Island, find Brendan Carlyle, and get him to talk. It was that easy, a weekend jaunt. Except it was completely implausible. Beyond the practical questions—would Carlyle be there? Would he say anything? Did he *know* anything?—loomed the greater issue of the flight itself. Because Touché, it became clear, had meant that *he'd* be doing the flying. I was petrified of planes and only boarded them heavily medicated and under extreme circumstances—family funerals, destination weddings, and trips to Vegas. It was a question of physics, equations of weight and balance that defied logic. *Wake turbulence, air pockets, wind shear, bird strikes:* these were the phrases, the *fears*, that consumed me every time I gazed down on the earth from thirty thousand feet, and all the alcohol and Ambien in the world couldn't dull them.

All of which is to say that the prospect of a Friday-morning flight to Fishers Island with Touché at the controls wasn't entirely appealing. In fact, it was harrowing. I'd never been in a private plane before, and I'd told Touché as much the night before.

"Ah, yes," he answered, "then this is exactly what you need. You can sit in the cockpit, be my copilot. Then you'll see how easy it is, how *routine.*"

"Amtrak is routine," I'd responded. But he had a point. What better remedy than facing my anxiety head-on, with a newly minted pilot in a single-engine plane? Still, I made one excuse after another until Touché said, "Fine, let's forget the whole thing." Which is when I remembered the whole thing—the bigger picture, the tiny photograph. That something would come of it was a long shot, of course. But even if Paige Roderick proved nothing more than a pretext for an island getaway, that was fine with me. Anything beat another weekend in the scorching summer city.

When Touché had told me Essex County was a private airport, I'd conjured images of a wind sock astride a dirt runway. As we finally pulled up, though, more than an hour late, I saw hangars, a tower, even a terminal. I grabbed my bag and gave the cabbie five bucks on top of the $95 fare. He spit at my feet as he drove off.

The "terminal"—a dozen cushioned seats and a tiny information counter—could have been a doctor's waiting room, but for the two men in pilot shirts sipping coffee near the door that doubled as a gate.

"If you're looking for Julian, he's out there working on his engine," one of them said, pointing at a group of planes parked in the near distance. His friend laughed. I didn't.

Almost a decade had passed since 9/11, and still it felt disturbing—almost illegal—to be walking through a door and out onto an airport tarmac. The midday clouds had evaporated and the sun was ascendant; I could feel the concrete give a bit underfoot. Up ahead, a dozen aircraft of varying sizes sat neatly in rows. I spotted Touché through the glare, climbing down the steps of a small Cessna. When he got to the bottom, he made his way to the tip of the plane, where, to my horror, he dipped his head under the open hood of what must have been the engine. The pilot hadn't been kidding.

"What the hell are you doing?" I shouted.

Touché reemerged from the engine block, careful not to bang his head. He was holding a screwdriver. "Glad you could make it. Did you walk?"

"Traffic."

"Well, put your bag in the cabin and come help me."

"With what?"

"Routine maintenance."

"Routine maintenance? Don't you have *people* for that kind of stuff?"

"Just hurry. We'd be there already if you'd been on time."

Resigned to my impending demise, I climbed into the plane and looked around. The cramped four-seater smelled strongly of gasoline and old leather. Flight time was less than an hour, but still. I clambered back down the steps and joined Touché, or at least the visible part of him.

"The fucking thing's tiny."

"Do me a favor," he said, from inside the engine. "Check the oil, will you? It's directly opposite me, you'll see it."

I didn't move. Touché poked his head up, annoyed. "What's wrong with you? It's the same as a car. There's a—what do you call it?—a *dipstick.*"

"My God. You're serious."

I walked around the propeller to the other side, where another cover lay open, baring the aircraft's inner workings. The dipstick was right in front of me. I pulled it out, wiped it on the bottom of my jeans, then put it back in and pulled it out again.

"*It's at three!*" I shouted, over the fuselage.

"*Out of what?*"

"*What do you mean, 'out of what'?*"

"*I mean three out of what?*"

I looked down at the rod in my now greasy hand, and like every dipstick I'd ever seen, it went to ten.

"*Ten!*"

There was silence.

"*Is that good or bad?*" I shouted.

"*It should get us there*" came the reply, followed by the slamming of the engine cover on the other side. A moment later, Touché was standing beside me.

"I'm not going," I said.

"Of course you are." He snatched the dipstick from my hand and put it back in himself, then slammed the cover closed.

"I don't know how to say this. Actually, I do. I'm not flying in this piece of shit. I don't care if you've had ten thousand hours in the air, and all the—"

"Ah, Aidan, stop being a baby. I was kidding about the oil."

"No you weren't."

Touché thought for a moment. "Fine. I'll go alone. You can stay here and wait for another e-mail that will never come. Or you can be *proactive.*" With that, he climbed up into his machine. He knew I'd follow him; in the end, everyone followed him. I took a deep breath and started up the stairs.

Touché twisted knobs and read gauges while I strapped myself into the copilot's seat. Then he stood up, pulled the steps into the plane, and with a straight face recited the location of emergency exits and life jackets in the event of various catastrophes. "Sorry," he said, as he sat back down. "I have to say all that."

Through the small windshield, I watched the rotor slice through the air, once, twice, then catch with a dull roar that immediately rendered communication impossible. Touché motioned toward a Vietnam-era headset hanging in front of me. I put it on and the world fell silent.

"Better, no?" His voice in the earphones was calm, almost soothing.

"This isn't fun for me," I responded, but he didn't react. Instead he pointed at a button on the console.

"Press this to talk."

We were moving now, *taxiing*. I pressed the button. "Please tell me you actually know what you're—" I was cut off. A third voice was talking, spewing forth a sequence of Whiskeys and Tangos that Touché repeated back as he turned onto the runway and slowly pushed the throttle. The engine gained power, and when we came to speed, my friend pulled lightly on the yoke and lifted us into the sky. It was like pulling a water-skier from a lake. Once, then again, he received coded instructions, and we banked smoothly and ascended. Below us, north Jersey spread out like green carpeting, stained in places but still lush.

Touché pressed his button. "You don't look so bad. Why all the fuss before?"

"It's okay to talk? I don't want to interrupt some critical ground-to-air directive."

"Your headset is only wired internally. You can hear everything coming in but can only talk to me."

Up ahead, the Hudson River slithered its way north, or maybe south, and I couldn't help but think about that US Airways jet that had glided to a miraculous water landing two winters back. Did Touché know how to glide? We turned east and suddenly there was Manhattan, the slender middle finger of the American fist, glittering so damn brightly I had to look away.

"Hold on," said Touché. "We're flying over the Palisades. Sometimes the air gets choppy." Seconds later, we swooned, down and then right back up, before returning to humming tranquillity.

There was a rhythm to flying. We moved up the coast and were passed from tower to tower—Stamford, Norwalk, Bridgeport, New Haven. Touché had filed a flight plan, so each new region of the sky was expecting us. The radio back-and-forths were friendly, jocular, *routine*. It's the word I kept coming back to. I relaxed and looked out over Long Island, which from my perch looked small and manageable, the harbors and vineyards of the North Fork, the mansions and azure pools of the—

"Tell me what we're doing," said Touché's voice in my ears.

"What do you mean?"

Touché pointed at his headset and then at the button in front of me. I pushed it and repeated myself.

"I mean," Touché said, "is any of this real? A girl like that. Do you honestly believe she could be involved?"

"I don't know. It seems unlikely, doesn't it?"

"If someone really had information about her, wouldn't they go directly to the police or FBI? Certainly, they wouldn't e-mail some amateur blogger—"

"Hey, I get paid," I said, but I'd forgotten to press the button again.

"—which means that whoever's sending the messages, your Mr. Empires Fall, is also likely to be involved."

"But isn't that a bit obvious? Why take the risk?"

"It's not a risk if the e-mail can't be traced back to the source," Touché said. "And I'm assuming it can't be?"

"Probably not. There are ways to cover your tracks online, from using public computers and proxy servers to data wiping and virtual tunneling. But that stuff's not my strong suit."

Touché furrowed his brow. "Perhaps they sent you the photo because they assumed you'd post it immediately."

"But why wouldn't *I* call the cops?"

"That's a good question. Why haven't you?"

Which is how we left it. Everything open to interpretation. But at least Touché was intrigued. Or maybe he was just bored. Maybe he was already planning to fly to Fishers Island and just wanted company. With Touché, it was best not to ask. And anyway, we were beginning our descent. I could see the island in front of us, a thin spit of land two miles off the coast of Connecticut. The airwaves had gone quiet.

"Why isn't anyone talking to us?" I asked.

"There's no tower. It's just a little landing strip. The military built it during World War Two."

"Then who guides us in?"

"You're the copilot," Touché said, grinning.

I could see the runway, an impossibly short strip of concrete on the western tip of the island. But we were well centered, and as I bit my lip and dug my fists into the seat, Touché brought us down. Slowly. Smoothly. Safely. Nothing to it.

He cozied the craft up beside the only other plane at the airfield and cut the engine. A minute later—and not a moment too soon— I stepped gingerly down the stairs onto the weed-strewn tarmac. Touché was still shutting things down, so I put in a quick call to Derrick. In my absence—I'd told him I was going to a wedding—my boss had agreed to take the reins of Roorback for the day (after that I'd be off the hook until Monday, as I didn't usually post on weekends). Like most publishers, he didn't mind occasionally sullying his hands on the content side of life, if only to seem involved. As a precaution, the night before, I'd moved the two EmpiresFall e-mails from my Roorback account to my personal account (though they were probably still on the server if someone was really looking). As for the possibility of another missive arriving while I was gone, I could only hope Derrick wouldn't notice it amid the hundreds of others clogging up my in-box. If he even checked my Roorback account at all.

To my relief, Derrick sounded normal when he answered the phone. In fact, he sounded like he was having a ball. "Just sitting here lobbing little grenades at the haughty fourth estate," he said.

"Isn't it fun?"

"For a day, yes. But make sure you're back Monday morning."

"I will be."

"Where are you again?" he asked.

"Fishers Island."

"Florida?"

"Long Island Sound."

"Never heard of it."

"I think that's the point," I said.

When Touché had secured the plane (with little blocks on either side of the wheels, as if the thing might roll away), I followed him to a battle-scarred Grand Wagoneer with wood-paneled siding.

"Your car's here. What a stroke of luck."

"Isn't it?"

We threw our bags in the back and were soon turning onto the island's main road.

"So I did a little research last night," I said.

"And?"

"There's a lot of old money here."

"So old there's no bank. No hotels or restaurants either. They don't want another Nantucket."

Touché recited a quick history of the island, the upshot being that the small group of industrialists—the Du Ponts among them—that had originally bought it had somehow managed, through a century of family infighting and sweeping societal change, to maintain control of their little paradise.

"How often do you come up here?" I asked.

"Once, maybe twice a year. It's all I can handle. The people. You'll see."

Except there were no people, just land, lush and wild. The road wound through meadows and tangled forest, then, out of nowhere, we came upon a guardhouse. Touché waved to the man inside and we kept going.

"Welcome to the private side of the island," Touché said.

"I thought the whole thing was private."

"There are levels to these things."

We pressed on, past ponds and coves, glimpses of water, sailboats shimmering in the sun. Then the road bent sharply and the trees opened to reveal a series of golf holes surrounding an elegant clubhouse. The fairways were crowded with men in outfits of unfathomable patterns and hues. "The Club Championship is this weekend, which is why I'm fairly sure we'll run into Mr. Carlyle."

"He's a golfer?"

"Everyone up here's a golfer."

We continued past the parking lot, filled with cars from another era—vintage Mustangs and diesel-powered Mercedeses—and on toward the end of the island.

"No Ferraris or Hummers, at least."

"The landed gentry has its upside," Touché said.

That he somehow said this without sounding like an asshole was a tribute, not only to the statement's veracity, but to my friend's obvious indifference to his surroundings. Touché thrived on creativity, diversity, the manic hum of humankind. Fishers Island was the opposite of all that. It was comfort, idleness, boredom . . . golf.

It was also real estate. I had never been anyplace I could rightly call a compound until we turned into Touché's crushed-shell driveway. My God, the place was magnificent. The main house, which backed up to a bluff overlooking the sound, was painted white and peeling in places, but looked all the more elegant for the deterioration. And the surrounding grounds—which were immaculate—hosted a barn, a pool, and a well-kept grass tennis court. *Grass.*

We parked, eventually, and walked inside. Touché led me up a winding staircase to the third floor and pointed down a row of open doors. "That's your wing. I'll meet you downstairs in an hour." With that he turned and loped away. I wandered down my assigned hall and settled on a corner suite lined with books and windows. I let some air into the room and then collapsed upon the massive bed.

I woke up during the falling part of an airplane dream. I could hear my heart pounding in the dead silence of the house. How long had I been asleep? An hour? Two? Outside, the air had cooled and flags were whipping in the wind. It was the time of day when my father used to lay his thumb along the horizon, and if part of the sun disappeared behind it, he'd announce it was cocktail hour. I was young then. He no longer made such distinctions.

I showered, shaved, and slipped on an Izod and an old pair of khakis I'd dug up for the occasion. I searched the house, but Touché was nowhere to be found, so I made myself a gin and tonic and settled into a wicker chair on the front porch. What a life. Yet Touché saw right through it. This side of his family, his *American* side, was something he hardly acknowledged. But in truth he'd been living in the States for almost twenty years now. In an effort to keep him out of harm's way, Santo had shipped his only son off to a famous prep school outside Washington, D.C., then on to UCLA. Touché rarely discussed his time in Los Angeles; I'm guessing he liked it a little too much. All that money and panache in a town like that. It took him five years to get his diploma, and one more to recover from the exertion. He sniffed around the movie business for a while, but little came of it. So he decamped to his parents' apartment in New York and applied to NYU—right across the street—for grad school. While I, like so many others, saw journalism as something concrete in a suddenly arbitrary world, I think Touché saw it in simpler terms— as the old aristocratic fallback. Apparently, journalism was once an honorable profession.

I don't mean to say that my friend lacked beliefs; it was just tough to know what they were. Certainly, Touché identified with his Venezuelan roots, if not in revolutionary terms, then with a subtle anti-Americanism that lingered around the edges of his person. That his father was risking his life for a political cause, that he would take it *that far*, no doubt had an impact on his son. But what of his mother? She almost never came up. Du Pont, to Touché, was just another name in a world of big names. What were the odds two families like the Touchés and Du Ponts would come together? I used to wonder, back when we first met and I didn't know the odds were actually quite good. The rich do get richer, I realize that now. Between Dalton and Middlebury I'd known plenty of well-heeled offspring, but no one like Touché. He was too wealthy to understand money, to realize it was the permanent focal point of everyone else's existence. Debt, like public transportation, just wasn't part of his world.

His way of dealing with monetary imbalance was simply to pay for everyone, all the time. But he did more than that. He was a patron in every way, and the Washington Square apartment was his clubhouse. You never knew who might be there. Claire Danes. Will Sheff. Drew Barrymore. Mark Ruffalo. Jenny Lewis. European beauties over on United Nations contracts. Pasty-faced guitarists from the latest British invasion. He'd funded any number of projects—from political documentaries to conceptual clothing lines—and had lent his name to countless benefits without becoming overexposed. Being around him made you feel as if you'd made it in some way. Smoking a cigarette with Zadie Smith, a joint with Joss Stone. And the best part? He didn't give a damn about any of it. Which is why the whole thing worked, and why it never lasted. With Touché, the rules of friendship were different, unpredictable. We'd see each other for days on end, and just when I thought we were inseparable, I wouldn't hear from him for

months. Eventually, I'd get a choppy voice mail from a European airport or a hurried text from another hemisphere, and there we'd be, a
day later, sipping scotch in that living room . . . or flying up to Fishers
on the trail of a terrorist.

I saw him, then, pedaling toward the house on a beat-up bicycle.
He was completely at ease, at home in the world, his world, and I
was suddenly thrilled that we were in this together. My cause had
become his cause, and it made our mission seem less absurd. Chasing Paige Roderick wasn't a lark anymore, and even if it was, who
cared? A beautiful sunset was coming, and we had nothing better
to do.

He waved and dismounted, leaving the bike on the ground like a
ten-year-old.

"I talked to our man," he said, as he climbed the steps and took a
seat beside me.

"*Brendan Carlyle?* How'd you find him?"

"I thought he might be hanging around the clubhouse after his
round, so I rode over, and sure enough, there he was, sitting with a
few other guys, drinking beer and replaying his match, shot by shot."

"What'd you say?"

"I slapped him on the shoulder and said hello. We'd heard of each
other from all the summers we spent up here as kids, so it wasn't too
strange. Turns out he's a banker at Goldman and lives down in Tribeca.
I told him we'd be at the Pequot later."

"And?"

"He said he'd buy us a drink."

The Pequot was the only bar on Fishers Island. Touché found a parking
spot and cut the engine (though it was still sputtering when we walked
inside). The main barroom had a vaguely nautical theme and didn't
aim for anything grander, though a smaller annex played host to pool
tables and several sit-down video-game machines that I didn't notice
at first, thanks to a sea of polo shirts and pastel skirts, penny loaf-
ers and flip-flops. Fashion, clearly, didn't summer on Fishers Island. It
was the time of night when the old guard, in their whale-print pants
and cashmere sweaters, gave way to their children, already arriving

in waves from bonfires and beachfront dinner parties. As "Beat It" played and Touché chatted up a pretty redheaded bartender with a heavy Irish accent, I wandered around in search of the jukebox. What I found instead was a flashing disco dance floor full of lead-footed bodies.

"Grim, isn't it?" Touché said, coming up behind me.

"Must be inbreeding."

"Ah, yes," he replied, in a tone that signaled both tacit agreement and the end of the exchange. He handed me a beer.

"Quite the staff," I said, nodding back toward the bar.

"It's the same every summer. Australians, Irish, a few Eastern Europeans. They fly them in to be cooks and caterers, though the more adventurous girls always end up working here. It makes for an intriguing—what do the English call it?—*upstairs-downstairs* situation."

On the dance floor the old and the young had come together in a blur of Nantucket Red and Lilly Pulitzer green, fake white teeth and fake white pearls. Or maybe the pearls were real. In a far corner a thirtysomething woman was teaching an old man in seersucker pants some form of the pretzel.

"Daughter or wife?" I asked Touché, but he was looking across the room.

"There's Brendan. With that group of guys that just walked in."

I followed my friend's gaze. The photograph hadn't lied. Brendan was traditionally good-looking, and his clothes—dark jeans and a fitted button-down shirt—were casual but considered. Progressively preppy. What you saw, it seemed, was what you got, and what we had in Brendan Carlyle was a guy with a lot going for him.

He bought a drink and headed into the game room. We followed. The tables were all in use, so we found a booth with a view of the parking lot. It didn't take long.

"Julian!"

"Ah, Brendan. Come join us."

Brendan left his buddies and slid in beside me. Touché made introductions, then raised his glass: "To the golf tournament. Tell us how it's going."

"Please, no," Brendan said, rolling his eyes. "I won't bore you."

We all raised our glasses anyway, and the conversation drifted into more familiar territory. Apartments, jobs, restaurants, bars: New York. We were two years into the deepest recession of our lifetimes, but you wouldn't know it listening to Brendan. He worked late, ate out most nights, collected contemporary photography, and got up to Fishers when he could.

"How about you guys?" he asked.

"Aidan's a blogger," Touché said, with measured amusement. "He skewers the media all day and drinks with them all night."

"How does that work?" Brendan asked.

"It's tricky," I answered.

Just then, the redheaded bartender appeared and asked Touché— as if Brendan and I weren't even there—if we wanted another round. "On the house," she said.

"Well, how could we say no to that?" Touché responded. The two of them locked eyes, then the girl smiled, embarrassed, and said she'd be right back.

"Impressive," Brendan said, when she was out of earshot. "You got her out from behind the bar."

"Ah, please," said Touché. "I remember that beautiful girl you showed up with a while back."

"When?"

"I don't know. A year or two ago? You brought her to one of those big galas at the club. There was a picture of the two of you in the news-letter. My mother keeps those things lying around the house."

"I haven't invited a girl up here in three years," Brendan said.

"Could have been then. Or maybe it wasn't you. No matter."

"Was she tall? Long, dark hair?"

"Sounds right," Touché said, nonchalantly watching a nearby pool game.

"Yeah, her name was Paige. Interesting girl. We'd been dating a while, so I asked her to come up. Big mistake, as it turns out. I played golf every morning, and she got stuck at the beach with a bunch of young Upper East Side moms. She wasn't too thrilled. Not her scene. I think we lasted a month after that."

"Aidan likes the difficult ones as well," Touché said, his gaze returning to the table. He proceeded to explain in gleeful detail my very public relationship with Cressida. Why was he changing the subject? We'd finally been getting somewhere.

"I think I've read a few of her columns," Brendan was saying.

"Aren't they great?" Touché said. "Especially now that you've met the poor bastard on the other side?"

"He's funny," I said to Brendan.

"He is," Brendan agreed.

"I brought a girl up here for a weekend once," Touché continued. "An actress I knew from L.A. She'd had it after one night so I took her across the water to Foxwoods."

"With Paige it was more of a political thing," Brendan said. "At the big Saturday-night dinner, we were sitting with Jerry Auchincloss and his wife, and Sandy Dreyfuss, Martin Phipps, a few others, and Phipps said something about Iraq, how it was getting distorted by the media. It was a throwaway line, a knee-jerk opinion, but Paige went off. Really took the guy to task. I think her father had been in the army, or her brother, I can't remember. Anyway, it shut the table up."

"Where was she from?" Touché asked.

"North Carolina, originally. The mountains. We were going to drive down there later that summer, but her parents came up to New York instead. Nice people. We had dinner in the Village, but Paige and I were pretty much over by then. I heard she moved to D.C. to work for a think tank or something. But I haven't talked to her since we broke up."

"Irish car bombs," said a female voice, and we looked up to see the bartender balancing a tray of drinks above us. "Pint of Guinness with a shot of whiskey inside. I got one for everyone, including me."

We all downed them, then the bartender wiped her lips, collected the glasses, and sashayed away.

"On that note . . ." Brendan put his hands on the table and slid out of the booth. "Let's all get together in the city sometime. Julian, I've heard about your parties."

"You'll have to come to one," Touché said. "Though they're sadly tamer these days."

We shook hands and said our good-byes. Touché and I lingered at the table a minute longer, then got up and made our way through the barroom and out the front door.

"So?" I asked, as soon as we were in the car.

"It sure sounds like Paige," Touché said. "Except if she's such a radical, why would she date a guy like that? He's perfectly nice, but . . ."

The sky was dark and starless. We turned onto the same coiling road we'd taken from the airport, but Touché handled the curves perfectly, curves he'd no doubt memorized as a drunken teen, on this exact drive, at this very hour. When we reached the house, he disappeared into the cellar and returned with a bottle of Château d'Yquem. He poured the sweet, syrupy wine into two small glasses, and we fell into the living room furniture, like men twice our age.

The Touchés believed strongly in nightcaps; it was a time of conspiracies and last chances, a brief respite from a world that presented more questions than answers.

"You should call her house in North Carolina," Touché said.

"Why? She won't be there."

"But her parents might be."

"And what would I say? 'Hi, Mrs. Roderick, this is Aidan Cole. I'm sitting here with my fellow journalism-school dropout Julian Touché, and we—' "

"Hey, I graduated."

" '—were just wondering if there's any chance your daughter blew a hole in the side of a building on Madison Avenue last weekend.' "

"Ah, Aidan. A little optimism would go a long way." Touché sipped his wine and cleared his throat. "When you call, you should pretend you're him."

"Who?"

"Brendan Carlyle. Say you've lost Paige's home number and are trying to get in touch with her. Didn't Brendan say he got along well with her parents?"

"But I don't sound like him."

"They won't remember. It was three years ago."

The doorbell rang, and I whirled around quickly, almost spilling my wine. Standing on the other side of the screen door was the bartender.

"Come in, come in," Touché said, getting up to greet her.

"I got off early," she said, opening the door and stepping tentatively inside. "I thought you said this would be a party."

"An intimate one; the best kind. Here, you need a drink."

She took off her windbreaker and threw it on a chair. Her low-cut, white shirt was stained from her night's work. "Hi again," she said to me, before following Touché into the kitchen. Had they met before, or had this rendezvous just come together tonight? It was a question better left unasked. I got up and joined them. The girl was leaning on the island counter, shifting her weight from one bare leg to another. She undid a clip and a frothy mess of hair fell down over her shoulders just as Touché handed her a glass of wine. Trying not to sound too obvious, I begged off to bed.

Upstairs, marginally drunk, I tried to check e-mails on my phone, but could get no signal. I was stranded in the off-line world, reduced to browsing a bookshelf. A weathered hardcover copy of *Franny and Zooey* caught my attention. I hadn't read Salinger since high school, but how, in that house, after that night, could I pass up a little Glass family disaffection? I opened it up to the title page. It was signed: *To Santo, My New York City comrade, Your friend, Jerry, 5/24/62.* Figured.

I was asleep before Franny got off the train in New Haven.

Touché was cooking breakfast when I got downstairs the next morning.

"Big day," he said, flipping an egg.

"Big night," I replied, looking around. "Is she still here?"

"It's ten thirty. She left hours ago."

"You never told me your dad knew Salinger."

"Did he?"

"He signed a book for him upstairs."

Touché shrugged and pointed the pan at an atlas on the kitchen table. It was open to North Carolina. Beside it lay a sheet of paper listing dozens of names and numbers.

"Our Irish friend was snoring, so I got up and spent some time on the phone with a nice lady from Verizon. There are twenty-three Rodericks in western North Carolina. Only eleven are listed as couples. It's a—how do you say—*shot in the dark*, but . . ."

"How do you not know *shot in the dark*?"

"Tell me," Touché said, "how many languages can *you* speak?"

"But you're American, for Christ's sake."

"How about some coffee? You sound a bit testy."

More like nervous. This was beginning to resemble a real investigation. The kind that could lead somewhere. Is that what I really wanted? Answers? Or was Paige better as a concept—an American myth, a subversive ideal. I sat down and Touché put a plate of eggs in front of me. With a fork in one hand and a pen in the other, I started writing a script, but Touché thought I'd sound more natural without one. So I winged it.

The first call: Charles and Merly Roderick, from a town called Hickory. I dialed and a woman answered. I asked if Paige was there. "Sorry, wrong number."

"Lower your voice a little," Touché said. "Brendan, he's more . . . *like this*."

I took another bite of eggs and cleared my throat. Edward and Lynn Roderick of Mars Hill. No answer. No answering machine. "Deep in the mountains," Touché said, eyeing the atlas. "Lucky they have a phone."

And on down the list. Florence Roderick of Blowing Rock. Gene and Sylvie of Asheville. Hank and Mimi of Cullowhee. Carl of Kings Mountain. Touché had listened to Brendan carefully, for every town on the list was west of Winston-Salem. But it didn't matter: ten calls and nothing. Just answering machines, wrong numbers, and an old man with a heavy accent—Walter Roderick of Forest City—who told me to go fuck myself.

"I've never been there," Touché said. "To the Smoky Mountains."

"Me either." I dialed another number. "I think it's pretty remote."

"Where did they film *Deliverance*?"

A woman answered the phone. "Hi, is Paige there?" I asked.

"That's a great movie," he continued.

"May I ask who's calling?" the woman said. I shot a look at Touché, then scanned the sheet. *Lawton and Ellery Roderick—Maggie Valley*.

"Is this Mrs. Roderick?"

"It is . . ."

"This is Paige's old friend Brendan Carlyle. Do you remember? We met a few years ago in New York."

"Oh, Brendan, of course! What a nice time we had. How are you?"

Touché was staring at me.

"I'm fine, thank you. I was . . . well, I hate to bother you, but I lost Paige's number, and since I still had this one written down, I . . . um . . . well, I was hoping to get back in touch with her before too much time passed."

Shut up, Touché mouthed. He was right. Let her do the talking.

"It was good of you to call," Mrs. Roderick said. "I'm sure Paige would love to hear from you, but we . . . that is, Lawton and I . . . to tell you the truth we're not sure where she is at the moment. She told us she was going to visit friends for a few weeks, and, well, it's been several months. Of course, I'm sure she's fine, you know her."

There was a commotion in the background, a male voice, low but insistent, then Mrs. Roderick again: "Brendan, could you hold on a moment?"

"Sure." More muffled conversation. She was talking to someone with her hand over the mouthpiece. Touché looked at me impatiently.

Then the line crackled back to life. "Brendan, this is Lawton Roderick here."

"Hello, sir."

"My wife's putting a happy face on all this, but the fact is we're real worried about Paige. She's a big girl, and Lord knows she's always had a mind of her own, but she's never disappeared like this. I'm assuming you have no idea where she is?"

"No, I haven't talked to her in ages."

"Well, if you hear anything . . ."

"Of course," I said.

There was a pause on the other end of the line. I waited.

"Brendan?" Mr. Roderick said, finally.

"Yes?"

"There is one thing." His voice was tentative now, unsure of itself. "We got a call here at the house two weeks back from a number with a Vermont area code. I picked up the phone and . . . nothing. I mean, someone was there, but they didn't speak. When the line went dead, I called the number back but no one answered. I wouldn't have thought much of it, especially since we don't know anyone in Vermont, but"—he sighed heavily—"it was our son Bobby's birthday that day, and Ellery, she feels strongly that . . ."

"It could have been Paige?"

"Call it a woman's intuition." He tried to chuckle, then gave up.

"Do you still have the number?"

"Sure, but I doubt it'll do much good. I've called it a dozen times, but no one answers. I even tried to trace it through the phone company, but they said they couldn't do anything because it wasn't a residential or business number, whatever that means."

"Would you mind giving it to me? Maybe I can . . . I don't know"—I didn't know—"look into it and see if anything comes up."

"Can't see as it'd hurt. It's . . . are you ready?"

"Oh, yes."

I wrote it down carefully, repeated it back, and thanked him.

"Maybe I'll be thanking you," he said, and then hung up.

Touché looked at the digits and frowned. "Should we try it?" he asked.

"Of course!" I took a deep breath and dialed the number. It rang. And rang. For more than a minute. There was no answering machine. Finally, I gave up.

"Probably a pay phone," Touché said. "And that means we're . . . what's the word?"

"Screwed?"

We put our plates in the sink and relocated to the porch. Fresh air and all that. For half an hour we talked through ideas, loose theories that led nowhere. Why wouldn't Paige just call her brother directly? Why wouldn't she at least say hello to her father? Or, if she was in real trouble, why call anyone at all? We had no answers. After a period of silence, Touché sighed heavily, then announced that we were stuck. At a dead end. Unless another e-mail message surfaced, there was nothing to do now but move on with our lives.

"Just think," he continued. "On Monday you can write about the whole saga. Post the photo, the e-mails, tell the entire story. Maybe it'll lead to something. Probably, it'll turn out to be a joke. Either way, it'll get you some attention." With that, he picked up a magazine and started working on a crossword.

He was right. We'd been lucky and luck runs out. I stared out over the water and thought of my crumbling apartment on my broken street; I thought of my girlfriend and her tales of love gone wrong; and as a light breeze cooled the porch and fluttered distant sails, I thought of the thousands of blog posts that lay before me, years of momentary significance adding up to nothing in particular.

"I need to check in with Derrick," I said. "See how the rest of yesterday went."

"Feel free to use the house phone," Touché said, without looking up.

But I didn't know my boss's number by heart. I lived in short bursts of communication—blogging, texting, speed dial. Derrick was #4. I went upstairs and found my cell phone charging on the bedside table next to *Franny and Zooey*. I put the book back on the shelf where I'd found it, between *Peyton Place* and *Butterfield 8*.

Butterfield 8!

As a teenager in New York, I'd come across John O'Hara's Depression-era classic on our living room bookshelf and asked my father what the title meant. My parents had just started fighting, and happy for conversation that didn't involve his increasingly unclear whereabouts, my father explained that *BUtterfield* had once been the phone exchange for the Upper East Side. When he was a kid, he said, each two-letter exchange had had its own mnemonic name—288 became BU8, which became BUtterfield 8, etc.—that was supposed to make phone numbers easier to memorize. The names often grew from neighborhood characteristics—anything from surrounding streets (*ORchard* for the Lower East Side, *WHitehall* for the Financial District) to prominent families (*WAtkins* in Chelsea, *ENdicott* on the Upper West Side) to area reputation (*ALgonquin* for Greenwich Village, *BEowulf* near Columbia). The exchange system was phased out beginning in the 1960s (they'd run out of phone numbers), but in many places the numerical prefixes had stayed the same, especially in rural areas where populations hadn't grown. In other words . . .

I bounded down the stairs and almost ran into the screen door.

"What's a four-letter word for 'an imitator'?" Touché asked, pen in mouth.

"I think I know how to find Paige." I pointed at the phone number I'd scribbled down. "The prefix . . . it might still correspond to a specific town." Touché had no idea what I was talking about, so I quickly explained the old exchange system.

"But it doesn't work like that anymore," my friend said skeptically. "People move and keep their numbers."

"Not always. I mean, we should at least try."

"Go ahead," he said, looking back down at the puzzle.

I grabbed the phone in the kitchen and dialed Vermont directory assistance. I asked the recorded voice for a live one, and a moment later a woman came on the line.

"Hi," I said. "If I gave you the prefix to a phone number, could you tell me the town it corresponds to?"

"What is it?"

"Four nine six."

There was tapping on a keyboard, then: "Waitsfield."

"You're kidding."

"That's what it says here. Is there a number you'd like me to conn—"

"No, thank you." I hung up and hurried back outside.

"Well?" Touché raised his eyebrows.

"Waitsfield, Vermont. It's a ski town in the Green Mountains. We used to drive up there when I was a kid. It's where Sugarbush is, and Mad River Glen."

"I'm more familiar with Courchevel and Gstaad."

I waited for something more, but Touché just sat there.

"So what do you say? It's only Saturday. We could crank up the plane and head north. Do you need to file a new flight plan or something?"

"I can't go."

"Come on, just for one night. We're *close*. We've got her now."

"Do we?" Touché said, suddenly fixing his gaze on me. "All we've got is the name of a town that some girl we've never seen or spoken to *might* have made a call from. Let's look at the big picture here. You received an anonymous *e-mail*. Nothing more. I'm beginning to think we launched into this without thinking it through."

"I *have* been think—"

"And what if it *is* her? Have you considered that? What if you somehow do find her, and over a nice glass of chardonnay she admits she builds bombs in her free time? Then you're *involved*. Then you have to turn her in. And even if you don't get in trouble for having failed to alert the police sooner, your life from that point on . . . it will always be that one thing. You'll never escape it. Even heroism is a kind of infamy." With that he got up, slapped me on the back, and walked inside.

"What the fuck are you talking about?" I called after him. I felt dazed and a bit dizzy. Then, like a summer storm, the feeling passed, and I knew exactly what I was going to do. "When does the ferry to New London leave? I can catch a train from there, right?"

PAIGE

· • • • • • • • · • •

THE HEAT CAME THE SECOND WEEK OF JULY, SCORCHING DAYS, ONE AFTER another. Leaves browned and hardened like toast. Streams slowed to faucet trickles. The house, a place for winter pleasures, had no air-conditioning and by midmonth was almost unbearable (Lindsay kept promising to buy a stand-up fan in town, but it hadn't yet appeared). I imagine it was sweltering in the garage, too, but when Keith came in for lunch—shirtless, shoeless, caked in sweat and grime—he never mentioned the temperature. So I pressed on, uncomplaining.

My role was evolving, the concrete replacing the conceptual. No longer roaming the Internet link by random link, I now searched for specific *targets*. Studies, trends, and forecasts. Articles, interviews, and essays. The trick, the crucial necessity, was to navigate cyberspace without leaving a trail. It was something I'd never had to worry about in my real-life research jobs, and once again, Keith showed me the way. He had a background in technology. He had a background in life. The wired world was a dangerous place, he told me, its endless pages filled with deceptively benign-sounding cookies, bugs, and logs. The cookies—ID tags embedded in user hard drives—could be disabled; the real problems were the Web bugs and log files. The bugs monitored page visits; the logs recorded server activity. The only way to bypass these was to blend in by avoiding search engines and local ISPs.

But that was only the beginning. We downloaded nothing and saved nothing (I took handwritten notes). We stayed away from e-mail, from blogs, from YouTube; from well-known tracking sites and any-where else that might arouse suspicion—government or university sites; extremist sites; anything originating from the Middle East. Instead, I roamed the outskirts of information, picking up scraps, shards here and there.

Who were these targets, these objects of our dangerous affections? They were the people and institutions that pulled America's strings, and played them, too, played them so well we'd been lulled to sleep by their soothing sounds—that soft thrum of capitalism. We wanted to expose the wretched underside of the global energy supersystem. Does it sound grandiose? Perhaps. But we believed it was achievable and became more so with every passing day, every careful click, every filled-up notebook.

Lindsay gave us our first hard lead. Since we had no television, she'd started watching webcasts on the laptop—mostly news shows and sitcoms. Keith didn't love the practice but couldn't say exactly why, so it continued. One sweltering night, while I made dinner and Keith studied ordnance manuals on the couch, Lindsay settled in to watch one of the network news shows. I could hear it in the kitchen, but not until I saw Lindsay furiously scribbling notes did I begin paying attention. The segment was on Texas Consolidated, Inc., one of the world's most profitable oil companies. TCI had just posted the largest single-quarter profit in the history of the New York Stock Exchange, and here, now, was their CEO—on the back deck of his 120-foot yacht—calmly explaining that every penny was justified. He spread his arms as wide as the surrounding water and spoke of millions of happy investors, and of hundreds of millions more that relied on him to keep their cars running, their houses heated. He clearly expected an easy time of it—a few pesky questions about executive compensation or going green, then a smooth glide to the finish. Instead, the correspondent surprised him with a ques-tion about TCI's operations in Ecuador. I knew that saga well thanks to my work in Washington, and I hurried over to watch. From the early 1970s, when oil was first discovered in the fragile Amazonian region known as the Northern Oriente, to the early 1990s, when drilling finally stopped, Texas Consolidated had pumped over $30 billion out of the ground. The bounty was split between TCI and the cabal of Quito politicians and generals who had allowed them in. Not a dime made it back to the poverty-ravished Andean tribes who had previously lived on and farmed that land. Stuck out at sea with his inquisitor, a sudden prisoner of his own wealth, the CEO called TCI's Ecuadorian adventure ancient history, but the correspondent was only getting started. What about the aftermath, she asked: the ruptured pipelines and toxic wastewater; the unlined sludge pits that seeped into aquifers; and the deforestation that stripped bare not just the land but the indigenous people who had inhabited the rain forests for as long as anyone had lived anywhere?

Bobbing three stories above the water, the CEO stared disdainfully at the correspondent. That's not my problem, he stated dispassionately.

But how can you say that? she persisted. Since the discovery of oil, Ecuador's national debt has increased from $200 million to $13 billion, while the poverty rate has risen seventy percent. And that's not your problem?

His anger evident, the CEO motioned to someone off-camera. Words were exchanged, then the camera was dislodged and the interview ended abruptly. Keith had joined us by now, and we watched the wrap-up in stony silence. When it was over, Lindsay wheeled around to face us. Let's blow up that guy's house, she said.

I looked at Keith.

Sounds like a plan, he said.

I'm being serious, Lindsay said.

So am I, Keith responded.

And so it was. Later, at dinner, Lindsay laid out the scenario—a glorious August morning on the East End of Long Island rocked by an explosion felt from Sag Harbor to Amagansett. Just think, she said. The height of the high season! A huge fucking bang and a thousand porcelain brunch plates smash to pieces.

But the plates were only the beginning. We all started chiming in, imagining the moment—men striding down Maidstone fairways; women power walking to morning bridge games; bloated trust-fund sons sleeping off marathon nights; skeletal daughters slinking home in dance-club tube tops; morning swims and morning papers; bodies already tanning on boats and beaches; small talk at farmers' markets; big talk at real estate offices—all of this . . . this *idleness* suddenly rocked by its opposite, a wake-up call that would reverberate through the hedgerows of Further Lane for generations to come.

Even Keith was grinning now.

Early the next morning I started reading everything I could find on the man. Through property records I found his Hamptons address (one of seven worldwide) and plugged it into Virtual World. The house was highly vulnerable; it bordered the beach and was surrounded on the three other sides by low trees and dune brush. Perfect cover: we wouldn't even have to break in. We could plant a bomb up against the foundation walls and the whole place would come down. The CEO was the scheduled headline speaker at the Global Energy Conference in Stockholm during the last weekend of August, which would, in theory, mean far fewer people coming and going from the house. I printed out maps and wrote up an analysis that looked a lot like my old reports at the institute. Back then, of course, I was trying to save the world, not ignite it.

At dinner the following night, I presented my findings. Lindsay flipped through the pages, vibrating with excitement. Keith remained stoic. He circled sentences and made margin notes. Then he sat back and thought while Lindsay and I cleared the table. When we were done, we moved to the living room. Keith cleared his throat.

I'm afraid it's not worth it, he said.

Why? Lindsay and I asked, in unison.

Think about it. The bomb goes off. What then? There'll be a few days of headlines, interviews with concerned neighbors and famous friends. When the commotion dies down and the police still haven't made an arrest, TCI's publicity machine will get out in front of things; they'll turn this guy into the biggest victim you've ever seen, the ultimate martyr of American achievement. Hell, before it's all over, people will be sending him money to rebuild. We need to find a target that won't elicit sympathy, an institution rather than an individual. And we need the Action itself to disrupt, to uncover, to *change* whatever iniquity has come before. We can't afford to lose in the court of public opinion.

I digested Keith's words and slowly realized they made sense. We'd been caught up in the moment. Lindsay understood as well, although it took her the rest of the night to get over her disappointment. When I came downstairs the next day, she was sitting at the laptop, watching the segment again.

He's still a fucking asshole, she said.

I burned up the TCI report and started over. A week passed, then two. I began taking walks in the mornings, when the world was still damp and pregnant with promise. Often, in those early days, Keith and I met for lunch on the deck. Sandwiches and salads. We'd talk about my work—never his—swatting ideas back and forth like shuttlecocks. Keith was thinking big thoughts, and still he was careful, measured, considered. Everything was about reaction and response. Tone and perception. He thought several steps ahead, could envision exactly what would happen, how things would turn out. It was a rare gift, foresight of that magnitude, and it had been the key to his success (Lindsay once said he'd have been a mainstay on the FBI's Most Wanted list if he existed in official circles as anything more than a rumor). Keith simply knew what he was doing. And he knew why. We were moving toward some kind of national reckoning. We all felt it. America had passed an invisible tipping point, had strayed too far from the noble tenets of its founding, and taking it back would require drastic measures.

So I barely raised an eyebrow the first time Keith mentioned it. We were eating on the deck, under the shade of the house, the air heavy and pressing against us. Keith, in cutoff jeans and running sneakers, was poking at his food with a plastic fork when he suddenly looked up and asked if I'd ever heard of Indian Point?

I nodded. It's a nuclear power plant on the Hudson River. They use it in all those worst-case scenarios because it's so close to the city.

That's right, Keith said. And I've been thinking . . . maybe we could use it in our own little scenario.

His idea, like all of his ideas, was tied to a larger theory. He knew the world was a place of truces and compromises, marginal friend-ships, uneasy alliances. He understood every shade of gray, from darkest coal to silver lining, and the complex issue of nuclear power contained them all. We'd talked about it before, and I remember being surprised by his views. It was a question of time, he'd told me. America needed to move beyond fossil fuels and foreign oil imme-diately, but it would take decades of research and implementation to effectively harness the weather or find some purer source of power. Nuclear energy could fill the gap, could save the century. It was reli-able, affordable, produced domestically, and environmentally clean (until, of course, it wasn't). Mostly, though, it was inevitable. The developed world would pass through a short nuclear age on the way to someplace better.

It's already happening in Europe, he said.

Now, as the sun beat down on us, I sat dead still and listened to words so unsettling, so massive in meaning, that it was all I could do to process them. Keith led me inside and spread out several sheets on the dining room table. They were photocopied blueprints of Indian Point. I stared at them wide-eyed, but instead of demand-ing to know—as any normal person would have—how he'd got his hands on them, I helped him smooth the corners down. They were incredibly detailed, and showed not only the plant's reactors and buildings, but its perimeter—the walls, the fences, the gates—and surrounding area. Keith had already pencil-marked various loca-tions with the letters *POE* (place of exploit), and now he pointed at one and circled it.

The reactors are protected by the Feds and the NRC, he said, which means heavy walls and well-trained guards, but the rest is left to rent-a-cops hired by the company that runs the plant. Look here, by the cliffs above the river. It's just barbed-wire fencing. I'm sure there are sensors, too, but it's like aviation radar—you just have to stay low.

But, Keith, I said.

Hold on. Just hear me out. The point is to save lives, not take them.

By blowing up a nuclear facility?

Not exactly. I mean, yes, but not the reactors. What I'm talk-ing about is a small, controlled explosion right . . . here, Keith said, pointing to a blank area surrounded by unmarked warehouse-type buildings. See, it's a good two hundred yards from the reactor walls. Nothing would actually get damaged.

Then why do it?

Come on, he said. Think it through. He looked at me expectantly, a teacher waiting for an answer.

Well, obviously they'd immediately shut down the plant, I ventured. And if the government didn't keep it closed indefinitely, then the community would.

Exactly, Keith replied. Which is something, considering Indian Point's location and safety record, that should have happened years ago.

But I don't understand. We'd be killing the very cause we're promoting. Look at Three Mile Island: the smallest of reactor meltdowns and it crippled the American nuclear industry for decades. Have they even commissioned a new reactor since then?

Nuclear energy fell out of favor long before 1979, Keith said. But, yes, I get your point. And that's why we'd release a communiqué clearly stating the reason behind our action: safety. Just think about it. Every plant in the country would immediately reevaluate and drastically ramp up security procedures. The Feds would set new mandates and regulations. We'd avert a major catastrophe by creating a very minor one. Not even.

And you honestly think we can detonate a bomb *inside* the grounds?

Yes, I do. Because nuclear power plants still operate under the old model of keeping radiation in, not keeping people out. We'll breach the outer fencing with a remote-controlled device, so we won't have to enter the facility ourselves.

You're talking about some kind of toy?

Sure, Keith said, a grin spreading across his face. Why not? A miniature dump truck or something. We just tape a payload onto the back and off she goes. . . .

And so, a half hour later, off *I* went. This was a tougher assignment—most websites of interest were government-run—but the information was out there, and slowly I found it. I needed to know what happened in the buildings closest to the potential blast site, so I found the layouts of six other nuclear plants and compared them to Indian Point.

It didn't take long for a problem to emerge, in the form of spent uranium. Keith had assumed the used-up nuclear fuel was trucked away. But that wasn't the case. There was still no federal depository for radioactive by-product, so most plants, including Indian Point, kept their waste on-site. But where? Since spent uranium was every bit as radioactive as the live stuff, it was stored in underwater tanks protected by impervious steel structures and positioned far from the reactors. These by-product buildings were labeled on some of the other layouts (in one Alabama plant, the building was actually shaded a lovely nuclear yellow), but the location of Indian Point's spent fuel wasn't clear. Three buildings were large enough to contain waste operations, and unfortunately two of them bordered Keith's courtyard-like ground zero. Radioactive material wasn't flammable like gasoline—it wouldn't ignite or explode—but it didn't matter. To my mind, even the possibility of instability, of a leak or spill caused by our Action, made everything else moot. If we couldn't eliminate the nuclear-fuel equation—and I spent several days trying—then we couldn't move forward.

Presented with the evidence, Keith finally, grudgingly, agreed.

I can't say I was disappointed. The idea had disturbed me from the get-go. Part of it was the unfeasibility of the Action itself. But what really got me was Keith's and Lindsay's blasé approach. Lindsay had come home the day Keith brought it up and, after hearing him out, quickly endorsed the plan. Her big blue eyes lit up and that was it. No one acknowledged that we were flirting with the ultimate taboo, the climactic chapter in everyone's private book of fear. Were we truly willing to go that far? I'd found Keith's arguments theoretically sound, but still . . . something goes wrong with a bomb and a town house explodes; something goes wrong with uranium and mankind pays a price.

The mood in the house changed during our nuclear flirtation. Maybe the word itself was too much. It was a psychic wound, a word meant for nightmares, for death, and just as it hung over America, so it hung over us. The air turned stale. Our tempers grew taut. Keith had

said our Actions should speak for themselves, but now he was talking about communiqués, explanations—brochures to highlight the
destruction. But, afterward, *we* were suddenly the ones who couldn't
communicate. Keith squirreled himself away in the garage for three
days. I think he even slept in there. Then, one searing afternoon, he
slipped up behind me as I sat at the computer.

Find anything interesting? he asked.

I must have jumped half a foot.

Stop fucking scaring me like that, I said.

Soon, though, I did find something interesting: an article—on
Slate—about the construction of a pan-Asian oil pipeline. It mentioned a company called Indigo Holdings as the money behind
the project. The name sounded familiar but I couldn't immediately
place it. Had I come across Indigo during my time in D.C.? Or was
it the name alone that caught my eye? I started nosing around,
and almost immediately things fell into place. The company, I discovered, was a giant consortium—part private equity firm, part
global consultancy—that operated at the crowded (and confusing)
intersection where government, military, and industry met. Three
masters to manipulate, to play off one another, with a single unambiguous goal: the generation of obscene amounts of money. Indigo
relied heavily on access to power, and its board was littered with
former presidents and prime ministers, Allahs and sheikhs, CEOs
and generals—a veritable private-sector (and privately held) administration. They went to great lengths to avoid the press, but nothing
so lucrative could operate completely in the shadows. The more I
read about their international projects, the easier it became to imagine them as a target. For oil was their objective, the engine behind
every investment, every shady inside deal. Here was the military-
industrial complex at its obscene best. The nightmare endgame of
the capitalist state. Corrupt as man could get.

Indigo was the grand stage we'd been looking for, and Keith knew
it, too. He'd heard of them in the same vague and unsettling light,
and as I delved deeper, he started sitting with me, taking notes like
a stenographer. If we hit them hard, he said, the media spotlight

would linger long after the violent fact. And best of all, though they were headquartered in D.C., they had a smaller presence in New York. The location wasn't ideal—it was in a Madison Avenue office tower above the famed department store Barneys—but we'd figure something out.

We were restless now. Time sped up, the days got shorter. We were finally moving toward something definable, a worthy adversary, an ideal target. When Lindsay showed up one night with the long-awaited fan, we forgot to turn it on for several days.

The heat was still everywhere, but we no longer noticed.

AIDAN

- • • ● ● ● ● • • • ●

IT'S DECEMBER 25, ACCORDING TO THE CLOCK RADIO ON MY WRITING DESK. I'M
kidding; it's not that bad. I'm aware of the date. I follow politics. I know
how the Jets are doing. And I stay on top of the ongoing search for us.
Newsreaders and sports announcers: in the absence of others, these
voices have become my friends.

Not that I've been completely alone. My handlers, Jim and Carol,
continue, despite the snow, to stop by twice a week like clockwork—Jim
on Tuesday nights; Carol, Fridays. (After discussing it, they've agreed to
let me use their names, which only confirms what I already knew: that
Jim and Carol aren't their real names at all.) They come armed with supplies, but it's their conversation I crave—Movement news, mostly, but
other stuff, too, the latest movies, town meetings, anything they'll tell
me. That's how monotonous my life has been.

Until yesterday, that is.

I was in the woods behind the house when I heard a noise. More
precisely, I was attempting to cut down a Christmas tree. Why? Because
I'd always had one, even in that stunted studio on Weehawken Street. It
was my only nod to tradition in an otherwise transitional existence, and
I went so far as to throw an annual tree-decorating party, the apparent
sincerity of which never failed to amuse my friends. I know what you're
thinking: I'm compensating for a broken family. And, sure, you're prob-

ably right (my parents, in those early West Side days, took Christmas seriously in every way but biblically, and I was always the spoiled benefactor). We all carry with us the remains of our younger selves, some of us sadly, but most gratefully, for the world seemed whole then, the universe entire, and the less we understood, the more it made sense. So there I was, yesterday morning, in a coppice of pines, trying, and failing, to chop one down. The ax (which I'd discovered in the basement) was quite dull, but I figured it would get the job done. Of course, I'd failed to realize the trunks would be frozen. And I'd forgotten I had no work gloves or snow boots (to say nothing, on the chance it got that far, of a tree stand or ornaments).

Maybe I just needed to get out of the house.

I'd been at it almost an hour with only blisters and loose bark to show for my efforts when I heard the muffled—but distinct—sound of a car door slamming. It caught me off guard, for I hadn't heard anyone drive up. Anyway, there *shouldn't* have been anyone driving up, since Carol, who was due to stop by later, never appeared before sundown. Dropping the ax in the snow, I bounded through the trees to the edge of the clearing behind the house and glimpsed the backside of a man navigating the icy path that led around to the front door. When he disappeared from view, I moved closer, until I was only about twenty yards from his car—an early-model Jeep Cherokee. In-state plates, no bumper stickers, no extra lights or special gadgets . . . nothing official-looking. Who the hell was this? The front door to the house was locked, so unless his plan was to break in, he'd be back soon enough. I repositioned myself behind a tree, and a minute later there he was, retracing his footsteps through the snow. I could see him now, a distinguished-looking man with bushy eyebrows and wisps of white hair curling out from under an ear-flapped cap. He looked like a local town elder. He looked like trouble. Carefully negotiating the icy path, he opened the driver-side door and began rooting around inside the Cherokee. Christ, I thought. He's got a crowbar in there; he's going to smash a window or jimmy a door. But he emerged with something else: a single sheet of paper. Again, he walked around the side of the house; again, he came back a minute later. This time, he started his engine, turned the Jeep around, and followed his own tire tracks back down the hill.

I waited awhile, because that's what I'd been taught to do, and when no one else appeared, I followed his footprints to the front door. The paper was folded in half and hanging from the mail slot. I picked it up like a jury summons, which is to say, unenthusiastically. Because it couldn't be good.

The words were scrawled in black marker:

> *Neighbor(s) - Please join us tonight for Christmas carols and cocktails, 6–9 p.m. We look forward to meeting you—Carl and Nancy Henderson (2 houses down on the left, look for the colored lights on the lamp post).*

I turned around and slumped down on the snowy stoop. Before me lay rolling hills like clouds, soft and white and endless. Was this endless, this high-wire life, expecting the worst of man and instead receiving his best? It was the simplest of acts—inviting a neighbor over on Christmas Eve—yet it floored me. I could never go, but how badly I suddenly wanted to. Just mingling in a warm room, drink in hand, making small talk with strangers. But wait. How had Carl Henderson known I was here? This house, as I said, sits at the end of a long, private drive that winds up through woods and grazing fields. There are three other houses on the road, though I haven't thought much about them since the day I was dropped off. Neighbors are always a consideration, of course—people are nosy—but the houses are far enough apart that they've never struck me as a problem. What business, after all, would anyone have driving farther *up* a private road? Well, now I knew. Carl, or perhaps his wife, must have noticed Jim and Carol coming and going and thought they were living here. And the more the merrier at Christmastime. What was wrong with that? Nothing. Everything.

I was cold and wet and increasingly despondent. I went inside and changed, then sat down and tried to write. But it was useless. As the little things so often do, Carl's note had set off a larger internal crisis. Loneliness, Paige told me once, was just another way of feeling sorry for yourself, and I'd taken her words to heart, allaying that lurking demon by staying busy, by *writing*. But now I stared at my notebooks and wondered what exactly I was doing. Was Paige, wherever she was, still writing her story?

And did our words even matter beyond their morbid salaciousness? Paige has always had clear reasons—comprehensible motivations—for her actions, but mine are less definable and, perhaps, defensible. Which brings me to the question I've been grappling with for months (and one you'll start asking soon enough). *Why?* Why did I do what I did? Ruin my life (or did I salvage it?). It happened fast, as you'll see, but that's no excuse. I knew what was going on. I made decisions—or didn't—freely. But it has taken these words, this attempted explanation—or rationalization—to truly understand what my life was, and what it is now, and how that most improbable line from one to the other was drawn. Call it memoir therapy. Call it an honest accounting. There's a first time for everything.

It's Christmas Day. So here's a present to myself. Another chapter finished, another window opened to the world. Keep writing. The fresh air does you good, kid.

PAIGE

. . . ●●●●●● . . ●●

THE GOAL WAS NEW YORK BY NOON, SO WE LEFT AT FIRST LIGHT. I SUGGESTED the Thruway, but Keith thought coming south through New England would be faster, so that's what we did—I-91 through Springfield and Hartford and on down to the bucolic Merritt Parkway.

Keith kept looking off into the surrounding woods.

I've always loved this road, he said. It's really beautiful.

He was right: the winding, canopied parkway was beautiful, the *day* was beautiful, all expectation. This was it, our big reconnaissance trip, the beginning of whatever was to come. I would be *the front*, the person who'd appear in public. Part preparation, part improvisation, it was a role I'd played well in North Carolina. But this was New York, and though I'd once called the city home, it was a different place now—taller, prettier, more angular. It was aging well, the recession having left it physically— if not financially—unscarred. We made good time and came in down the West Side, the sun high over the Hudson, past sailboat marinas and massive cruise ships, their white sterns sticking out beyond the piers, as if mooning all points west. Yes, New York still had attitude, but it was a different kind of us-against-the-world—more Donald Trump, less Lou Reed.

We turned east onto Twenty-third Street and sliced across town. New high-rises consuming Chelsea. Baby strollers three deep on Village sidewalks. SoHo like the world's largest duty-free shop, all perfume and fine leather. And then the Lower East Side. I'd lived on Stanton and Suffolk for a few years after 9/11, when the neighborhood was still scruffy and marginal, when figures lurked in doorways and women walked in groups at night. But it was turning, even then. Gentrification reaches out like a welcoming hand, block by dirty block, until the grip gets too tight and you can't get away. Boutique jewelry stores, then boutique hotels. I left before the turnover was complete, before the last of the Bowery flophouses and Italian butchers closed for good, before Delancey Street became less a border than a boulevard.

Now people were everywhere, lounging half-naked outside coffee shops and frozen-yogurt stores. Some ersatz version of America had invaded these narrow tenement streets. American Eagle. American Apparel. American boys and girls drinking American beers in their snap-button cowboy shirts and Daisy Duke shorts. Grow the legend large enough and the country becomes it. Keith was watching the road. I wanted to ask if he'd ever lived in New York, but he was busy glancing in mirrors, and anyway his experience in the city would have been so different from mine. I'd moved here straight from UNC, a fresh-faced girl chasing rumors of a counterculture. But what I found was conformity, endemic apathy. The counterculture, such as it was at the dawn of the twenty-first century, seemed like the only segment of society that *wasn't* changing. Sure, kids still came to New York from everywhere else, seeking thrills and some loose kind of meaning. But how quickly they discovered themselves—settled into satisfaction, cozied up to success. And it's hard to rage against that.

The streets were playgrounds. They were malls. We turned right on Allen and right again onto East Broadway where it crosses under the Manhattan Bridge, and only then did a different city emerge. We'd come into a narrow pocket on the edge of Chinatown, an immigrant neighborhood that sloped toward the river like it might never find its footing. Life down here was lived in the open. Drying clothes billowed from fire escapes. Asian men huddled over games passed down through centuries. Women watched or shuffled past, weighed down not by what they carried but something heavier—the hard slog of it all. It felt very far away.

But that was the point. Keith turned left on Catherine Street and proceeded slowly past project-lined blocks I'd never known existed. Henry Street. Madison. Monroe. We were hard against the East River now, could glimpse the crumbling docks and fish stalls of a long-forgotten world. Keith made another left, at Water Street, then turned back up the hill onto Market. This was the oldest part of the island, the streets thin as arteries, and when we found a parking spot, it was all Keith could do to wedge us in. He waited a minute before turning the engine off, but we hadn't been tailed.

We're going over there, he said, nodding at a graffiti-covered apartment building halfway up the block. Fourth floor, the window by the fire escape. I've got keys, we'll pretend we're a couple.

No one's going to ask, I said.

But if someone does.

We walked past the building's two street-level businesses—a filthy fish market and a boarded-up fabric store—and climbed the front steps. Keith knew which keys went with which locks, and once we were inside, we hurried up the dark stairwell, turning our faces from the peepholes we passed. The air smelled like rotting fish and something else—boiled vegetables, tangled roots, foreign soil. Poverty. Keith stopped outside the apartment and listened a moment before opening the door and turning on the light. A narrow hallway opened into a small room with bare walls and a grimy window partially hidden by blinds. A low table separated two cots, and a sleeping bag sat waiting for us at the foot of each bed. There was a bathroom near the front door, but no kitchen—just a coffeemaker, hot plate, and mini-fridge stacked in a corner. Outside, a train rumbled across the bridge on its way to Brooklyn.

Keith raised the blinds with a flourish, but the fire escape still obscured much of the light. Sorry about the view, he said.

Any other exits?

There's a basement door that leads to a back alley. The building's full of illegals coming and going at all hours, so it's usually just wedged open. But we've never had any trouble down here, so use the front entrance unless there's an emergency. It'll be much less conspicuous.

We. Keith had said there would be a set of architectural plans for 660 Madison Avenue waiting for us, and sure enough, there they were—rolled up in a corner of the hallway closet. I could only imagine how they'd gotten there—the amazing precision of the whole thing—and for a moment it made me think we couldn't fail. We spread the sheets across the floor and got to work. Someone who wasn't an architect had scrawled comments here and there—along with arrows, question marks, exclamation points—and Keith went through them all carefully. I took notes, and by the late afternoon we'd finalized our plan. It was straightforward: I'd go up to Barneys at lunchtime the next day. A Saturday in summer: there'd be plenty of people around, so blending in wouldn't be a problem. There looked to be several ways into the office building from the adjoining department store, which meant we could conceivably avoid using the ground-floor lobby. I needed to examine these shared corridors firsthand, determine accessibility, memorize details—locks and lighting, stairwells and elevators, security cameras and personnel. And all without raising suspicions. I'd have to look the part.

Around five thirty, I left Keith to his calculations and set out for the vintage stores on Ludlow and Orchard. Shop after shop of pretty girls, all teeth and tans. They made me nervous. No, they couldn't help me. No, I wasn't looking for anything in particular. Just another skin to hide behind.

I bought a modest, knee-length skirt, a sleeveless top, and low heels I could walk—or run—in. I paid in cash. Dusk descended as I started back, a golden New York twilight, the kind you noticed and slowed to admire. The bars had opened their doors to the street, and out poured the voices of early drinkers, the latest jukebox favorites, and a river of summer laughter, easy and free-flowing. It was the sound of a city I'd always imagined but never quite found.

The laughter, I mean, and all that fitting in.

I picked up sandwiches, cigarettes, and a six-pack of beer at a bodega near the apartment, then walked a square-block perimeter before entering the building. Keith was talking on his cell phone when I came in, his voice stern, almost angry. When he saw me, he stopped in midsentence. In the moment before he snapped the phone shut, I heard a man's faint shouting through the earpiece.

What was that about? I asked.

Nothing. Let's see what you bought.

I paused a moment, then took the skirt and top out and held them up.

Feel free to try them on, he said, grinning.

It's okay, they fit.

We worked a few more hours, going through contingencies until we'd passed the point of effectiveness. Keith got up and opened two of the beers. We clinked bottles and exhaled for the first time all day. Soon, we started talking, carefully at first, then more freely. Scraps of things—childhood stories, trips we'd taken, people we'd known. Maybe they were real names, maybe not, it didn't matter. I lit a cigarette and he sat down beside me to share it. He looked content. A man in his element, inasmuch as Keith could be "in" anything. It had grown dark outside, and the lightbulb above us pulsed like a movie prop. We sat with our backs against the far bed, listening to the trains on the bridge.

Keith told me where he'd grown up: Jacksonville, Mobile, Virginia Beach.

A military brat, I said, and he nodded.

Parents split up, I said, and he nodded again.

You buy into that world or you get out, he said. My mom got out in Virginia. I hung in until San Diego. I was sixteen.

Young still.

I guess, Keith replied.

Did he know about my family's background? Beyond Bobby, I mean? It wasn't so different: three generations of war, of duty and slowly mounting despair. You give so much, and then you give everything. The moment was becoming charged, discomfiting, and to fill the silence I began to talk again, about surprises, about growing up and discovering how much of life takes its form in opposites. Patriotism. Courage. Love. You think they mean one thing when in fact they mean something else entirely. But I didn't get far because it happened then: Keith put his hand on mine. And I froze.

It felt as light as a promise, and as crushing as the moment it's broken.

What was he doing?

Physically, not much. Just sitting there as if it hadn't happened, wasn't *happening,* at that moment. I became aware of my breathing, the seconds moving past. Yet the world was still with me. And all that talk, about our project, our mission, our Action, being so much more important than the individuals involved. The mighty sum of its lesser parts. The lectures about emotions, desires, beliefs—how these were to be shunted aside or abolished altogether for the greater good. Just like our pasts, our histories, our lives up to now. What I felt was not anger or disappointment but something less definitive, a kind of far-off regret. Why was I there? Why had I been chosen? Was it this? Would it always be this? Fear crept into me. I was scared to move. His fingers were stroking mine, softly, almost imperceptibly. He put his arm around my shoulder, his hand dangling near my breast; the other found my leg, my bare thigh, the inside of it, under my denim skirt. He wasn't gripping me hard, but I felt his fingers on my skin, and with it the horrid rush of the familiar, men I'd been with, in one city or another, and the ensuing lies and disappointments, months of anxious sighing, hoping even as I sank away, the bottom deeper every time, and the end always the same.

But this was supposed to be different. A passion born of something nobler than desire. The three of us had reached an understanding on that first day in the car and agreed to let it take us where it would, a place beyond the physical. . . . Keith was looking at me. He began to pull me toward him. I could see it in his eyes: this was no joke or drunken aside. It was betrayal.

No, I said.

I pulled roughly away and stood up without a word. Keith didn't try to stop me. He just watched as I walked into the bathroom and locked the door. I sat on the edge of the tub and rubbed my face. A deep weariness came over me—a traveler's exhaustion, a soldier's exhaustion. That I could be so wrong, so utterly naïve. I'd chosen, finally, after years, to believe in someone. I thought I'd found a place where my value was more than skin deep, and now . . . and now . . .

How long was I in there? Twenty minutes? Thirty? At some point I got up and tied my hair back. I washed my face in the small sink, then walked back into the main room. Keith had turned the light out, but I could still see his trim form stretched across the cot nearest the door. He was pretending to be asleep. I tiptoed past him to the other bed. The eyes, the charisma, the overwhelming sense of danger that announced him, surrounded him, defined him. Had a woman ever said no before?

The city outside was as quiet as I'd ever heard it. Everything just waiting.

I slept in my clothes that night, as Keith had trained me to do.

When I woke in the morning, he was gone, along with his overnight bag and the plans. The *plans*. The only evidence of his having been there at all were the empty beer bottles, the rolled-up sleeping bag, and the unfortunate memories that now came flooding back. I hurried to the window and looked through the fire escape to the street below.

There was no car. Or there was a car, parked where we'd parked, but it wasn't ours. I scanned the street again, then the buildings opposite, looking for anything unusual, human movement or the lack of it, but it was still early. The storefronts were shuttered, the street mostly empty. And so, several months into my new life, I performed my first reckless act. I found the cigarettes—he hadn't taken those—opened the window, and climbed out onto the fire escape. I was exposing myself to anyone who might be watching, but I suddenly didn't care. I sat there, as I'd once sat as a child, legs pulled in against me, shirt over my knees. It's how I used to try to disappear.

Call it a tribute to my training that my first thought was about the Action—what time I should leave for Barneys. Before the anger. Before the realization that I'd been abandoned in a safe house with no car and no money and absolutely no idea how to proceed. Was I safe? Had I ever been safe? It had been a long time since I'd felt this helpless, this dependent on another person—a man who believed in the unconditional, a man with a theory of a perfect world. There was no such thing.

The city came to me and I breathed it in. Garbage, soap, and the scents of the Orient. I couldn't go back to Maggie Valley. I was no longer the daughter my parents knew. Or thought they knew. It was too late, and too dangerous. The Indigo Action would go down or something else would, and I'd be named as an accomplice, or worse. We'd always talked about breaking clean from the past, but it was impossible to vanish completely. There were people in North Carolina, activists I'd run with in the months after Bobby died, who knew I was with Keith. Someone would talk. I stubbed my cigarette out on the black iron railing. I had to move, but where? I thought about the night before. Such grand ambitions ruined by the smallest of gestures. Human urges and pride. Just then, the sun broke free of the buildings across the street and I realized . . . *I can still walk away.* If I can get to the Port Authority, I can hop a bus to—

There he was! In the car at the corner. Blinker on, about to turn onto Market Street. He looked up through the windshield and saw me. I didn't move. I couldn't think. I watched him drive slowly past the building and park up the street. Keith didn't look up again. He got out, locked the car, and, with a shopping bag in one arm and his overnight bag in the other, started walking toward the building. I should have been relieved. Instead, I felt a kind of dull dread. My stomach churned as he opened the door four flights below me. I climbed back inside and closed the window.

Keith was grinning when he walked in.

You're up, he said.

Casually, he unloaded bagels and two cups of coffee, as if all our days started like this, years of mornings in this very apartment, the two of us smoking and eating and wiping crumbs from each other's mouths.

I probably don't need to tell you, he continued, it's not a great idea to sit out—

Where were you?

He stopped moving. Running errands, he said calmly.

Well fucking let me know next time.

You were still asleep. And anyway, I was gone less than an hour. Keith dropped the subject and started spreading cream cheese on a bagel. As if nothing had happened. As if last night hadn't happened. I knew he'd never apologize.

After that, we fell back into form. What other choice was there? I could yell or ignore him, but what would that accomplish? He'd been getting his revenge. Or maybe he really did have things to do. But why take the car? Why take the plans? We ate, then spread the plans out and went over everything once more. I tried to clear my head.

When we were done, he looked at me sternly, like a teacher, like a parent. Are you ready? he asked.

Yes, I said.

Because we only get one shot at this.

I showered and changed and Keith drove me uptown. We made small talk, then stopped talking altogether. Did I seem nervous? When I got out, a few blocks south of Barneys, I strode casually up Madison in my flattering top and fashionable skirt like a thousand other well-heeled women on that warm summer day. I peered idly through store windows, my eyes sizing up the mannequins, my mind completely on the task before me. I glanced over at 660 Madison as I walked up the east side of the avenue. It was a strange structure, tiered and asymmetrical. On the plans it had been listed by its original name, the Getty Building, and when Keith saw that, his eyes had grown wide.

Perfect, he said. They built it with oil money.

There is nothing to be gained by going into detail here, so I'll keep it brief. I crossed Madison at Sixty-first Street and entered Barneys without making eye contact with the doorman. I ambled over to the bank of elevators on my left, staying close to people, groups, crowds. When the doors slid open, I stood in the back corner with my head down as eager shoppers piled in after me. I got off on a high floor and went to work, memorizing layouts and the position of things—saleswomen, racks, and registers. I observed patterns, the flow of foot traffic, the floor manager's habits, the guards' routes. I even saw someone shoplift: that's how focused I was. Yet to see me, as I wandered contentedly from one department to the next, you'd have thought I was only interested in the clothes, one more gust in the whirlwind of avarice and consumerism. And then you'd have lost track of me altogether, as I slipped unnoticed past a row of dressing rooms and through a plain white door that led even higher.

AIDAN

· · • · • • • • • • · · • •

strident moan. I climbed the stairs to the top deck and went to the rail to wave good-bye, but Touché was already driving off. Just as well, I thought. We'd gone the entire length of Fishers Island without mentioning Paige Roderick once. Instead, he'd chatted up inclines and joked around curves, anything to avoid acknowledging the sudden awkwardness between us. I'd never seen him shy away from anything, especially an adventure like this. What the hell was wrong with him?

The ferry slipped through the harbor and into open water. It was only a fifteen-minute trip to Connecticut, time enough to call my mother. When she didn't pick up, I left a message: "Hope you're home tonight, because I'm on my way up to see you. I need a good meal. And a comfortable bed. And your car. Not necessarily in that order. Love you and see you soon. Like in four hours."

The train station was less than a hundred yards from the dock in New London, and Amtrak's Northeast Regional was already there, waiting, apparently, for me and the half dozen other ferry transfers. I bought a ticket and climbed into the closest car. At this hour, on a sunny Saturday afternoon in August, the train was mostly empty. I found a window seat and was soon gazing out across warehouses and factories, the remains of Connecticut's modest coastal industry. Connecticut: the state depressed me. I could never get through it without thinking of my poor father, the country tenderfoot, stuck up there in Litchfield with young Julie. How was he getting along? I'd know soon enough. His sixtieth birthday was a few weeks away, and I'd promised to drive up, have dinner, and spend the night. At least his bar would be well stocked.

Determined to put my stepmother out of mind, I dug out the paper I'd taken from Touché's front stoop—the Saturday *Times* and part of Sunday's that had arrived early—and flipped out of habit to the more "cultural" sections: Arts & Leisure, Styles, Travel, the Book Review, and the Magazine. These were a gold mine for a blogger like me. Entire days of material could be culled from wedding announcements, scathing reviews, and supposed trend pieces hyping some already outmoded craze or fashion. Then, of course, there was Cressida's column. I thumbed intently through the *Magazine*, but she appeared, thankfully, to have the week off (her relationship pieces only ran once or twice a month). When nothing else caught my eye, I picked the Saturday paper back up and opened it to the national news.

How had I not seen it earlier? It was the lead story:

ULTRA-PRIVATE INVESTMENT GROUP EYED AS EXTREMIST BOMBING TARGET

By C. J. EDGERTON

Indigo Holdings, a powerful but little-known private equity firm with offices on the fourteenth floor of 660 Madison Avenue, was the likely target of the bomb that exploded on the fifteenth floor of that building early last Sunday morning, FBI officials close to the investigation said on Friday.

The officials, who asked not to be identified citing the active nature of the case, also confirmed reports that Islamic extremists plotted and carried out the attack, but stressed that no credible individuals or groups have claimed responsibility or yet been named as suspects.

The bomb, which detonated at 3:45 a.m. in the studios of fashion designer Claudio Valencia, left a large hole in the side of the building and scattered debris over a two-block radius. No injuries or fatalities were reported.

The New York City Police Department, which has been

criticized for what many see as a stalled investigation, released a statement Friday calling Mr. Valencia a "victim of circumstance." When asked late yesterday about Indigo Holdings, department spokesman Len Jacobs would not comment specifically, saying only that "the NYPD is actively investigating all leads."

Based in Washington, D.C., Indigo Holdings invests in corporations operating in the energy, aerospace, and defense industries. Many have contracts with the U.S. government in Iraq or Afghanistan. Since the Indigo Group is privately held, it is not required by law to report earnings and other financial information, and it is not clear how many people work in the company's New York offices.

"Certainly, Indigo fits the profile of a company that could be targeted in some kind of anti-West attack," said Riley Cooper, a terrorism expert at the Rand Corporation. "They operate in the shadowy Golden Triangle where government, defense and corporate interests collide. Or, in their case, coincide."

Contacted by phone in Washington, an Indigo spokesman refused to comment on any aspect of this article.

There are 32 companies listed in the lobby directory of 660 Madison Avenue, and Indigo Holdings is not among them. According to a building employee, who spoke on condition of anonymity, there is no sign outside their suite on the fourteenth floor. "It's just like this known thing," the employee said. "If there's a package for Indigo . . . you call a number and they send someone down. They don't like people coming upstairs."

One theory being discussed by officials involves a feature common to New York buildings, including 660 Madison Avenue: a missing thirteenth floor. "It is possible that someone climbing a stairwell at night could have miscounted the flights, thus believing the fifteenth floor was in actuality the fourteenth floor," said the FBI source.

The shopping wasn't so good. The blowout sale was on the wrong floor. Oh my God. Reflexively, I took my phone out to call Derrick. Or Cressida. But then I took a deep breath and put it back in my pocket. I didn't want them involved. Not yet.

My plan was to switch trains in Yonkers and take the Adirondack line up to Rhinecliff. My mother hadn't called back, which was mildly worrying, but cell phones weren't her forte, and anyway, there'd be cabs at the station. I had second thoughts only once, waiting on the platform, the city so close I could feel it in the air. Home. It wasn't too late to turn around, only a matter of changing tracks. The pointlessness of the pursuit no longer bothered me. The opposite did: the mounting evidence. Whatever had scared Touché away. But I stayed where I was, and when the train came I climbed aboard and immediately began feeling better. More sure of myself. Maybe it was the simple decision to do something.

I couldn't sleep and then I could, and when I opened my eyes again, the conductor was tapping my shoulder. The sun was lower. We were pulling into a station.

"Don't forget your bag," the man was saying.

"This is Rhinecliff?"

"It is."

I hopped down and walked with a handful of others through the quaint stone station house. It was a wistful place, that room—what waiting room isn't?—and our heels on the hard floor echoed back through decades of teary departures and solitary arrivals. Outside, three cabs were parked off to the side, their owners huddled nearby. One of them broke reluctantly off as I approached, and motioned toward his backseat.

"Where to?"

"A town called Shady," I said. "Just past Woodstock."

"I know where it is."

He didn't speak again, and that was fine; I was on a down cycle with cabs. We followed River Road along the Hudson, which was wide and tranquil this far north, as if catching its breath before the final run to the city and the sea. It was a grand landscape, everything manicured beyond perfection: the vast lawns behind split-rail fences, green even in the fading light; the mansions and horse fields on not-so-distant hillsides; and the old carriage barns by the road, paint peeling on purpose, rustic in that wealthy way. We took 199 across the river, skirted Kingston, and eventually picked up 28 at the base of the Catskills. The weekend estates of Dutchess County gave way to roadside enterprise—diners, gun shops, gas stations. We turned at the sign for Woodstock and wound into the hills, the night. I tried my mother again, and this time she picked up.

"Aidan, where have you been?" she asked. I could hear noise in the background.

"Did you get my message?"

"No, did you leave one? You know me and those machines. They're endlessly beeping."

"Then check them."

"I haven't had time. I've got people over, a little party."

"Well, that's why I'm calling. Do you have room for one more?"

Shady was a small hamlet outside Woodstock, a patch of land between road signs. Its famous neighbor had seen ups and downs, renewals and revivals, attempts at tourism and campaigns against it, but Shady just plugged along in a timeless limbo that worked fine for my mother and her friends. If Woodstock, with its head shops and hemp boutiques, was a kind of hippie Disneyland (and it was: forty years after the concert—which actually took place an hour away in Bethel—they were still pouring in), the surrounding valley was a haven for the more sensible left, people who'd chosen a certain kind of life and stuck stubbornly to it while the rest of the country grew muscular and unrecognizable.

My mother's 1860s farmhouse near the base of Overlook Mountain was encircled by what had once been grazing fields. Now, though, the fields—clearings, really—were planted not with hay but strange monolithic sculptures of varying shapes and proportion, the work of my mother's close friend Simon Krauss (yes, *that* Simon Krauss). Driving past them felt like entering some new dimension, and on cue the cabbie slowed down and stared at the looming objects in the twilight.

"What the fuck?" he said.

I paid the burgeoning art critic and watched him drive off. The top of my mother's driveway looked like a used-Subaru dealership, the cars all dented and splattered with mud. I could see their owners through the dining-room window, eight people at a lively table, everyone happily talking and gesturing—a film with no sound, just before the plot takes off. My mother and Simon were seated at opposite ends of the table, monitoring the proceedings like lifeguards on a public beach. I opened the screen door and walked in, choosing to do so just as my mother disappeared into the kitchen. My sudden presence caused a chain reaction. A woman I'd never seen before gasped, and immediately six strangers turned around to face the intruder. Simon saved the moment.

"Aidan," he said, his voice low and reassuring. The congregation looked at him, then back at me.

"Hey," I said, waving to the room.

"This is Susan's son," Simon continued, rising to come shake my hand.

My mother walked back in, holding a bottle of wine. When she saw me, she made that face that mothers the world over make when a wayward child has returned home—joy mixed with a reflexive kind of worry. Mostly, though, it was joy. With the exception of two days at Christmas, I hadn't seen her in more than a year. I just never felt comfortable with her upstate friends. They were relics of an era long past, preserved like rare animal bones and just as brittle. Even then, as Simon made introductions—my mother had hugged me and set off to find an extra chair—it seemed as if I were meeting the same person six different times, a person who'd retreated from some larger life to gain a voice in a smaller one, traded in the big ideas for a sense of diminished achievement. They combated globalization by drinking free-trade coffee, rescued the environment one energy-saving lightbulb at a time. Call it what you want—paring down, going local, *dropping out*—but I could never shake the feeling that such peace of mind came at the price of significance.

I'd interrupted a debate concerning the development of the nearby Awosting Reserve, and as I settled in beside my mother, the talk began anew. It was a well-worn issue, marked by a decade of lawsuits and protests and bumper-sticker campaigns, and soon everyone was talking over one another, their separate voices rising in unison like some great classical crescendo. For they were all on the same side! I focused on the only two at the table who remained silent.

My mother, ever the host, kept coming and going, clearing and replenishing. She'd never been able to sit still, and the constant movement had served her well. Her lean, handsome features glowed in the candlelight, and although she'd aged in the last few years—lines and veins were cropping up and out—she'd retained the energy of her city days. And the elegance, too. She wore blouses and fitted slacks, even a wrap dress now and then, but it was a subtle glamour, subdued, perhaps, so as not to upstage the various earth tones of her oft-sandaled guests.

Beauty is beauty, in town or country, and Simon must have thought the same, for he watched my mother with wry bemusement as the racket around them grew with every refilled glass. His silence emanated a kind of authority, and after a while it seemed the guests were performing for his benefit. And awaiting his verdict. But I admired his reserve, as I admired him. Sure, he was famous—at least in art circles—but he was also a good friend to my mother, a partner of sorts, sometimes in love, increasingly in life. They'd been together, in their way, for years now.

She likes to say their friendship started with a bang. Really, it was a screen door slamming shut. She had just moved to Shady—this was a decade ago—and boxes and artwork from the New York apartment sat stacked against the walls. As I recall, she was unpacking plates in the kitchen when she heard the noise, and rather than grab a knife or run out the back door, my mother, out of some misguided understanding of country life, waltzed into the front hall to see which friendly neighbor had brought over an apple pie or communist pamphlet. But the only thing the hulking man in the foyer had with him was a duffel bag. For Simon Krauss thought he'd just come home.

Where he'd been and how long he'd been gone, I have no idea, but it must have been months, because Simon's former landlord had put the house up for sale and my mother had bought it soon thereafter. Most of Simon's shit had been moved to a storage unit, with the exception of a few industrial-size creations scattered across the property.

Simon and my mother slowly pieced together this chain of events and, in the process, became fast friends. I can see the scene perfectly, my mother sitting this strange man down in the kitchen to announce that the steel monstrosities littering her lawn—for she couldn't have known what they'd be worth, *were* worth—could stay, and furthermore, that he could work on them whenever he wanted. And that's exactly what happened. Simon found a house down the road somewhere (I've still never been there) and worked out a deal to keep using the barn behind my mother's house as his studio. I wonder how long it took her to figure out who he was. Certainly, Simon wouldn't have let on, for he was a man of few words, and the one he used least of all was *I*.

So who was he? A late bloomer, apparently. I'm guessing he was some kind of bohemian when he was younger. He'd traveled extensively, had lived all over the States—both coasts and a few places in the middle. Art came later, in his forties, and proved to be his calling. When my mother met him, he'd already made a name for himself as a disciple of Donald Judd's and Richard Serra's. These were men who dreamed in massive scale, who saw the earth as pliable, a natural canvas to be critiqued through addition, through change: great shapes and adjusted environments. In those early years, I'd drive down from Middlebury for a night and there he'd be in the barn out back, with a blowtorch and helmet, bending some enormous metal plate. The noise would be deafening, and still he could always sense my presence. Usually, he stopped whatever he was doing and grabbed two beers from a cooler he kept nearby.

I came to like him a great deal. The artist in residence was good to my mother, became her confidant, her protector. It was never overtly physical. I'm guessing they had both tired of the traditional approach to relationships (I know my mother had), and this worked better, was less complicated. They came together by living apart.

I watched them closely at the dinner table that night as their guests slowly talked themselves out. At some point my mother gave Simon a slight nod, and a moment later he weighed in on the debate at hand, at once lending it validity and bringing it to a close. He stood up and clapped his calloused hands together. There'd be more nights for talking. These were issues that would never end, people who would never let them.

Buoyant with belief, tipsy with wine, the couples filed out to their Subarus, steeling themselves for the short, drunken drives home. In the doorway, the three of us waved awkwardly after them, aware, perhaps, of what we must have looked like in that sea of headlights—a kind of family.

We settled into the living room with what was left in our glasses.

"So I was thinking of heading up to Vermont for a day or two," I said.

"And you want a car?" my mother asked.

"I guess. I mean, I could rent one."

"Don't be silly. You can take mine. We have Simon's van."

"You're sure it's okay?"

"Of course, though I wish I'd had a bit more notice. I would have cleaned it."

"What's going on in Vermont?" Simon asked.

"Just visiting an old friend from school. You know, get out of the city."

"I see," he said.

"How *is* the city?" my mother inquired. "After that horrible bombing and everything?"

"It was hardly 9/11," I answered. "Although they can't figure out who did it, which is slightly unnerving."

"What does your friend from the *Times* say?" my mother asked.

"You mean Cressida?"

"Yes."

"We've been dating for more than a year, Mom. You should know her name."

"If you ever brought her up here, I might learn it."

"Well, we haven't discussed it much. The bombing, I mean. It's not really her beat." I took a sip of wine and became aware of Simon watching me. Was I that bad a liar? I tried to change the subject.

"Any new sculpt—"

"How's the blogging business?" he asked, talking over me, so that for a moment I wasn't sure I'd heard him right. Was he joking? Simon didn't even like computers. It was part of some larger philosophy he had about synthetic systems and their place in the natural world.

"I'm not sure *business* is the right word," I said, feeling suddenly defensive. "Though I guess it's a paycheck." My face was going flush.

No one spoke for a while. Finally Simon got up and stretched. "Well, it's good to see you," he said, looking me in the eye. He shook my hand and kissed my mother. "I think it's past my bedtime. Have a safe trip, Aidan. And say hello on your way back down." With that, he took his keys and walked outside. The screen door banged shut behind him.

"I should get that fixed one of these days," my mother said.

PAIGE

· · • • • • • • • · · •

IT WAS MIDNIGHT WHEN WE GOT BACK TO THE HOUSE. THE LIGHTS WERE OFF, but Lindsay had waited up, and she came running out to greet us. We were both exhausted (we'd driven back the same way we'd come down, Keith taciturn behind the wheel as I scribbled pages of notes, everything I'd seen and could remember), but we stayed up with her, recounting the trip and its seeming success. She looked ecstatic.

Lindsay didn't notice the change in Keith amid the excitement, but I did. He was wounded. We lived in a world of high symbolism, and Keith, who stood for so much, had been laid low by desire. A weak moment in the strongest of lives, though in truth, after three months I'd learned little more of his life—its facts and particulars—than what I've so far related. Of Lindsay's, I'd learned even less. Yet, the three of us had grown incredibly close. We could now anticipate each other's thoughts so precisely that hours often passed without someone finding cause to speak. It was an incongruous situation—our intimate present, our mysterious pasts—the result of a need-to-know policy that placed our personal histories more or less off-limits. It was a simple matter of plausible deniability, and I kept telling myself it made sense. But I should have known better. In reality, I was the only one in the dark. Keith and Lindsay had been together for years.

The days that followed—two weeks of them—were filled with endless detail and repetition. But we were focused. We each had our assignments and carried them out with a determination that bordered on competitive—who could do more with less sleep. It was Lindsay's turn now: she and Keith would make the real run together while I stayed home to guard the house. It was the only way. Despite the precautions I'd taken in New York, my movements had no doubt been recorded on dozens of security cameras and surveillance systems—not just in Barneys, but in shops, on streets, everywhere. Lindsay was a fresh face, and she knew what she was doing. I spent hours filling her in on everything I'd seen and learned, everything, that is, except for what had happened—or hadn't—between Keith and me in that dark room. She had enough to worry about.

We went through the plan again and again, until the chain of events was so familiar we couldn't imagine what might go wrong. This was all Keith, of course—it's what he did best—and as he led us flawlessly through our final preparations, I did *my* best to put the incident on Market Street behind us. We were buoyant, driven, gripped by momentum. Most important, in those crucial days leading up to the bombing, we never once doubted what we were about to do—at least out loud. In truth, I thought about it constantly, obsessively. I was, by now, completely resolute in my rationale: Indigo was exactly the kind of target I'd envisioned going after when I agreed to join Keith. I found the company and its operations despicable, and it wasn't difficult to connect their shadowy activities to the larger national narrative (to which my brother was a footnote). But no matter how strong my motivations, I still blanched at the bomb itself. I just couldn't put the thing out of mind, and the cold, steely fact of it took a daily toll. I stayed away from the garage, and stopped asking Keith how things were progressing—the fuse tests and all that. Fairly well, I guess. We were still alive.

The night before they left for New York, I braced myself and went out there. I had to see, just once, what we'd wrought. I knocked three times on the garage's side door, then twice, then once, and said my name. I heard footsteps, and a moment later Keith opened the door. If he was surprised to see me, he didn't let on. Instead, he moved aside and let me in. I saw it immediately: a silver metal suitcase, powerfully illuminated from above, lying open on a worktable in the center of the space. Keith turned and gazed at his luminous handiwork the way a new father might stare at his infant child—in awe of his own creation.

Wish you could come with us, he said.

It was the first time I'd ever heard him lie.

A few hours later, the suitcase strapped carefully in place, I watched from the window as Keith and Lindsay pulled slowly out of the driveway. They'd been confident and upbeat to the last. Was it bravery? Was it bravado? Both, I thought, but mostly it was stubborn, unwavering belief. Admirable, dangerous belief. For some time I stood there, looking at the place where their car had last been, wondering what I should be feeling. Then I walked over to the desk and got back to work.

There was plenty to do. For weeks, we'd been accumulating paperwork for the identities we'd be assuming after the Action. Our deceased-baby birth certificates had led to Social Security cards, passports, and driver's licenses. Lindsay even had a library card. Now I needed to put the finishing touches on my backstory.

Keith was Todd Anderson. Lindsay was Laura Bellamy. My new name was Isabel Clarke. A, B, C: it made the memorizing easier.

The real Isabel Clarke had been born in a San Francisco hospital and never made it out. So I just pretended she had. In my version, she'd grown up in a split-level house in the Avenues north of Golden Gate Park. Middle-class upbringing, then a few years of community college before the money ran out. She met a man and moved with him across the bay to Sausalito (a town I'd once visited and could describe if I had to), and when he disappeared one night without warning, she'd stayed there, kind of burrowed in. Isabel took graphic-design classes and started freelancing. She steered clear of relationships, had no kids, no terrible secrets or dynamic past—no reason in particular to show up in a Google search. I imagined her living a quiet, sunny life of coffee shops, yoga classes, and weekend jaunts into the city. Then something happened. She picked up and moved East. To Vermont. It was ennui, I decided: the fading gloss of the California dream. But the reasons hardly mattered. What did was the paperwork, and now I had it. Isabel Clarke officially existed. Again.

All that was the hard part. The physical change would be far less

daunting, even fun. Or so I thought. It made no sense to go blond—
my roots would show within days—so I focused on style and length.
For years, my hair had cascaded haphazardly down past my shoulders.
Now, though, I cut it almost tomboy short in the bathroom mirror
(though I kept the sweeping bangs to cover my eyes). As a finishing touch, I dyed it a few cautious shades lighter—dark chocolate to
something milkier.

When I'd finished cleaning the sink, I went downstairs and opened
a beer. Keith and Lindsay would be walking into that Chinatown
apartment soon, where they'd spend a few restless hours going over
the details of the Action one last time. If it all went well, the bomb
would be planted by early evening and set to go off six hours later,
when the upper floors of the building were empty. Soon thereafter,
the two of them would come tearing back into the driveway, full of
adrenaline and the rush of the world between their ears. A long night
lay ahead so I tried to sleep a few hours, but it was no use. Instead I
read and played solitaire. At some point, I moved over to the computer and started clicking on anything that might take my mind off
things. Absurd celebrity scandals. Inane gossip blogs. The ceaseless
chatter of a culture in decline.

At 3:25 a.m., twenty minutes before detonation time, I opened the
news sites—CNN, MSNBC, Fox, Drudge, NY1. For half an hour I
clicked between them, refreshing the headlines every few seconds. It
was silent all around me, yet it seemed I was at the center of a thousand moving pieces. A muted timer ticking in a utility closet. A car
streaking home in the New England night. A city sleeping through its
last minutes of peace. Everything lay before me like a giant puzzle that
only I could put together. For the first time in my life, I knew exactly
what was about to happen.

MSNBC broke it. EXPLOSION ROCKS MIDTOWN BUILDING, FIRES
RAGING, announced a large banner at the top of the page. It seemed,
on the screen, like any another wretched headline, tragic but also far
away, someone else's horrific problem. I felt only numbness. MSNBC
had it for six minutes before the torrent came. Words, audio, and
finally shaky helicopter video. By 4:15 a.m., every network had someone live at the scene. For a while I couldn't see much; it was raining in
New York, and between that and the darkness and smoke, the build-

ing remained a shadowy background presence. But the story moved every which way. First it was Con Ed. Then it was Al Qaeda. Then no one had any idea who it was. I watched for any mention of casualties. We'd done everything we could think of to eliminate that possibility, but no plan was foolproof. A person sneaking around? An employee working late? A mistake, in other words. A victim. Of murder.

That was the chance we took, the awful risk we lived with.

As the smoke began clearing with the morning's first light, the blast site became visible. Firemen were moving around inside; the reflective bands on their jackets flashed when the cameras zoomed in close. I studied the damage, what was gone, and still there. Because something seemed off. I stared past the color-coded alerts and terror advisories taking up so much of the screen, the endless updates and breaking developments. And then I knew. The hole in the building: *it was on the fifteenth floor.*

Indigo's offices were on *fourteen.*

I counted the floors of 660 Madison again and again as the camera panned out and almost missed a bleary-eyed reporter confirm what I'd been waiting to hear: no one had died or even been injured. I leaned back and exhaled, and right on cue, a car turned into the driveway. It was them. Keith parked out of sight of the road, and together they came bounding up to the house, beaming like newlyweds. I greeted them at the door.

Are you guys clean? I asked.

Spotless, Lindsay answered. I got in and out, no problem.

Keith hurried to the laptop. Have they mentioned Indigo yet?

No, I said. They keep talking about Barneys, as if it takes up the whole building.

They'll figure it out.

Well, that's the thing, I said, looking from Keith to Lindsay and back again. I'm not sure, but I think we might have a problem.

It's always the smallest detail. The busted brake light. The earring left under the pillow. Or the simple fact that many buildings don't have thirteen floors. Lindsay made the mistake, but any of us could have caught it.

I put on coffee and the three of us sat down to work through what had gone wrong. A dark stairwell, a small-beamed flashlight, the mask she was wearing. Lindsay had counted the flights in her head, she told us, because there were no floor numbers next to the exit doors (I couldn't remember if that was true).

I went to the computer and began searching the building's online rental records. It didn't take long.

It looks like the office we hit is some kind of fashion showroom, I said.

Was, Keith said.

Was.

Well, there's nothing we can do now, he said, but wait for someone to make the connection. The thing exploded directly above Indigo. They'll have sustained a lot of damage, too, and plenty of people will be sniffing around. I'm not that worried.

Then should we open the champagne we bought? Lindsay asked.

Sure, Keith said.

By the way, Lindsay added, turning to me. I like your hair. I meant to tell you.

And so we drank champagne while New York City smoldered. While mothers watched television and held their children close. While the government increased its threat level and a president vowed revenge. At some point on that Sunday morning, the rain reached us. Lindsay went outside and held her arms wide as it soaked her through. Keith joined her. They clinked glasses and he spun her around. Then, without hesitating, he looked through the sliding-glass door and beckoned to me. I couldn't tell if he was sincere, but I needed to believe he was. We would be three or we would be none, and so I walked outside and raised my glass to theirs.

I told you, Keith said.

What?

That we could do this.

I always believed you.

And the bomb, it went off without a hitch. The timer, the wiring, everything worked perfectly. Did you see the hole in the building? It was really . . . beautiful.

He wiped the rain from his face and drank straight from the bottle, his last word still hanging in the heavy air. It sounded familiar. And then I knew. Keith had gazed into the woods on the Merritt Parkway and said the same thing.

Nature and violence and a man who found beauty in both.

This, then, was the point of no return. We were violent criminals now, enemies of the state (even if the state didn't yet know it). When Keith and Lindsay finally went to bed, I stayed on the deck to watch the day creep in. The woods had come alive after the rains, and I tried to hitch the moment to a happier memory. But the past seemed unreachable. I couldn't find Bobby, couldn't see his face. Only then did the full gravity of what we'd done hit me. It hit me so hard I sat down against the side of that soaking house and started shaking.

AIDAN

· · · ● ● ● ● ● · · ● ●

MY MOTHER COOKED BREAKFAST AND WE ATE TOGETHER AT THE KITCHEN table. Bacon and eggs and lots of coffee. I wasn't much for a.m. chitchat, so she did the honors, catching me up on her summer—volunteer work, travel plans, news of family friends. She seemed content. She'd navigated middle age so gracefully. How old was she? Sixty-one or sixty-two. The perfect time to find happiness, I thought. I was anxious to hit the road, but shrugged off my more petulant self and stayed awhile and listened and afterward was glad I did.

I left around 10:30 a.m. Simon's van was in the driveway, and I thought of him, back there in the barn, trying to shape the unshapable. Maybe he'd be a good man to talk to about Paige Roderick. But what could a sculptor tell me about a terrorist? No, Touché had made me gun-shy. This was my story for now. I climbed into my mother's Subaru and pointed it north.

The New York Thruway on that heat-choked Sunday morning was eerily empty. The radio offered only church sermons and right-wing talk shows, and when I could no longer tell them apart, I started sifting through my mother's ancient CDs—Anne Murray, Dan Fogelberg, Loggins & Messina, some bizarre-looking duo named the Captain & Tennille. I settled on Gordon Lightfoot.

I didn't have a plan, exactly, but I didn't care. I was exhilarated; no more planes or trains. The simple act of driving seemed fresh and exotic, even if the route was familiar—that straight shot up the spine of New York State, then winding back roads into Vermont. We used to make the trip half a dozen times every winter when I was kid. We'd set off from the city late on a Friday afternoon, my mother packing the station wagon, then swinging down to Midtown, where my father, waiting impatiently on some predetermined street corner, would hop behind the wheel and proceed to take his latest, greatest shortcut out of Manhattan. From there it was a race against the coming night, a bulky radar detector our only ally, Dylan and Johnny Cash our only friends.

Now, as then, I stopped for a quick bite in Glens Falls, then took Route 4 east toward the state line. Nothing had changed. The towns—Fort Anne, Whitehall—dated back to the Revolutionary War and had suffered through any number of American booms and busts—railroads, industry, farming, tourism. As a child I'd been whisked past their empty storefronts under cover of night, but now, unsheathed in daylight, they appeared beyond redemption or repair. I shivered as I drove past the maximum-security Comstock Prison—now the Great Meadow Correctional Facility—lording over a nearby hillside like an ominous warning.

The landscape changed as I crossed into Vermont. Dead fields came to life in flourishes of color. Small towns bustled with people. The Mad River Valley was tucked away in the Green Mountains, two-thirds of the way up the state. It was a near mystical place of steep slopes and steady snows and, better still, was tough to get to, a fact of geography that kept the worst of the weekend ski warriors away (their caravans stopped at Stratton and Killington—the full-service resorts farther south). The Subaru ground its way up the Lincoln Gap and coasted down the other side, past boarded-up inns and alpine lodges, then Mad River Glen, its legendary single chairlift hibernating in the heat. But the valley's workhorse was Sugarbush, and through the trees I could catch glimpses of its crisscrossing trails hanging high above the valley. It was one of the largest ski areas in the East, and for a time, in the 1960s, the most glamorous. They called it Mascara Mountain back then, in tribute to the wealthy New Yorkers who journeyed up in booze-filled buses for long weekends of excess on- and off-piste. Soon, though, the in-crowds moved on—to the Rockies, the Bugaboos, the Alps—and the Mad River Valley never quite recovered (which explains why my young, cash-strapped parents, and later, their college-aged son, could afford to ski there).

I'd never seen the valley in summer, the thousand shades of green and the overgrown nearness of it all. I passed an ancient lumber mill, crossed a small bridge, and found myself at the intersection of Routes 17 and 100. To my left was the village of Waitsfield, but I'd save that for later. I needed a place to stay, so I turned right and a mile down the road spotted a cluster of weathered cabins spread among a grove of trees. The Mad Mountain Motel. I turned into the driveway and parked in the near-empty lot.

I rang the counter bell once, then again, and finally a petite woman well into her seventies appeared through a side door. I asked for something cheap and quiet.

"All the same price," she rasped. "Up here for the fair?"

"Excuse me?"

"The livestock fair. Best in the state."

I nodded, not sure what to say, then handed her my credit card. She ran it through an old machine.

"Cabin six," she said. "Last one on the left."

She gave me a key along with my card, and I shouldered my bag and took off on foot. Cabin six was on the edge of the property, a good thirty yards beyond its closest neighbor. It was a glorified wood hut, the inside all brown—even the bedspread. There were no glass windows, just screens with shutters, but they wrapped around three sides and kept the cabin from being too gloomy. No air conditioner either, so I opened everything up including the back door. I stepped outside, but there wasn't much to see—just a gravel path that led past a forlorn flower bed and disappeared into the base of a hill.

Now what? I sat on the corner of the lumpy bed and considered my options. I felt like Paige was close. Like I was close. Yet the valley spread out for miles in every direction. And so I would, too. I showered under a lukewarm trickle and changed into the nicer of my two shirts. I thought about calling Cressida again, but drove into town instead. It was almost 5 p.m.

Waitsfield had shrunk since my college days, but the supermarket was still there, anchoring the modest strip mall along Route 100. It had been years since I'd been to a real grocery store (I bought my food at delis), and I weaved around kids and shopping carts in a state of bewilderment. This must be where *she* shops, I kept thinking. I imagined her darting down the aisles in a baseball cap and sunglasses, like a celebrity or a battered wife, then keeping her head down as she paid in cash. When *I* reached the checkout line, I realized I'd accumulated only potato chips and a couple of bottles of red wine (there was no fridge in the cabin for beer). Two lanes were open, two cashiers: an almost anorexic-looking blond woman about my age, and a ruddy-cheeked young man so full of overachieving spirit (he kept scanning items so fast they didn't register) he must have been angling for management. I got in his line.

"Having a party?" he asked, when it was my turn. He smiled and ran the bottles through until they caught. "There's a liquor store down the road if you're looking for the hard stuff. We can't sell it. State law."

"How'd you know I'm not local?"

"Small town in summer," he said, as I gave him a twenty.

"Well, speaking of that . . ." I reached into my pocket and produced a copy of the Barneys photo I'd printed out back in New York. "You don't know a girl named Paige Roderick, do you? She's an old friend of mine, and I heard she was living around here."

He studied the photograph closely, then gave me my change and looked again.

"Can't see her face too well," he said. "But still, I'd remember someone like that. If you really think she's in the valley, try a bar down the road called the Purple Moon. It's where everyone goes."

"I will. Thanks." He handed back the picture and I began walking out, but something didn't feel right. I turned around, wondering if I'd forgotten a bag, but I had everything, and the kid was already busy with the next customer.

The only thing to do was go door-to-door. The hardware store, the Internet café, the Ski & Sports Warehouse where the stoner behind the counter stared at the photograph as if he might know something, then looked up and said, "Sorry, dude, haven't seen her. But she looks pretty hot." I tried the shopping center across the street. Pharmacy, toy store, real estate office. And then the bookstore. It was the only other place I could imagine her—leafing through the earnest musings of Señor Guevara.

But it was closed.

What was I doing? Chasing a character I'd invented through the landscapes of my youth. The truth was, I barely recognized the single-minded person I'd become. I guess I'd never taken anything so far. But now there was nowhere left to go. Did I give up then? I think so, yes. I drove to the Purple Moon (it was on the way back to the motel) to get a drink and curse this brief foray into fiction.

The place was half-full and a ball game was under way on the TV behind the bar—the Mets and Sox at Fenway. Sunday-night inter-league baseball. That was something, at least. When the bartender finally came over, I ordered a Ketel One and tonic.

"Stoli's our best," she said dispassionately.

"Sure, fine."

I had one, then another, tipping well each time, and finally the bartender began to thaw. I switched to beer and ordered a cheeseburger. When she brought my food over, I took out the picture. I had nothing to lose.

"She's an old friend," I said. "Moved up here to get away for a while."

"If she's a friend, why don't you have her number?" She looked at me, pleased.

"We've lost touch."

"Well, you're not a cop, obviously, so I'll tell you the truth: I've never seen her. And I see everyone, sooner or later. It's not that big a town."

"That's what I keep hearing."

I switched back to vodka. It was only the fourth inning.

Chirping birds and a buzzing cell phone and the sun pouring in through the screens as if the world were in a microwave. I was lying in my boxers above the sheets, and still I was sweating. And then I began to remember . . . the drunken drive back from the bar and . . . oh, no . . . the midnight text to Derrick. What did I say? I picked up my phone to check.

D . . . Srry so late but fam emrgncy mother till tues. Wll cll tmrw. A

Not even predictive texting could help me. I'd never stuck him with Roorback for an extended period before, let alone at the last minute. I was pushing things too far.

It was Monday morning. I had calls to make and texts to answer and who knows how many e-mails piling up. I showered and dressed, then drove to the Internet café, where I ordered the largest Green Mountain Roasters they had. When a computer came free, I sat down to catch up with the world. Nothing new on Indigo. Nothing on the bombing at all. I spent a half hour going through Derrick's posts from Friday. They weren't funny, and the commenters were getting restless. I needed to get home. Paige Roderick had been a long shot, and long shots don't come in.

When I walked back into the cabin, I felt that same eerie sensation I'd experienced earlier in the supermarket. Nothing was missing—I'd brought hardly anything with me—but . . . the back door. I'd left it partly open to get some air circulating, and now it was closed. Maybe it was the wind, except there was no wind. Just heat. No maid yet either, as the bed was still unmade. Well, whatever. I packed up and went to check out.

There was no real rush, so I drove slowly, peering down roads and into driveways, already nostalgic for the day before, the week before, when finding Paige had seemed truly possible. Now, I just felt like an idiot. Touché had been right. I'd allowed myself to get swept up in something so blatantly . . . *hopeful*. There was a small backup where Route 100 met 17, and I waited my turn as a line of cars snaked slowly past in front of me, cars packed with people, kids and grandparents— families. A cop was stationed at the intersection, and I rolled down the window as I inched closer.

"What's going on?" I asked, when I reached him.

"First day of the fair. Always a mess." He waved me forward. There was a pause in the passing traffic. I could turn left and head back south, or—

I put my blinker on and turned right, with everyone else. What the hell? I'd never been to a real county fair before. And I wouldn't reach the city until dark anyway. What difference would two more hours make?

The tents started a mile up the road. I parked in a field, then bought a $15 ticket at the front gate. Booths and rides fanned out in every direction. Signs advertised the Waterwheel Park, the Hayseed Theatre, the Woodsman's Forest. A public address system announced a steady stream of impending events—Sheep Dog Trials, a Pig Scramble, something called a Fireman's Muster. The midway, lined with food stalls and freak shows, seemed a good place to start. It was the pulsing main artery of the fair, already alive with carnival barkers and confidence men honing their pitches for the week to come. I stopped to watch a little boy shoot baskets. He was trying so damn hard, but the whole thing was rigged, of course, the ball too big or the hoop too small, and shot after shot hit the rim and clanked away. But the prizes were *right there*, superheroes and stuffed animals so close you could almost touch them. When the boy was out of basketballs, he looked up at his father and another dollar came out. A crowd had formed to root the kid on, everyone disregarding the laws of physics and common sense, because it *could* happen, *was* possible, it would just take luck, or perfection—

Someone was behind me. Too close. A hand grasped my arm above the elbow. I started to turn, then heard a voice in my ear, stern and steady.

And everything else fell away.

PAIGE

· · ● ● ● ● ● ● · · ● ●

KEITH CAME RUNNING IN FROM THE GARAGE AND LAUNCHED HIMSELF THROUGH the open deck door and into the kitchen.

The car keys, he said, breathing hard. His face was a study in opposing forces—agitation and self-control, anger tempered by experience.

They're on the mantel. Why?

Got a text from Lindsay. The emergency code.

What happened?

I don't know. I'm going to meet her right now. You need to wipe the house down. If one of us isn't back in two hours, then get out of here. We'll meet behind the Downhill Edge. Take the bike.

And then he was gone. We'd run through this scenario over and over in our first weeks here, and I was ready. I donned a pair of surgical gloves and got started. Tables, counters, windows, doors: any flat surface. Plates, glasses, dirty silverware. I rushed from room to room, rounding up our personal effects and stuffing them into a single garbage bag (that's how lightly we lived). Keith had taught us to see the house as a grid, and now I walked it, foot by foot, downstairs then up, dusting, wiping, cleaning. Bathrooms were the worst; one loose fingerprint could mean everything. It took forty minutes, but I got it done, and as I pondered the next problem—namely, how to inconspicuously carry a large garbage bag filled with clothes to a meeting point three miles away on a mountain bike—I heard a car in the driveway. Panic hit me like an uppercut. But there was nothing I could do; it was one of them, or it wasn't. I held my breath, then peered out the window.

Lindsay's blond hair was bobbing up toward the house. I exhaled. I'd never been so thrilled to see her, to see *anyone,* though I tried not to show it. I walked over and opened the door with a dishrag.

Don't touch anything, I said.

You finished? That was fast.

What's going on?

Funny you should ask, because that's exactly what *we're* wondering, she said. Some guy showed up at Shaw's two hours ago looking for you.

That's not possible.

Paige, I saw him. He came through Tyler's lane with a couple of bottles of wine and then asked him if he knew a girl named Paige Roderick.

He actually said my name?

Yes. And he had a picture.

What?

I couldn't get a good look at it without being obvious, but I think it was you. I mean, he said it was.

Fuck.

I know.

And Tyler?

He said he'd never seen you before. Which he hasn't. So there's that, at least.

What'd the guy look like?

Our age, maybe a few years older. A little scruffy, good jeans, cool shirt . . . definitely not a local. He was kind of put together. He had a *look* . . . like he could have been someone you know.

He can't be.

Are you sure?

Please.

Well, he seemed pretty determined. I waited till he'd walked out, then told the manager I was feeling sick. I texted Keith from Tyler's cellphone and caught up with the guy as he was getting into his car— it's a Subaru with New York plates, by the way. Paige, he was going store to store, showing your picture to everyone he saw. He ended up at the Purple Moon. Keith's there now. We have to go meet him.

Are we coming back?

I don't know.

We took one last quick walk through the house, then carried the trash bag out to the car. For a moment we both stopped and looked at the garage.

What do you think? Lindsay asked.

I think we shouldn't worry about it. Keith always uses gloves when he's in there. Anyway, I don't have a key.

Really? Lindsay said. You should get one.

Lindsay backed out of the driveway and we started down the hill. Someone wielding my name and picture was sitting in a bar a few miles away. I rolled the window down and began searching for an explanation.

You should roll that back up, Lindsay said, just in case.

Seven silent minutes later, we turned into the Purple Moon's dusty parking lot and pulled up beside Keith's car. Lindsay kept the engine running. Keith must be inside, she said. Stay here, one of us will be right back. With that, she hopped out, walked across the lot, and disappeared through the front door of the bar. I climbed behind the wheel and stared at the neon window signs as my mind raced through dozens of faces, men I'd known, and boys; lovers and friends; coworkers from New York, from Washington; activists from Carolina. Could it be a stranger? But how was that possible?

A minute passed, maybe two, then the front door opened and Keith walked outside. He stretched his arms, rolled his neck around, and came strolling toward me. When he reached the car, I unlocked the passenger door and he climbed in. Without so much as a nod, he took out his cell phone, pushed a button, and handed it to me.

Know this guy? he asked.

The image was dark and unfocused. I couldn't make anything out. Here, zoom in.

I did as he asked, and now a few figures emerged from the photographic gloom. Bodies on bar stools.

He's the one on the end, Keith said. I got him while he was watching the ball game.

This is the only picture?

Were you expecting a photo shoot?

Sorry.

I stared hard at the glowing image. Keith stared hard at me. He wanted answers. I'd always been good with faces, and when I spoke again, it was with certainty.

Keith, I said, I've never seen him before.

He looked at me a moment more, into one eye, then the other.

I figured as much, he said, because I don't think he's laid eyes on you either.

And you're sure he's not with the Feds or something?

I don't think so. He was drinking. And he didn't look the part. No beeper, no badge, no gun. The only thing he had on him was a Xeroxed photo. I tried to get a look when he showed the bartender but couldn't. She said she'd never seen you—assuming it *was* you.

Well, I've never been in there.

I know.

I handed the phone back. Keith snapped it closed and stuffed it in his pocket.

I'm really sorry about all this, I said. But I have no idea who—

Paige, come on. It could have been any one of us. And, besides, he doesn't know you actually *are* here, so we're okay for now. I told Lindsay to tail him in the other car to wherever he's staying. Lets the two of us get back to the house and figure this out.

So we're not splitting?

Not unless we have to.

Fine, I said, putting the car in reverse. I turned on the lights, pulled onto the road, and drove us back up the hill. Keith stared into the twilight.

Some way to live, he said.

It was a long night, and we spent most of it cross-legged on the carpet in the living room, revisiting our last few months. We wore socks and gloves, just in case. Keith was sure the guy was from New York—there was the license plate, plus he'd been rooting for the Mets—so we went back through the two days we'd spent in Manhattan, hour by hour—people on the street, faces in passing cars—but came up empty.

When we finally took a break, Keith grabbed a flashlight and went outside. He said he'd be back soon, but I knew better. The garage had a hold on him. Barely a week had passed since the Indigo Action, and already he was hard at work on his next device. He said the middle of the night was the only time he could truly focus, but Lindsay and I worried he'd nod off surrounded by all those wires and timers and, well . . . Every few days, I woke up dazed from a dream that had just ended with a horrific bang.

Exhausted, I stretched out on the couch and closed my eyes. A ten-minute nap was all I had in mind, but more than two hours passed before Keith shook me awake.

Come on, it's almost four in the morning.

What's going on? I asked, sitting up quickly.

I've been assessing our situation.

And?

I need more time.

To cover our tracks?

To finish things. He nodded in the direction of the garage.

Oh, I said. I'd been trying to clear my head, and Keith's simple statement did it. He acted as if it were a model airplane he was assembling in there. Perhaps that was the only way to approach it.

Also, Keith continued, Lindsay called me. From a pay phone down the road from some place called the Mad Mountain Motel. She's staking out his cabin.

I'll go relieve her.

Okay, good. But, Paige, just watching this guy isn't going to be enough. We need to find out who he is, and why he's here.

How do you suggest I do that?

Keith stared at me intently. It was the same look he'd given me the night we first met—half-charm, half-challenge. Before, I'd have taken the bait, answered my own question with determined resolve. Now, I did my best to ignore him. I walked into the kitchen and picked up the car keys.

Park in the restaurant lot next door to the motel, Keith said, trailing after me. She'll meet you there.

What if he leaves?

The motel?

The valley.

You can't let him. Not without getting some answers.

Fine, I said, walking outside. Keith began to speak again, but I was already shutting the door behind me.

It's not that he wasn't right. It's that he was. And he always knew it.

For the second time that night, I headed down the hill. This time I was alone. This time I could keep driving. Over the mountains and far away. No, I couldn't. More faces came and went, before I settled on Keith's. The look in his eyes: it was different now, more desperate. My headlights cut through the lingering darkness, the roads as empty as the ski slopes they serviced. A mile down 100 I saw the motel sign. I drove past it and took the next left, into an empty gravel lot in front of a boarded-up restaurant called the Castle Rock Tavern. Closed for the season or forever, it was hard to tell. Lindsay's car was parked beside a dumpster around back. I pulled up beside it, cut the lights, and waited.

When she knocked on the passenger window two minutes later, I was so startled I hit the gas with the car still in park, but quickly recovered and unlocked her door.

What the hell are you doing? Lindsay hissed, getting in.

I didn't see you.

I came down the path over there, she said, pointing through the windshield. It snakes up the hill behind the cabins. When it's light you'll be able to watch him without being seen. He's in the one closest to us—number six. He hasn't come out all night.

Okay, I said.

How's Keith?

A little nervous. He's been in the garage tinkering.

He doesn't like surprises, Lindsay said.

I know. He thinks we should stay in the house for now, but it depends on who this guy is. I need to find out.

How?

Not sure yet, I said.

Well, be careful. She squeezed my arm and hopped out. A moment later her car came quietly to life and she was gone. I got out, locked the doors, and set off in the direction Lindsay had indicated. It took a little time to find the path, but soon enough I was creeping through the scattered trees and up a small hill. When I saw the cabin below me, I settled in behind some bushes and waited.

It all came back to me as I crouched there: the way the woods could play with time. Make it seem more vital. We used to camp out all night, Bobby recounting old stories as the wind rustled through treetops— local legends of convicts and bootleggers, outlaws who knew the back-country better then any pursuer. There was always someone famous hiding out in the Smoky Mountains. When I was growing up, it was Eric Rudolph, the antiabortionist who set that bomb off at the Atlanta Olympics. Bobby was enthralled by him, or at least the idea of him— his determination, his savvy. He eluded hundreds of FBI agents and teams of dogs. At one point, they even brought in trackers. They finally caught him, the year after I graduated from college, dumpster-diving behind a supermarket in Murphy. An ignominious end, but the legend had been solidified, along with an idea. That a person could still outwit an army.

Now, but for opposing beliefs, I was Eric Rudolph. Alone in the forest, tracking the trackers, a world still to change.

Dawn came—bees and birds, squirrels, a family of deer, then man and his machines, cars and early-morning trucks out on the road. Evolution in order, small to large, meek to menacing.

I knew what was happening. This was my mess and I had to clean it up. Whoever this guy was hadn't used Keith's name or Lindsay's; he'd used mine. I was at least partially exposed, and therefore a danger to the group. But if a chasm was developing between the three of us, its depth was limited. Because things had happened now, and we were all culpable. Was there any choice but to stay together?

At 8:05 a.m. a man appeared in the back doorway of the cabin. I crouched down low, but he wasn't looking in my direction. No, he was yawning, stretching, waking up. He wore a short-sleeved Cuban shirt, off-white and untucked, with jeans and gray sneakers. His messy brown hair had recently been towel-dried. He was tall and moderately thin and not too tan; all in all, he looked like the type of guy I'd made an effort to stay away from—the attractive ex-frat boy who'd lived in New York long enough to adopt a little style at the expense of substance. I watched him mat his hair down and walk back inside. The cabin had screens for windows, and if I could get close enough, I might be able to peek in. I started down the hill and had crept about ten yards when the front door slammed shut. There he was, walking along the path toward the office. If he was checking out, I had just enough time to race back to the car and tail him. But he didn't have a bag with him, which meant—I hoped—that he wasn't leaving for good. I took a chance and let him go. When I heard his car start, followed by a crunch of gravel as it edged toward the road, I hurried down the hill and across the small clearing to the back door. It had been left ajar, and the hinges creaked as I slipped inside. The room was hot and surprisingly messy—or maybe I'd just lived too long in meticulous exactitude. A backpack sat on the bed; boxers and socks were scattered across the floor. So he *would* be back. If he was going into town for coffee, I had ten or fifteen minutes. I gave myself five.

I slipped on my gloves and emptied the backpack onto the bed. A dirty T-shirt, bathing suit, flip-flops, more boxers, khakis, a pair of cargo shorts. I went through the pockets. A few dollar bills and a matchbook from a Greenwich Village restaurant called Malatesta. I opened it and found scribbled directions to an address in Essex County, New Jersey. No BlackBerry, no business cards, no address book. I stuffed everything back inside and turned my attention to the room. The bureau and closet were empty, and the only thing on the coffee table was a copy of the local newspaper. Then I saw it, a slip of paper on the floor near the base of the bed. I bent down and picked it up: an Amtrak receipt—New London to Yonkers—dated two days before. In the upper corner was a name: *Aidan Cole*. I said it out loud, as if that might trigger my memory, but it didn't. I'd never heard it before. How long had I been in the cabin? Two minutes? Three? I peered outside. All was quiet. I put the receipt back exactly as I'd found it, then searched the desk, the nightstand, the folds in the cheap, stained couch. Then I walked into the bathroom. A puddle had formed on the floor beside the shower (the bath mat hung undisturbed on the towel bar), and the mirror was still fogged up. A travel kit sat unzipped on the sink, and I picked through Q-tips and Chap-Stick and small packs of Advil. I felt something in the side pouch, a prescription bottle. Xanax, and most of them were gone. But the label! This time, Aidan's name came with an address: *5 Weehawken St., New York, NY, 10014*. Weehawken Street? Where was that? I tucked the bottle back away. I'd been there five minutes, maybe more. I took one last careful look around the worn-out room, as if the rotting walls might yield some secret explanation for Aidan's presence. But they remained silent. I slipped outside, closed the back door, and retreated to my perch on the hill.

He appeared a half hour later and, as he had earlier, came out back and looked around. But this time he was frowning. There was no way he could see me, but I froze anyway. I didn't move or breathe until I heard the screen door slam shut.

When he walked outside again, it was through the front, and he had the backpack slung over his shoulder. Had he discovered some-thing, or was he giving up and going home? He ambled down the path toward the office; I hurried back to the car and pulled around to the front of the restaurant lot. I didn't have to wait long. Fifty yards to my right, he nosed his Subaru out into the road and started toward town. I let a car pass, then followed. The road seemed busy for a Mon-day morning, and the traffic began to back up as we approached the intersection of Routes 100 and 17. Then I saw the cop at the corner. Was he just directing traffic or . . . I locked the doors. We came to a dead stop as the officer let a stream of cars pass in front of us. Then it was our turn. We inched forward. Five cars away, then four, and three. The officer stopped our line again. Aidan's car was at the head of it, his window down. The cop leaned in close. They were *talking*. Fran-tic, I looked for an escape. The shoulder was wide enough if I needed it, but suddenly Aidan was moving again, taking a right—heading *north*. The woman in front of me put her left blinker on, then turned that way. And now I was at the intersection, the cop directly outside my window. Should I make eye contact? Yes? No? No. I smiled slightly as I passed him, trying to look distracted. I could feel his eyes on me, could feel my face turning red, but I kept moving forward, one rota-tion at a time, and finally turned right without incident. I was directly behind Aidan, practically on his bumper, the two of us moving at a crawl. Where were all these people going? I thought about shielding my face, but pulling the visor down might catch his eye. A glint in the mirror. That's what this had come to.

I should have realized the livestock fair was to blame (Lindsay had mentioned it), but I didn't until I saw the signs for parking. Cars were turning off the road. And now *Aidan's* blinker was on. He was going to join them. We both were.

AIDAN

· · • • ● ● ● ● • · ● ●

I knew who it was before I even turned around. Her voice was calm but forceful, just as I'd have imagined it.

"I said, 'What do you want?'" She tightened her grip on my arm, and I didn't try to shake her off. I was frozen in place beside her. We were packed in a tight semicircle in front of the basketball booth, kids squealing, shouting, pleading with parents. I opened my mouth.

"I . . ."

I tried to collect myself, but my face was turning crimson. Most of hers, meanwhile, was hidden behind large aviators, as it had been in the photograph. She'd cut her hair and was wearing very different clothes, but it had to be her. The fantasy come to life.

It hit me then: what this *meant*. The danger *I* might be in. How long had she been following me? And were there others? I wanted to look around, but couldn't take my eyes off her for fear that . . . what? She'd disappear? Suddenly, I couldn't remember why I'd come looking for her in the first place. Or what I'd do if I found her.

"I . . ."

What had she asked me? I was losing my grip on the progression of events. I wondered again if this might be a gag, the joke to end all jokes, a new reality show meant to test the boundaries of my sanity—

"Fucking say something," she said, still gripping my arm.

"Are you Paige Roderick?"

"Who are you?"

"Aidan Cole."

"What do you want?"

"To talk to you."

Paige looked around quickly. People were everywhere.

"Are you alone?" she asked.

"Yes. Are you?" It was all I could manage. Rote dialogue. Words she expected.

"We can't stay here. Follow me, but at a distance."

With that, she let go of my arm, kind of discarded it, and started walking quickly through the crowd. I almost lost her right away and had to jog a few steps to catch sight of her again. She was taller than I'd imagined and was wearing a plain V-neck T-shirt and cords. Brown cords. In August. Why was I thinking about fashion? Because I couldn't think about anything else. Bumper cars. Pirate ships. A creaking Tilt-A-Whirl. We ducked off the midway and entered the live-stock area, rows of clapboard barns housing goats and pigs and giant horses. A cow-milking exhibition. A sheep-shearing contest. The State Bucksawing Championship was getting under way at the Woodman's Center, and a crowd of large men dressed in Carhartt milled around outside. We kept walking—past the Alpaca Farm, the Dairy Tent, and finally the jam-packed Ox-Pulling Pavilion—until we found ourselves alone beside a split-rail fence that marked the edge of the property. Beyond us lay a patchy meadow overrun with tents and trucks and trailers. The fair's ugly underbelly.

"So talk," she said.

"I'm not sure where to begin."

"Let me help you. Who do you work for? How did you find me? And what the fuck do you want?" She was leaning against the fence, her right foot propped up on the lowest rail, as if she might hop it at any moment and disappear among the generators and clothing lines spanning the temporary trailer park.

"I don't work for anyone. Not like that. I'm . . . I'm a blogger."

"A what?"

"A blogger. Someone who—"

"I know what a blogger is."

"Well, then."

She was staring at me, through me, her jaw locked in place. And still I couldn't quite make her out behind the glasses, the sweeping bangs, the elusive movements that held the potential of sudden flight.

"I . . . I received an anonymous e-mail about the recent bombing in New York, and it said you were involved."

"What else did it say?"

"That's it."

"I don't believe you."

"*Were* you involved?" I asked.

"Who sent it?"

"I told you, it was anonymous."

"Listen," she said. "I'll take off. I'll take off right now if you don't start answering my fucking questions."

"Will you calm down for a second? If I were going to turn you in, *don't you think I already would have*?"

I hadn't meant to say this. It just came out, but the words had a visible effect on her. Slowly, she took her foot off the railing and edged closer, as if this were something approaching a normal conversation.

"Don't raise your voice," she said.

"There's no one around."

"That's what I thought, then you showed up. Now tell me exactly what the e-mails said."

And so I did. And then I told her more. Why not? It's not as if I knew that much. She stood stoic against the fence, listening closely as I explained (without using names or incriminating details) how I'd tracked her down. She interrupted only twice. When I mentioned the bomb going off on the wrong floor, she asked when, *exactly,* I'd received that e-mail, and what, *exactly,* it had said. And a few minutes later, when I told her I'd spoken with her parents, she asked how they'd sounded. Otherwise, she remained silent until I'd finished, at which point she turned to take in our surroundings. Paused in profile, my ingrained image of Paige Roderick finally fell away, and the woman herself came into focus: the long legs, the narrow waist, and a blossoming upper body—broad shoulders and full breasts—evident (albeit to a trained eye) even under the loose T-shirt. And still, it came back to her face, vaguely European—Dutch perhaps—in its eccentric beauty. She had a wide mouth and full lips and a high forehead like some ultimate crowning achievement. Only her eyes remained a mystery.

Ten seconds passed, maybe more, and just as it seemed she was going to speak, a roar went up inside the Ox-Pulling Pavilion. We both looked over at the giant tent.

"They're done in there," she said. "I have to go."

"Wait."

"For what?"

"I just told you everything, and you haven't—"

"Listen." She stared straight at me. "Just go back to wherever you're from and forget we ever met."

The hordes began trickling out, a few already wandering in our direction. Paige looked around again, then hopped the fence in a single scissorlike motion.

"Tell me where you're staying," I said. "We can talk this through."

"Fuck off."

"I won't call the cops. I won't say anything, I promise."

"What is it you want? Money?"

"I want your story."

"My *story*?"

"Yes."

"For your stupid website? I swear it's people like you that—"

"That what? Anyone else would have posted your picture or called the FBI as soon as they saw it. You know, under the circumstances, you might consider showing me the benefit of—"

"So why haven't you? Huh? I don't understand. If it's notoriety you want. I can't think of a better way to get famous then turning in an alleged terrorist." She was raw with anger, and I paused a moment before I spoke again.

"I don't want notoriety. I want to understand."

"How we did it?"

"*Why* you did it."

We had crossed a line, accepted for a moment the hypothetical crime that had brought us together. She must have felt it, too. She adjusted her sunglasses and took another glance at the exiting crowd.

"I don't believe you," she said.

"Well, I'm telling the truth. For a long time I didn't believe in any of this myself. In you, I mean. All I had was the fucking photograph."

"Do you have it now?"

"Yeah, sure." I reached into my pocket and handed it to her. The printout was crumpled, the back covered with nonsensical notations—numbers and addresses, the raw statistics of this anomalous pursuit. She unfolded it slowly, as if it held great value. "I don't have the best printer, so it's not as clear as the image on-screen—"

But she wasn't listening, hadn't heard a word. No, she was staring at herself crossing Madison Avenue as if confronting irrefutable proof of the afterlife. Just as I was about to speak again, she looked up at me. The color had drained from her face, all the robustness, the life. She handed the page back and without so much as a parting word she turned and strode quickly across the field toward the sprawl of trailers.

When I called after her, she began to run.

PAIGE

THE DUST WAS THE SAME, A CLAY-COLORED GRIME THAT LOOSED ITSELF FROM ten thousand trampling feet and stuck fast to your clothes, your skin. The sounds were the same, and the sweet smells and rust-dappled rides built a generation ago. Even the dispirited animals, which you'd think would vary by region, were the same in Vermont as they were at the Haywood County Fair in Waynesville, North Carolina. We used to go every September, the four of us setting off at some impossibly early hour so my mother could join the other Maggie Valley women in the morning skillet throw. The men would cheer from the sidelines as the frying pans took flight amid a volley of laughter. But after twenty minutes of being ignored, the husbands inevitably drifted away, taking their bouncing children with them. I don't know where the other families went—to see the giant pigs, probably—but they never came with us. Our destination was a secret even from my mother. Bobby always took charge, my father and I struggling to keep up as he led us to the unkempt corner of the fairgrounds that housed the freak show. There they were, the bearded lady and the Siamese twins, the midgets and magicians, and the man who hammered nails up his nose. They operated in ill-lit booths, peddling their aptitudes and appendages to the young, the curious, the gullible. Bobby and I were all three, and yet we hardly even glanced at these lesser attractions, for our hearts belonged to the man behind bars at the end of the alley. He was huge, a seven-foot-tall leviathan, spitting and snarling and drooling down the front of his filthy shirt. And still, we always snuck up close to read the story posted on the cage. For what a story it was. He was called the Smoky Mountain Man, and after a lifetime in the wild he had wandered into a backwater in the most remote part of the state and begun terrorizing its citizens. He broke into houses, even stole rotten children. But he never stole from the poor. And the children were always returned without a scratch. It didn't matter. The government began a manhunt that spanned two decades and claimed a dozen lives, and finally they caught him. That his jail cell was a flimsy sideshow cage at a regional state fair was a fact Bobby and I never questioned. We were too young to know the world that way. We believed in him, *identified* with him. He was the shadow just beyond the foot of my bed, the noise in the woods where the backyard ended.

Then one year it rained. The skillet throw had no-shows, so the Maggie Valley squad was forced to draft my father. When Bobby and I complained, he told us we could go see the Smoky Mountain Man by ourselves. *If we were careful.* My brother was eight, I was seven, but we never gave it a second thought. We scampered fearlessly through the puddles until we reached the freak show, and the ominous cage at the end of the alley. The place was deserted. And the Mountain Man? He was sitting in the back of his cell, legs crossed . . . reading a book! He didn't see us or, anyway, didn't look up. Bobby was stricken, but quickly recovered. He took my arm and we backed away. This is our chance, he said urgently, as the rain streaked down his cheeks. I didn't know what he was talking about. Still, I let him lead me around to the rear of the cage, which was covered by a heavy tarp. Bobby peered inside. It was pitch-black.

Let's get out of here, I said.

Hold on. I have an idea. Bobby pulled aside the canvas curtain and stepped into the darkness. *I'm going to set him free.*

Before I could respond, my brother was gone. I heard his tentative footsteps, and then only rain on the canvas. I was standing on a service pathway behind the booths and tents. No one else was around. No one to witness what would happen next. I wanted to cry, but what good would that do? And who would care? From somewhere inside the cage I heard a knock, and the squeak of hinges, *a door opening*. There were muffled voices, Bobby's and another. I'd never heard the Mountain Man speak, and I imagined roars like thunder, but his voice sounded calm and measured. For a moment, I thought I heard laughter. Then silence. Had Bobby been attacked? Killed? *Eaten?* I was about to run back around to the front, but then came footsteps, and a familiar voice calling my name. *I'm here,* I said. The canvas ruffled, then parted, and there was my brother, looking brave as ever, but confused, and a little bit lost.

He wouldn't come with me, Bobby said. Then he shrugged a sad little shrug and we started back toward the grown-ups.

The following year was our last, for we'd become skeptics. We saw glue on the ground near the bearded lady. And noticed a blanket positioned over the twins' attached torsos. The Mountain Man was still there, as always, but we didn't go see him. We were finally old enough to understand what had happened, and already too old to talk about it. It didn't matter. Our heroes now were the mountain men still at large.

Here they were, a generation later, the sideshow performers of my youth. The acts were different, the grotesque faces new, but their calls and come-ons were the same. And they still haunted me. I followed Aidan Cole down the midway as memories of Bobby and the Mountain Man came rushing back. My brother often broke my train of thought, but the moment was too critical and I fought hard to stay in the present.

What was Aidan doing? For one thing, he didn't seem to be looking for me. Maybe he'd given up and come to enjoy the fair: a good walk, some fresh air before heading back to New York. He sauntered along, absorbing the atmosphere, like a man taking his first steps in a new city. The situation seemed so improbable. He appeared completely unthreatening, and yet he radiated danger, veritably pulsed with it. I came up close behind him as he stopped to watch a little boy shoot baskets. A crowd had formed, offering distraction, providing protection. The safety of large numbers. This was the moment, and I tried to block out the risk. Exposure, capture, the end of everything. I could still turn around, retreat to the house and tell Keith we'd been made. We'd be free and clean in half an hour, no prints, no traces. Just pack up the new bomb and move on—another house, another garage. I knew how Keith worked; he gave himself options. We'd vanish into the heart of the country we were trying to expose, trying to save. But I couldn't turn around now. *I* had to know who this man was, this bridge between my lives. Because I thought I'd burned them all.

I grabbed his arm and he didn't pull away. He was understandably astonished, yet he made no move toward—or from—me. I'd been ready to run, but as he stood there groping for words, I knew I wouldn't have to. He was no cop, no agent, no bounty hunter. There was nothing hard about him. His eyes were deep and blue in the sunlight, his wavy, brown hair too wild for Wall Street, too tame for the arts. His clothes—the jeans, the shirt, the hip sneakers—were slightly less than a statement. He was ruggedly handsome, but seemed uneasy in the outdoors; athletic having never played a sport; well-groomed without relying on products. I wondered what worlds he orbited, what scenes he slinked around. Then I wondered if anything truly terrible had ever happened to him. Because it didn't look like it.

Fucking say something, I told him.

I was angry. Everything was flooding back now, a decade of witnessed indifference, the selfish manifest destiny of a generation I'd failed to fit into. And so I'd chosen this other way, this contrarian anti-life. Now this, too, was being threatened.

When he finally opened his mouth, he said my name and I almost broke. I hadn't heard it from a stranger in so long. When I knew he wouldn't run—he was as interested in me as I was in him—I led him through the crowds toward the back of the fairgrounds. It would be safer there, past the animals, past the people. I found a place near the sprawling carny camp, where I could escape if I had to.

But he proved easier than I thought. He talked right away—a convoluted story about some vague, anonymous e-mails he claimed to have received that connected me to the bombing. By name, by *photograph*. All this work, these months of planning, of methodical calculation and attention to every detail, and some blogger (for that's what he said he was, a *professional blogger*) with too much time on his hands finds me in three days. Through my parents, no less! I didn't believe him. He had that city sheen, acquired over years of small talk around small tables; he was all practice and polish, and it was impossible to see underneath to where his motives might lie. But when I pushed him, he pushed back, said he'd have gone to the cops already if that was his intention. And when I mentioned blackmail, he looked almost disappointed, as if I'd let him down. The timing, though: it didn't make sense. Whoever sent the e-mails claimed we'd bombed the wrong floor several days before that fact came to light—and then only as a theory—in the *Times*.

And still I was fine until he showed me the photograph. It was no random picture, no casual crowd shot. It was a close-up of me, crossing Madison Avenue after walking out of Barneys that day. Who could have taken it? Who knew I was there? These were questions I couldn't begin to answer. And didn't want to.

For there was only one answer. And it was as unacceptable as it was implausible.

People were pouring out of nearby tents. Sure, there was safety in numbers, unless you no longer trusted anyone. Unless you found yourself all alone.

Which is when I ran.

AIDAN

· · ●●●●●● · · ●

FOR YEARS I'D LEAVE NEW YORK, AND WITHIN A DAY OR TWO, NO MATTER where I was, I'd start craving all I'd left behind. There was a velocity to the city, a careening inevitability that became addictive. Everyone I knew felt it—the great rush of plans and possibilities—and we lived accordingly. What was it exactly? It was everything vibrating at once: streets and restaurants and parties and clothes and lofts and stores and cabs and subways and, of course, people—the native, the foreign, the old, and the young, everywhere the young, a never-ending spectacle of fresh faces and lithe bodies to befriend and despise, to love and to leave. And at some point it was all supposed to slow down, ease up, as our younger selves gave way to commitment and responsibility. But that had yet to happen. We all kept running around. As the music changed and films came and went. As skirts got longer and then shorter. As places opened and closed and opened again. Some of us turned thirty. Some forty. And if the money never quite came—never enough, anyway—no one truly seemed to care.

But three nights on the road and I didn't miss anyone, or anything. Not Cressida or Touché. Not the wired world or the brick-and-mortar city. It was as if I'd finally left its gravitational pull, its far-reaching effects. But what to do now? I pondered the question all the way back to my mother's house. She was cooking dinner when I pulled in, and she asked me to stay. But I just couldn't. If I wasn't longing for New York, I couldn't hang out in Shady either. My mother's life was so simple and safe. There she was, listening to NPR as she stirred pots and uncorked wine. And the rest of the cast was bound to show up sooner or later, ready for another one-sided debate about whatever graced the cover of the latest *Utne Reader*. The radical world had moved past these people, and I had glimpsed its new face, beautiful and troubling as it was. My mother called a cab to take me to the station. I had a few minutes, so I went looking for Simon. He was where he always was, in the barn, blowtorch in hand, frowning at a piece of steel. He raised his face mask when he saw me.

"How'd everything go?" he asked. "You had good weather."

"Pretty good, yeah. It was hot."

He put the torch down and came over to shake my hand. "Staying the night?"

"No, I have to get back."

"Sure," he said, nodding, and I couldn't tell how he meant it.

"How's my mother doing?"

"Happy. I think she's happy."

"Me, too. I mean, I think she is, too." I was flustered. Every conversation with Simon went like this. Small talk and easy listening. And it was frustrating because I really respected the guy. I wanted him to take me seriously, and here we were discussing the weather. I didn't pretend to know about his art or his family or his past, but I knew what he was *like*. I'd witnessed the quiet charisma, experienced the subtle charm, and I knew how strongly my mother felt about him—about his kindness (if not exactly his warmth) and obvious intellect. And I was sure he felt the same for her.

Then it struck me again, the idea that I could talk to Simon, that I trusted him. Surely, somewhere in a past as vague and intriguing as his, he'd known people like Paige. Activists and worse. Maybe he could help me understand her mind-set, explain how a seemingly sane person could take her beliefs so far. If, indeed, that's what she'd done. But, no, I'd just sound ridiculous; the whole affair was so improbable. Besides, Simon was an artist who lived in the woods and worked in a barn. He was almost completely disengaged from modern society. Wasn't Paige the opposite?

We said our good-byes then, and he slapped me on the back. "Take care," he said, and I told him I would. When, partway across the lawn, I looked back at the barn, he was staring at his steel plates again, hands on his hips, a puzzled look on his face.

And so the city.

It didn't bode well for my relationship that when faced with work, friends, or lover, I chose lover last. Work meant money. And friends didn't yell at me. I spent my first morning back in New York blogging. Derrick's texts had turned menacing, all caps and explanation points. He'd filled in for two days, and the novelty had worn off. I knew how he felt. But it was my job, so I went back to it. I scoured the blogosphere, the news sites, and the daily papers, searching for anything I could run with. I posted my weekly wrap-up (though it was now Tuesday), a few celebrity sightings, and a semi-amusing commenter story about a lost weekend in Bushwick. Next, I scanned my in-box, but found nothing earth-shattering, nothing substantive . . . nothing from EmpiresFall. Who was I kidding? That's what I was looking for. I couldn't get away from it. From her. At 2:30 p.m., I stopped for lunch. Eight posts, three of them lazy links to other sites. I checked the stats: 53,723 unique visitors since 9 a.m. Numbers like that once buoyed my confidence; now they just sapped it. All those people, running out the clock in their barren little cubicles, looking for cheap laughs, idle gossip, anything they could repeat later over martinis and melting candles. I had a story for them. A tale that would blow those candles right out. And still, I didn't write a word of it.

Four more posts. I uploaded them and turned my laptop off. No standing by, no hibernating: *off.* I couldn't think through that low hum. I turned the air off, too, and opened my windows to the late-afternoon stink of Weehawken Street. A yawning garbage truck. Car horns on the West Side Highway. The city, moment by moment, a place of tacit agreements, short-term leases, nonbinding contracts, *instant gratification.* And still nothing ever changed.

I hadn't thought it through this far. Past finding her, I mean. If I wasn't going to turn her in or expose her on Roorback, what exactly was I going to do? Share what I knew with a reporter? With Cressida?

Or keep digging myself? But where should I start? The story had run its course. I'd found her, then let her get away, and I didn't even know why. So I did what I always did in a bind: I texted Touché. He was involved in this, too, whether he liked it or not. When he promptly called back (he thought texting was for teenagers) and invited me over, I put on my sneakers and left right away.

Dusk set in as I made my way to Washington Square. It had been some time since I'd been to Touché's apartment, but the splendid routine was the same. Ellis, the ageless doorman, called upstairs, then led me across to the gated elevator ("the first residential model Otis ever made"). He ushered me in, turned the key, and a minute later—a minute filled with seamless urban small talk—he threw the gate open with a flourish and I stepped into the Touché family "pied-à-terre."

"Vodka or gin?" came a familiar voice from somewhere up ahead.

"Vodka!"

"Ah, yes, of course. Americans don't drink gin anymore."

"You're American, too," I called out, following the voice toward the kitchen.

"Don't remind me," he said, as ice fell into glasses. "I'll be out in a minute."

I wandered into the living room and over to a circular oak table that in some earlier time had hosted Santo Touché's legendary card games. Now, it hosted his son's decidedly less glamorous computer setup. Normally a free moment and a Wi-Fi connection would have me tapping my way online, but now I stared at the screen with the kind of seething animosity we save for those people and objects that come to control our lives against our will or better judgment.

Touché shouldered his way through the swinging door, drinks in hand, and laughed when he saw me hovering over the monitor. "Going through withdrawal?"

"Shakes and hallucinations."

I took the drink he proffered and we clinked glasses—Fishers Island tumblers.

"You and your virtual world," Touché said. "A man cannot exist in two realms at once, remember." He sank into the nearest leather armchair. I made my way to the adjacent couch.

"You love your aphorisms, don't you? Whose is that? Let me guess: your fellow countryman Márquez."

"You think everything must come from somewhere else."

"It's called history."

"An American giving history lessons." Touché took a sip of his drink and crossed his legs. "Márquez, by the way, is Colombian."

This is what we did—parried around the important subjects of our lives like fencers. Like friends. We spent years waiting for something exciting to happen, and when we suddenly found ourselves at the center of a major story, it took us three drinks apiece to bring it up. It was as if the very mention of Paige Roderick, or the mind-numbing possibilities she represented, might shatter the facade of small lies and exaggerations we'd constructed around our own lives so as to give them meaning.

This, at least, is what I was feeling. Touché was feeling something else. He was talking about a *theater* actress he'd met, a flaxen-haired thespian named Brontë or Briony or some such, whom he'd just seen in the new Alan Bennett play on Minetta Lane, and how afterward they'd strolled down to Da Silvano for a late-night bite and a bottle of Barolo, and wasn't it perfect when pretty girls lived up to their savory names—

"I found Paige."

My friend sat up in his chair. "I thought as much."

"Do you want to know about it?"

"Have you told anyone else? Have you told Cressida?"

"No."

Touché frowned at his glass. "I suppose I know too much not to know the rest."

"Can I trust you?"

"*Aidan.*"

"I'm just saying."

"Well, you needn't."

"Because I don't know what to do. That's why I've come to . . . I could use some advice. She was *involved,* Julian. I talked to her."

"You *what*? She admitted to the bombing? Here, start from the beginning. From when I dropped you off at the ferry."

So I did. I told him what had happened, everything I knew or could surmise (except for what she looked like in person, because Touché could so easily be sidetracked), concluding with a careful rendering of the encounter at the fair.

"Is that it?" Touché asked, when I'd finished, almost half an hour later. "That's all she said? I wouldn't call that a confession."

"Well, it sure was something. And, anyway, the point is that she exists. I tracked her down. Actually, *she* tracked *me* down. Which means she—or they—must have a whole system in place up there. Lookouts, infiltrators . . ."

"I still think it may be a joke, a . . . how do you say . . ."

"Prank?"

"Yes."

"But who would try to pull something like this? And why?"

"Because it doesn't make sense any other way," Touché said. "Seriously, what are we talking about here? A beautiful woman, a beautiful *American* woman—young and smart and with every door open to her—becomes involved in an act of terror, in this *time,* in this *country,* and we—you and I—are the only two who know about it? Come on, Aidan. It's not the way of things."

I didn't answer. What was there to say?

Touché stood up to refill our glasses (for the third time). I was getting drunk. Why was I there? What was it I wanted Touché to *do,* exactly, besides believe me? Maybe that was enough for now. No, it wasn't enough. I needed his counsel because he of all people would understand the reactionary mind—its motives and machinations, its next moves. Touché was a product of political turmoil and the outmoded—or at least un-American—belief that a government could be toppled, a country overthrown. And if my friend could comprehend mass insurrection, he could certainly get his head around a young extremist with a fetish for violence. Or whatever the hell she was.

He came back with the drinks.

"So, she was beautiful?"

"Yeah. I guess."

"Like the photograph?"

"Tell me something," I said. "Why didn't you come to Vermont?"

"Aidan, I can't spend my life flying friends up and down the East Coast. I had things I had to—"

"Oh, bullshit. I wasn't asking you to take me to some beach party in Bar Harbor. This was real and you knew it. You knew it back on Fishers when—"

"*So what if I did.* Huh? You want the truth, Aidan? Here it is: this isn't my business. And it's not yours either. Of course I knew you might be onto something. But we're not talking about an ordinary crime here. We're talking about treason. Do you know what that is? Do you have any idea at all? It happens to be the only crime specifically mentioned in your precious Constitution, and *you* could be charged with it *right now*. I'm sorry, I hate to sound so dire but—"

"Treason is an act against a government."

"A nation. Not a government. There's a difference."

"Well, I'm not the one blowing up buildings, Julian."

"Yes, but apparently you know who is, and that's just the same . . ." His voice trailed off. He took a sip of his drink and pushed his thick, dark hair off his forehead. "Let me tell you something now, and then we won't speak of it again. It's the story of my father's best friend, Eduardo López. They grew up together, same private schools, same wealthy neighborhood. The López family owned textile factories and was very respected in Caracas. Soon, they became politically involved, as my family did—as every family did that had something to lose—and when Eduardo came of age, he was sent to school in America. Dartmouth, I believe. My father, as you know, was at Harvard. This was the fashion of the time. Now, of course, we're sent to America out of necessity: it's the one place Chávez can't touch us. It was Eduardo López who introduced my father to my mother—at a regatta in Newport—and that's an act not quickly forgotten where I'm from. Eduardo and my father remained the best of friends for a long time. Even after Chávez took over in '98 and they grew apart politically."

"What do you mean?"

"The López family businesses remained untouched while my father's concerns—the mines and all that—were nationalized. It was nothing more than chance: the mines were deemed valuable to the state. Eduardo stayed in Caracas and became an economic adviser to

Chávez; my father chose to speak out against the socialists and was forced to flee south. Even so, the two friends talked every week, as if nothing had happened.

"And then there was the coup. Everyone wanted it. Even the Caracas police sided with the rebels. My father, of course, was heavily involved as a liaison between the old guard—his people—and the labor unions who also supported change. He tried hard to convert his friend to the cause—he even told him of the coup beforehand, when it would happen, and how—but if Eduardo had no love for Chávez, he had no stomach for revolution either. Two days before the uprising, Eduardo left Caracas with his family to wait things out at his country estate. As it turns out, Chávez was back in power before the week was over, and when the dust cleared—or smoke . . . do you say *dust* or *smoke*?"

"Either, I guess. Was there actual smoke?"

"Some. There was shooting."

"So smoke."

"Okay, when the smoke cleared, Chávez went on a rampage. He went after everyone he thought might have betrayed him. The lucky ones were imprisoned after show trials. The others disappeared."

"Such a fine South American tradition, your disappearances."

"Ah, yes, we learned from the best," Touché said, clearing his throat. "But let me get to the point now. Which is Eduardo López. Which is the *death* of Eduardo López. Because that's what happened, Aidan. He came back to Caracas and Hugo Chávez had him killed. Shot dead on the street by men in masks. And why? Because he knew of the coup in advance and didn't speak up. He never lifted a finger against Chávez. Never participated in the plots against him. And still . . ."

"Jesus."

"Which, to answer your question, is why I hesitate to learn too much about your lovely friend."

"But you were all gung ho in the beginning."

"People are always gung ho in the beginning. In the same way they're liberal when they're young. To be honest, a part of me thinks you should tell everything to Cressida and let her take it from there. Or the two of you could break the story together. A *grand exposé*. It could do wonders for your relationship."

"And the other part?"

"The other part . . ." Touché shifted in his seat. He picked up his drink and held it in his hands, and when he spoke again, his voice was so quiet and intense that if I'd heard it over the phone, I wouldn't have recognized its owner.

"The other part thinks that you . . . could *help* her."

"You mean, get involved?"

"God no. You don't even understand what she's doing. Or why. But it's hard to feel sorry for Indigo Holdings, no? If that was indeed her intended target. What I'm talking about is *indirect* support—a ride somewhere or a place to stay. That is, if you ever see her again. And I don't say this because I believe in her methods—political violence is a worn-out theory, my friend, a black hole of misplaced idealism. It's a thing that scars great nations. But too much prosperity can ruin them."

Touché stood up and started pacing the room. "I'm speaking of the American malaise. The triumph of the wealthy: complete disengagement, derived not from admirable self-sufficiency but sickening self-regard. Fishers Island. Nantucket. The Hamptons. This is wealth of another kind. And the new money is more dangerous than the old. Look at Palm Beach. Look at Aspen. Look at our cities, Aidan. A hole has been ripped in the fabric of the American middle class, and still Manhattan is like a theme park, but safer even, and more homogeneous. And, yes, I realize I'm part of the problem. I go along with it all. I laugh at golf stories and speak mindlessly of real estate at cocktail parties. But what choice do I have? We are the walking dead, my friend: America's winners. Too tired making money to *live*. And the rest of the country? Too tired living to fight." Touché sat on the edge of an armchair and leaned toward me, conspiratorially. "Eduardo López sent my father a book once, by the Italian anarchist Alfredo Bonanno. This was in the months before the coup, when politics was still intoxicating and the future might belong to anyone. The book was meant as a counterargument to unrestrained free enterprise, but my father was bothered by its theories and put it aside. I found it in his office during one of my visits, and intrigued—for my father is many things but most definitely *not* an anarchist—I skimmed it. Only one sentence was underlined. I still remember it, for my father had scrawled a giant question mark in the margin: 'Beyond the crises, beyond other problems of underdevelopment, beyond poverty and hunger, the last fight that capital will have to put up, the decisive one, is the fight against boredom.' And you know what? That makes a certain sense to me. Something at the end of prosperity is broken."

We sat there a moment. I wasn't sure what to say, and Touché seemed none too sure of what he'd *just* said. Then, as if dismissing his own sudden depth, he stood back up and waved his hand through the air as if brushing away a fly.

"But enough of this," he announced. "You shouldn't listen to me. I suffer from that foolish pessimism particular to South Americans. Read your friend Márquez, you'll understand." He started walking toward the kitchen. "I'm thinking of throwing a party on Friday night. Some music people. If you and Cressida are on speaking terms, you should bring her. If not, I'll introduce you around."

And just like that, we came back to ourselves, to our roles, our lives—alluring and glamorous and utterly vapid. I left Touché's apartment sometime later, drunk on big ideas and vodka, and caught a cab back to deserted Weehawken Street. It was almost three in the morning. It was always almost three in the morning. I climbed the stairs and fiddled with the locks, and when I got inside I paced around awhile, unsteady and unsettled. I turned on the TV, opened a bottle of wine, and dialed Cressida's number. We'd gone five days without speaking, and when you're in a relationship, five days is four too long. It was my fault, this extended silence, proliferating as each day passed, making it that much more difficult to initiate contact. The issue of her columns had lived its half-life and fallen away. This was something else now. A contest. Cressida had become an adversary—in life and love.

She didn't pick up. I tried again, and this time left a message.

My windows were still open, and the wind must have changed for I could suddenly smell the river. I had the idea then of walking back outside and across the highway to the edge of the island. I could lean out over the lapping water like a million young men before me, men who'd encircled themselves in this city of angles and sought out answers in the bleakness before dawn. Because the odds evened out at night. The clock reset itself, the opposition rested. I'd never been to the waterfront at that hour, alone under a universe I couldn't see.

I wasn't the kind of person who howled at the moon. And I didn't that night either. No, I sat there drinking cheap wine, gazing at a televised war, soldiers slogging through some dusty desert, and to this day I have no idea what I was watching—what battle in what country. Was it the news, a documentary, a movie? At some point I got up to pour another drink, but the bottle was empty. And it was this unfortunate fact that led me back outside to hail another cab. It was 3:45 a.m. Surely Cressida would have wine, or answers, one or the other, it didn't matter which.

PAIGE

· · ● ● ● ● ● ● · ● ●

WHEN I RELATED THE STORY, I WAS CAREFUL TO LEAVE OUT CERTAIN
specifics—Aidan's name, address, and the name of his blog. It was more
than an issue of trust; I needed something—*anything*—that no one else
had. I was tired of being the one in the dark. Keith listened intently until
I was finished, then rubbed his growing beard.

Will he stay quiet? Lindsay asked.

I think he has so far, I said.

Except now he knows you exist.

Yes, but I didn't say anything incriminating.

It sounds like you didn't deny anything either, Lindsay responded.

Whose side are you on?

I'm just saying.

What? What are you saying?

Lindsay glanced at Keith. I'm saying you've put us in real danger.

Really? Wow! That was almost an original thought.

Excuse me?

Girls, Keith said.

Girls? I repeated. Who the fuck do you— I stopped, abruptly, and
stood up. The cigarettes were on the kitchen counter. Calm as I could,
I took them and walked out to the deck. I managed to close the sliding door without slamming it, all the while thinking of that well-worn

Kipling line about keeping your head while everyone around you is losing theirs. The poem was about becoming a man, and Bobby, the earliest of bloomers, taped it to his wall when he was eleven or twelve. I used to read it when he wasn't around. And then one day he took it down. I guess he didn't need someone else telling him how to grow up. Later, in college, I bought Kipling's collected works at a used-book sale, and I still have it—or did, when I had things. It's funny what we cling to.

But even Kipling couldn't assuage me. These were the same people who'd originally suggested I confront Aidan Cole, and now, now that questions were piling up like leaves set to burn, I was being blamed. It could have been any one of us captured in that photograph. That's what I kept telling myself. I lit a cigarette and took a deep drag. Behind me, the door slid open, and Lindsay stepped outside. She was barefoot.

I'm sorry, she said solemnly. I shouldn't have—

Don't. I mean, don't apologize. We're all under pressure.

It was a stale response, but noncombative, and all I could manage just then. Lindsay produced one of those wrinkly smiles that so often lead to tears. But the tears didn't materialize. Instead she came over and hugged me, her bony arms wrapping tightly around my body. I must have reciprocated, though I can't remember. I was too busy wondering if Keith had sent her out to do this, too.

Lindsay went back inside. I stayed on the deck until I'd calmed down enough to be around them again. When I walked in, Lindsay was draped across the couch. Keith was at the computer.

Well, I'm exhausted, Lindsay said almost immediately. I'll leave you two to . . . you know . . . and with that she climbed the stairs and disappeared. I, for one, didn't know. And so I waited.

I don't understand what's in it for him, Keith said finally. If he's not a journalist, why not just go to the cops and wash his hands of the whole thing? Hell, he'd be a *hero*.

He said the word with all the disdain it deserved.

I stepped down into the sunken living room and took Lindsay's vacated seat on the couch. Keith followed me, but opted for a nearby chair. He was wearing a grubby white T-shirt and jeans. His hair was growing out, but not as fast as his beard, which was becoming a straggly, knotted mess. It made his eyes look small.

Tell me what's going on, I said. Who's behind this?

What do you mean?

Oh, come on, Keith. There's only one possible explanation for who sent those e-mails and took my picture. Someone's been dropping bread crumbs that eventually led this guy to our doorstep. Someone who knows what we're up to. Someone on the inside.

There are plenty of other expla—

Stop it! Just stop talking.

I couldn't look at him anymore so I stood up and began pacing. Then I wheeled around and glared at him. He didn't look away.

Is it you? I asked flatly.

Is what me?

Are you doing this? Is Lindsay?

Of course not. What sense does that make? If *you* get caught, *we* get caught.

Okay, so it's coming from whoever's supporting us. Our so-called patrons.

That's impossible, Keith said.

Really? Do you know what I think would be impossible? To be photographed coming out of Barneys if someone didn't know I was *in* Barneys. Or, for that matter, to know the bomb went off on the wrong floor *before* the *Times* article was published.

You don't think someone could have figured that out? Jesus, *the fucking* Times *figured it out*. Obviously, we weren't going after that ridiculous little fag designer—

Fag? Nice.

—or maybe your new boyfriend is lying. Have you thought about that? Look, Paige, I don't have every answer. If that's what you want, you're in the wrong business.

You don't have *any* answers.

I'm sorry, you know perfectly well that I can't talk about the Movement—either individual names or the larger structure. It should be enough to know I trust these people completely. I trust them with my life. And Lindsay's life. And *your* life, Paige. They believe in us, and for good reason: look at what we've *done*. What we're *doing*. And who we're doing it to: *Indigo Holdings*. They're a household name, now. Have you seen the press they've been getting since that *Times* piece ran? Everyone's piling on. It's like Enron. Do you remember that, or were you too young?

I wasn't too young, I said.

But do you know how that happened? An enterprising reporter wrote a magazine article that dared to question the practices of a company everyone else was heralding. That one piece led to a dozen others, then a hundred others, and then the house of cards came down. Enron was a public company, and still it took a year to get to the bottom of things. What we did took a week. We were impolite, but we had to be. It was the only way to make people listen. What I'm saying, Paige, is that our strategy *works*. If we're careful, it works. Tell me what the downside is. Besides the danger. Besides what it's doing to us. If we can just come back together, find a way to move forward, we can . . . oh, you know what we can do.

His eyes were wide again, and affecting. Was this a performance or the real thing? Was there a difference anymore? Had there ever been? Keith was a man who could rally an army if the lighting was right. And, of course, it was right just then, at the end of the day, cicadas starting to sing. I could feel myself backing away from the precipice I'd been edging toward. I'd searched a long time, in different cities and capacities, for . . . what? A sense of purpose and significance, sure, but everyone is casting about for these things. I'd been working to reform a culture and country that changes imperceptibly if it changes at all. A system built on compromise and control, where there's no room for idealism, for grace. Losing Bobby had freed me to step outside my small world, and Keith had allowed me to stay there, on the fringes, and to find a life—the kind I no longer had to turn from, or apologize for. Here was one last chance to embrace that grand idea that things could get better, that they *would* get better, if we set out to make them so. What was the alternative?

The three of us sat down to breakfast the next morning and talked through our options. Continuing in one way or continuing in another. We would have to move. We'd been in the house too long, and if one person had found us, others would be close behind.

So: leave immediately or stay a few days longer. There'd be another house ready in a week, Keith told us, in a town a few hours south. He'd be done with his work in the garage by then, but was that too long? We all lived with the same uneasy feeling, the sound of passing cars at night. That any one of them could stop. Movement was the only constant in our lives, dropping everything and starting over. We could leave the next day, stay at campsites and motels until the new place was ready. We could find more cars, just as reliable and utterly unmemorable as the two we had.

It was time to go, but we didn't go. In the end, Keith just wasn't ready, and we wouldn't push him. Maybe we feared the unknown or trusted Keith too much. For me, though, it came down to Aidan Cole. I believed his appearance was an isolated incident. And somehow I just knew he wouldn't talk. It was a feeling based on the flimsiest of evidence, and yet I felt it strongly. He wasn't the one I was worried about.

A week, then. Keith began working even harder. Days and nights in the garage. Lindsay gave notice at work so as not to raise eyebrows by simply disappearing. She made dinner most evenings when she got home, buzzing manically around the kitchen like a fly. Like a wasp. She always made a tray for Keith and took it down to the garage.

How's he doing? I finally asked. I hadn't seen him for two days.

Good. Why?

He shouldn't be working like this.

He knows his limits, she said breezily.

He does?

Lindsay didn't respond.

I spent my time online. There had been little talk of the next target, so I got a head start. I made lists of vulnerable government facilities and military installations, but mostly I focused on corporate America—gluttonous oil companies, weapons manufacturers, bailed-out financial firms. The building blocks of a crooked republic. I liked to believe they were becoming our niche, our expertise, these secretive giants. I filled more notebooks with statistics—horrible facts and figures—and for a while it kept me busy. For a while I could ignore what was happening around me. Or what wasn't. Two more days passed without my laying eyes on Keith. Once, in the middle of the night, I heard him climbing the creaking stairs, but I stayed in bed.

It was as if confronting him, or even appearing to care, meant losing whatever silent war was being waged. How had it come to this? In the same way everything terrible happens: slowly, then all at once.

On Saturday night he came in for dinner. It was Labor Day weekend, though no one cared. Keith's beard was even fuller now—like Steve McQueen's in his sad final years. His work shirt was unbuttoned halfway down his chest. And his hands were filthy. The person in front of me bore no resemblance to the man I'd met in North Carolina. This was more than a disguise. Keith, always meticulous, ever aware, was letting himself go. He opened a beer and sat down at the head of the table. Lindsay served him a large helping of salad, then put the bowl down and took a seat beside him. I looked at the bowl and then at her. She picked it back up and served herself.

Paige showed me some articles about Indigo, Lindsay said. There's a new one almost every day now. Keith took a bite of lettuce, the fork momentarily disappearing into the scruff where his lips had once been. They're raising all these questions about improprieties, she continued. Illegal weapons deals. Secret offshore accounts. Even the *Wall Street Journal* is onto the story. It's exactly what we wanted.

We waited while Keith chewed. He chewed and I assume he swallowed, then he reached for his beer and swallowed some of that, too.

We should talk about the next Action, he said finally.

Okay, Lindsay replied. She turned to me expectantly.

I've been focusing in on a few companies, I said. Let me get my notes and—

Don't, Keith said.

What?

There's no need. I've figured it out.

Figured what out?

Our next move.

But we do these things together, I said.

Lindsay stopped smiling.

The media, Keith announced, stabbing at a tomato. It's time to shoot the messenger.

You're not serious.

Keith put his fork down and leaned toward me. Do I look like I'm not serious?

I'm not sure what you look like anymore, I said.

He laughed, as if to break the tension.

I'm not kidding, I said. You're scaring me.

Paige, said Lindsay.

It's okay, Keith said calmly. If you'll just hear me out.

Not if you're going to suggest blowing up a newsroom somewhere.

No, not a newsroom. A company headquarters. He put his elbows on the table and clasped his hands together. I'm talking about N3.

I looked from Keith to Lindsay. She was already focused on me, as if awaiting my reaction.

Lindsay, do you already know about this?

About what?

The National News Network.

I think Keith mentioned something.

When?

Come on, I thought we'd gotten over all this nonsense, Keith said dismissively.

So did I.

Can I at least explain my thinking? Keith said.

You can do whatever you want, I told him.

Lindsay stood up to clear the plates as Keith began to speak. So, she'd heard this part, too. The part about a fourth estate turned docile, a press catering to demographics and caving to power. Did I want specifics? Keith asked. Because he could give me a lifetime of specifics. But why not start with Iraq—since that's why I was there—and Bush's final press conference before the invasion, the White House correspondents reduced to a state of childlike wonder by the awesome spectacle of it all, the million machinations of an empire readying for war, and the reporters who could speak at all lobbing out softballs about new weapons systems—high-speed tanks and missiles accurate to the meter. They asked how long it would take, hours or days, and who might be next. Shock and awe. Remember that? Rumsfeld, that charlatan, seizing control not of the war but the *tone* of the war, and they lapped it up, every last thin-lipped line. But the best part? Deciding to send *them* over as well. Let's turn those pesky reporters into harmless travel writers by embedding them with the troops. Oh, it was brilliant, and by the time the war went wrong, they were back home, safe and sound, picking sand out of their teeth between bites of escargots at Café Luxembourg. Or go back further: the *Times* and WMD. Was that the so-called *liberal media* at work? No, it was *a reaction to the charge* is what it was. The fucking media bending over backwards *not* to be liberal. That's how scared they are of criticism. Everything needs two sides now, equal time. Some deranged grade-school principal in Wichita tears a picture of monkeys out of the textbooks, and the next day forty news trucks are parked outside. And no one's saying, Wait a minute, this is insane. No, they're saying, Here's the other side of the story! But there is no other side to evolution. Some things *just are.*

Keith was standing now, arms out like a preacher as he spoke of regression, the new administration moving to the center, the safe ground in an economic tempest, thus insuring the asinine issues Americans had argued over for years—guns and gay marriage, the beginning of life and the end of it, an ongoing refusal to address, hell, to *accept,* global warming—would continue to comprise our national debate. These were things the modern world had moved past. There was no death penalty in Japan. People didn't shoot each other in Canada. Western Europe was moving past religion, and the armies of the world were melting away, to say nothing of the ice caps, and where were we? Half of Congress thinks Darwin may have been wrong, and my God, no one calls them out. No one says, Enough! Instead, the reporters rush back to write the story by deadline. Is that a liberal press? Is that a biased media? If only they *were* liberal. Or independent. Or even just thoughtful; I'd take thoughtful. What happened to the intelligentsia? Our best and brightest have become our pert and prettiest. Suck-ups to power, or even the idea of it. Just watch that repulsive White House Press Dinner sometime. But it's not just D.C. It's Hollywood. It's New York. Who's the most sought-after party guest on the Upper East Side? *Fucking Kissinger!* America's greatest war criminal becomes cuddly old Henry, staring at surgically enhanced socialite cleavage as he offers his bon mots and sips scotch with hands shaking from the blood of half a million men.

Fear, Keith said. They try to make us scared, keep us scared. The press, the politicians, the left as bad as the right. He quoted Rousseau then, something about opportunity and obligation. He was speaking not of *them* now, but of *us.* What *we* had to do. How we'd take the very worst offender, the National News Network, and use their strategy of spreading fear against them. *We'd* be the other side of the argument they pretended to hold so dear.

Was there poetry in any of this? Certainly there was truth, but bombing the nation's delivery mechanism, even if it was broken . . . well, it would be like shooting the postman because you were sick of junk mail. Even N3, with its tongue-in-cheek news coverage, its faux patriotism and propagandist talk-show hosts. Keith had been right about Indigo, but did that give him the authority to proceed unchallenged? I stayed quiet as he spoke because this wasn't a discussion. It was a lecture. An explanation for a decision reached in a vacuum. In a garage with a bomb. What he was looking for was not input but agreement, consent, and the only bone he tossed me was logistical. I could help decide when and where. Because it was already going to happen.

Two more days went by and no one came for us. Keith holed up in his concrete lair; Lindsay scanned food at the supermarket. There was no sign of Aidan Cole. He'd come and gone, and sometimes, in the severed otherness of our reality, it was hard to believe he'd ever been there at all. I checked his blog incessantly, but he posted nothing significant, nothing about us. He wasn't even covering the bombing anymore. It was old news. And the world moved madly on.

I got back to research. N3 occupied the first twenty floors of a building (owned by its parent company) on West Fifty-first Street. The sets for the brainless morning shows and flag-draped newscasts were on the ground floor, allowing tourists to gather every dawn and dusk to lend the broadcasts that faux-everyman feel that had come to contaminate modern media. I found the building's layout among some online real-estate-leasing records and used the telephone extensions listed on the company website to locate the offices of senior management (x0706 meant seventh floor, sixth office from reception, etc.). I printed out everything from programming times to studio-usage schedules. It didn't take long. Was it a lack of information or a lack of intensity on my part? Because none of this felt right. And Keith had offered no more guidance. He just came in one day, picked up my pile of notes and printouts, and walked back to the garage.

On a sunny Saturday morning, five days after we were supposed to have packed up and left, Keith announced that he and Lindsay were driving down to scout the target in New York. Another reconnaissance trip, this one without me. When they got back, we'd leave.

You'll clean the house like last time?

Sure, I said. What about the garage?

Leave it be.

He went out to inspect the car—Lindsay's this time. Tires, headlights, blinkers, a quick check of the engine. He looked, from the window where I stood watching, like a real mechanic, his jeans stained, his T-shirt yellowed under the arms and streaked with something metallic. His hair was slicked back, which only accentuated the beard. He was waiting for Lindsay, who was working the early-morning shift. It was her last day, and afterward she was going to get her hair cut and dyed (something she'd refrained from doing, so as not to raise eyebrows at work). She pulled in a little before 1 p.m., sporting a cute red bob. It kind of worked for her, and when we were alone inside I told her as much. She giggled like a girl and squeezed my arm, then chattered incessantly as she threw a few things in an overnight bag. I took a chance and asked what she really thought of the N3 plan.

Which is when she shut up.

Keith came in to say good-bye. He'd changed into a fresh dress shirt, but instead of looking clean-cut, he just looked weird, unstable: bipolar.

The beard, I said. It's becoming conspicuous.

It's a disguise.

I know, but it's not working.

We'll be back tomorrow night, he said, ignoring me. And then . . . and then a fresh start. With that he nodded and walked outside. Lindsay was leaning against her car, waiting for him. He said something to her. She looked over at me and waved good-bye.

I went through it all again. Tiles and mirrors, toilets and drains. Hair in the shower, toothpaste in the sink. When they found the house, they would probably already know who we were. Still, I cleaned. There was nothing else to do. When I finished, I drifted over to the computer and checked the news sites for the latest on Indigo, but nothing came up. Soon enough I was browsing Roorback, looking for clues. An explanation. Keith had a point: Why was Aidan risking so much when he could risk nothing and become famous? Isn't that what people like him wanted, that one great story to dine out on?

How long was I online? Three hours? Four? An afternoon spent reading sardonic posts—a celebration of useless information that epitomized the reasons I'd fled New York, then Washington, then, finally, myself.

It was getting dark out. I'd been claustrophobic for weeks, but now, left alone in a house where I could touch no surfaces, left alone to guard a locked bomb factory, the feeling overwhelmed me. I walked outside and sat down in the grass. The universe was contracting, the stars like stars in a planetarium—penned in. A terrible thought dawned on me, and when it came clear, when I realized I'd probably just been set up, it was far too late to do anything about it. I'd been a fool. Keith had packed his muse into the car and together they'd vanished, as they'd first appeared, another couple on another road. And why *should* they come back? I was a liability now—personally and professionally. I lit a cigarette. Had I failed or had Keith? I'd followed the rules as he'd crumbled under their weight. I'd stayed consistent while he'd transformed before my eyes, become everything he'd preached against. A fateful moment of lust and our tight and vital lives had come apart. Now he was off to precipitate an Action he couldn't justify, an Action planned so loosely, so quickly, that it seemed the work of another man entirely. Was he even going to New York? Or had he lied about that, too? He was gone and Lindsay was gone and I'd been left as a sacrifice to the gods, or worse, the authorities, because they were coming, weren't they? Keith knew it and so he fled. They would come roaring in with vests and helmets and a hundred guns, and if they didn't shoot me on sight, they'd take me in, an enemy combatant. The perfect proof that terror takes all forms.

But didn't Keith think I'd talk? Rat them out as he'd ratted on me (because, really, who else could it have been)? I could broker a deal with the Feds, tell them all I knew, except *I knew nothing*. I'd wandered blind through these last months, stupidly equating my doubts with some lack of faith or courage. Maybe Keith was betting I'd stay loyal to the end—the confession room with the two-way mirror. Meanwhile, they could set off the N3 bomb, then a dozen more, and truly turn the country around. Was that our purpose? Did we ever even have one—an endgame, I mean?

I was becoming paranoid, unhinged. I lit another cigarette from the end of the first. I'd never smoked like this, like I needed to, but I inhaled and for a moment felt better. I didn't have an addictive personality, had never smoked much weed or binged on cocaine, yet I was now an extremist, a person who had forcefully stepped over the lines that defined contemporary life, and then turned around and tried to erase them. That I would come to crave something would follow, but *cigarettes*? Still, it was a way to stay occupied, the endless fiddling with matches and lighters. I stood up and the nicotine rushed to my head. My eyes had adjusted to the dark and I could see the outline of the woods, hear the rustle and crunch of what lay beyond, nature repositioning itself—if the noises were natural at all. Turning then, I saw the garage, a black square in the near distance, eerie and foreboding. I paused, took one last drag, and went back inside.

I was wired. I lay on my mattress fully clothed (gloves on my hands, shoes on my feet), tossing and turning like a child on the last night of summer. Occasionally, I could hear a car out on the road, and in that netherworld of half dreams I imagined it pulling into the driveway, then my name through a bullhorn, and the flood of lights . . .

I woke with the dawn, sat straight up and listened for anything out of place. But the world was silent. I went downstairs and slid open the glass door. A collection of cigarette butts lay on the ground in front of me, a testament to questions unanswered. I needed to go somewhere, anywhere, if only for a little while. Leaving the property was against the rules, but did they even apply anymore? I unzipped my bag, found some shorts and a loose T-shirt, and put them on. Then I locked the house and ventured into the dewy northern morning. The heat wave hadn't broken, but a breeze had come up and it was still early enough to be almost comfortable. I turned right at the end of the drive and walked awhile. Then I ran. The air felt like pure oxygen; I swallowed it in gulps and, for the first time in ages, felt temporarily unburdened of a world that had tightened like a cinch around my head. It was only 7 a.m. and not a single car had passed, but I didn't want to press my luck so I turned around before the first intersection and started walking back. I walked with my hands on my hips, and gradually the adrenaline was replaced by a lesser, if equally pleasant, high. The trees were an almost rain-forest green, and I could hear a stream through the roadside brush. I thought briefly of going to investigate, but I wanted to get home before it got too—

Someone was behind me—a car, I mean—coming around a corner. There was no time to take cover; I barely managed to turn my head from the road as it went by. The car was a late-model Lexus, silver and almost silent, and I thought it might pass without incident until I spotted the blinker, and the brake lights. I was less than two hundred yards from the house, but that didn't matter. It was too late to take off. We had outs for every situation, dialogues we'd conceived over dozens of dinners and committed to memory by morning. It was a never-ending night of improv, this living underground, and all you could do was try to keep up the illusion, no matter how unbelievable it might be. Because your life—my life—depended on it. Depended on overcoming moments just like this, a car backing up, its white reverse lights portending any number of dangers, any number of fates. Then the window coming down, and a man leaning over to say something that could end it all.

Need a ride to town? he asked. I'm heading down to pick up the paper.

He was old, seventy-five or eighty, with silver hair and large glasses, and, oh, how I suddenly loved him, even as I smiled and said, Thank you, no, I need the exercise. Even as he smiled back and said, Okay, just checking, be safe now. And then he drove off, his car quiet as central air.

Shaken, breathing deeply, I ran the rest of the way home and collapsed onto the bench that framed the deck. I closed my eyes, and when I opened them, I found myself gazing once again at the garage. Even bathed in sunlight, it was as lifeless and forbidding as any place I'd ever seen. That's when I knew.

I had to go in there.

If the bomb was gone, I'd know for sure they weren't coming back.

The toolbox, like everything else, was packed up and sitting by the front door. I opened it and (wearing gloves again) rooted around until I found Keith's lockpicking tools. The heavy-duty key lock on the garage door would be too strong for bolt cutters, and too advanced for a tension wrench and hook pick. That left only one option: bumping it. I'd learned to use a bump key back in Carolina, but I'd never mastered the procedure, and anyway, months had passed since then. I found it near the bottom of the kit, a small key like any other, until you looked closer and saw the shaved-down grooves, designed to tickle the stacks of a tumbler lock until the driver pins separated from the key pins. It only happened for the briefest of moments, but if you were applying exactly the right amount of force in exactly the right place—and it really was a question of finesse—the cylinder would turn and the lock would (sometimes) come undone.

Key in hand, I walked out to the garage. The art of lock bumping was still in its infancy, and I knew of only two models—high-end BiLocks and Kwiksets—that were truly tamperproof. Keith had gone with a Medeco Biaxial, a lock advertised as impenetrable, though imperfect was more accurate. I took a deep breath and slid the key in until only one notch was left showing. Using the base of my right hand, I bumped it into the lock while applying pressure to the back of the plug. It took several tries; but then it gave. The cylinder clicked and the pins parted. I was in.

It had been weeks since I glimpsed the first bomb—spotlit like a marquee invention at its trade-show unveiling—and the inside of the garage had changed since then; I could tell that right away, before my eyes even adjusted to the darkness. The air was cool and smelled like . . . what . . . battery acid and metallic burn. Like blood, if blood had a smell. I felt for the light switch without stepping inside, my fingers reaching along the cold wall, and when I found it, there was this instant when nothing happened. Booby trap, I thought: I've walked right into it, been outsmarted again.

But then the lights came up. I stepped inside. Keith had divided the space with a makeshift sheet-metal barricade. The foreground had been arranged into a cocoonlike shelter, with a small rug, books and clothes, blankets and pillows. On the other side of the wall, the photographer's light shone down like before. I'd convinced myself by then that the bomb was gone because Keith was gone; his bombs were his children, and he'd never leave them behind. Still, drawn to the light like a girl in a horror movie, I stepped tentatively around the barricade. The garage was a place to tread lightly.

What I saw first was the periphery, the dynamite crates along the wall, the tools on tables, and then the yards of wiring, insulation, crimpers and canisters, lengths of pipe, fuses and detonators, springs like miniature Slinkys. I saw half a dozen hand grenades in a milk crate. Above them, hanging by a leather strap, an assault rifle. It was sleek, and smaller than I'd have thought, and I would have gone and picked it up had I not been distracted by the spotlit metal suitcase, propped open like the hood of a car. *How could it still be here?* I walked over and peered into it. Keith preferred suitcase devices, and now I understood why: it was light and easy to carry, but it was also insulated. The bomb components lay in hard foam padding. The Tovallaced dynamite sticks were tightly bunched together on one side of the case; on the other, carefully cut into the foam, was a dry-cell battery and a small timer. Both were connected by a series of wires to what I presumed was a blasting cap lying somewhere below the dynamite. That was it: one, two, three. I started backing away, wondering what this meant—how I could be so wrong—when I noticed something else, a space between the padding and the case itself. It was a kind of trough, a secret little moat covered with electrical tape. Except a corner was still exposed. I bent down and looked inside, and I will never forget what I saw. The lining was jammed full of things, awful things, nails and ball bearings and cut glass; splinters and fragments and shards—*shrapnel*—set to blast out in all directions. This was no attention-getting explosive. This was a weapon meant for murder.

AIDAN

· · ● ● ● ● ● ● · · ● ●

I REMEMBER THE POSTPARTY SMELL, STICKY AND STALE, CIGARETTE SMOKE and alcohol. The TV was on, rerunning some MTV or VH1 awards show—a sea of pumped-up breasts bursting forth from cinched and clinging dresses into Cressida's otherwise dark living space. On the coffee table sat two glasses of red wine beside a half-full bottle left uncorked. And what else? Scattered heels, an unemptied ashtray, unopened bills, old invitations. Flowers wilted in carafe pitchers, fashion magazines stacked in piles on the floor, and against a wall near the windows, a surfboard, still pristine white, purchased by Cressida during some other boyfriend's regime. All of this was visible within the television's glowing jurisdiction.

I listened for sounds of life beyond the drone of air conditioners and the late-night voices wafting up from the street. A stereo played softly behind someone's door, one of those whimpering emo bands—Bright Eyes or Beirut—and with it, softer still, came a man's snoring, peaceful and rhythmic—the breathing of a boyfriend, not a one-night stand. It wasn't coming from Cressida's room, of that much I was sure. Even in my drunken state it never crossed my mind that she might cheat on me. She was tenacious and driven, and when she found what she wanted, she didn't let go lightly. It was a pure, almost Catholic kind of loyalty, and it both soothed and scared me. "Imagine the breakup," Touché once said, and now I did, often.

I was outside her bedroom door. I'd called from the corner, and after five minutes of pleading she'd buzzed me in. I could picture her scowling as she sat up in bed, her jaw clenched, those cheeks of English rose all tight and drained of color. She was in there waiting to pounce.

I knocked softly and pushed the door open. The lights were out, the blinds drawn.

"Hey," I said into the darkness. "The TV's still on out here."

There was no answer. But I could go with this, use the silence to my advantage. I'd sneak up and kiss her gently, and that would be enough; we'd sort the rest out in the morning. I inched toward her bed, waiting for my eyes to adjust. It was probably what she wanted anyway, sex without apologies or complicated excuses, without the bullshit of the larger relationship. For sex, after a certain age, was something you could separate out. Why? Because older women enjoyed it more than younger women. A simple fact on the surface of things, and yet I'd come to believe it was the answer to a thousand mysteries of the female mind. It was a matter of experience. It was a question of need. It was years of wasted hope and disappointment, of saving sex for last, then realizing, as one's twenties ended, that the bedroom was the best part. The only honest part. You could take what you wanted and save the sniveling, the emotion, the messy issues of loyalty and attachment—of *life*—for later. Or never. The selfish modern woman joining the egotistical modern man in an attempt to stave off what was once inevitable—the slow melancholy of marriage and children—and prolong her golden, irresponsible youth.

And where did that leave us, guys like Touché and me, who once counted on the ticking clock as an ally? Time was no longer on our side, and this had rendered the map of modern love almost useless. We were confused, but also intrigued. We had a paragon now, an archetype—the chic, detached urban woman, perched on the slippery summit between youth and experience—and we chased after her, after *the idea* of her, endlessly. Of course, this being New York, we occasionally got distracted. By whom? By girls who were too young: fine-boned MFA students from the New School, confident and ambitious and impossibly busy doing nothing at all; by iron-haired junior publicists typing dirty texts into well-thumbed BlackBerrys as they cabbed it to the next event; by cherubic Sam Shepard devotees poring over Xeroxed plays and agent call sheets before you'd even opened your eyes in the morning. And by women who were too old: slightly manic divorcées, still pretty but overcompensating, forcing themselves to stay out and drink more than they ever did in their twenties; and Botoxed former debutantes with famous last names that never quite excused them from the absurdity of their lifestyles; and wild-eyed Brooklyn artists with ink sleeves and lingering habits who seemed to never give a fuck about anything, and, it turned out, really didn't give a fuck about anything. These women came in and out of our lives in gusts of passion, if not love, because love was for the other kind. Love was for the one still out there, the one who'd lived but was not yet jaded, who understood pleasure but respected its limits, who came from someplace else but was making it here—on her own, preferably, but, hell, whom were we kidding, a nice family never hurt. We were looking for a woman who glided through life but paused to read the great books (or at least a few of them); who was social but slightly alternative; who knew all the places to go but almost never did. A woman who had great taste and nice tits and a bit of a temper. Touché liked curves. I wasn't so picky.

Cressida was as close as I'd come. I reminded myself of this every time our little two-car train derailed, and I reminded myself again as I advanced across her spinning bedroom.

"Cressida?" I whispered.

All this in-a-perfect-world shit, and yet we'd reached our early thirties, the great age of compromise, of finally understanding that the ideal was an abstract concept.

"Cressida?"

I reached out and felt for her—

"*Ow!*" I'd stubbed my toe on something, the corner of her bed frame, and a second later the pain arrived. "*Fuck!*"

"*Shhh!*" Cressida hissed. "*You'll wake up the whole bloody house.*"

"Well, turn a goddamn light on."

"Only if you'll use it to leave."

I collapsed onto the bed and rubbed my toe. I could see her now, the outline of her, sitting up much as I'd imagined, her arms tensed at her sides, palms digging into the pillows. She looked scared and angry at the same time.

"This isn't a good idea, Aidan. It's the middle of the night and you're—"

"I'm not drunk."

"Oh, please, don't be boring."

She said this sometimes and it drove me crazy. *Don't be boring.* Who the hell was ever trying to be boring? It was so condescending, especially with that haughty British accent. *Don't be boooring.* It was an insult, a warning, a dare. There was nothing worse than being told you were just like everyone else.

And fine, maybe this was a bad cliché, showing up loaded at 4 a.m. after disappearing for days with no explanation, but I wasn't there to talk or grovel or apologize. I was there to fuck my girlfriend. And this is what I set about attempting to do. I brushed off her comment—my actions would take care of that—and slid over to the middle of the bed. Then I pulled her toward me. She didn't resist. She didn't take me in her arms either. She just lay still, waiting. She was wearing a T-shirt and lacy—what did she call them?—*boy shorts.* I brushed a hand over her modest breasts, their firmness pleasantly familiar, the way they kept their shape as she lay on her back. I started sighing in her ear as my hand slid down her stomach, all the way down, over the lace and then . . . under. My sighs became words and I related them in a dry-mouthed whisper. Things we'd done, things we hadn't. And I had her now; her hand replaced mine, her fingers spelled my fingers. I moved quickly to catch up, disrobing in a tangle of pants and socks and boxers, then there I was, back in her ear, murmuring improbable ideas, impossible ideas. Concepts and geometry. We were under the sheet, fumbling, her hand on me now, and then she was on top, and then I was on top, and I was thinking of how long it had been since I'd gone down on her, and how, for a while—a month or two—she'd soldiered gamely on, pleasuring me without reciprocation until that, too, had ended, and the sex itself evolved from the main event to the only event. And to think . . . we'd started out gracefully, the naked hours filled with curiosity and communication, responsible exploration, pointed pleasure. It all ended: wore off, got old. Replacements were sought—not different partners, of course, but different *acts.* If it were drugs, we'd have bought more; if it were blackjack, we'd have doubled down, gone for broke; but with sex, it was something else, something

deeper and more carnal. What had begun as simple "lovemaking"—
she on top, say, slowing writhing as I cupped her breasts, her hips, eyes
locked on her eyes, entertaining vaguely spiritual thoughts of eternity,
that life could always be so good—receded over many months or was,
more accurately, intruded upon by more primal urges, the struggle
for power and acceptance merging with a childlike desire to see how
far we—how far *I*—could take things, what exactly I could get away
with. The opposite of evolution. Animal instincts. Hard sex. She on
the bottom, legs over my shoulders, over her shoulders, tits pressed
together, the whole thing raw and sloppy and slightly embarrassing
afterward. This is what lovemaking had become, and what it now
became again. A sex columnist reduced to the act itself. There was no
talk of the other, no sense of timing. We weren't in this together; it was
the ultimate act of the self-involved. And the thing is . . . *it felt so good.*
Good enough to forget for a time the various slights and frictions of
our relationship. And that was exactly the idea.

Her eyes were closed as I pushed against her, so I closed mine as
well. And a familiar film started playing in my head . . . the third part
of a trilogy that had premiered more than a year ago. The first installment, at the beginning of things, had just one performer, an actress of
exquisite talents and wonder, a supple, apple-cheeked woman captured
in all of her sensual splendor—the fitted work shirts, the leather pants
with the lace-up zipper, and the Halloween costumes . . . oh, Cressida's Halloween costumes, always adhering to the less-is-so-much-
more principle . . . and yet these moments were more than a montage
of short-breathed lust, for this first film was about the woman, too,
the very best of her, and mixed among the visual stimulators were
salient memories, the perfect early days of our romance—the rooftop
cocktails and shared bathroom bumps, the cautious debates and gig-
gly juvenility, the mornings in bed with our laptops as we read each
other's work out loud . . . all of this captured in snapshots spliced into a
dazzling reel that played as we made love, a movie so lifelike that when
I opened my eyes—and I did open them back then, all the time—the
star, lost in her own reveries, looked every bit as beautiful as her big-
screen likeness. That first film played for months, and then the sequel
came out. Though in many ways identical to the first, some new characters had been added. Scarlett Johansson, for instance, and the hostess

at the Spotted Pig, and certain beguiling coffee-shop regulars, bare-legged in short skirts, and even, now and then, an old flame, captured in close-up at the height of her sexual powers. These faces, these *bodies,* all found screen time alongside Cressida, and though they had lesser billing, they gave the star a run for her money, thus complicating what had been a happy, straightforward plot. But Cressida being upstaged seemed only a minor detail until the third and final installment was released. Because now she had all but disappeared, been banished, like so many starlets before her, in favor of younger, sexier upstarts, a breathtaking parade of skin. And the tone had changed, too: it was rougher, edgier, one man's vision of an increasingly stark, if stunningly beautiful, world. There was no plot anymore, no theme, only a high-speed collage, more flip-book than film, sordid pop culture and porn, chaos. Ah, but the choices! If variety was absent in my real life, it now governed my imagination, and so it was that drunken night in Cressida's room, as she softly moaned below me (no doubt lost in her own cinematic ecstasy). But I couldn't settle on anything, and soon I was having trouble with the physical act itself. I could feel myself fading. Cressida pulled me toward her and took charge, offering suggestions, giving orders. She was close, and so, in an act as magnanimous as I could manage, I tried to hang on until she got there. I sped up, the bed now hitting the wall, but the film was playing too fast for the projector. Desperately, I searched for a spark, an image to build around, and then there it was, a flicker of familiarity, brown hair and piercing eyes, a pretty girl crossing a busy street, and it didn't matter that she was clothed because I was onto something, had found an actress with staying power, and it wasn't hard to change locations, trade in Madison Avenue for beaches, for bars, for the bedroom, her outfit coming slowly off, the revolutionary uncovered, her gorgeous mysteries exposed—

We came together, Cressida gasping intensely, then catching her breath, and afterward we lay there in silence. Minutes passed. I could see her column now: SHOCK & AWE—MAKEUP SEX WITHOUT THE FIGHT. Finally, she began digging herself out of the dark corner of the mattress she'd been driven into. She peeled the sheets from her sweaty skin as if peeling a Band-Aid from a wound she hoped had healed. I rolled onto my back, thought briefly of getting up to find a towel, then didn't bother.

"Good timing," I said.

"For once."

I moved to put my arm around her, but she inched away.

"Come on," I said, "can't we just enjoy the moment without—"

"Did you come here to apologize?"

"For what?"

"For *what*? Being an asshole, for starters. You disappear for days and then show up drunk in the middle of the night demanding to get laid."

"I didn't *demand* anything. You're the one who was just barking out orders."

"Oh, fuck off. That's not what I was talking about and you know it. Where were you? Are you seeing someone else?"

"No."

"Is this about those names you gave me at Malatesta? Because nothing came of those. In fact, that whole dinner was bizarre."

"What are you talking about?"

She sat up, facing me. "I'm talking about this, us. What's *happening* with us?"

"I don't know."

"Because I feel like I'm putting in all the effort here."

"That's not true," I said weakly.

"Do you even care anymore? About our relationship? About your job? Roorback's been nothing but shit for a week now. At least you used to care about not caring. Now you've given up on everything—"

I wanted to close my eyes again. It was so much better like that.

"—and it's embarrassing. Do you think my friends don't notice? They don't trust you anymore, Aidan. I mean, what am I supposed to say when they ask where you are? And who you're with?"

"Oh, you've never been at a loss for words."

"Really? Right, then. Here are five more: *Get the fuck out!*"

"That's only—"

"*Now!*"

PAIGE

· · • • • • • • • · · • •

I DROVE REFLEXIVELY, UNCONSCIOUSLY, SEEING NOTHING BUT SNAPSHOTS
of life before—

Bobby hugging me good-bye, handsome, soothing, self-assured.

Keith that first night I met him, bright eyed and full of wonder.

The way we come to trust people, men. The old schoolyard game,
falling backward from a height and knowing we'll be caught. They didn't
tell us it would never be so easy again. They didn't tell us everything
afterward would be a futile attempt to get back to that perfect moment,
the risk and certain reward.

Months of tightly wound precision, the thought before the step,
everything analyzed, every word and glance and action. I'd had enough
sense to take the money and a knife from the emergency drawer in the
kitchen, then I'd packed the laptop, the printer, and what few clothes
I had into the car. It was the car we'd driven up in months before,
through the broken country, the three of us so bent on fixing it. And
now.

I stopped for gas at a Kwik-Mart near Albany. There were no other
customers so I pulled around back and, using the car as cover, smashed
the laptop and printer on the ground, then put the pieces into a garbage
bag and tossed it into a dumpster. Everything except the hard drive: I'd
get rid of that later.

A Sunday afternoon in September and the two-lane Thruway was crowded. Still, I kept glancing across the divider. It was ridiculous, I knew. Keith always took the other route, I-91 up through Connecticut and Massachusetts, and anyway, what were the chances I'd spot their car among the thousands of others heading north? It was starting already, the sordid truth of life on the run. Relentless anxiety. Perpetual paranoia. I needed to think more clearly, become more observant. But how soon before that led to paralysis? It's hard to move when you see danger in every direction.

This was how I passed the time, with pointless games of what-if. The rest was too much to contemplate. All that had happened and still might. Movement was important, the simple act of driving. And so was the luxury of a destination. Because I knew where I was going. I'd looked up Weehawken Street before I left, and on the screen, from above, it had looked like a rotting alley, a dilapidated wharf slum that had, for whatever reason, fallen through the cracks of the sprouting metropolis. Did he really live there? And did he live alone? Every question raised a dozen more, each more troubling, more menacing, than the last. But I no longer cared. This was my only real option. If you could even call it that.

So breathe. Roll the window down. The air was cooler now; it carried remedies and resolutions. I turned on the radio—not NPR or the news, but music, an indie station out of Amherst. I didn't know the bands, but I'd never really known the bands. What was the point? They came and went so fast, you could spend a lifetime trying to keep up.

Two more hours to the bridge, then a straight shot down the West Side. I remembered a massive parking complex on a pier near Houston Street, an archaic structure with a ceiling that leaked greenish ooze (I'd borrowed an old coworker's car one weekend, years ago, and this was where she'd stored it). It was a sinister place, but now it might be a godsend if it still existed. I could park in some distant corner, then remove the license plates and scratch off the VIN inside the driver's door (it would be weeks, maybe months, before someone called a tow truck or the cops). Then I'd throw the hard drive into the Hudson, clean myself up, and walk over to Weehawken Street.

What would Aidan Cole say? Would it all end there, on that desolate block, with a curbside confrontation? Or would he invite me upstairs, then barricade me in? Behind the wheel, I felt for the knife in my pocket. It was a switchblade, but that was better than nothing. It was only a deterrent anyway. I would never use it, could nev

I just . . . theres a man outside thewindow where I'm writing thi

SOM EONES HERE . .

AIDAN

· · ●●●●●● · ·●

THERE HAD BEEN AN UPRISING OF SORTS, A GROUP OF PROMINENT ROORBACK commenters who'd banded together to admonish—or should I say abuse—me for what they perceived as a serious dip in the quality, and quantity, of my recent posts. For a while I'd ignored them, but their comments only grew more vocal, so I changed course and announced one morning that the battle had been joined. I fought back hard, railing against the most earnest and insipid among them, then "executing" the worst offenders by revoking their participatory privileges. It raised everyone's game. Dozens of pithy comments, mine included, now streamed down from every post, endless back-and-forths that often threatened, like some protracted David Foster Wallace footnote, to supersede the original text. Roorback was becoming an online cesspool, slowly draining and dangerously atrophic—except everyone was a little bit brilliant, what with the embedded literary allusions and clever turns of phrase, the meta-references and nuanced understanding of irony. To think all this energy was being wasted in the comments section of a low-culture blog. Or did that make us high-culture? Only one way to find out: throw the question to the wolves and let them chew on it awhile.

Derrick, of course, loved the increased audience participation. It livened up the site, made it truly *interactive*. He'd figure a way to monetize the trend soon enough.

"But they're basically all complaining," I told him, when he called late one Sunday afternoon to encourage me.

"Good, play that up. The commotion, the noise. Let's be rude and rile feathers."

"But if I spend all day fucking around with commenters, it'll mean less original content," I told him, glimpsing an opening.

"Fine, the comments are funnier anyway."

I took this lying down. Quite literally. I was spread across the length of my thrift-store couch, laptop on lap, muted ball game on TV, monitoring comments and prewriting the next day's posts. I'd promised my father I would drive up to help him celebrate his sixtieth birthday in Litchfield the following evening, and that meant getting the next day's quota written and uploaded before I skipped town after lunch. I wasn't worried; I'd found my blogging groove again. I'd been back from Vermont less than two weeks, but already my memories of Paige were beginning to falter. I'm not saying I was questioning events as they'd occurred, but what had occurred was so utterly bizarre that the whole thing seemed, well, *unlikely,* and never more so than at that moment, as I tried to proofread a paragraph while Derrick chattered away in my ear about Roorback's upcoming redesign—*more ad space, a broader platform, changing demographics.* To think he'd almost fired me the day after my ill-advised visit to Cressida's apartment, when Roorback.com had lain dormant for hours while I slept off a hangover that no pills or further poisons could remedy. Instead, he'd chosen to deliver a stern warning, and I had heeded it, fallen in line, gotten back to work. This was my life after all, like it or not.

We were still on the phone when the buzzer rang.

"Who's that?" Derrick asked.

"I don't know. Chinese, probably."

"You're ordering dinner? It's only five thirty."

"Lunch," I said. "I'll call you back." I hung up and walked over to the front door. I hadn't ordered any food; I just couldn't deal with Derrick. Who was this then? Cressida? No, she still wasn't speaking to me. Touché? He never visited anyone; people came to him. Most likely, it was some other marginally employed friend dropping by because he was in the neighborhood and knew I'd be home. It was the West Village, after all, and I was a blogger. Perfect prey for the Sunday drinker.

I pressed the TALK button, said, "Hello?"

There was no response. Maybe some derelict was trying to get into the foyer for a nap. Things like that still happened on Weehawken Street. Everything did. I sat back down on the couch and reached for my laptop.

The buzzer sounded again. Shrill and insistent. I marched back over to the door. *"What?"* I snapped into the box on the wall.

Nothing.

"Who is this?"

No answer.

I went to the window and opened it. Leaning out as far as I could, I scanned the street below. The sidewalks were deserted. With the exception of two men loitering near the back door of the old Badlands Video store—and as shady as they looked, they were too far away to be the culprits—the entire block was empty. Maybe the buzzer was screwed up.

I fell back onto the couch. I had more blog posts to write, and I needed to call Derrick back, but the Mets bullpen had loaded the bases and my phone was vibrating with texts concerning the evening's usual palimpsest of parties and get-togethers. I was thinking of heading to Brooklyn for a night of barhopping on Smith Street with some blogger friends. It was cheaper on that side of the river, and the girls, all ink and dye, more alluringly unique—

The buzzer, *again*! Louder still, and longer. That's it! I sprang up and out the door, took the steps three at a time, and was downstairs in fifteen seconds. I charged through the security door and the front door, and then I was outside, gazing upon exactly the same scene I'd just observed from the window. No one was around. Even the Badlands duo were gone. What the fuck? I put my hands on my hips and looked up at the sky. It was a cool, clear early-autumn day, and the sun was lingering mercifully over New Jersey, as if the state might need the extra light.

When I looked back down I saw her. She was leaning against the side of the long-abandoned gay bar across the street, a small duffel bag strewn over her shoulder, wearing skinny jeans and a snug V-neck T-shirt, and in that way that frivolous thoughts often precede important ones, I marveled at her chameleon existence, altering to fit every new environment. And then I realized what this meant, that none of this was over, and the thought paralyzed me. On some subconscious level I'd assumed that *I* was in control: if I didn't write about Paige Roderick, she would slowly fade out of existence. But here she was, casually crossing toward me. As if she lived here, too.

"Are you alone?" she asked, when she reached the sidewalk.

I looked around.

"Upstairs, I mean."

"Yes."

"No roommates?"

"It's a studio."

"What floor?"

"The top."

"There any other way out?"

"The roof, but the emergency exit door's been locked for years."

She considered this for a moment, distastefully.

"Also, hello," I said, coming around. "How are you? Nice to see you again."

She ignored me. "If I come up, how do I know you won't call the cops?"

"I might if you keep asking me that question."

Paige smiled, but so slightly that if I hadn't been staring at her, I would have missed it. I was still astonished, and not at all certain this wasn't some kind of setup. But that didn't make sense. Nothing did.

"I'll follow you inside," she said, looking down the empty block.

I could have said no, of course, could have turned around, run upstairs, and called the police. But looking back on it, I don't think that even crossed my mind. Instead, I was thinking we had to get off the street, get somewhere safe, and if that meant my apartment, then fine. What were my motivations? I could tell you they were pure or impure, but they were neither. I was only reacting. I was scared.

So in she came, trailing behind me up the stairwell, her vintage Converse high-tops so quiet that twice I turned around to make sure she was still there. At my front door she paused, steeling herself to cross the threshold, relinquish a degree of control. "It's okay," I said, trying to sound reassuring. She stepped inside and the door closed behind her.

We stood there awkwardly. Ten minutes earlier I'd been monitoring a commenter debate over which Jonas brother was more likely to end up in rehab, and now . . .

"Here, sit," I said, gesturing at the couch.

"I'm fine." She was still near the door. I had no idea what to do. I almost wanted to put on music, open some wine, make small talk—the reflex of so many bachelor years in New York, to make the girl comfortable, set her at ease: *keep her there.* I was disconcerted, and not, initially, by the many questions and complexities surrounding her sudden appearance, but, again, by the simple fact of her beauty. It was entrancing. Her deep brown eyes flitted about the apartment, taking in each poorly painted wall, glancing into dusty corners, then up at my sleeping loft. Watching her, I thought I saw a trace of desperation, and all at once I realized the trouble *she* must be in. To be coming here. To me.

"Do you want some water or something?"

She didn't respond. She was still scanning the room, and I turned away to let her judge me in privacy. It didn't take long, and I can only imagine the conclusions she reached—the ball game still on, the laptop surrounded by tortilla chips and cheap magazines, old newspapers stacked on an old chair, and the absurdly small bookshelf lacking in anything substan—

"I'm not sure how to do this," she said. "How to talk to you."

"About what?" I asked dumbly.

"I need you to do something. But first I need to know *why.* I just . . . it doesn't make sense. You ardently pursue me, and then, when you've actually tracked me down, you don't go public or tell the cops. Do you know the trouble you could be in? What if the Feds came crashing through your door and found us here together? What if I'd been tailed or something?"

"Were you?"

"Of course not."

"How do you know?"

Paige walked over to the counter that separated my small kitchen from the rest of the space (such as it was). She pulled out a bar stool and balanced against it.

"Twenty-five years," she said. "Minimum. That's the punishment for harboring a suspected terrorist."

"Are you trying to scare me?"

"Yes."

"But I don't even know what you did."

"That's not what you said back at the fair."

"I was bluffing."

I came over and took a seat on the only other stool. It was almost like we were flirting, neither of us sure how to get past preliminaries to the substance of the situation. The horrible enormity of it. It must sound strange, I know, but Paige's involvement in the bombing never seemed less likely than at that moment, when she was closest.

"Tell me why you came here," I said.

"Do you smoke?"

"Not really. I don't have any, if that's what you're asking."

"Okay then, a beer?"

"Sure."

I walked around the counter and opened the fridge. Several Miller Lites lay strewn across the bottom shelf. I grabbed two, twisted off their caps, and slid one across the cheap Formica. I almost said *Cheers,* then thought better of it.

"So tell me," I tried again. I was still in the kitchen, the counter between us.

She took a long sip, like a sip in a commercial, and when she put the bottle down, she pushed her long bangs to the side of her face. "A lack of better options, I guess."

"That's the name of a friend of mine's band. But with a *the.* The Lack of Better Options."

"Cute," she said.

"Do you live here, in New York, in more . . . um . . . *normal* circumstances?"

"No. I did, once."

"What part of town?"

"Seriously? *That's* what you want to know?"

"I'm just making conversation. You're not exactly chatty."

She exhaled audibly, then swiveled on the stool and faced me head-on. "Okay. Listen carefully. I'm going to tell you what I know about the bombing, and I want you to break the story on Roorback."

"*What?*"

"I want you to expose me. Expose the entire operation."

"But that would be suicide."

"Perhaps, but if you don't . . . well, if you don't, it'll get much worse."

"What do you mean?"

"There's another bomb," she said, in the same even tone that an ex-girlfriend had once used to tell me she was pregnant. "And this one . . . I need to stop it, stop *them*."

"Your *compatriots*?"

"They were, yes."

"And you, what, grew a conscience? Lost your nerve? Found the Lord?"

Paige smiled introspectively. "You make it all sound like a whim, a little phase. Tell me, Aidan—it is Aidan, right?—when was the last time you believed in something?"

"I believed you were real, and then I chased you across New England."

She sighed. I waited. "I'm sorry, you're right. I didn't mean to sound accusatory. It's just that . . ." She cleared her throat. "We were talking about the bomb. The next one. It's supposed to go off this coming Saturday night. If I tell you what I know, will you post it?"

"Why the sudden reversal?"

"Because this one's designed to kill."

We took things slowly. Information. Revelation. She was backing off a precipice and hadn't yet found solid ground. A place to rest. I turned off the TV and tried to tidy up on the fly, cursing myself for having no candles or aromatic anythings. It was such a guy's place, but she didn't seem to notice. When I finally sat down on the couch, she moved there, too, taking a seat at the far end so as to keep the space between us—the *worlds* between us—intact.

"Is it always so noisy?" she asked, looking out through the open window. The sky was darker now and empty over the river.

"I guess. With the highway and all. I can close the window."

"No, it's fine. I'm just not used to it anymore."

"Talk about not used to things. You should have seen me in Vermont, this cabin I had back in the woods."

"I did," she said.

She grinned, but it was cursory. She was already someplace else. I waited, and when she started to speak, I didn't interrupt. Her story began in North Carolina, with a ragtag group of environmental activists, then migrated north. She spoke in short bursts—Keith and Lindsay; targets and Actions—and it sounded, from her lips, like a logical progression of events. Until you placed them in a larger context. Until you actually realized what she was talking about, trying to accomplish: awaken a country by violently exposing its sinister soul. It was beyond the realm of rational human behavior. Yet she seemed, as she recounted her exploits, far saner than most people I knew. As for the bombing itself? However despicable the method, it was hard to argue with the results. America was now keenly attuned to Indigo's sins. The way Paige and her cohorts had played the press was brilliant, and for an unsettling moment, I glimpsed common ground between us—that deep and abiding distrust of the media. But, Jesus, the ways we'd gone about addressing it!

Paige began to relax. She settled into the cushions, accepted some chips and salsa. And she kept talking, unburdening herself: Internet protocols, dynamite runs, fake identities. She explained the growing rift between her and the others, the human toll of so much pressure. Then she told me about the shrapnel-sprinkled bomb. And what it was meant for. She stiffened, bracing as if for judgment. But she already knew what I thought. My open mouth, my visible shock, said it all.

She'd arrived back at the reason she'd come: the Roorback exposé. It was the only way she could stop the next Action without turning herself in.

"I want you to write the truth about everything," she said, "except for this—my being here. Tell them you got the information out of me up in Vermont and have spent the intervening time trying to confirm the details. And one more thing: don't post the story for at least twenty-four hours. I need a head start."

"Where are you—?"

"*Don't*. It's best that way. Just do exactly what I told you and you'll be on the *Today* show before the week's out. Now, do you have any questions? Because it's important you get the facts right."

"No." I had a million.

"Okay, then." She put her hand out and I shook it. It felt more like a dare than a deal. "I'm going now."

"*Wait,*" I said. "You can spend the night. Take the bed, I'll sleep on the couch."

"Thanks, but I need to keep moving."

"Come on. It's getting late. You'll be safer here than anywhere else. I'll write your story first thing in the morning, and you can proof it yourself. Plus, I'm renting a car to drive up to Connecticut tomorrow, so I can give you a ride out of the city."

She cocked her head to the side. Had she hoped I'd ask her to stay? I couldn't tell. "You're really not expecting anyone?"

"Now? No. This isn't a hotel."

I could see her thinking, weighing risks. The scale hung low on both sides.

"I need a cigarette."

"I'll get you some."

"And a shower."

"Go right ahead."

She rubbed her eyes, then brushed her bangs back again.

"You won't fuck me over?"

"I won't, I promise."

Maybe she believed me. Or maybe she had nowhere else to go. Either way, her demeanor changed. She sank back into the couch and drew her legs up under her.

"Do you want some wine?" I asked.

"Sure."

I walked over to the kitchen, opened a bottle of red, and poured two glasses. Then I scanned through iTunes and landed on Bowie's "Life on Mars?" Applicable, I thought, clicking PLAY.

I brought the wine over, handed her a glass, and retreated to my side of the couch. We sipped in awkward silence. What, I wondered, had led her so astray, this perfect daughter of America? She'd glossed over that part—the beginning, the idyllic before. I was about to ask about her childhood, but she beat me to it.

"It's your turn to talk," she said.

"What do you want to know?"

"Whatever you want to tell me. Start with your family."

And so I did. Like Shakespeare, I began with the secondary characters—my parents' current spouses and lovers—and went from there, working backward through time. It seemed easier that way, and less complicated. Julie and my father, Simon and my mother. Paige gazed back and forth between me and the window, *through* me and the window, but I had the feeling she was listening intently. At some point on the reverse time line, I arrived at my city childhood, that liberal-family ideal, then further back still, to my parents' early activism, hoping it might stir Paige. But it didn't. The gap was too great, the past too far away.

I got up and changed the music. A Brooklyn band she'd never heard of. I floated the idea of ordering food, and Paige responded enthusiastically, even perching beside me on the couch as I shuffled through a dozen menus (we settled on a down-market pizza place because they also sold cigarettes). It was the first time we'd been together for more than a few seconds without something between us—cushions or a countertop. She was feeling more comfortable.

The buzzer rang a half hour later. I went down to intercept the deliveryman, and when I got back, Paige was scrolling through the music on my computer.

"I can't remember the last time I went to a concert," she said.

"Well, you can't go now."

"Oh, I don't know. Crowds can be the safest places."

"You wouldn't even let the pizza guy come upstairs."

"Fair enough." She smiled, mouth wide, teeth so white, so American.

I brought two of my three existing plates over to the coffee table and we ate. For a while we talked about what everyone else talks about, books and movies, who'd gotten married, who'd died. She knew a lot, her long days online more than compensating for her off-the-grid seclusion. I poured more wine, and when she went to the bathroom, I dimmed the lights just a bit. If she noticed—of course she noticed— she didn't say anything. The conversation slowly devolved, from the uptown of my youth to the downtown of the present, and that's when she began retreating, her eyes glassing over—that thousand-yard stare in a three-hundred-square-foot room. When I asked a question and she didn't respond at all, I put my glass down and said her name.

"Sorry," she said, snapping out of wherever she'd been.

"It's okay. We can talk later."

"No, no. It's just . . . God . . . you must think I'm crazy."

"Not crazy. But I can't pretend to understand. Why, I mean."

"I don't expect you to," she said quietly, as if it were all too much to articulate.

"Fine. We can keep talking about nothing if you want. I'm good at it, believe me. I can go all night."

"But what *would* you understand? What do you *want* to understand? I've read Roorback, Aidan. You don't see the world I see. Our experiences are so different—what we've lost, and loved. And still love. Do you really want my worldview? Because it's pretty bleak these days. Everything I once saw as a problem with others—the numbness, the detachment, the disillusionment that came with being American— everything I once sought to fix . . . I'm coming now to feel myself. The horrible realization that you really can't change anything or trust any- one. We've become a nation that buckles down and endures instead of rearing up, instead of revolting against unacceptable circumstances. And why? Because no one will lead the way: the poor are too weighed down by the task of survival, and the wealthy will never challenge a system that's taken such good care of their interes—"

"Come on, seriously, not that old argument. The rich do plenty."

"They marry trophy wives and move to Connecticut."

"And what, besides the obvious, is the problem with that?" I asked. "My father's allowed to do what he wants. He worked his whole life to earn the privilege. You can't just invent a revolution because people are complacent. Tell me, what's so bad out there? Most people actually get by. Sure, they've got their meth labs and their shitty mortgages, but *they manage.* Christ, America's one big sprawling suburb, and it's hard for me to look at it and conclude that the system—capitalism or democracy or whatever you're fighting—doesn't work for the majority of the people."

"And a majority is enough?"

"In a strikingly imperfect world? Yes, a majority is fucking great. Look, I'm not saying we've perfected anything here, but, hell, half the rest of the planet's in flames."

Paige lit a cigarette and leaned forward, into the argument, as if trying to swallow it. Did I sound as stupid as I feared, spouting watery platitudes straight out of freshman poli-sci? But how else to talk politics with a stranger, or present a middle ground to a fanatic? Yet, in truth, I couldn't remember the last time I'd had a conversation like this. Thousands of hours huddled over drinks in bars, thousands more serving them, and all that time *talking* . . . but about what exactly? Sure there'd been a groundswell of hope surrounding Obama a few years back, visions of a fresh start and all that, but hope always ended badly in America, or at least got bogged down in Congress. Really, I wondered—indeed had adopted as a mantra—what was the point of getting involved at all? If the American game wasn't rigged, per se, it was certainly out of our hands.

"Look," I said, "systemic change is an earned thing, fought for over decades. That way, the big victories—civil rights, say, or legalized abortion—are nearly impossible to overturn, and major policy mistakes, like Prohibition, or Vietnam, or, to some extent, Iraq, don't come along that often, and don't cripple us when they do."

"To some extent?"

"Well, recognizing that there are viable arguments for and against. Not that I was pro-war"—Paige had stubbed out her cigarette and was getting up, brushing off her jeans—"I mean, Afghanistan, obviously, we should have, but . . . where are you going?"

She'd grabbed her duffel bag and started looking around the room for anything else. Evidence of her presence in such contemptible company. There was none.

"I'm sorry. I can't do this, can't stay here. It's my fault, I should never have come."

"Wait, what did I say?" I stood up, dumbfounded.

She was moving toward the door. "I was trying to understand, on your level, on any level, but—"

"You can't go out there. They'll find you and—"

"—it turns out you're just like everyone else I've met in this city, in *every* city, completely oblivious until it's too late—"

"—that'll be it. You don't have a car now or any place to stay."

"—and only then do you wake up and see the empty horror of the whole thing—"

"Paige."

"—only when it's you they bankrupt, only when—"

"*Paige!*"

"—it's your brother they kill."

We were both standing by the door. At some point, as we'd spoken over each other, I had grabbed her wrist, and now I let it go. She looked at the reddening marks on her skin and said nothing. Her hair was hiding her eyes, her tears.

"Will you . . ." I started. "I'm sorry . . . I . . . your brother died?"

She didn't answer. I reached for her, but she raised her arms protectively.

"Please," I said, as softly as I could. "Come sit. There's nowhere to go. Not tonight."

She shifted her weight, one leg to the other, and sighed, long and heavy. It was the saddest sound, the sound of a person who'd reached the end, then realized she had to continue. And so she did, one step at a time, back to the couch. She put her face in her hands and let the tears flow freely. I poured her a glass of water, rounded up the rest of the napkins that had come with the food (of course I had no paper towels), and brought them over. I'd have left her alone, but there was no place to retreat to, so I just sat down next to her and tried not to cause more damage.

"I'm sorry," she said, managing an embarrassed smile. "This is the first time I've cried in ages, but . . . it's been such a long year."

And I said, "I know." I wanted to tell her to *just let it out*. But how do you say that to someone like her? Anyway, she was starting to laugh, in that wrenching female way that can come after tears, opposite emotions following one another so brutally quickly.

"I don't suppose you have any hair clips," she said, pushing her bangs back off her forehead again. She picked up a napkin. "I shouldn't have said any of that. About you. About my brother. *But he's why, Aidan.*"

"Tell me what happened."

"Do you really want to know? Do you really want any of this? Me, here? Because it's not too late. I can still . . ." But it was too late, and she knew it. She took a sip of water, slipped off her shoes, and this time, when she began to speak, she started at the beginning.

With her father. And her mother. He was a soldier back from Vietnam. She was a wife who had waited. Paige's parents had grown up in the mountains, and after the war they settled down there. They had a son, then a daughter, both bouncy and curious, test cases for a developing theory of how to live. Paige's father was no radical—he would end up working for years as a floor manager at the BorgWarner plant in Asheville—and yet he felt America had somehow let him down, in wartime and peace, its shortsighted policies steering the world toward some not-too-distant cataclysm. So he focused his family on what *could* be known and understood—the land itself—and brother and sister, a year apart but together in all else, spent their youth outdoors, the boy a champion of the physical world, the girl capable, too, but shy, and more bookish. . . .

Paige was lapsing into a Southern accent, and I told her so. She smiled as she caught the insinuation: that the layers were beginning to peel.

"Keith was big on stamping out our roots," she said. "It was another way to blend in, become some formless other. Accents, habits, hobbies. We even had different names, though Lindsay's the only one who actually had to use hers. Mine's Isabel Clarke, which is what you should call me if we're ever in public."

"Isabel Clarke," I repeated. The words produced a thrilling shudder.

Paige filled me in on Isabel's San Francisco backstory, then returned to her own, which had entered a phase familiar to me: a series of unfocused college years, followed by a move to New York, where she rented an apartment on the hip and vulgar Lower East Side—my town, my people.

"This was the year after 9/11," she said.

"I was living in Brooklyn back then. Williamsburg."

"I could have guessed."

"But I was in your neighborhood a lot, too," I told her. "Luna Lounge, Motor City, Casimir." The idea that we'd been circling in the same spheres, that in previous incarnations we might have brushed past each other in a restaurant, on a sidewalk—except a previous incarnation assumes some kind of metamorphosis. And I'd just been carousing on Rivington Street a few nights before.

"I didn't go out much," Paige said. "Or I did in the beginning, but . . . I don't know, I was working a lot."

"Where?"

"At the Earth Initiative. It's a research institute funded by a group of billionaire entrepreneur-turned-philanthropists."

"The Gang of Six," I said.

"Well, then, you know."

"It's in the news all the time."

"Exactly," Paige said, smirking. And now it was my turn to pick up the insinuation. "I read an article about their global-warming campaign when I was a senior at UNC and then wrote to the director, Carl Cleary, asking for a job. When I didn't hear back, I called his office and pretended I was Angelina Jolie's assistant. I guess I knew even then what these people responded to, because a minute later I had Cleary's private e-mail, which I then used to let him know he shouldn't be blowing off politically engaged twenty-one-year-olds. He should be *meeting* with them, *talking* to them . . ."

"Let me guess: he hired you on the spot."

"Yup. To be their Web researcher, scouring blogs, videos, articles . . . anything pertaining to the causes we championed—alternative fuels, poverty reduction, disease control, debt cancellation. It was the dream job. Suddenly, instead of sex-crazed college kids, I was surrounded by these brilliant young people with a very different kind of energy, people who not only thought about the future, but believed it was malleable: if we just worked hard enough and shouted loud enough, the rest of America would come around. We armed ourselves with statistics and projections and wrote brilliant position papers that became keynote addresses in Davos, in Aspen, anywhere that money met with good intentions. But our *timing* was off. The world after 9/11 had more immediate concerns, like self-preservation, like revenge. It's hard to fight smallpox in Africa when you're worried about anthrax coming in the mail or dirty bombs detonating down the street. And then, of course, there was Iraq . . . and *still* there's Iraq . . . and it was just so hard to be *heard,* through the war and all it bred, the patriotism and cynicism, half the nation jumping feverishly on board, the other half turning shamefully away. Or *not* shamefully. Just not caring at all. The worse the war, the better the mood! Americans stuffing themselves on food and pleasure, on voyeurism and celebrity. So I guess it was inevitable that Carl Cleary would hit the road with Bono, with Beckham—"

"With Angelina Jolie."

"Indeed," Paige said. "We need sex to sell even poverty initiatives."

"Well, you were doing a lot more than the rest of us. I spent my first decade in New York making drinks and banner ads. I couldn't even get through journalism school."

"Oh, dear."

"Right?"

"But, Aidan, I wanted those things, too. Or not *those* things exactly, but something like them. A life I could recognize, slip into. Normal stuff: dating, dinners, shopping. Don't get me wrong, I had boyfriends—a painter, a city planner, even a banker—"

"Brendan Carlyle. I met him."

"That's right. I can't believe you tracked him down. Anyway, I kept trying, but I just never quite *fit in*. Story of my life, I guess. I wasn't glossy enough, and when I was, it was an act. The Pucci dresses. The skinny jeans. See?" She rubbed her thighs. "I'd go to dinner parties and pick at them under the table, like the denim was the problem. And above the table all the talk was about work: fashion and real estate, publishing and PR. I felt like I had to keep my job a secret lest I *bore* people. And so I gradually built up this animosity toward everything. I stopped going out. What was the point? Just to get laid? My neighborhood had become a film set, and my generation, all these kids skidding and stumbling through the time of their lives, had let the decade get away. Or maybe, I finally decided, the problem was me. Which is when I left for grad school in D.C. The Johns Hopkins School of Advanced International Studies. It's full of aspiring diplomats and spies. But they had a good development program, and I wanted to work on third-world environmental problems."

"Did you?"

"Eventually, yes. After two years in school—and fifty-five thousand in student loans—I found a job at an environmental-policy think tank called the Carver Institute. My business card read DEVELOPING NATIONS INITIATIVES ANALYST, and yet I never got to leave the country. I could speak for hours about the seasonal air quality in Bangladesh, but not a word about the place itself. What it looked like, smelled like. It took me six months to figure out that think tanks were really just retirement homes for history's political also-rans, and still,

I stayed three years, working twelve-hour days, just giving myself over to causes. But no one was paying attention—not the U.S. government, and consequently, not the rest of the world. I mean, how could the Bush administration sit there with a straight face and ask the Chinese to burn less coal? Or demand that India raise emissions standards?" Paige paused. "Bobby was stationed overseas by then, and I used to come home to my shitty Dupont Circle apartment and watch the news and . . ." She turned her palms faceup—a reflexive pleading, an unwitting prayer. Her soft, dark eyes, glassy ponds again, threatened to spill over with every rippling thought.

"We don't have to talk about this," I said. "It's late."

But she shook her head stubbornly, almost violently, and I knew that whatever she was about to tell me was being said for the first time. Wasn't it always easier to confide in a stranger? Or was I now a friend? I poured what remained of the wine into our empty glasses, but she didn't notice.

"You have to remember," she began, feeling her way along, "that Bobby was the son of a soldier. And no matter what else happens in your life, that fact stays with you, especially if you're a man. None of his friends thought he should go. They were all antiwar, and so was my brother, to an extent. He was still at Appalachian State when 9/11 happened, and it changed his thinking, turned it a bit. In all our years together, I'd never heard him defend the government; his relationship to America was more physical, even spiritual, as if he'd reached an understanding with the land itself and didn't much care who laid a larger claim to it. But when I came home that first Thanksgiving after the attacks, there were tinges of patriotism in his dinner-table opinions. And afterwards, he and my father would stay up late, talking in the study, arguing with ghosts. Painful history. Wars fought and to come. This was before Iraq, of course, when Afghanistan was the only looming battleground, and Bobby told us he was thinking about the National Guard. He could get money for school, he said, and when he graduated, still be more or less a normal citizen. If he got called up—and really, what were the chances?—Afghanistan, to his mind, was a worthy fight. My father wasn't so sure. Every war seemed worthy before people started dying, he said. But, in the end, Bobby prevailed. We'd been raised to abhor organized religion, and Al Qaeda and the Taliban represented its horrific extreme. My brother believed they qualified as enemies in a way that domino-effect communists never quite had.

"And then, as soon as he signed his papers, Iraq came along, and Bobby and half a million others were suddenly trapped like lab rats, awaiting a fate they'd never fathomed. The greatest bait and switch in American history, my father called it, but still, we weren't overly worried. Iraq would be a video game played by generals with joysticks: find Saddam and it was over. Bobby finished his last two years of school and took a job as a park ranger. He spent his Saturdays at the local armory and every few months drove down to Gastonia for more formal weapons training. But that was the extent of it. The wars dragged on. Other National Guard units were fighting, but another year passed without Bobby being contacted. What an awful time, the never knowing, like some endless game of Russian roulette. It's weird to say, but when the call finally came, it was almost a relief. Bobby was living up in Boone with his friend Carter Gattling, and they were basically off the grid—no phone, no TV, no Internet—but my dad drove up there, against every instinct he had, and got him. I flew back home the weekend before he left for Fort Dix, and between the Raleigh airport and Maggie Valley I must have driven past a hundred yellow ribbons and SUPPORT OUR TROOPS signs. It was as if every house had a child in uniform, and I guess that should have been comforting—that we weren't alone—but it just made everything worse. This was the end of 2005, and the news seemed so bleak; the war had turned, and the idiots who'd authored it had been reelected. Here it was, exactly what my father had feared, but still he put on a brave face. We all did. The North Carolina National Guard was part of the 505th Engineer Combat Battalion, which served as support—'round out,' they call it—for the 101st Airborne. Bobby was being deployed to Kirkuk, near Kurdistan. Back then, Kirkuk was one of the war's few success stories, and his company had orders to keep it that way. That meant patrolling borders and training Iraqi soldiers, but also building schools, polling stations, community centers. Most of the hard fighting would be south of him, in Baghdad and Fallujah. There was nothing to worry about, he told us the night before he left, as my parents and I moved food around our plates. He'd be doing the same thing he'd been doing up in Boone: policing the wilderness. Only now he'd have a better uniform.

"And he was right," Paige continued. "He got through his first tour without a scratch. In his e-mails to me, he actually sounded like he was getting something out of it. The rebuilding process, the starting over. He befriended Iraqi families—traded gifts, accepted blessings—even stayed in touch with them when he finally came home."

"To Carolina?"

"Yeah. Fifteen months overseas and he slipped back into his old life like it was a sock. Same job, same friends, same apartment. He came to see me in D.C., and I marveled at how comfortable he was moving between his army life and his antiwar friends. The awful truth of the larger picture. The hopeful moments of the smaller ones. He was trying to arrange for an orphaned Iraqi boy to be brought over, a child whose parents had been killed by American bombs. Bobby's unit had taken the kid under its wing as a kind of amulet, a reminder of the good they could do. But the boy disappeared from a refugee camp before the red tape could be cut, and Bobby, he was just so . . . *deflated*. That he couldn't help one troubled kid in a nation full of them. In '08 he got called for his second tour, and there was never a question as to whether he'd go. Other guardsmen were deserting, guys he knew and respected, but Iraq had gotten under my brother's skin in a way I'll never understand. At home, there were more late-night talks, a father and son with a war between them—a war fading quickly from America's consciousness. Part of it was the recession, part pure exhaustion. The surge had mostly worked, and the only thing that remained was to shore up the Iraqi army, then get the hell out. But wars never end as scheduled, especially stalemates. Thousands died in Vietnam while politicians argued over wording, how to position the retreat. The insurgency never quit in Southeast Asia, and it hadn't quit in Iraq either. The most dangerous time for soldiers, my father once said, is when their country forgets they're still fighting."

It was quiet out on Weehawken Street. What time was it? I had no idea. Reality had fallen away. There was only Paige now, her agonizing truth revealing itself in slow motion. All that remained was the awful end.

And so she steeled herself to carry through. The tears were flowing again, tears as sad and brave as any I could imagine. She described the broken land Bobby returned to: nothing standing, nothing left.

His unit worked for a year, taking it town by town—digging wells and clearing rubble. He wrote when he could and called every few weeks, his despondency coming clear through the crackle and static of the satellite phone. Something terrible was going to happen.

Then it did.

"The army incident report called it a 'perfect ambush,'" Paige said. "A roadside bomb exploding in a gutted village north of Mosul. The bodies and debris from the lead truck blocked the narrow street, and the remaining vehicles in Bobby's convoy had no choice but to try to back out. The snipers opened fire immediately, from windows and rooftops, from everywhere. They blew out the tires, then took aim at the men. A dozen heavily armed Americans—my brother among them—fired back through the smoke, and soon the fight moved from the streets to the surrounding buildings, room by room, the insurgents fading through walls, into tunnels, underneath the endless sand.

"A period of time passed with no shooting, and I've always wondered if the Americans let their guard down. In the investigation that followed, the battalion leader said he thought they'd cleared the area, but there was a lot of confusion, obviously. They were commandeering an abandoned house when someone heard a noise upstairs. The soldiers followed the sound, peering around corners, weapons twitching, ready for the first sign of movement, anything, anything at all, and then they turned another corner . . ."

Paige stopped, and when she spoke again, it was without emotion.

"Several weapons discharged in the chaos, but the army never did identify the shooter. The killer. It didn't really matter; his uniform was enough. That he was one of ours. After that, what difference does it make?"

I went over to her then, put my hand on her shoulder, *around* her shoulder, and when we hugged, it was like the hug at the end of time, or the dawn of it, when there's nothing left to say because we know too much, or we know nothing, and maybe that's the same thing. At some point, red-eyed and exhausted, Paige stretched her feet out and lay down. I spread a blanket over her and turned the lights off. Then I climbed the ladder to bed. God only knows what she was thinking about, dreaming about: *what she knew*. I couldn't digest what I'd heard, beyond the awful facts, and then I could, just one thing: the fact of her, lying there, when she could have been anywhere.

I lay awake in my bed beneath the ceiling. Paige lay across the room in the darkness. When I'd tried to shut the window—the breeze off the river had picked up—she'd stopped me, and now, in the silence, I realized why: *she wanted to hear them coming.* The thought shook me. That someone could live like that. I listened for her breathing, her movements, because there's no way she could have fallen right asleep. Alone and on the run. In a stranger's house, in a city of millions, every person a potential threat, the one who could snatch away her freedom. But didn't she have it coming? New York was only returning the favor for the damage she'd done, physically and psychologically. A building bombed and a city made to face itself again, face the questions that still lingered—about our larger lives, risk and safety and the order of things. For a few days she had shocked us back to reality, she had terrified us to our core.

The grinding night. Another hour passed. I felt rushed and overwhelmed, at odds with everything. What was I doing? What had I done? Men were spilling out of the bars onto Christopher Street, their laughter echoing up the block. Cars charged up the highway toward the all-night dance clubs in Chelsea. Everything I should have asked, coming at me now. Questions about consequences, about power and authority; about how this all would end. What a strange sensation, being in that room with her. It was something I could feel, right there in the pitch-black, a kind of pulsing glow, coming not from the radioactive woman on the couch, but from somewhere else. Inside me.

AIDAN

. . . ● ● ● ● ● ● . ● ● . . .

"AIDAN."

I opened my eyes, barely conscious. Where was I? In my own bed, it seemed, and alone, so who just called my name? And what happened last—

"Aidan, come on, wake up."

"I am. Awake."

PAIGE RODERICK! I sat up and bumped my head on the ceiling as I peered bleary-eyed into the room below. She was sitting at the kitchen counter, writing something on the notepad I used for messages.

"You always get up so late?" she asked, without looking up.

"What time is it?"

"Seven fifteen."

"Christ."

"You'd make a terrible radical, sleeping so soundly."

"Yeah, well . . ." She had changed shirts, though the jeans and sneakers were the same. And her hair was wet: she'd *showered*. How had I slept through that? I climbed down carefully and put coffee on. The apartment smelled like shampoo; it smelled like hope. Paige asked if she could get online. I motioned to my laptop, and soon she was clicking through news headlines.

"Just public sites," she said. "Don't worry, I won't log in to anything."

How long had I slept? Two hours? Three? I felt exhausted. I needed to assess things, regroup, so I excused myself to take a shower of my own. Freed from her immediate presence, her engulfing physicality, I stood under a stream of hot water, closed my eyes, and tried to clear my head. . . . And then it hit me, nearly knocked me over: *that she'd actually done it!* She really had set off a bomb, and still I hadn't turned her away, or turned her in. But *why*? There is no absolute answer, even in hindsight. I knew I was acting foolishly, and I understood, at least hypothetically, the potential consequences of my decisions. But neither fact had dissuaded me (after all, I hadn't been involved in—or in any way condoned—what she'd done and could therefore, I believed, still claim some kind of ignorance). I was just going with the drift of things, as I had—as everyone I knew had—for years. At the same time, I began to take hold of my situation. I felt sharper and more present, and if I could pinpoint a moment, not when my mind-set changed, but when the *potential* for that change occurred, perhaps it was then, wet and still waking, as the awe and confusion began to wash away. And if the reasons I attached to my thinking weren't exactly pure—I was acting out of hormonal self-interest as much as any muscular altruism—well, at least I was doing something. Or about to. I had never been in a position to play savior before, and as scared as I was—and I was terrified—the role appealed to me.

Let me put it another way: I suddenly couldn't bear the thought of her leaving.

I dried off and dressed and emerged from the bathroom. She was reading through what she'd just written, her back to me.

"I've listed the key points you should include," she said, without turning around. "Everything I know about the N3 Action, and enough about Indigo so the authorities will believe you. And now I need to go. Thanks for, you know . . ." She nodded toward the couch, immaculate now, the blanket folded on the armrest as if a soldier had slept there.

"*Stay.*"

"It's okay, I don't need a ride anywhere."

"I mean . . . for longer."

She sighed. "This isn't a game, Aidan. Just do what we discussed. Post the thing when you get back tomorrow. That'll give me enough time to get away. The Feds will show up here pretty quickly after it appears, but just do as they say and you'll be fine. I wiped down the counter and the couch area while you were showering, so they won't find any prints."

She picked up her bag and took a last look around the room.

"What if I *don't* write it?"

Paige went still. "Then people will die."

"And if I do, Keith and Lindsay will just come out of hiding with their hands up and call it a day? From what you've told me, I seriously doubt it."

"Yes, but they'll have been *exposed*. By tomorrow night, their names and faces will decorate every precinct wall in the city. There'll be a manhunt under way. And N3's headquarters? They won't be able to get near the place. It'll be a fortress."

"But the cops will be looking for you, too."

"I'll take my chances. Anyway . . . it's not like I'm innocent in all this."

"You weren't trying to kill people either."

"No. Somewhere back there, I was trying to help them." For a moment she looked wistful, lost, but just as quickly she recovered and started for the door. "It's too early for this conversation. Or too late. Just write the post. If it makes you feel better, don't include my photograph. They'll dig it up later, though, in your hard drive or on Roorback's server. They'll find pictures of Keith and Lindsay, too. Everyone exists somewhere else, even them."

"*Stay,*" I said, again. "Until I get back."

"*No.*"

"Fine, but I'm not writing anything. Not yet."

Where was this coming from? It was more than desire, I realized. It was the culmination of months—of years—of hyperactive stasis, running in circles on an oval-shaped island, twelve posts a day, four parties a week, and a personal life in permanent flux. A decade had passed in the back of countless cabs, at fancy dinners and midnight pizzerias; the drug dipping and surprisingly functional alcoholism that consumed our nights and destroyed our mornings; nothing stimulating, nothing surprising, our thirties spreading out before us like our twenties, but with the lessons still unlearned. We were a tough lot to teach. We only listened to ourselves.

I keep saying *we,* when what I mean is *I.*

I was thinking of everything. I wasn't thinking at all.

"What are you trying to do?" she said, her voice suddenly flat as a steppe.

"There has to be another way. One that doesn't involve you ruining your life."

"No, I mean . . ." She was gesturing toward me, past me. I turned around. I had unintentionally—or at least subconsciously—gravitated to the front of the apartment and was now standing between Paige and the door.

"Oh, I didn't mean to . . . here, you can go, of course, if you want, I was just . . ." I turned sideways, made a sweeping motion with my arm. She didn't move, which I took as a sign to keep talking. "I was just thinking," I sputtered, "that, well, maybe you—maybe *we*—could, I don't know, try to stop Keith ourselves. Before he plants the bomb."

She frowned. "I have no idea where he is."

"So, we'll figure it out. Look, I'll only be in Connecticut one night. You can stay here, relax, sleep, figure things out, whatever. And if you haven't come up with something by the time I get back tomorrow morning, then I'll write the blog post. There'll still be time. You said it yourself: the original action was planned for this coming Saturday night."

"It's not safe, Aidan."

"Outside this door is where it's not safe. Do you even have a place to go?"

"I meant that it's not safe for *you,*" she said, ignoring my question. "Having me here. Everything's coming undone. Forget the cops for a second. And the FBI. We still don't know who sent you my picture. It's just . . . it's not the time to sit tight."

No, it wasn't. I'd been sitting tight my entire life.

Paige had this sweet, sour look on her face, at once tender and slightly patronizing. Or maybe she really was conflicted. Because she still wasn't moving.

"One more night," I said. "And when I get back, if Keith and Lindsay haven't been caught, or you haven't come up with another way to stop them, I'll write the post, and then you . . . you can disappear forever."

She rolled her neck and rubbed her eyes. She looked outside, then back at me. "I wish you'd listen to what I'm saying."

"I have been listening."

"This isn't what I want."

"I realize."

She sighed. I waited.

"Fine," she said. "Do you have anything for breakfast?"

We ate eggs and drank coffee, and afterward I uploaded the posts I'd written before Paige showed up, time-stamping them to appear at intervals throughout the day (the last thing I needed was Derrick on my case). I didn't want to leave the apartment and let this strange dream reach its inevitable end. Still, there was my life, and in the late morning I told Paige I needed to run a few errands, then head over to Charles Street to pick up my rental car. She could come, of course, but—

"Aidan, no."

"I didn't think so. Make yourself at home then. I'll bring back some lunch."

"Okay," she said. "I'll be here."

And so I donned a hoodie and left her. The morning was crisp and cloudless . . . and suddenly surreal. How disconcerting it had been, the two of us in that small apartment together, like the morning after a one-night stand—the shy backpedaling after the drunken deed, knowing everything and nothing, too much and too little. I walked east on Christopher, past dog walkers and squealing schoolchildren, past mothers pushing babies, past a cop at the entrance to the PATH. I nodded to him out of habit, then, a half block later, cursed my stupidity. I was at the corner of Hudson Street and had forgotten what I needed to do. Drugstore, wine store, supermarket. Spare keys at the hardware store (Cressida had my other set), a stop-off at the dry cleaner. I hurried from place to place, two lists in my head, for two lives—mine and Paige's, the mundane and the outlandish. I was drawn to her, both *because of* and *despite* who she was, what she believed. But what *did* she believe? How much of all this was a symptom of her grief? And how much came from the woman underneath? Suddenly, I wanted to run home and ask her, run home and see her, just run home. But I stayed out, stayed away. Give her space, some time to breathe, or bolt. I considered heading over to Paul Smith to find my father a birthday present, but like every man with money and a young wife, he was almost impossible to shop for, stuck as he was between styles and generations, the acceptable and unseemly. Taste, which had once emanated from him, was no longer in evidence in Litchfield. Indeed, the last time I'd been up to see him, a year ago, he'd worn nothing but blowsy golf shirts and pleated slacks. He was getting old.

The thought cowed me. And made me miss him. I gave up on shopping and made my way to the Dollar Rent A Car on Charles Street. Through the glass door I could see the woman behind the front desk. I paused. Should I really be leaving Paige? For that matter, should I be handing my driver's license over to someone with a computer? Yes, and yes. What had Touché called it? *Indirect support.* That's all I was offering. Nothing more. I wouldn't let her rough landing into my life completely disrupt it. And I wouldn't become paranoid either. Of course I could hand over my license. My name wasn't on any lists. I wasn't the one setting off bombs. I could write a single blog post and be free and clear of any trouble.

Fifteen minutes later I was sitting behind the wheel of a soulless Chrysler Sebring. If the Dollar woman had suspected I was harboring a terrorist, she certainly hadn't let on. In fact, she'd offered to upgrade me to a PT Cruiser (I'd politely declined). I turned west and weaved my way through Village streets that never quite pointed in the right direction. Would Paige be there when I got back? I'd been gone more than an hour, plenty of time to take off if that was her plan. And what if she'd stolen something, cash or my computer, or worse, been somehow tracked or traced? By the time I turned onto Weehawken Street I half-expected the block to be cordoned off, cop cars pulled up on sidewalks, a crowd, reporters, cameras.

But the street was empty, as usual. I parked nearby, grabbed my shirts and groceries, and walked briskly home. When I opened the door, Paige looked up from the couch. She was writing a letter, an art book serving as a makeshift table on her lap.

"It's to my parents," she said, when I asked. "Don't worry. I won't mail it from around here."

"Okay, good," I said, as if I might have suggested that precaution myself. "I got you a salad. I thought you might be a vegetarian or something so . . ."

"Thanks. I'm not."

I started fiddling with things. Plastic forks and napkins, and the hangers from the dry cleaner, which had attached themselves to everything I was holding. Paige went back to her letter, as if this were the most normal day two people could spend together.

"Have you been in contact with them?" I asked.

"My mom and dad? Not really. Just the pay-phone call they told you about—to hear their voices, let them know I was alive. It was stupid; I shouldn't have done it. But I'm glad they realized it was me."

"Why'd you hang up? You think their phone's tapped?"

"It's possible."

"But it's okay to write them now?"

"Probably not, but it may be the last chance I get. Plus, you were talking about your father's birthday . . ." She let the thought die.

I got lunch together, and we ate quickly. Then I packed a small overnight bag. I had to get going, and anyway, Paige had turned quiet.

"Are you sure I should leave you alone?" I asked.

"Yeah, sorry. I'm just . . . I'm thinking about Keith."

"How to find him, you mean?"

"Maybe. I don't know."

"Why don't I call you when I get to Litchfield."

"Okay, but wait until later tonight, after dinner." She peered at me through her hair, like a boy looking through the woods. "Let's say ten o'clock. Let it ring twice, then hang up and call back right away. Use your dad's house phone, not your cell."

"Meaning . . . ?" I felt for the phone in my pocket.

"Meaning let's not take unnecessary chances."

"And what if you don't answer?"

She brushed her hair aside. "Then stay up there."

AIDAN

· · · ● · ● ● ● ● ● · ● ●

THE MONDAY-AFTERNOON TRAFFIC WAS LIGHT LEAVING MANHATTAN, AND I rolled my window down to take in the breeze off the river. It felt good to be on the road, and then, as I crossed the northern tip of the island, it suddenly didn't. I almost turned around in White Plains, and again as I merged onto I-84. What was I doing, leaving Paige alone at a moment like that? Did she even think I'd come back? My mind raced every which way as my car continued north, but by the time I reached Danbury I'd acquitted myself of any wrongdoing. I had done what I could. The rest was up to her. Of the larger picture I remained decidedly ignorant. Like a junkie—and as a bartender I'd known plenty of them—the vague awareness of my tenuous situation was accompanied not only by denial, but also a strange euphoria, and I didn't want the feeling to end. Besides, I told myself, again and again, I could always write the Roorback post and wriggle free of any trouble or blame. It was like a get-out-of-jail-free card, and it made me play more fearlessly. For this still felt like a game. Make-believe.

I turned off the highway and tried to shift my attention from the mess I'd left behind to the mess that lay ahead. My father and Julie lived in a century-old lake house surrounded by horse farms and rolling hills. It was hard to think of a more picturesque place for a couple to retire to after decades in the city, but Julie hadn't spent decades in the city. She was only a year older than me. A reformed party girl. An absentee mother. And the only (half) Asian I'd ever seen in Litchfield County. For several years now I'd been trying to figure out what she was doing living a rural life she clearly hated, with a man she didn't love. Was money that important? Or was she running from something?

Julie wasn't responsible for my parents' divorce (that title went to a "Porsche Girl" my father met at an auto-show advertising dinner while I was in college). No, she came several years and women later, after my father had squeezed everything he could from his extended midlife crisis and settled, creased and furrowed, into semiretirement outside Litchfield. It was during this period that I grew closest to him, the two of us stung by recent—repeated—failures (I'd just dropped out of NYU), but with all of life suddenly open to us. We saw each other every month, even took a road trip together. We were becoming friends.

Then Julie appeared. They met for the first time at a Midtown-hotel lounge where my father was entertaining a table of big-shot marketing people. Julie was their cocktail waitress, and somehow numbers were exchanged. She played it perfectly after that, stretched the chase out over several months so as to serve up her spicy past in digestible morsels. There were her children, for instance, two twin girls and a boy—ages six, six, and five—who lived with their father in Nassau County, begging the question—

Oh, there were so many questions it was hard to know where to begin.

As is a son's obligation, I'd rebelled against every stage of their courtship, from the sordid Phil Spector–ness of their initial meeting, through the dark days of the engagement, and on to the awkward wedding itself, which officially completed my father's reduction to cliché. He had doomed himself to play out the string with a washed-up stripper—because at some point, with her tits and attitude, Julie *must* have been a stripper—and that was just too much to bear. I refused to accept his new reality—or mine—and instead defaulted to a strategy of mordant disregard to get me through my Litchfield visits. This further distanced me from my father, of course, while exacerbating the significant tension and discord already present in the house. Still, I couldn't help myself. It was a rough situation. And I'd never been much of a bigger person.

Whether by accident or not, my father's birthday fell on one of the few weeks all year that Julie played host to her kids. Which is why he always begged me to come—even sprang for the rental car. And I couldn't blame him. They—Amber, Ashley, and their brother, Jordan (some real Asian-American names for you)—were miniature hooligans who pillaged with no fear of reprisal. Everyone ignored them, or tried to, except poor Loretta, the Honduran maid, whose job it was to keep them under control.

"She'd have better luck in the green-card lottery," my father muttered, after one particularly difficult night a few years back.

The poor guy, turning sixty in a cyclone. But he would try to rally while I reverted to form, did what I always did: mock Julie's mindless small talk at dinner, and after she'd drunkenly gone to bed, slowly shake my head in disdain as my father sipped his scotch and kept the conversation away from anything personal or approaching important. Indeed, it was only out of some enduring filial respect that I hadn't yet asked the question that hovered over his house like an electric cloud—that being what the hell my father's thirty-four-year-old wife had done to lose custody of her three confused children. Because something pretty unbelievable must have happened.

Two cars—two *vehicles*—were parked in the driveway. The tiny Prius belonged to the long-suffering Loretta, keeper of secrets and nominal order. Beside the Prius sat another hybrid, this one brand-new and bright red, and it would have been exciting news, would have marked an evolution in family environmental thinking, if it weren't a massive Escalade, complete with step-up running boards and what looked like monster-truck tires. The thing was so wide the rearview mirrors had necks. I could only shake my head. That they'd gone to the trouble of buying the hybrid somehow made it worse.

I walked into the house and was immediately assaulted by the piercing screams of my young stepsiblings. They were in the den, jumping up and down on the couches while a TV gunfight droned on in the background. This is what a Yoko Ono karaoke party must sound like, I thought, as I turned and walked the other way. I found Loretta in the kitchen, watching a Spanish game show as she tended to a pot of vegetables. She was momentarily startled, but recovered enough to say, "Hallo." *"Hola,"* I responded, and from there we fumbled through each other's languages until I came to understand that my father and Julie were at the golf club.

"Practice," Loretta said, making an odd attempt at a golf swing.

A shriek alit from the other room, so loud it echoed.

"La casa mucho noisy," I said pathetically. "No wonder *señor et señorita* left."

"Señor-a," Loretta said. "No *señorita."* We grinned in some kind of collusion.

I couldn't wait around at the house, not with *Romper Room* in full swing, so I set off across town to find them. My father had joined the Torrington Country Club before Julie appeared on the scene, so the membership—a genteel roster of aging blue bloods—had no choice but to tolerate her plunging dinner dresses, skintight tennis whites, and thong bikinis at the children's pool (I hadn't seen her golf outfit yet). The wives wouldn't speak to her, of course, and the husbands weren't allowed to, but Julie didn't give a shit. She thought the place was hilarious. It's the one thing I liked about her.

I parked in the members lot and walked past the clubhouse to the driving range. I spotted Julie right away, at the far end of a row of comically clothed bodies hacking at stationary golf balls. She was wearing a sleeveless white top and a blue daisy-print miniskirt that barely reached her thighs. A matching choker added just the right touch of S&M to the proceedings, while allowing for an unobstructed view of her wondrous breasts. I stopped a moment to take in the scene, its lavish, unadulterated spectacle. Julie was taking a lesson from the head pro, who was down on one knee, like an on-deck hitter, patiently placing balls on tees, while my stepmother, still fit as a showgirl, stood up tall, spread her legs past shoulder-width, and took abbreviated swipes at the earth with some kind of high iron. In the four swings I witnessed, she made contact—with the golf ball—exactly half the time. The problem was simple to diagnose: her assets were a liability. She couldn't swing her arms without her tits getting in the way. Not that anyone cared. This performance had nothing to do with sport, and everything to do with a thirty-four-year-old seductress stuck in the middle of nowhere with a sixty-year-old retiree. It was only a matter of time—weeks by the look of it—before a dock boy or yoga instructor or this golf pro here began complicating matters—if it wasn't already happening.

And my father? you might ask. He was a few spots down, hitting wedge shots at a crooked flag a hundred yards away. Could he be that oblivious? Or did he truly not care about the swirl of activity surrounding his wife? Christ, maybe he actually enjoyed it, in some perverse Hugh Hefner–ish way. I don't know. It was hard enough to view from a distance, this tragic final act of an American life, without delving under the sheets for the particulars. The total detachment. The absence of self-awareness. Or was it *too much* self-awareness? Had my father won or given up?

Bill Cole stayed poised over the ball as I approached him, but he must have sensed I was there, for his awkward swing produced a hand-rattling shank that sliced off toward the trees at all deliberate speed. He grimaced and looked up.

"Happy birthday," I said.

"*Aidan*. How are you? So sorry we weren't home."

"Don't worry about it." We shook hands and sort of patted each other on the back at the same time. A hybrid hug, I thought.

"It's just that Julie had a lesson scheduled—"

"I see that."

"—and we were getting in Loretta's way. She's cooking dinner for us. Did you see the kids?" Something weird was happening. Two trickles of sweat had escaped from under his cap and were now wandering down past his ear. Except they were . . . *black*. Was his cap dirty or something? "Here, come say hello to your stepmother."

"I don't want to interrupt."

"No, no."

We made our way down the firing line. In front of us, Julie swung and missed and giggled; the pro chuckled along with her, but stood up abruptly when he saw us. Julie turned around, and what Touché once described as "the greatest fake smile in the stepmother business" now spread across her face. She held her arms out, shirt stretched taut, and I stepped up to her. Her breasts felt like water balloons that could only give so much before bursting, which is not to say I didn't test them. Indeed, we held on a beat too long, the moment heightened by sweat and perfume and the audience that was watching. She knew what she was doing. She knew that if I saw her in some Brooklyn bar (or, more likely, a Vegas lounge), I, like any man, would have been all over her. And who knows what she would have done then. We let go, and I backed away.

A few minutes later, her lesson came to a merciful end, and the four of us paraded toward the pro shop. Flustered after our encounter, I had somehow picked up Julie's golf bag and was now carrying it like a caddy, while the pro spoke—apparently seriously—about Julie's swing-plane.

One night, I thought. Just one night.

I followed my father's vintage MG along Route 4 toward Woodbridge Lake. The air was dry and cool with the wind, and I realized I'd gone almost two hours without thinking, without obsessing, about Paige. Which is exactly what I started to do. But then we stopped at an intersection and something in the lead car caught my eye; the top was down and my father had taken his cap off, and his hair was . . . *darker.* That's what it was! The bastard was *dyeing* it.

A frazzled-looking Loretta was waiting for us when we turned into the driveway. She began speaking rapidly in Spanish, which no one understood, but the gist of it was that Ashley or Amber (did Loretta get them confused as well? Did *Julie*?) had got loose in my father's study and knocked one of his prized advertising awards off the shelf.

"A CLIO?" my father asked, before realizing Loretta (and Julie, for that matter) would have no idea what he was talking about.

"Is broken," Loretta said.

My father brushed past her into the house. The kids were nowhere to be heard.

"Want a drink?" Julie asked. "I'll make a pitcher of margaritas before I shower."

"You've got him drinking margaritas?" I asked.

"I meant for you and me. He's strictly whisky or wine."

"Whisky *and* wine."

She managed a watery smile. She was tossing me a lifeline, not jumping in my boat.

"Fuck!" my father shouted, from somewhere above us. *"The god-damn kids, Julie!"* Julie ignored him, but I ventured upstairs to observe the damage and found him squinting up at an empty space amid a row of awards on the top shelf of his bookcase. He had a gold statuette in one hand, its detached base in the other. "How the hell did they get up there?" he asked, genuinely flummoxed.

I took the black base from him and read the engraving aloud: "Absolut Vodka, U.S. Print, Winner, 1986."

"How about that?" he said, calming down. "It was a big deal back in the day."

"I'm sure."

"Speaking of, how's your mother?"

The question caught me off guard. "Good," I said. "Peaceful."

"Lucky her. She still with that artist guy?"

"I guess, yeah. But he has his own place."

"Well, tell her to marry him so the goddamn gravy train can come to an end. I've got enough expenses around here without shelling out for her every month."

With that, he set the broken CLIO on his desk and we went downstairs. We were well into cocktail hour now, and I watched as my father measured out a few fingers of Maker's Mark while Julie poured the margaritas. It was the most focused I'd seen them. Somewhere in the house, a child yelled. My father shook his head. Julie looked at him and shook hers. Drink in hand, I escaped outside.

The view across the lake was spectacular. Out in the middle, a lone water-skier cut smoothly across the surface. A fisherman trolled quietly in a nearby cove. And a pair of loons—were they loons?—bobbed up and down a few yards from our dock. Nature rolled endlessly out in every direction, and yet it seemed somehow manageable, containable, as if physical splendor might still be enough to counteract man's many evils. I tried to tune out the rush and swirl of events. The kids arguing in the house behind me. My father shouting for his wife. And Derrick, whom I'd never gotten around to calling back. To say nothing of Cressida. The late-day sun was warm on my face and the margarita was strong and cold; New York seemed like another planet, orbiting, perhaps, but a long way off. Only Paige stayed with me.

What I thought about then was the Fishers Island photograph she'd posed for with Brendan. And how completely dissimilar that Paige had seemed from the outlaw version currently occupying my apartment. Had she changed so much? Or was she both of those people (or neither of them)? Appearances: I'd spent my working life judging them, and the rest of the time keeping them up. What good had come of my efforts? For me? For anyone else? Tonight, I decided, I'd bite my tongue. Refrain from piling on. My father and Julie were somehow getting by, and maybe, for them, that was enough. Who was I to say it wasn't?

The big birthday dinner consisted of watery leek soup followed by tasteless pasta drowned in vegetables. Julie had turned a classic meat-and-potatoes man into some kind of organic nibbler. And still my father hadn't lost much weight. I tasted the soup, then put my spoon down and caught his eye. He shrugged. The kids, who started at the table with us, soon escaped to the counter stools and settled in to watch *Scarface* on the kitchen television. No one said anything about it until Pacino unleashed a particularly famous volley of oaths that caused my father to arch his eyebrows in the direction of his wife.

"Ashley," Julie said, "watch the language." To which Ashley responded, "I didn't say it," which was true enough. And the TV stayed on.

Julie, I noticed, became increasingly irritable the closer she came to her children, and now she shoveled down beets and peppers in a frenzy of agitation. She was all cleaved out in a deep-scoop sweater dress, but my father barely gave the ensemble a second look. He twirled his pasta around his plate and lobbed me halfhearted questions about New York. Julie cut him off to ask about Cressida. Though she'd never actually admitted it, Julie was an avid online reader of both Roorback and my possibly former girlfriend's dating columns. I stumbled through an answer as she opened another bottle of wine and began some kind of private drinking game, taking a long gulp every time Pacino snorted a line. My father asked what I thought of the new "hybrid" in the driveway, and I was formulating a response when Julie, surely drunk now, put her glass down and said, "Can you believe they finally caught those Muslims?"

"What Muslims?" my father asked.

"The ones who bombed Barneys. I heard it on the radio when I was upstairs getting dressed earlier. Three Pakistanis and one from somewhere else."

She said this as if her ancestors had arrived on the *Mayflower;* in fact, Julie's Vietnamese mother had arrived on a 1973 Pan Am flight from Thailand, the ticket paid for by a U.S. marine (Julie's father) who had saved her from a village he'd then helped destroy.

No matter. *Muslims?*

"What are you talking about?" I said, more sharply than I meant to.

"I don't know. Go listen yourself. I was just *making conversation.*" She eyed her husband, as if *making conversation* was exactly what he'd asked her to attempt. "Loretta bought a birthday cake at the store if anyone wants any." With that, Julie stood up, presumably to mute Pacino, who was in full machine-gun phase, but she walked past the TV and disappeared into the house.

"Four Muslims," my father said. "That'll be the talk of the town. Good thing you don't cover real news. They'd be calling you back to the city."

"Still, I better check on things," I said, getting up.

"Can't it wait?" my father asked, eyeing the empty table, then the kids.

"I'll only be a few minutes."

I bounded up the stairs to my father's office and clicked my way to nytimes.com. There it was, a brief, recently posted article near the top of the home page. I read it quickly, but there wasn't much additional information—just four Muslims (the fourth was an Indonesian) arrested in an apartment above a chop shop in Flushing, Queens. I opened my e-mail. The most recent was from Touché; he'd linked to the same story, then added *WTF?* underneath. Which about summed it up. It was nine forty-five. Fifteen minutes until I called Paige. She'd know what was going on. I heard my father trudging across the living room downstairs. How had four Muslims entered the picture? Did Paige know them? Or was there—and why was I just thinking of this for the first time—a chance that Paige had been lying this whole time? I rubbed my temples and watched the minutes pass slowly by.

When the hour finally struck, I picked up the phone and listened for anything out of the ordinary—clicks or beeps or tiny interruptions. There were none, so I dialed my home number. The phone rang, once, twice, then I hung up, as instructed. I dialed again. It rang again. Isabel. Call her Isabel. I'd thought about circumnavigating my father's house to make sure no one was expecting a call, or about to make one, but I didn't want certain parties to know I was so desperate to use the phone. And so—

Paige wasn't picking up, which was impossible. She had to be there. Five rings. Six. *Seven*. I waited, like some pathetic lover, for another minute. Then I hung up and called one more time, just to be sure. Nothing.

What the hell was happening? Had she finally fled? Or turned herself in? Or had news of the arrests somehow changed the game plan? Maybe the Feds had raided my studio, had been right there huddled around the ringing phone. They'd traced the call and would come tearing into my father's driveway at any moment. Well, fuck it. They could have me. I wasn't about to take off running.

Back downstairs, the dishes lay piled in the sink, awaiting Loretta. The kids were gone, maybe even in bed. I wandered over to the bar, poured myself a small Maker's Mark, and found my father in the library off the den. He was reading the paper of record.

"You get the *Times* up here?" I asked, flopping down in the only other chair.

"God, you sound like Julie, who seems to think we live in Lapland."

Julie wouldn't know what continent that was on, I didn't say. But how often I wished I had, wished I could shake the man out of the thick boozy fog that had rolled in some years ago. I looked around the room, his refuge, which Julie had painted a rich shade of teal. The built-in bookshelves were lined with war epics and presidential biographies that could have belonged to any well-off white man in any state. Above these, though, on the highest shelves, sat the aging books of his New York past, literary novels and liberal polemics written (and inscribed) by old friends. They were the only things he'd taken from our West Side apartment, and now they sat by the ceiling, unreachable without a ladder, unreadable without remembering—

The phone rang. My father shook out the paper, exasperated. "That'll be for Julie. Probably her masseuse calling to confirm whatever she's got scheduled for tomorrow."

"Dad?"

"Hmm?"

"Can I talk to you about something?"

"Sure," he said, without looking up.

"Well . . . I guess I just want to apol—"

"Aidan!" Julie shouted, from upstairs. *"It's for you!"*

"Who is it?" I shouted back.

For a moment there was no answer, and I imagined her gleefully falling into conversation with Touché or even Cressida—whoever'd tracked me down up here.

"Isabel."

"A new one?" my father muttered. "Why doesn't she call your cell—" But I was already up and out of the room. The closest phone with any privacy was back in the kitchen, and I shouted up to Julie—wherever she was—to hang up when I got on.

"I wasn't planning on listening in," she yelled back, then I heard her apologize into the phone. I cringed—those two speaking!—and almost out of breath picked up the phone and pressed TALK.

"I've got it, Julie, thanks," I said.

"Whatever," Julie replied. Then there was a click.

"Are you sure it's just you?" Paige asked. There was background noise. She was outside somewhere.

"Yes. Are you okay? I tried calling the apartment but—"

"Listen to me," she said, with urgency. "Do you know a thin British girl with reddish hair and freckles who apparently has keys to your place?"

"Yeah. My girlfriend. Or ex. We've been—"

"Fuck, Aidan! You think you could have mentioned she'd be dropping by? Is there any way she'd know who I am?"

"No," I said quickly. "Why? What happened?"

"She *saw* me. I was in your apartment earlier and the intercom buzzed."

"You didn't answer, right?"

"Of course not. And I couldn't risk looking out the window, so I opened your door and listened down the stairwell. I heard someone come into the building, then what sounded like a woman's boots climbing the first flight. If whoever it was had a key to the downstairs door, she probably had a key to *your* door, so I grabbed my wallet and my bag and got out. I couldn't go up because you said the roof was locked, so I had to go down. She was still on the second-floor landing, so there's no way she could have seen which door I'd just come out of. We passed each other on the third floor. I didn't get a great look at her, obviously, because I didn't want to make eye contact, so I just muttered the requisite "Hello," and she did the same in what sounded like a British accent. And then . . . then she looked back over her shoulder. Like *she recognized me*."

"And she went into my apartment?"

"I think so. I pretended to leave the building, even slammed the downstairs door and everything, but I stayed in the foyer and listened. She knocked a few times and I heard your door opening. Aidan, who is she? And what was she doing?"

"She doesn't know anything. We had a fight a few weeks ago and kind of ended things. We haven't spoken since. Her name's Cressida."

"*Cressida? Cressida Kent? The* Times *reporter?*"

"Yeah. How do you know who she is?"

"Because I *read the paper*! Because how many Cressidas are there? Because . . . oh, Aidan, you're dating a *New York Times* reporter?"

"Look, it'll be okay. Where are you now?"

"It *won't* be okay. I'm at a pay phone on Fourteenth and Seventh. I can't go back to Weehawken Street. It's too hot now. The whole city's too hot."

"But did you see the news? They picked up four Muslim guys in connection with the Indigo bombing."

"What? What are you talking about? I haven't seen any news in hours. Are you sure? My God, that's terrible."

"They had nothing to do with it?"

"Four Muslim men? Of course not." She sounded annoyed that I'd asked. "Either the Feds made a mistake, or, more likely, they're trying to cover their asses."

"Maybe it'll give you some breathing room," I said hopefully.

"The only thing it'll give me is an even better reason to turn myself in."

"*No*, Paige. Just wait. I'll come back right now. It's a disaster up here anyway."

"But haven't you been drinking all night?"

"Then I'll leave first thing in the morning and be in the city by nine. We'll figure it out, I promise."

"I have nowhere to stay."

"How about this," I said, in a voice almost too calm to be my own. "There's a place two blocks away from you called the Liberty Inn. It's on the West Side Highway. They rent rooms by the hour, so they won't ask a lot of questions. Check in and just stay put. I'll come straight there. I won't even go home first."

Paige paused a moment before answering.

"Okay, fine. But, Aidan, there's something you need to understand."

"What?"

"*You can't go back to Weehawken Street now either, even if you want to*. Not until this plays out. One way or the other. Now I've got to go."

"Wait, what do you mean?" But she'd already hung up.

I put the phone down and sat there. Now what? Renegade strands of pasta lay coiled on the countertop. I took a breath. My apartment was the only thing I really had, and even that was rented. Paige had warned me—had *begged* me—to post her story, and I hadn't listened. Or I had. I had listened, and understood, and made a choice. And I wasn't upset. Instead, I wanted to get in the car and go fix things.

My father was reading, his drink a memory, melting ice. I offered to refill it, and he shrugged. "Sure, why not?" Back and forth I went through the oddly silent house, and when we once again had drinks in our hands (mine was mostly water), my father lifted his glass. I did the same.

"A bit hectic tonight," he said. He sighed, then took a sip.

And just like that, I wanted to hug him. I was in trouble, and he was my father. *Still* my father. A man who'd lived his life with the top down and endured the consequences with a kind of obstinate fatalism. I could have used that quality then. That unflappability. Suddenly I had the same feeling I'd had that day in the barn with Simon Krauss, the desperate need to confess, unburden myself . . . *get some help*. But what did we understand of each other anymore? A father winding down and a son spinning in place. *Stay up there*, Paige had said, but as I gazed at my father's once handsome profile—his unnatural hair, his jaw set like plaster, his copper skin reptilian-dry—I just didn't see any way in. If this was how the American success story ended—with complete and utter disconnection—then I wanted no part of it.

"Dad, I have to get back first thing in the morning."

"Mmm. I could tell something was up. The bombing?"

"Yeah. Things are going a bit crazy."

"That's why I moved up here. To get the hell away from all that nonsense. The politics of fear and terror. At some point you just have to throw in the towel."

"What about fighting back?"

My father took another sip and chuckled. "Tried that once, doesn't work." He looked through the window, toward the gray outline of the water, but only for a moment. There was all the space in the world out there, but no room for what could have been.

He wouldn't understand, but I said it anyway: "I might not see you for a while."

"Oh, nonsense. I'll come down to the city this winter. We'll grab some dinner, me and you. Is '21' still open?"

"I think so."

"Then it's a date."

He stood up and we shook hands, and, yes, we hugged. Then he went upstairs to bed. I stretched out on the couch, but couldn't sleep. At some point I turned on a light and started leafing through my father's old novels. Love and loss, life and death: mankind's enduring themes laid bare on brittle pages. Soon, I was back on the road, in the last lonely hour of night. I almost turned my lights off to drive by the stars, and a month before I would have. But now such a small act of insurrection seemed less than liberating. Besides, I couldn't risk it. If I wasn't yet wanted by the law, I *was* needed at home. The feeling thrilled me. I buzzed with energy and for a while forgot the danger I was in. And the lie that I had told.

For there *was* a chance Cressida had seen Paige before. In that Fishers Island photograph. The one she gave me that night at Malatesta.

AIDAN

· · · ●●●●●● · · ●●

LAST NIGHT, JIM AND CAROL TOLD ME ABOUT PAIGE. IT WAS THE FIRST TIME MY handlers had visited the house together, and immediately I knew something wasn't right. Jim took a seat on the couch and frowned at the fireplace while Carol made tea in the kitchen. I sat in a nearby chair and tried to mask my impatience.

When Carol came in, she set steaming mugs in front of each of us, then sat next to Jim and squeezed his leg.

"You don't do much besides microwave, do you, Aidan? I could write my name in the dust on that stovetop."

"Your real one or fake one?"

"Ha ha."

Jim took a sip of tea and started talking. From what he'd heard—and they were only rumors, he stressed, completely unverified—Paige had been hiding out in the Midwest—Ohio or Indiana. They'd found her an apartment in a busy college town, somewhere near the main strip so she could walk places (neither one of us has a car, not yet, because the paperwork—the title transfers, the registrations and insurance—is almost tougher to produce than human papers, our passports and Social Security cards).

"For whatever reason," Jim continued, "she began frequenting a nearby Internet café. It was a risk, of course, adopting a routine like that, but she must have felt safe enough to chance it. Or maybe she just needed to get outside, you know . . ." He shrugged, and in that instant I realized I'd been right about Jim and Carol. At some point, probably decades ago, they'd lived as I now live—furtively, invisibly. And they knew exactly what it felt like, spending day after day—and now month after month—cooped up, in hiding. It's the knowledge that gets you, the maddening knowledge that just up the street or over the hill, life is proceeding apace. How many frozen mornings I've woken up and almost walked down the driveway and back into the world. But I know I can't.

I listened closely to what Jim said, hung on every word. Paige had been writing in her apartment, using a secondhand computer and printer. She had everything she needed; and she had nothing at all. And so the café, the Internet: *information*. On the mounting case against us. On the larger case against the country. Perhaps it was just being around people, overhearing conversations, idle chatter: parents with children, students with ideas. I live with that feeling, too—craving the very civilization I've turned my back on. But don't confuse that for regret.

"Apparently," Jim said, "she went out one morning and never came home. Something unexpected must have happened because she left all her stuff behind."

"And there were no messages or clues?"

"Not that we're aware of, Aidan. She just disappeared."

"Well, we'd have heard about it if she got picked up," I said. "It would have been all over the news."

"I know."

"Which means she's still out there."

"No one knows what it means," Carol said quietly.

They stayed a while longer, to make sure I was okay. I didn't ask them anything more. They'd told me what they knew, or at least what they could.

"There is one more thing." Jim stole a glance at his partner.

"Can't wait," I said.

"You've made the FBI's Ten Most Wanted list."

"They still have that?" I asked, surprised. "I thought it was just the TV show now."

"Maybe that's next. Anyway, congratulations."

With that, they stepped out into the February snow. It was seven degrees, according to the glazed thermometer hanging by the door. What would I do now? Knowing that Paige was okay had kept me going—and kept me writing. I'd come to think of our dual narratives as unrequited love letters, fervently baring our true feelings—words we wished we'd spoken and one day still might. But now what? I'd never imagined her in trouble. On the run again.

I walked into the empty living room and watched Jim's car inch cautiously down the driveway, the brake lights slowly disappearing into the whiteness, then the dark.

She was out there somewhere. Or worse, she wasn't.

AIDAN

· · · ● ● ● ● ● · ● ●

I TOOK A CAB FROM THE RENTAL-CAR OFFICE TO FOURTEENTH AND TENTH. IT was still early, before nine, and the West Side restaurants and galleries were all shuttered. I got out on a curb under the High Line and looked around tentatively. Already, I felt like a fugitive, divorced from my life. If being unable to go home had briefly felt thrilling, it now terrified me. Everything had happened so quickly. Two days. I'd been on benders that long, a few of which, I realized then, had at some unspeakable hour involved the hotel in front of me.

I walked into the lobby, such as it was, and stopped at the front desk. It was like an art-house ticket booth, and I waited for the clerk to acknowledge me. He was a small, rueful man who clung tightly to a studied nonchalance, and when he finally looked up and heard me ask for an Isabel Clarke, he eyed his list of guests as if he might fall asleep before he reached the bottom. "Your name?"

"What?"

"Your name."

"Uh . . . Aidan."

Shit. Should I have made something up? Of course I should have. But how would Paige have known it was me? The clerk punched a few numbers into his phone, waited a moment, then repeated my name and hung up. He eyed the backpack on my shoulder, wondering, I suppose, if I might be that rare breed that stayed a night or two.

"Room twenty-four," he said. "Up the stairs and down the hall."

The lobby resembled a city-hospital waiting room, right down to the bolted-in chairs and vaguely chemical smell. I walked past a sign reading THE LIBERTY INN: YOUR RENDEZVOUS FOR ROMANCE and found the staircase opposite the bar, which was already stirring with early life. If I were ever a real writer, I thought, this is where I'd come hang out—get a whole book of short stories in a single day.

Room 24 was at the end of the narrow hall. Paige must have been eyeing me through the keyhole because she opened the door before I knocked. "You told the guy downstairs your real name," she said, quickly checking the hallway, then closing the door. "You can't do that."

"I know. Sorry."

I put my backpack down and looked around. The curtains were closed and the lights were on. The Liberty Inn had run with the prevailing theme since the last time I'd been there (or maybe I just hadn't noticed back then): the king-size bed, still the center of activity, was accentuated now by a cushioned headboard the shape and color of two plump lips; a floor-to-ceiling mirror ran along an entire wall; and on another, a hand-painted mural depicted a gaudy tangle of naked bodies.

"The only thing this room hasn't seen is luggage," I said.

It was a lame joke, but Paige let it pass. She'd changed her appearance, gone even more native, with tousled black hair and matching dark-framed glasses.

I tried again: "You look like you've moved a few L-stops further into Brooklyn."

"I had a little time to kill," she said, pulling self-consciously at a loose strand above her ear. "There's dye all over the bathroom sink, but I'll clean it up."

"It's alluring," I told her. And it was. But I'd embarrassed her by saying so, and just like that, our situation caught up to us. We were strangers on the run hiding out in a sex hotel. It seemed impossible, but there it was. There *we* were. I sat down on the bed.

I knew she was changing the subject before she opened her mouth. "No problems with the rental car, I take it? Or your credit card?"

"I don't think so."

"Okay, good." She paused. "Thanks for coming back."

"Sounds like I missed a lot. I'm sorry about Cressida."

"Why was she going to your apartment?"

"I'm not sure. Probably to return my keys. We haven't been on great terms, and I was supposed to call her, but, well, you showed up and"—and here it went—"Paige . . . there's something I need to tell you."

"What?"

"There's a possibility, a small one, that Cressida *did* recognize you."

Paige sat down beside me. She was wearing jeans and a white tank top with lace trim. I turned to talk directly to her, but she continued facing forward, her forearms on her thighs, waiting. So I told her, again, about that dinner at Malatesta, this time including details I'd left out before—the names I'd used to fool Cressida, and the folders, and then the photographs.

I said, "I didn't mention this before because I didn't think it was important. And I'm not sure it's important now. The picture of you and what's his name on Fishers Island was just one of many. There were three or four pages worth of photographs, a dozen Paige Rodericks that Cressida had dug up from across America. I only noticed you because I'd seen the Madison Avenue photo. And even then I almost missed it."

"I *knew* it. Cressida's reaction, that double take she did on the stairs . . . it was like she'd suddenly remembered."

"I really doubt it. The chances are just—"

"Chances get you killed," Paige said.

"Here, I'll call her." I took my phone out. "I'll be able to tell if she thinks something's up. She's not exactly subtle."

"*Wait! What are you doing?*" Paige snatched the phone out of my hand and turned it off. "You can't use this anymore. I told you that before you left."

"You didn't *tell me*. You kind of hinted at it."

"Jesus, Aidan, come on."

"I can't even call friends?"

"*No,*" she practically shouted, before catching herself. "No, you can't, because it may be tapped. Especially after yesterday. Don't you understand the significance of your girlfriend's little visit? It means . . . it means *there's no going back.* They'll be looking for *both* of us now. That's our reality. It's why I begged you to do what I asked, write that damn post and be done with me. And you wouldn't listen."

"For good reason."

"I'm not sure there's such a thing anymore." Paige stood up and walked over to the built-in wall desk, then turned around and flipped my phone back to me. "But now that you're *in* this, there are some things I need to tell you, because we can't afford even one mistake from here on out."

And for the next hour she gave me a crash course on survival—how to live on the run, or try. The importance of details. Faces and voices. Clothing and accessories. Names, addresses, license plates. She explained the dangers of cell phones and technology. Stay out of photographs and off the Internet. No landlines either. Public phones were slightly better, because even if the number you were calling was tapped, you usually had time, a minute or two, before a trace could kick in. I sat speechless on the bed, thinking this was how it was in movies—this kind of talk in this kind of room. But on-screen the desperation always led to desire, lust, sex. In reality, I felt anxious and sick to my stomach, because now, finally, it was sinking in. Nowhere was safe.

"*Hey*," she said. "Are you listening? This is important. We have to assume Cressida knows about us, but we need to find out for sure." Paige looked around the room. "And we have to find another place to stay. This one's a little . . . *obvious*."

"Well, I took some money out on the way over here. Four hundred bucks, which is pretty much all I've got. Figured I wouldn't be doing much banking for a while."

"That's right. No ATM cards and no credit cards."

"What you're trying to say is that you're impressed with my forethought."

"Vastly."

"Because I've got another idea," I said. "About a place to stay. How about Touché's apartment? Just for a night while we work all this out. Hell, he already knows about us, so he'll be cool with it. He likes living dangerously. He grew up with it."

"Among the Fishers Island outlaws? Aidan, you talk about this guy like he's some *foquismo* revolutionary. Don't fall in love with the accent. Exiled aristocrats are the same the world over: always with the people until they climb back into power."

"Just trust me."

"I have. I am." She reached into the front pocket of her jeans and with some effort pulled out a phone card. "Here, use this to call Cressida. And your friend Julian, too. I got it up north so it's clean. Find a pay phone a few blocks away. Don't stay on long, but don't sound rushed either. And no messages. Sorry, I don't mean to baby you."

"It's fine," I said. And it was. It was nice.

I left my cell phone, took the room key, and kept my head down until I was outside. Only then did I realize how close I was to Cressida's loft on Gansevoort Street. She'd be at work on a Tuesday morning, but still, there were roommates. There was anyone, really. The city felt shrunken and overly familiar. I started up Tenth Avenue into Chelsea and had walked several blocks before I finally spotted a bank of phones. I huddled in against the middle one like a bum sleeping on his feet. So Cressida first. I punched in all the digits and it started ringing. I imagined her in the newsroom, whipping her phone out, checking the number, and, not recognizing it, impatiently answering anyway. Reporters always answered. Except she didn't. I hung up when it went to voice mail. Should I call her office line? Call the *New York Times*? No, that wasn't a good idea. There was no way Cressida could have put any of this together, but still . . . I moved on to Touché. As it happened, his was the only other number I knew by heart. Again it rang. Again no answer. This time I waited for the beep: "Hey, it's Aidan. I just got back from Litchfield, which was a delight, as always, and have a favor to ask. Call me, or I'll try you again later. It's important. Okay, talk soon."

I placed the receiver in its cradle and immediately realized my mistake. *No messages.* Paige had drilled that into my head not fifteen minutes before! But this was Touché, and if anyone was discreet it was . . . oh, she wouldn't accept that excuse. What was I doing? I wasn't cut out for this. I can still write the post, I kept telling myself, and everything would sort itself out from there—Keith and Lindsay, the N3 plan. I could single-handedly stop the bombing, then go back to how things were, and Paige, well—

I don't know what tripped me up: the thought of returning to my life or the thought of Paige leaving it.

● ● ·

When I got back to the room, she was watching N3's coverage of the bombing arrests in Queens. The hapless Muslims had been dubbed the Flushing Four, and their mug-shot expressions, at once confused and defiant, could have come from terrorist central casting. I told her what had happened: that Cressida, for the first time in her life, hadn't answered her phone; and neither had Touché, though that wasn't such a surprise.

"I left him a message," I said, and watched her shoulders sink. *But you don't understand, he's on our side,* I wanted to tell her. *It is possible to have friends, allies, still, after everything.* But I held my tongue.

"Aidan, we need to get out of here. We're too exposed."

"You mean leave the city?"

"No, not yet. Because Keith is here, or will be. I'm sure of it. All this nonsense"—she pointed at the TV, at the talking heads screaming bloody murder—"this will only encourage him, spur him on. Most people would see it as a chance to get out, their crime being pinned on others. But it'll only make Keith more determined. I mean, look at those poor people."

"I still can't believe they're totally innocent," I said, as they were perp-walked across the screen.

"Crazy, isn't it, the things your precious country is capable of?"

"Yeah, yeah." Paige was in the chair so I sat on the bed and slipped my shoes off.

"You should take a nap," she said.

"I'm fine."

"Well, you look tired. And we're not going anywhere until it's dark."

"You have a plan?"

"Maybe."

She didn't elaborate. So I didn't push her. Anyway, she was right. I was exhausted. I'd barely slept for a day and a half, and who knew when I'd get my next chance. Now there's a thought, I thought, as Paige started flipping through news channels. I turned my cell phone on and placed it next to me on the nightstand. Then I propped myself up on some pillows and stretched out across the bed. The TV droned on like city traffic. At some point Paige stood up and turned off the overhead light. I started to tell her she didn't have to, but was asleep before the words came out.

Either Paige said my name or I dreamed it. Anyway, I opened my eyes. Wolf Blitzer was talking. The room was still dark. And Paige was still in the chair. I couldn't have slept more than fifteen or twenty minutes. Except . . . the sun was low over Jersey City.

"Paige, did you . . ."

"You're alive," she said, without turning around.

"I think so. How long—"

"Coming up on four hours."

"Jesus." I sat up. "Did Julian call?"

"I don't think so." I checked my phone; he hadn't. Neither, for that matter, had Cressida, or Derrick, or anyone else. It was like I'd dropped out of time. I sat up, still getting my bearings.

"We need to leave soon," Paige said.

"Do I have time to take a shower?"

"Yes, but keep it short."

Paige turned off the TV and began cleaning the room. I walked past her into the bathroom and shut the door.

I stripped down and stood under the falling water. Why hadn't Touché called back? He felt like my last tether to the known world, and I suddenly craved his soothing, big-picture perspective. Anyone's perspective. Where were we going? Had Paige figured something out, or were we just trying to stay ahead of whoever might be after us? But no one was after us. Still, the thought was sobering. I'll give this one more day, I decided. At the most.

Stepping out of the shower, I realized I'd left my backpack with my clean clothes out on the bureau. Could I walk out there in my towel? How bizarre this forced intimacy was, the two of us like characters in some short-story assignment, strangers feeling their way through a crisis. And let's throw in some action words—*passion,* perhaps, and *potential; risk* and *peril.* And *impossible.* Because that's what this was. That's what *we* were. Oh, hell. I wrapped the small towel around my waist, opened the door, and walked across the room. She was sitting on the bed. I don't think she even looked up. Another bridge crossed. To nowhere.

When I came out the second time, I was mostly dressed. Paige had changed, too—into a blousy, long-sleeved top.

"I went shopping while you were lounging around your father's country club," she said, slipping on her high-tops. She ripped a Club Monaco price tag off her sleeve, then took it into the bathroom and flushed it down the toilet.

"What's wrong with the garbage? The maid won't care where you shopped."

"Come on, think it through. Say we're traced back to here, and the cops show up before housecleaning does. They find the price tag in the trash and fan out to every Club Monaco in Manhattan, including the one on Prince Street where I bought this. They watch the security tapes, and, hey, there I am—new haircut, new glasses, new clothes. An hour later I'm on the news and we're in deep trouble. Not that we aren't already."

"I see."

"I hope so. Because that's how you need to start thinking."

We left after Paige wiped down the room. After she donned a knit hat and scarf. After my phone still hadn't rung. She walked downstairs, and I followed her five minutes later, stopping at the front desk to pay for the room in cash. The clerk didn't ask why we weren't spending the night. He didn't ask anything at all.

We reconvened at the corner of Fourteenth and Washington, in a sliver of darkness amid the glowing high-end boutiques. She nodded at a pay phone I'd passed up earlier, and I slipped over and tried Touché one last time. It rang through to voice mail.

"Okay, then, let's go," Paige said. She started walking toward Ninth Avenue.

"Hey, wait. We can't walk. I know too many people around here."

"But there are cameras in the subway stations and most of the cabs."

"Where are we going?"

"The other side of town."

"How about the bus?"

"Cameras there, too."

Across the cobblestone street a string of taxis and limos were dropping people off at some bottle-service lounge. "A town car, then," I said, and before Paige could answer, I was dodging through traffic with my hand raised. Illegal liveries were everywhere in Manhattan, stealing market share from their yellow-cab cousins. The ride was superior but it came at a steeper price. I knocked on the first tinted window I saw.

"How much to the East Side?"

"Twenty-five."

"Come on, I live here."

"Twenty."

"Fine." I hopped in the back, pointed at the tall, bespectacled girl across the street, and a moment later Paige was sliding in next to me.

"Chatham Square," she told the driver. "And could you turn on the radio?" The man glanced into the mirror as he tuned in a techno station, but Paige had sunk into her seat and he couldn't see her face.

"Chatham Square?" I asked, once the music was loud enough. "At the bottom of the Bowery? What's down there?"

"Shhh."

We turned right onto Hudson, merged onto Bleecker, and began a descent into the depths of the island. Soon we were in Chinatown, somewhere near the original Five Points. I spotted Winnie's, a late-night karaoke dive that had always seemed like the outermost edge of civilization. But it wasn't; the city pushed on, to the south and east, and so did we, across Bayard and down Mott. Where were we?

"This is good right here," Paige said. She opened the door and stepped out onto Worth Street while I paid the driver. I tipped him well and he drove away having never fully seen us. I turned to find Paige, but my eyes landed on the terrifying skyline behind her. For there, in the ominous gloaming, stood the hulking facades of the criminal justice system—Police Headquarters, a series of courthouses, and then the dreaded Tombs. How convenient, I thought: every stage of the process, from arrest to incarceration. East was the only way to go. East into the immigrant netherworld between bridges. We skirted chaotic Chatham Square, Paige wrapped up like a fashionable mummy in her hat and scarf, and started down the hill toward the water. It felt like another country, or several, for the grim faces that shuffled past us hailed from every broken part of the planet. We made a left onto Henry Street, the tenements trading lots with city housing—poor and poorer—and stopped at the corner of Market. Before us stood the massive Manhattan Bridge overpass, a structure that should have symbolized escape, but seemed instead a barrier, a wall, the farthest thing from a way out.

"Over there," Paige said, motioning toward a grimy, graffiti-covered apartment building across the street. "The fourth-floor window by the fire escape. The one with the blinds down. Keith uses it as a staging area before the Actions."

"And you think he and Lindsay might be here?"

"No, not yet. The blinds would be open. That's Keith's signal to the handlers that we're there. But I think he'll show up at some point. And I can get us inside."

"You said you have no idea who these handlers are?"

"No. In theory, the less we know about who's involved the better."

"So what if Keith shows up while we're in there?"

"That's the point. We're trying to *stop* him, remember? Which involves *finding* him first. And this place is our only shot. If he doesn't show up, then Roorback it is."

"I hope so," I said, and left it at that. But I was worried. I'd posted nothing on Roorback for more than twenty-four hours now, and Derrick was surely seething. If he finally followed through on his threats to fire me, he might change the site log-in to freeze me out. But wouldn't he call me first? Maybe he'd been trying; I had no way to tell. In the car, Paige had ordered me to turn my phone off and keep it off. Apparently, they could track cell signals without any calls being made at all. But enough. When I finally posted Paige's story, all would be forgiven in the eyes of the law.

"Come on," Paige said. "We can't stand on the corner all night like crossing guards."

More like dealers, I thought, peering around at our shadowy environs. It felt as if a thousand eyes were on us, yet I saw none of them. We walked to the end of the block, turned left, and then left again, onto Mechanics Alley, a rugged little lane running between the rear of the building and the giant bridge support behind it. A body moved in the darkness up ahead. Someone holding something. I stopped. Paige took my arm.

"It's okay. It's just the ground-floor fishmonger. He's hosing down his loading dock."

"It would help if there were streetlights," I said.

"Where's the fun in that?"

When the man retreated inside, we hurried past the back of his shop and stopped in front of a short set of stairs that led down to a basement door.

"Do you have a key?"

"It's not locked."

A piercing iron screech resounded high above us, scaring the hell out of me. It sounded like the end of the world, or at least the city, the infrastructure finally collapsing as we knew it would all along. But the screeching turned familiar, became a plaintive roar, as a Brooklyn-bound train passed on the bridge overhead. Paige glanced up the alley, then went down the steps and through the door. I followed after her.

We found ourselves in a damp basement hallway. The stench of rotten fish was overwhelming, and Paige put her scarf to her face before starting up the dilapidated staircase. Young men and old women scurried past as we climbed, avoiding us just as we avoided them. It was a building of phantoms. On the fourth floor, Paige turned down the hall and stopped outside the second door on the left. She put a finger to her lips and an ear to the door, for a minute, for two minutes, dead still. "Okay," she finally whispered. She handed me her duffel bag and pulled a strange-looking key from her pocket. Kneeling down, she pushed it in and out of the lock several times, delicately, patiently, like a marksman lining up a kill. She was listening for a click. For some reason I started holding my breath. Then there it was, the faintest of noises. She turned the knob and the door gave way.

Paige stood for a moment in the doorway, but the apartment was empty. I followed her inside.

The room was like the cheapest motel room you've ever seen—only it was half the size and almost completely bare. A narrow entrance hall with a bathroom on the right opened into a rectangular space just wide enough for two cots and a low, rectangular table between them. The walls and curtains were a murky off-white, and dark water stains dotted the ceiling like an archipelago. What little streetlight made it past the fire escape was choked off by the blinds and the filthy glass, and I had to take several steps toward the shapes in the corner before I recognized them as a minifridge, hot plate, and coffeemaker. Paige flipped a switch and a single bulb illuminated overhead. She motioned to me and put her index finger to her lips. *Bugs,* she mouthed, then started looking around. It didn't take long; there was almost nowhere to hide a listening device. When she was satisfied, she walked over and locked the front door behind us.

"Home sweet home," she announced, taking off her glasses, her disguise.

"Keith hasn't been here?" I asked.

"Doesn't look like it. And neither has the handler, or there'd be sleeping bags waiting like last time. N3 was originally planned for Saturday night, remember, so unless he's changed his schedule or really needs a place to crash, he won't be here until tomorrow at the earliest—and that'll still give him three days. He's not good all cooped up. Of course, he might be in Mexico for all I know." Paige walked back to the front door. "You comfortable?"

I'd just sat down on one of the beds. "Sure, why?"

"Because we can't keep the light on. If they do show up early, it'll scare them away."

With that, she flipped the switch and plunged us into darkness.

Mine was now a life of waiting: hours of boredom and seconds of terror. Like fighting fires, like fighting wars. I didn't believe in Paige's version of the world, but I believed in *her.* If we could just stop running, simply surviving, long enough to breathe again, I would do everything I could to pull her to safety. For something inside me had sparked and caught fire. And when that happens, you can defend any decision, justify any Action.

Slender streaks of gray light appeared through the blinds. Paige positioned herself by the window awhile, but eventually crept over to the cot closest to the door. Her silhouette seemed stolen from a teenage fantasy.

She dug out some snack packs from her bag and we talked as we ate. She told me about the last time she'd been in that room, how similar it had been—alone with a man in the near-dark—and yet how utterly different. She explained what Keith had done, or tried to do, and how that one act had opened her eyes to both his hypocrisy and her own inability to confront it. She'd been taken by him, by his bright-eyed passion, his endless persuasiveness, and become content within the confines of revolt. But the story of history's great charlatans always begins and ends with charisma, and if most were driven by money or power, Keith's vice was ego. Being the genius voice on the side of truth. And what things you could do from atop that moral high ground.

I thought I was beginning to understand her, just as my own life grew more obtuse. What was changing in me? There'd been no dramatic shift, no come-to-Jesus moment when I grasped the cursory nature of my existence. Rather, it was something I'd known all along. I had come to accept my life, my toxic cultural footprint, but if everyone was walking in the same direction, what did it matter? The idea of standing up, of revolting against something—*anything*—had never been a cogent or realistic option in the America I knew. And so I'd embraced, had *made a living from,* the ceaseless bloat—the publicists and spin doctors; the talking heads and network programmers; Hollywood and Washington. I went along with the screamers and hypocrites, gurus and preachers, everyone who talked *at* me and *past* me and *for* me while I stared blankly at TV screens and movie screens and computer screens, reality this and reality that, and of course the world had gotten away from me, from *us,* because complacency of one kind breeds complacency of every kind, and soon we're going along with wars and genocides because it's easier not to think about them, simpler not to get involved. We had experts for that kind of thing, and what could I possibly know about the great American illusion that they did not? I knew Paige was right to raise her hand and start asking questions. But how did one frame those questions exactly? How did one act upon one's knowledge?

At some point we slept, or I did. Paige, I'm guessing, stayed up a while more, thinking, plotting. How would Keith react if he found us here? And could she really talk him out of detonating another bomb? It sure didn't sound like it, not the way she'd described him earlier.

Would he have the thing with him?

That was my last coherent thought, and my first again upon waking, the trains on the bridge a perfect snooze alarm. Paige was still asleep. I thought of sneaking out to get us breakfast—I was starving—but she'd be awake the second my feet hit the floor. Then she woke up anyway.

"You'd make a terrible radical," I said, "sleeping so soundly."

"Ha ha." She rubbed her eyes. "I *am* a terrible radical. Look at us."

She had a point. If it was possible, the room in the half-light of morning had become even more depressing. You could see it now, how grimy it was, and how small. We showered—separately—using our dirty shirts as towels, then assessed the situation. We agreed I should venture out for supplies; Paige posed a greater risk of being recognized, and anyway, what would happen if Keith rolled in and I was here alone? I didn't want to find out.

We got some laundry together. Paige made a list of essentials: newspapers, food and water, blankets and pillows, plastic cups and plates, a flashlight, soap, towels, toilet paper, cigarettes. I made one, too: beer, wine, coffee, magazines . . . cigarettes.

"And I could pick up some lottery tickets," I said. "Because you never know."

She was looking at my list. "You're smoking now, too?"

"Can you think of a better time to start?"

It was still early when I left. I bought the papers and wandered around awhile before finding an open Laundromat on East Broadway. The night before, the streets had been a Benetton ad of races and religions, but now, watching our clothes spin dry, I was aware of being the only non-Asian in the place. Still, no one seemed to notice me. I flipped through the *Times,* the *Post,* the *News,* turning each page with a kind of dread. There were a few articles on the Flushing Four—including a piece in the *Times* about the mosque they'd regularly attended—but nothing, I noticed, connecting them to the bombing. And nothing about Paige either. Or Keith and Lindsay. Or, now, me.

When the clothes had dried, I stuffed them into my backpack and left. I bought some groceries at a bodega on Pike Street, then, remembering what Paige had told me about varying routes, started walking back toward the river. I was on the north side of the Manhattan Bridge now, and my plan was to make a right on one of these slender little streets—Monroe or Cherry—and arrive back at the apartment from the east. I'd made it a block when I came upon the Chinatown version of an Internet café—a clubby storefront dive with a neon @ sign in the window. None of the notices on the door were in English, but I looked inside anyway. A computer was free. I had to go online; it was as if the monitor had a tractor beam. As long as I didn't sign into any sites or check e-mail, I'd be fine, right? I paid the spiky-haired kid behind the desk five bucks for fifteen minutes and sat down beside a fish tank filled with water so murky I couldn't see inside. I started with the usual suspects: CNN, MSNBC, Drudge, the Huffington Post, the Daily Beast, and a few of the newsier blogs. Nothing. The world had moved on without us. Then I checked Roorback. I had to know what Derrick had done, how he'd handled my disappearance. Perhaps EmpiresFall had written again, in which case Derrick would surely have posted the message. I scrolled through the handful of entries he'd written in my absence. They had his fingerprints all over them—from the obvious jokes to the fatal lack of irony. He didn't trust his audience. Several commenters had inquired as to my whereabouts, but Derrick had ignored them. Everything, in fact, seemed like business as usual, suspiciously so. Fighting the urge to check my e-mail, I logged out and left. I felt dirty, as if I'd been splashing around with the fish that may or may not have existed a foot from my head.

I hurried back to the building, entered through the alley, and knocked on the apartment door as instructed.

"How come there's no peephole?" I asked, when she opened it.

"It's an old building. How come you took so long?"

She looked annoyed, like she'd been pacing, but seemed relieved when I told her there'd been no news of us, online or off ("I hope you didn't check your e—" "*No*"). And so we settled into our Wednesday morning. Crosswords and coffee. Newspapers and nicotine. We were huddling in a shelter awaiting a tempest, yet I can't remember being any more alive than I was then. Everything was unnatural and contradictory: the gravity and absurdity of our plight; the sureness and skepticism; the idle calm, the ever-present fear. And the two of us—reading and soon playing cards, like old friends, like new lovers—completely incapable of verbalizing even our most trivial feelings. Paige peeked through the blinds every few minutes, but there was no sign of Keith or Lindsay. Twice I asked her what would happen if and when they did show up. Twice she told me not to worry about it, that she would handle everything, but that just made me more nervous.

"How do you know he'll use the front entrance?"

"Because he has a *key* to the front entrance. People don't use alleyways unless they have a good reason. Like desperation."

I stopped asking questions after that. The afternoon passed, the air thickening, squeezing out the lingering light. When night fell in earnest, we opened beers to crack the tension. This time there was no talk of theory, of choices made and reasons why. Likewise, we stopped anticipating the future, how this all might end. Instead, we sat cross-legged on the floor and played gin by flashlight. At some point, we moved the game to her more comfortable mattress. She had changed into a black tank top, one I'd just washed, and it was so tight against her that her arms appeared to have punched through and escaped. It was almost pitch-dark in the room now. Paige was worried the flashlight beam might be seen from the street, so we turned it off and let our eyes adjust to the nothingness. She asked about Cressida, and I became conscious of my own voice, its droll timbre, nervously groping for a foothold. Then I stopped hedging and just told the truth, detailed our slow decline (or was it a rise to the surface, away from depth and emotion?). Paige was lying down, then we both were, side by side on our backs, just small talk now, nervous jokes, intriguing pauses. She told me about her childhood in the Smoky Mountains. I countered with harrowing stepmonster tales, masking their sting in humor, or trying to, until it was Paige's turn again, the two of us closer now, shoulders touching, and legs, barely, the way everything should start, with electric hints, and I must have dozed off because it only seemed a blissful minute or two later—though, again, it was hours—when she shook me awake and, before I could say a word, clasped a strong, soft hand over my mouth.

AIDAN

· · ●●●●●●● · · ●

WHAT HAD SHE HEARD? FOOTSTEPS? VOICES? I SAT UP IN THE DARKNESS. Paige was creeping barefoot toward the bathroom, the tired floorboards quietly cooperating. Then I heard it, too, the jangling of keys, followed immediately by another noise, closer, unmistakable: Paige opening a switchblade. My God. The front door was visible from the bed, and I watched paralyzed, helpless, as the lock began to turn. I was thinking *fire escape*. I was thinking *bum-rush*. I was thinking *blood*.

I couldn't think at all.

Why the knife if we were only here to talk?

Why not call out to Keith?

Why didn't I do something?

The door was opening, the weak light from the hallway framing a male figure. He stepped inside, taking the key from the lock, head down, arm stretching out, searching for the light switch. I could see part of Paige, tucked against the wall around the corner like a TV cop. Not five feet away. She was watching me, waiting—for what: a signal?—all of this in two seconds, the time it takes to breathe.

Then the light came on, and the man, sensing something, looked up, just as Paige raised her arm, blade showing, the scene a horror movie still.

He saw me. I saw him.

And I shouted, *"Simon, stop!"*

And Simon Krauss did exactly that, went dead still, the door slamming itself behind him. He looked at me in wonder, in disbelief, his mouth opening, forming words. Paige was staring at me, too, wild-eyed, desperate. *"Don't, Paige, I know him!"*

"Aidan," Simon managed, still motionless. *"And Paige? Paige Roderick? It's okay. I'm here to help."*

Paige stepped into the narrow hallway, the knife still in her hand, but lowered now, at her side. They faced each other, neither ceding ground nor moving closer.

"Who are you?" she asked evenly. Simon, seeing the knife, didn't answer immediately. Paige turned toward me without shifting her eyes from the man before her.

"He's my mother's friend," I said. "The one I told you about."

Paige frowned. "How could you . . . why did . . . you *called* someone?"

"No," I said.

"Then—"

"This is my apartment," Simon said, in that calm voice I knew well. Or thought I did. His eyes were still on the knife. "I'm on your side. I know what's going on."

"Well, someone better tell *me*, then," Paige said, still blocking the hallway.

Slowly, Simon took his cap off, and then his coat—

"Don't."

"I'm not armed."

"I think we can invite him in," I offered, but Paige ignored me. Instead, she closed the knife, put it in her pocket, and cautiously stepped up to Simon, who, without prompting, spread his arms. Paige patted him down, over his coat, then under. Simon stared serenely ahead, as if this happened all the time.

"Checking for a weapon or a wire?" he asked, when Paige had finished. She didn't answer. Instead, she turned and came back into the room. Simon, accepting this as an invitation, took his jacket off and followed her. I stood up and, having no idea what else to do, walked over and shook his hand.

"Surprised to see you here," he said to me.

"Okay, enough with the reunion," Paige said. "Who are you?"

"My name's Simon Krauss."

"He's a famous artist," I said.

"And your mother's boyfriend?" Paige asked.

"And Keith Sutter's . . . *patron*," Simon added, completing the ad hoc résumé.

There was silence then, everyone absorbing, working this out. Paige was still studying Simon, who looked, with his messy gray hair and stubbly beard, his faded jeans and rugged flannel shirt, as if he'd just put his blowtorch down.

"So you know where Keith is then?" Paige asked.

"I was hoping he'd be *here*," Simon answered, scanning the apartment the way Paige had scanned mine—in an instant. We were standing, the three of us, beside the table in the middle of the room, no one ready to commit to sitting, or anything else.

Paige wasn't done with him. "Tell me: if you know Keith so well, then what's his alias?"

"Todd Anderson," Simon said. "And Lindsay's Laura Bellamy. And you're, let's see, A, B, C . . . Clarke. Isabel Clarke."

Slowly, the tension in the room, the heaviness of the moment, evaporated. Paige exhaled. We all did. "Okay then," she said. "Sorry about the knife."

"How'd you know I wasn't Keith?" Simon asked.

"I wouldn't have heard Keith coming."

He chuckled. "I must be out of practice."

"When were you *in* practice?" I asked.

"We'll get to that," Simon said, "but first . . . do you two have a flashlight? The sun will be up soon, but still, we shouldn't use the overhead."

"Thanks for the tip," Paige said, pointing out the flashlight on the floor beside the bed. She walked to the window and snuck a peek though the blinds. Simon picked up the flashlight, turned it on, then reached up and unscrewed the ceiling bulb.

"Safer this way," he said.

"You bring sleeping bags with you again?" Paige asked.

"I didn't come here to change Keith's bedding. I came here to change his mind."

"About what?" Paige asked, her voice softening.

"The N3 Action."

"You know his plans?"

"As well as anyone," Simon answered. "Which doesn't necessarily mean much."

"No," Paige agreed. Simon handed her the flashlight, which I took as a sign of acquiescence. Or maybe he just realized it was hers. I was still utterly confused by Simon's presence, his apparently secret life. It was like finding out your father was a war hero, or had killed someone, or both.

"Can I ask what's going on?" I asked.

"I think I can answer that," Paige said, turning to address Simon. "You're EmpiresFall, aren't you?"

"No, he's not," I said.

Simon cleared his throat but remained silent, waiting for Paige to continue.

"Of course he is. What, Aidan, you think it's a coincidence that your mother's boyfriend just strolled in here off the street? That's another thing I should have told you. Coincidence: there's no such thing."

"She's right about that," Simon remarked.

"So what happened?" Paige asked. "Wait, let me guess. Keith starts making you nervous and you decide he has to be stopped. And I'm your sacrificial lamb. The photograph of me outside Barneys. You took that, right? But if you're going to blow the whistle, why on earth did you e-mail the photo to Aidan? Why not tip off the mainstream media? Or the Feds?"

"Because we don't squeal on our own. Not like that. Keith may be misguided—"

"Try unhinged," Paige said.

"—but he's still one of us. I didn't want any of you getting arrested, so I came up with the Roorback idea. I'd send you the photo, Aidan, and one of two things would happen. Probably, you'd think it was a joke and post it. Everyone would link to the thing, and it wouldn't take you long, Paige, trolling the Internet up there in Vermont, to realize your cover was blown and scrap the Action. The three of you could fold up shop and disappear with a head start. At least you'd have a fighting chance."

"Or?" I asked.

"Or you *wouldn't* post the photo," Simon said, "and you'd do a little digging yourself. Journalism, I think they call it. Maybe a picture of Paige would get you off your laptop and out into the world. Which is something you should have done ages ago."

"How'd you know *I* wouldn't call the cops?" I asked. "Or tell Cressida?"

"Because you'd never forgive yourself," Simon answered, and nodded toward Paige. "A girl like that."

Paige, who'd been listening intently, rolled her eyes back out to the street.

"So when I saw you at my mother's house, you knew what I was up to?"

"Of course. Though I was surprised it had gotten that far. I never thought you'd actually track Paige down. At best, you'd get close enough to spook her. Spook them. Instead, here we are. Your mother's going to kill me. We need to get you out of here."

"Tell me *she's* not a part of whatever it is you're doing," I said.

"No, no, she doesn't know about any of this. Let me . . . I should just make this clear: I love your mother a great deal, and would never put her in harm's way. Please remember that. Besides, she's never been *involved* like that. Even at Yale, from what she's told me, she always stuck to campus stuff: antiwar rallies and civil-rights sit-ins."

"As opposed to you?" Paige asked.

"As opposed to me," Simon answered.

"Well, I've got bad news for you in terms of the home front," Paige said. "It's a bit too late to put Aidan on a bus up to Woodstock."

"What do you mean?"

Paige told Simon about seeing Cressida in the stairwell, and from there we took turns filling him in on the rest: Fishers Island; the state fair; the Liberty Inn; and our plan to expose the N3 Action on Roorback if we couldn't find Keith soon. Simon listened carefully, his face creasing in concern, and what looked like regret. Was he blaming himself? He was, after all, responsible for the two of us being there. And Paige? Why wasn't she still spewing venom at the man who'd leaked her identity? Perhaps it was something they shared, these two, beyond searing passion and cool objectivity, this ability to steer around impediments, around tragedy. Is that what kept them alive to the damaged world? Or alive in it?

● ● ·

It was still so early, 6:30 a.m., and we took a few minutes to collect ourselves. Simon's sudden appearance had changed the parameters of our situation. But it also focused us. There were too many questions to ask, so we didn't ask them. Instead, we put on coffee and sat down around the table. Simon thought we should give it twenty-four hours; if Keith didn't come through the door by first light the following morning, then I was to go back to the Internet café and inform the world—or at least the Web—of his violent plan, while Simon snuck Paige out of the city.

And if Keith did appear, well, then we needed to be ready.

Simon knew a lot about N3 and, like Paige, believed there was a good chance Keith would still try to carry it out. It was now Thursday morning. The N3 Action had originally been planned for Saturday night, when the building would be least busy, and major Actions were not easily rescheduled. But a lot had changed since Simon and Keith had last spoken. Paige had split, for one. And the Flushing Four had been charged. And Keith and Lindsay had disappeared.

"I drove up to Mad River yesterday," Simon said, "and the house looked like it'd been deserted for months."

"Did you check the garage?" Paige asked.

"Yeah. It was empty."

Intercepting Keith in New York was Simon's last hope, as it was ours, and we could do nothing now but plan for the confrontation. I was thinking about Paige's knife, whether she'd have used it if Simon had been someone else. Then I thought about her, and the night before, the two of us together on the mattress. How much of it had been comfort, a simple matter of close quarters, and how much had been . . .

Enough. I poured coffee as Paige and Simon discussed contingencies—what would happen the moment Keith walked in, and what would happen after. Paige had been reticent when I'd pushed her on the subject, but with Simon she came alive. They were two professionals, speaking the same language. Neither believed it would get violent, but still, they ran through a half dozen potential scenarios. Paige stood up every few minutes to peek through the blinds, but the street below was quiet. Eventually, Simon leaned back and rubbed his hands together. "So now we wait," he said. He fished a phone out and began checking messages.

"I hope you know what you're doing with that thing," Paige told him.

"Don't worry, it's clean."

"And what about 'Simon Krauss'?"

"It's held up for thirty years."

"You're kidding."

"I should think," Simon said, "that under the circumstances, you'd be thrilled to know it's still possible to survive underground in America."

"You're saying I have a chance?" Paige asked with a wry smile. "What were you, a Weatherman or something?"

"As a matter of fact, I was," he said, putting his phone away. "Up through the Northwestern chapter of SDS. A part-time student and full-time agitator. I managed to get arrested at every march in Chicago, and I guess that's what the leadership was looking for—Bill Ayers, Bernardine Dohrn, Terry Robbins—someone with a natural aversion to authority, who thrived on all that us-against-the-world shit. The Weathermen measured a person's worth by how far he or she was willing to go. A lot of it was ego and bluster, and early on we alienated some people—"

"Like the entire student left," Paige said.

"Unfortunately, yes. But remember the historical moment, how much was happening and how quickly. Especially in Chicago. The Democratic Convention in '68, the SDS convention a year later, which Weather more or less hijacked. And then, of course, the Chicago Eight, the Days of Rage, and the murder of Fred Hampton, and all of this set against the background of Vietnam. That America could do such a thing . . . I'm sorry. I'm not sure how much you know about this stuff."

"A lot," Paige said.

"Not much," I said.

Simon shrugged. "It was a long time ago. We were kids, most of us, sons and daughters of Jews who'd had it hard, who'd survived European anti-Semitism and eventually found success on these shores. And when America cracked open just as we were coming of age, well, we decided we could fix it. We had the earnestness of intellectuals, the anger of the persecuted, the vanity of youth. And with the war and the assassinations, the music and the drugs, the *scene,* there was a feeling in the air that nothing was settled, that history could be budged, if only we had the guts to start pushing. It sounds naïve, *amusing* even, to talk about revolution in an age when nothing is vital, when America has accepted its own mediocrity, settled for a lesser version of itself— action replaced by sarcasm, cynicism, muted displeasure. . . ."

Simon was regarding me curiously.

"What?" I said.

"You've come a long way in two weeks."

"Not that far," I told him, grinning. "Just a mile across town."

"Indeed."

"What's your real name?" Paige asked.

"Jonathan Glassman. Or at least it was until March of 1970."

"The town-house explosion," Paige said.

"What town-house?" I asked.

Simon told me the story. How wires got crossed in a basement. How three of his friends had died, and two others, dazed and ears ringing, disappeared into the crowd. Then all of them disappeared, went underground. "March, 1970," Simon said. "The beginning of the end. Because how effective could we be after that, with no central structure, with the police and FBI after us? We kept at it, of course, planting bombs and all the rest, but it was already too late. America wasn't going to turn, and our nascent revolution died a slow, splintered death. We shuffled from safe house to safe house, motel to motel. Some crossed into Canada or Mexico. Others cut deals and gave up—the lunatic fringe coming in from the cold. I spent the next few years on the run, from New York to Baltimore to D.C., and then out West."

"The Weather Underground set bombs off in all of those cities," Paige said.

Simon raised his eyebrows. "You really do know your history. Alas, those Actions—the National Guard headquarters and the U.S. Capitol—they were the work of others. I came into my own in California, with the Presidio . . . and Timothy Leary."

"The acid guy?" I said.

"Yeah," Paige answered. "The Weathermen broke him out of prison and snuck him off to Europe."

"Africa, actually," Simon said. "A Black Panther compound in Algeria."

"And when Leary got busted again a few years later, he ratted everyone out to get a reduced sentence," Paige said, shaking her head.

"Well, yes and no. It certainly wasn't his shining moment, but he didn't tell the Feds everything. And he didn't give me up. By then—this was '75 or '76—I'd pretty much disassociated myself from Weather, or what was left of it. Everything had come to an inglorious end. The war was over, Watergate was through, and people were tired of fighting. Radicals had earned themselves a bad reputation. For years we'd shouted from the mountaintops, demanding a society free of class and racial divisions, and we'd never once descended from our lofty heights to meet anyone halfway. We'd forced our ideas down people's throats: a perfect world, liberated not just from the tyranny of government but from the constraints of our own minds. Hence the drugs, the mental manipulation, the endurance training, the orgies . . . Mandatory non-monogamy: Jesus."

"And yet here you are in a safe house thirty-five years later," Paige said.

"How about that."

"Why?"

"That's a good question. I suppose it has a lot to do with our friend Keith Sutter."

"You knew him back then?"

"No, he was much too young for all that. I spent the eighties bouncing around northern California. Different jobs. Different identities. Most of my friends had surfaced by then. The Feds had broken so many laws coming after us that they couldn't mount prosecutions. I'd have come up, too, reclaimed my name, sought out what was left of my family and friends, except . . . suddenly there was this art thing."

"*This art thing?*" I repeated. "Paige, his sculptures sell for tens of thousands."

"Occasionally."

"Yeah, well . . ."

The room was getting warm, but opening the window—even a

crack—wasn't an option (if Keith suspected we were there, Simon said, then he'd never come upstairs). It would be a long day, I could tell. Already Paige seemed anxious, pacing back and forth every few minutes to peek outside. Simon remained seated on the bed, but he was sweating. We all were.

"How'd it happen?" Paige asked. "You becoming an artist, I mean."

"I'd been working the wharf in San Francisco, but then the city renovated the waterfront and the tourists rolled in. They'd watch us unload the crab boats as they waited for the ferry to Alcatraz, and every so often I'd glance up and see a face I thought I knew—an old comrade reborn as a family man with a chubby wife and sunburned kids. It was probably just my imagination, but still, it was getting too dangerous with all those people milling around. So I took a job at a scrap yard in the East Bay—no questions asked, and they paid in cash. I worked under the lights at night, surrounded by acres and acres of scarred and twisted metal. Well, pretty soon the stuff took on a weird significance to me, and I began working with it in my free time, shearing and bending, searching for a kind of beauty in all that decay. The owner of the yard displayed one of my early monstrosities up by the entrance, and a few weeks later some art collector driving past in his BMW stopped and made an offer. And that was the beginning.

"I'd been living as Simon Krauss for a few years by then, and my IDs had held up well. It sounded like an artist's name—rough and a bit foreign—and I thought . . . maybe I can go with it, build a whole persona, become someone else forever. So I gave it a shot. I sold a few more pieces, then hooked on with a gallery in SoHo and moved to New York. I'd been in the Bay Area too long anyway. As it happens, the art world was the perfect cover. Every artist since Warhol has had a bullshit back-story, because it helps with the marketing. No one ever asked where I'd grown up or gone to school. They asked about my influences, what artists I hung around with, what women I slept with, and when I didn't answer, they liked that, too. Mystery sells most of all."

Simon stretched out his neck and arms. He was caught up in events of a magnitude I couldn't fathom, but there he sat, exuding a serenity that was almost contagious—until, that is, I glanced over at Paige, nervously tapping on her thighs, and remembered what was at stake, what could happen.

Anything. At any moment.

". . . So I found a warehouse space in Greenpoint," Simon was saying, "and buried myself in work. The eighties became the nineties. The galleries moved to Chelsea and artists got rich. America got rich—rich and lazy. And I watched it all at a comfortable remove. Sculpture like mine had become the rage, art on a grand scale, swollen and overwrought—like the money that came with it. Soon, people began tossing my name around with the legends of abstract expressionism. I was the next Richard Serra, the next David Smith. Heady stuff, though I never bought into it. I always thought it was luck—luck to be working in an artistic field with hardly any competition. Massive welded ironworks? Believe me, it's not for everyone. The downside was the publicity—the openings and interviews—which I endured to an extent, because the other option, reclusiveness, came with its own form of notoriety. Look at Salinger. Look at Joseph Cornell. I was as careful as humanly possible, but being recognized was inevitable. I always assumed it would be the Feds. Instead, it was Movement people—old friends at first, and then strangers. It was typewritten letters and tentative phone calls. A forgotten face at a gallery. A late-night knock on my door. Some had put their pasts behind them; one or two were still running. Most, though, I'd never met. They were young radicals who'd done their homework, the next generation of earnest contrarians, some sickened by the dot-com boom, others primed by the protests in Seattle, and somewhere along the way they'd heard my name whispered, like a secret password to the big time. The Weather Underground was suddenly in vogue again, but I didn't care. These were kids, green and ill-prepared, and I had nothing to tell them. I was out of that business."

"So that was it?" Paige asked, from her lookout post across the room. "You just turned your back on the world while you lived the high life?"

"Jesus, Paige, that's a bit harsh," I said. "He'd been on the run for almost thirty years. I think he'd done his time."

Simon winced. "Certainly that was part of it. I *was* tired of running, of pretending. And, yes, I'd fallen into this strange lucrative career, transparent as it was, as it *is*, but when you've spent your adult life working the docks and tarring roofs and frying eggs in boxcar diners, all because you cared too much, because you took *action* where others wouldn't, I'll just say my new circumstance was something of a pleasant change."

"I'm sorry," Paige said. "I didn't mean to—"

"No, don't be. Because you're right. I'd been saved by strangers time and time again when I was underground, and now here I was turning away the next generation. It took Iraq to finally wake me up, to make me realize there was something left to fight for. *Everything* left to fight for. And so I finally got involved. Just small-time stuff at first, meetings with the leaders of this group or that—ELF, ISM, UFPJ, even a revamped SDS. There was talk of carrying out an Action in the lead-up to the invasion, and then again at the Republican Convention in New York. But it never went anywhere; we weren't ready, and neither was the country. The Bush administration had done so many awful things, but the sad truth—and, Paige, please don't take this the wrong way—is that it would take something far worse than Iraq, perhaps worse than Vietnam, to bring about mass civil disobedience in America today. I'm talking about a total collapse of the financial system, or an unjust war with a body count in the hundreds of thousands. Iraq, no matter how drawn out, was never going to be that war. Not for Americans, anyway. Besides, we were gun-shy, us old-timers. We'd preached revolution and no one had listened. We'd brought the war home and no one had joined us. We'd come to realize we were wrong."

Paige shook her head. "How can you say you were wrong when—"

"Hold on, hold on," Simon said, raising his hand. "We were wrong about our goals, which were immature and ill-conceived. Revolution was always out of reach, and ultimately unnecessary. But what *had* worked, beyond any doubt, were our methods—the Actions themselves. The bombings achieved exactly what we hoped they would: they shone a spotlight on their targets. And in the end, they helped get us out of Vietnam. Sure, it took failure in the battlefield and ineptitude in Washington. It took speeches and marches and riots. *But it took bombs, too.* Every movement needs a jagged leading edge, a front line willing to sacrifice. It makes the second wave stronger and more legitimate. I believed it in 1970 and I still believe it forty years later: that targeted, nonlethal violence can be used for good. And I'm not the only one."

Simon sipped his coffee contemplatively. We waited, entranced.

"Iraq got worse," he continued, "and we got more serious. We spent late nights in the back of Greenpoint bars, discussing, debating, arguing, about what we might do—what we *could* do—to combat the War on Terror, that awful euphemism, catchphrase for all the massacres to come. For when the smoke cleared ten years from now, or fifty, and the world's survivors looked up through weary eyes to assess the damage, what would they say about America, about Americans? *That we should have stood up, should have tried harder.* And so a small group of us set out, once more, to do just that. We put the word out, carefully, to what few pockets of experienced resistance were left—people with the right skills and beliefs, the right temperament—and the name Keith Sutter came back, again and again. The ELF was the only legitimate group still carrying out Direct Actions, and they were brilliant at it— secretive in their planning and meticulous in their follow-through. What's more, they knew how to manipulate the press. I'd moved upstate by this point; I needed more space for my work, but I was also getting that old itch again—to keep moving, to avoid routines. There'd been too many meetings in Brooklyn and—"

"*Fuck,*" Paige hissed, and abruptly slid down under the window, out of view.

"What?" Simon jumped up and in an instant had joined her.

"The girl across the street. It might be Lindsay."

"Are you sure?"

"No. I just saw her for a second. Coming up the block. Skinny, right hair and height. She has a messenger bag over her shoulder."

"Was she looking up here?" Simon asked. "Did she see you?"

"I don't think so."

"Then take another peek."

Paige raised a slat ever so slightly and peered outside. I held my breath. I think Simon did, too.

"It's . . . wait . . . no . . . it's *not* her." Paige turned around and slumped to the floor. "Sorry, I thought . . ." She rubbed her eyes.

"You were being careful," Simon said.

"Yeah, but that doesn't mean the every pale, stringy girl in New York is Lindsay. I think I'm just tired."

"We're all tired," Simon told her. "Here, why don't I take a shift at the window and you can get some rest. I've been talking too much anyway."

"No, I'm fine. I promise. Keep going. I want to hear the rest."

Simon sat back down on the bed. Paige poured some water into cups and passed them out. The room was cramped, but almost pulsing with intensity.

"Okay then," Simon said. "Let's see. I rented what's now Aidan's mother's house in Shady—she was still in the city then—and went about blending in. It was a good base of operations, and I used my cover as an artist to begin organizing, planning, recruiting. I spent weeks at a time on the road. After one trip out West—when I met Keith for the first time—I came home to find Susan in my kitchen. Scared the hell out of me, though I'm sure I scared her more. We never really left each other after that, even as I tried to protect her from my more . . . *private* activities. It was because of her that I decided to work strictly behind the scenes. I was too old to be sneaking around anyway. It took months, and then years, but we eventually structured the same kind of loose organization that Weather—and later, the ELF— had successfully used, a series of cells each operating independently but with the same agenda: to bring American ineptness and injustice to light using any means necessary but one—we wouldn't hurt anyone. Not physically, at least. The Weather Underground never killed anyone—outside the group, I mean—and neither would we.

"Our first cell was in New York. The Bike Messengers, we called them, because that was their preferred mode of delivery. And then—"

"The bomb in Times Square a few years ago," Paige said, her eyes going wide. "Was that them?"

Simon smiled. "What do *you* think?"

"That guy rode into the world's biggest intersection and blew the door off that shitty recruiting station. He must have been caught on a hundred cameras, and still . . ."

"I remember," I said. "It was all over the news. They found the bike a few blocks south, but then the trail went cold."

"Indeed," Simon said, his tone carrying the pride of ownership. He extended an arm toward Paige, as if introducing her at a talent show. "And then we had the Carolina cell, which spawned Ms. Roderick here. Less extreme, perhaps, but no less effective."

"You were involved with us from the beginning?" Paige asked.

"Nominally, yes. We paid rents, sent supplies, and signed off on the Actions."

Back at the window, Paige peeked outside, then lit a cigarette.

"But Keith was always the focal point, the star, even early on. It took a lot of convincing to make him commit to anything outside the ELF, but when we said he could handpick his people, he agreed to work with us. Lindsay was a given—she'd been involved in ELF Actions for years and Keith trusted her. As for a third, well, we'd had you in mind since the paper factory."

"You were watching me that whole time?"

"From the moment you met up with Carter Gattling. You had everything—the brains, the fearlessness, and the . . . the *motivation*." Simon straightened up. "I'm very sorry about your brother, Paige. And while I'm at it, I'm sorry this has all ended so badly. Keith wasn't the man we thought he was."

"When did you realize it . . . that things weren't right?"

"When it was too late," Simon said. "I just . . . I should have seen the signs. Keith and I met every week after the three of you arrived in Vermont, at a Wal-Mart parking lot in Rutland. I gave him money; he gave me progress updates. Mostly though, we discussed the pros and cons of each potential Action. I was shocked when he brought up Indian Point. It was clearly too much of a risk, both in terms of the Action itself and the aftermath, but he was so in love with the idea. That should have been the first clue. I mean, breaking into a nuclear facility with a backpack full of explosives—"

"He was talking about a remote-control truck," Paige said.

"Even worse. I'm all for making a statement your first time out, but that wasn't it. Eventually, he backed away from that particular cliff—or maybe you dragged him away—and I let it go. He'd carried everything else off so brilliantly, like getting the dynamite: that was a stroke of genius. As was your Indigo idea. They were exactly the kind of target I'd envisioned going after, and the three of you almost pulled it off perfectly. It would have been a hell of a lot better than anything Weather ever did. Getting in and out of that building, with all that surveillance . . . I located the plans and did some recon of my own before you and Keith got down here. Those notes on the blueprints were mine. And I stayed around to make sure you didn't get in trouble. Keith didn't want me in the area—we were arguing on the phone when you walked in on him the night before, and continued in person the following morning—but it was your first major Action and I thought you needed support, even if you didn't know it. I followed you through the store, discreetly photographing security cameras and personnel, then snuck out just before you did. The Madison Avenue photo was the last one I took."

"I can't believe I didn't see you."

"It's nice to know I've still got a few moves left. That said, I'd have never imagined what happened next, the bomb exploding on the wrong floor. I watched the news in a stupor, shocked that Keith could have fucked up like that. But when we met in Rutland the following week, he was so pleased with himself. There'd been no casualties, after all, and surely the press would zero in on Indigo—which is eventually what happened. I told him he'd been damned lucky. Sloppy and careless and lucky—nothing more. And you know what he did, instead of apologizing? He claimed the elevator numbering hadn't been his responsibility. He blamed you and Lindsay, and it just . . . it *broke my heart,* because I'd seen it all before, the way people respond to sudden power: some with humility, others with a kind of righteousness. Lines blur at their extremes, and sometimes people crack. Keith cracked and I recognized it too late. When he mentioned his idea for N3, I begged him to forget it. *The media,* for Christ's sake. But he gave me a look I'll never forget. And when he got out of the car and slammed the door, I knew I'd have no choice but to try to stop him."

Our tenement building belonged to some other time and place. Shoeless footsteps pitter-pattered above us. Muted voices drifted through the thin walls as if underwater. And the smells, exotic foods and fish and waste, soon blended into a single tangy stink. When the heat finally became overwhelming, we opened the window a crack. Simon again offered to stand watch, but Paige would have none of it.

It was late morning when he snuck outside to check on his van (he'd parked legally on the street, but still . . .) and buy the papers. Paige and I didn't speak for a while after he left. She watched the street nervously; I lay on the bed thinking about Simon Krauss and the secrets we all lived with, or didn't. Was everyone somebody else? And what did it take to find that person, the one inside? For me, it took a picture. An ideal personified. I needed to tell her this, tell Paige what she meant to me. And I was just about to, I swear, but she was suddenly peering intently through the blinds, a frown clouding her face. Then she backed away, as if the glass were toxic.

"Something's wrong," she said.

AIDAN

· · • • • • • · · • ·

I HURRIED OVER TO THE WINDOW.

"Look," Paige said. "On the corner." The glass was streaky, but I could make out Simon coming toward us. He was hurrying, almost running, and looking around like a traffic cop.

"He's all agitated," I said.

"Like he's just seen something awful."

We moved together to the center of the room, facing the door, like fretful family members awaiting news from an emergency-room doctor. Simon's footsteps echoed up the stairwell and sounded down the hall, then he burst through the door, his face tight and ashen.

"What is it?" Paige said.

"The Drudge Report," he replied, producing his cell phone. He held it out to us. "I had Google alerts set for both your names, and when my pocket started vibrating like crazy, I knew . . ."

He didn't finish the thought. Paige took the phone and we sat down beside each other on the closest bed. She pressed the Internet icon. Drudge came up immediately.

"Oh, no," Paige said, and put her hand on my knee.

Our photographs loaded side by side on the top of the page. Above them loomed the headline:

THE BLOGGER AND THE BOMBSHELL:
NEW SUSPECTS IN INDIGO BOMBING.

Paige scrolled down the screen with a shaking finger.

**BONNIE & CLYDE DUO: GOSSIP WRITER AND
GLAMOROUS RADICAL
INTENSIVE POLICE AND FBI MANHUNT UNDERWAY
"FLUSHING FOUR" TO BE RELEASED, CHARGES DROPPED**

Thu Sept. 16 10:14:53 a.m. ET
World Exclusive
Must Credit DRUDGE REPORT

The New York Times *is set to publish a shocking article naming
two unlikely new suspects in last month's bombing in Manhattan,
the* DRUDGE REPORT *has learned. A massive police manhunt
is underway across the tristate area for Aidan Cole, 33, and Paige
Roderick, 29, who were last seen yesterday, checking out of the Liberty Inn, a notorious low-rent hotel in New York's West Village.*

*Cole was until yesterday the editor of the popular media and cul-
ture blog Roorback.com. Roderick had worked at the Earth Initiative in New York and the liberal Carver Institute in Washington,
D.C., before being let go in January. Her recent whereabouts have
been unknown.*

*According to an "acquaintance" of Cole's, the blogger became
obsessed with Roderick after receiving an e-mail (with the above
photograph attached) accusing her of the crime. Instead of
informing Roorback's publisher, Derrick Franklin, or contacting
authorities, Cole set off to track Roderick down himself. He found
her in Waitsfield, Vermont, where she confessed to being involved
(it is not known if she acted alone). Cole still failed to reach out
to police.*

In a fateful twist, Cole was dating Times *reporter Cressida Kent at
the time, and it was Kent who first alerted* Times *editors to Cole's
possible involvement with Roderick (the paper has allowed Kent
to help investigate the story, but because of potential conflicts, has*

assigned the actual writing to other reporters). Kent then reached out to Cole's "acquaintance," and convinced him or her to speak on record in exchange for anonymity. The "acquaintance" is also expected to receive immunity from any prosecution.

Cole contacted his "acquaintance" by phone on Tuesday, and left a message. Using GPS tracking, authorities were able to trace his cell phone to the Liberty Inn. By the time authorities arrived, however, Cole and Roderick, who had checked in under an assumed name, had checked out.

The Times *agreed to delay publication of the story until a press briefing today at noon, so police could keep the manhunt a secret. The decision angered several newsroom insiders, who claimed the article was ready in time for the Thursday-morning print edition.*

More . . .

The four Queens men arrested earlier this week in connection with the bombing were quietly released this morning and have been cleared of all charges. The men, all Muslims, were members of the Abubakr mosque in Flushing.

Late last night, according to WPTZ-TV News, the FBI raided a house near the Sugarbush ski resort in Waitsfield, Vermont. The property had recently been abandoned, and investigators were still combing the surrounding valley this morning.

Roorback publisher Derrick Franklin has provided the Times *with all online correspondence relating to the bombing, which includes the above photograph of Paige Roderick. Franklin told authorities he had no knowledge of the e-mails before the* Times *alerted him to their existence, as they had been sent to Cole's personal Roorback account.*

Developing . . .

Paige finished reading, waited for me, then scrolled back up to our pictures—hers, the iconic Madison Avenue glamour shot; mine, a drunken photo from a recent party that must have been provided by Cressida. In fact, I realized, looking closer, I'd had my arm around her in the original version, but she'd been cropped out (or had cropped herself out), so there I was grinning like a fool, with most of my arm missing.

"Are you okay?" Paige asked me.

"I think so. But it feels like they're talking about other people."

"I know," she said softly. She handed the phone back to Simon.

"Drudge must have gotten the article from someone at the *Times,*" Simon said.

"One of the 'angry newsroom insiders,'" I posited.

"Who's this 'acquaintance'?" Simon asked. "Your buddy Touché?"

"Has to be," I said, keenly aware that only two days before I'd been willing to put our lives in his hands. Paige could have called me on it, but didn't.

Simon sat down across from us. "Let's figure out what we do now."

"We wait," Paige said.

"No, no." Simon shook his head. "Keith won't come down here after this. It's far too risky. He'll find out about you two in the next few hours, if he hasn't already, and then he'll disappear. Or stay disappeared."

"You think he'll scrap the Action?" Paige asked.

Simon rubbed the stubble on his jawline. "Not necessarily. If you two had been caught, it'd be a different story. He'd have no choice but to scrap it because one of you might talk. But as things are . . ." Simon frowned.

"What?" Paige said.

"He may even try it tonight. Think about it. The Feds are closing in and he has no base of operations. But he has a bomb and one last chance to use it."

"And if it does go off," Paige followed, "everyone will think we're the de facto suspects, and Keith and Lindsay get away scot-free."

"Exactly," Simon said. "Which means we need to get out of the city right now. Before this press briefing. Before any more pictures of you two get out there. Before they ramp up security at the bridges and tunnels. There's a place in New Jersey, a farmhouse in Bernardsville, just off I-287. We use it occasionally for meetings. It's not perfect, but it'll work for a night or two while we sort out something better. I'll drive us out there. Here, let's straighten this place out and—"

"*No*," said Paige, quiet but forceful.

"But we have to move. You saw the Drudge thing. They're not far behind us. We're down to luck now."

"We've been careful," Paige said.

"*Really?*" said Simon, standing up. His eyes narrowed, his weathered face turned hard. "If you'd been careful, Cressida wouldn't have made you in that stairwell. If you'd been careful, Aidan wouldn't have left his idiot friend a message, and the FBI wouldn't be swarming the Liberty Inn right now."

"Hold on," I said. "All of that was my fau—"

"*Fuck that!*" Paige said. "Why don't you come out of retirement and see how long *you* last." She stood up and took a step toward Simon, the two of them suddenly nose to nose, and for a second I thought she might push him or, Christ, take some sort of swing. But she stopped short. "This isn't 1970. You can't just vanish. There are cameras everywhere, satellites and surveillance. They're watching the entire world. It's a miracle we're still going, so don't tell me to be more careful. Especially after what *you* did."

"And what did *I* do?" Simon asked, digging in.

"You threw me under a fucking bus for some supposed greater good."

"*You don't think stopping Keith is worth it?*" Simon said, his face reddening. "*You don't think I've done everything I possibly—*"

"*Enough!*" I shouted, finally standing up myself.

They both looked at me, startled. Simon bowed his head and took a step back. Paige moved over—as if out of habit now—to the window, then spun around to face us.

"I think stopping Keith is worth everything," she said calmly. "Which is why I'm not going out to New Jersey. Not yet."

Simon took a heavy breath. "Why can't you understand the danger you're—"

"He wants to kill people this time," Paige said. "Don't you know? The bomb's filled with shrapnel. I saw it myself. *That's* why I left."

Simon's mouth opened but nothing came out.

"Yeah," Paige said. "My thoughts exactly."

The Roorback option, though no one had said as much, was now gone. It had disappeared when two determined young women passed each other in a stairwell. And where did that leave me? Exactly where

I was: with Paige. On the far side of the American equation. Nothing was certain. Little was known. I listened, lost, as Paige and Simon argued in stage voices, trying not to be too loud. The contents of the bomb had clearly swayed Simon's thinking.

"I think Keith means it only as a harsh warning," he said. "I just . . . I can't imagine he'd intentionally hurt people, but still, this changes everything. We need to alert the authorities now. Place an anonymous call, feed them Keith and Lindsay's names, along with the sordid details of N3, and then get out of town."

"But what will that solve?" Paige asked. "It might save N3, temporarily, but they won't get Keith or Lindsay. No, the two of them will spot the extra security and be long gone. Their bomb will go off somewhere else, and then another one will, and sooner or later people will die and we'll still be suspects. We need to talk them out of it. *I* need to talk *him* out of it. I say we give it one last shot. He'll show up at N3 tonight, I'm almost sure of it, and if he doesn't, then we can call the cops. Either way, we'll regroup outside the city and figure out what to do."

I looked at Simon, and I saw in his eyes a kind of determined humanity. Keith had been his friend, his collaborator, the two of them working and dreaming together on a level I couldn't imagine. The sacrifices made, the risks taken, all in this foolish, brilliant, noble attempt to—what was his phrase?—*budge history*. And this is what it had come to. The opposition—immovable America—had once again proven too strong. It was time to retreat with as few casualties as possible.

So it was settled. We would stay. We would stay against every instinct we had to move, to run. Simon had come around to Paige's way of thinking. Or maybe it was the other way around. In any event, the arguing had ended, and the only thing that mattered now was stopping the bomb. They were both convinced that Keith would try it that night. After that the risk would be too great, the city too dangerous. We'd never hear from him again. Until, of course, we did: loudly.

We got back to work, the three of us around the table again. Paige had cracked the blinds, and the ensuing light, while hardly radiant, changed the mood. Simon went back out to his van and returned with a set of Google map grids detailing the blocks surrounding the National News Network's Midtown Manhattan headquarters. Paige had memorized the specifics of the Action back in Vermont, including the building's vital statistics, from the location of elevators and stairwells to the office of each senior executive. As well as lobbies and bathrooms, conference rooms and closets, and the expanse of ground-floor news sets and studios. What Paige didn't know (since she'd split before they'd returned) was what had happened on Keith and Lindsay's reconnaissance trip.

That's where Simon took charge.

"Keith told me everything," he explained. "The details down to the minute."

"When?" Paige asked.

"Last Sunday, on his way back up to Waitsfield after the N3 recon. We met in the Wal-Mart parking lot one last time. He wanted my help again, like on Indigo, but he didn't realize the extent of my opposition. He couldn't fathom I might turn against him—that the Roorback leak and Aidan's sudden appearance on the scene might be my doing. And he didn't know, Paige, that you would take off—had *already* taken off. He was still riding the adrenal success of Indigo, and he thought everyone would come around, everyone would *understand*, once he had a chance to explain himself.

"And that's exactly what he did," Simon continued. "He told me everything: how he'd canvassed the blocks surrounding N3's head-quarters, discreetly videotaping the outside of the building, the entrances and exits, the side-street loading docks, and further down Fifty-first Street, the studio emergency-exit door, which had been propped permanently open—like the alley door downstairs—by the company's nicotine hordes. Keith saw it immediately for what it was: *his way in*. Meanwhile, Lindsay, guidebook in hand, signed up for N3's Saturday-afternoon studio tour and slipped away when no one was looking. She spent hours sneaking around the building, marking not just placement and location, but employee flow, cleaning schedules, and security walk-arounds. She took the stairs up to the sixth floor, Executive Row, which by seven p.m. was deserted, as were the floors above and below. There were no cameras in the hallways, no internal motion detectors. The only part of the building that remained occupied at night was the twenty-four-hour news studio on the ground floor."

"Sounds easy compared to Barneys," Paige remarked, apparently seriously.

"That's what Keith said, too. And still I told him no. That it just felt wrong. You can't sway public opinion by attacking the media. It never works. But Keith wasn't listening. He said he'd be in touch, then got out of my car, walked over two rows to where Lindsay was waiting, and together they drove away."

Paige took careful notes as Simon talked, often asking him to repeat or clarify things. They discussed overnight security and cleaning schedules and concluded, as Keith would have, that the sixth floor at 2:15 a.m.—the original go time—would be just as empty on a weeknight as on a weekend. It was a dangerous assumption—despite Simon's hopeful premise, the makeup of the N3 bomb could also point to some secret darker plan to explode it at a busier hour—but in the absence of other information, it held firm. The day progressed, the room brightened. Soon, a strategy took shape, along with the necessary contingencies (and those two thought of everything: *if this, then this, or this, or this*). They decided almost right away that no confrontation could occur on the street. Instead, Simon—and it had to be Simon: our covers were blown—would wait inside the building while we acted as lookouts in the van. Lindsay (Keith always sent a girl in) wouldn't be hard to spot, as she'd be carrying the silver suitcase in a large messenger bag—a suitcase she would carefully carry upstairs, then place in the back of a storage closet across the hall from the chairman's office.

"But it'll never get that far," Simon said. "I'll stop her on the ground floor."

"What if she won't hand it over?" I asked.

"She will."

We took a break in the late afternoon, then went over everything again, and again, until it felt like I knew the National News Network's every back office and storage closet. And I wouldn't even be going inside. Finally, Simon proclaimed us as ready as we'd ever be, and we all reached for the cigarettes at once. We spent our last hour in that morbid room erasing any trace of ourselves. Even I pitched in, having witnessed this drill before. It was dark when we were done, darker still when Paige and I snuck down the staircase and out the basement door into Mechanics Alley. Simon, who'd got a head start, was waiting in his van. I'd seen it any number of times, parked around the side of my mother's house, but—how was this possible?—I'd never been inside. It was a typical workman's van, brown and battered, with tinted glass and rear doors that opened out. Simon used it to transport the raw materials of his art, but not until I climbed into the back did I realize the van was outfitted to serve another purpose as well. For what I saw looked more like the decked-out cabin of a modern yacht. Small appliances were tucked snugly under a cushioned sleeping bench, and behind the passenger's seat sat a built-in media system—TV, stereo, and wires running every which way. Two sleek walkie-talkies rested in specially made bases, and Paige knelt to pick one up.

"We used this type in Carolina," she said. "They were indispensable."

"I know, I sent them down there," Simon answered, putting the van in gear. "They're GPS enabled. And dead silent when they need to be."

Then we were moving. I took a seat on the bench while Paige balanced like a surfer in front of a tiny mirror and started applying heavy makeup, mounds of shine and shadow. We'd be continuing on to Jersey afterward, no matter what happened at N3, and Simon, worried about bridge and tunnel checkpoints, had insisted Paige and I leave the island separately. He would drive me in the van (they wouldn't be looking for two men), while Paige took the PATH to Jersey City, where we'd pick her up. It was risky, hence her transformation—this time into a suburban girl coming home from a late night at the clubs. "*You* won't even recognize me," she had said, and now, as I watched the makeover progress, I realized how right she was.

I, meanwhile, was wearing the same hoodie and jeans I'd had on for two days. My hair looked like an art installation dreamed up by a Cure fan.

"Should I do anything?" I asked, pinching my sweatshirt.

Paige regarded me through the darkness.

"You're fine like that. Your outfit goes with the van. Blue-collar on the outside."

From Canal Street we turned onto busy Sixth Avenue. Simon kept the radio off. The task before us was the only thing, and already there were glimpses of trouble—a cluster of cops standing on the corner of West Fourth, another group at Fourteenth. We kept to the middle lane, even when others opened up. Was it normal, this show of force? What about the squad cars parked side by side in Herald Square? Or the police van pulled up onto the Bryant Park sidewalk? I'd never noticed so many cops, but then again, I'd never been looking for them. Not like this. Simon didn't seem overly worried, so maybe this was just an average night. The thought gave me pause. What would I have been doing at 9:30 p.m. on an average Thursday night? I'd be at a couples dinner party in Boerum Hill, having been dragged there by Cressida and told to behave; or barhopping with bloggers through the last of the Alphabet City dives; or lounging on plush couches in the parlor room at Norwood, or the roof of Soho House, or, inevitably, Touché's apartment. Waiting for the light back at Fourteenth Street, I'd imagined flinging the van doors open and escaping to Café Loup or Bar Six. I knew the bartenders there, and at a half dozen other Village spots. But it was much too late for that.

And I didn't miss it anyway.

"How do I look?" Paige asked, grabbing my arm. Her eyes were swamped in blackness. She had cheeks like a geisha's. And her outfit: she'd slipped on a (Club Monaco) miniskirt and torn her tank top in all the right spots. And still, her lips carried the moment. They were a deep scarlet and looked as sticky as a stamp. She laughed. "Ridiculous, I know."

"I'd hardly say—"

"Okay," Simon called from up front. "Keep your eyes open for a place to park." We both moved forward and knelt behind the center console. Simon had turned left and was heading west on Fifty-first Street. Up ahead, spotlit like a launching pad, stood the eerie black hulk of N3's worldwide headquarters. We slowed down. The only legal parking was on the opposite side of the street, but it didn't matter: all the spots were taken anyway. We drove slowly past—glancing at the wedged-open exit door—and began circling the block.

"What about cameras?" I asked. "Can't they trace the van if we park too close?"

"It's got dead plates," Paige and Simon said at exactly the same time. They both grinned, which made me feel better.

We found a space the second time around. It wasn't perfect—a delivery truck parked in front of us blocked out the driver-side sight lines—but the person in the passenger seat would still have an unobstructed view of the building. Simon backed us in.

"What if Lindsay's in disguise?" he asked. "Changed her hair again or something."

"I'll still recognize her," Paige said.

Unbuckling his seat belt, Simon reached into the compartment between the two front seats and held up a pair of compact binoculars. "Here, these should help." With that, he slipped into the back and checked the mirror, though he hardly had to. In his ball cap, untucked shirt, and faded jeans, he was the very embodiment of a sleep-deprived overnight producer. The three of us leaned in close and went over everything one last time. Then we moved on to the equipment. Paige climbed up front and focused the binoculars on the building while Simon tested the two-way radios. Satisfied, he put one into his pocket and placed the other on the console between the two front seats. Then he wrote down the address of the farm in Bernardsville, New Jersey.

"Just in case," he said, handing me the piece of paper.

When the sidewalk was clear, Simon hopped out. We watched him walk briskly toward the smokers' door, where four studio-tech types— three men and a woman—stood in a loose circle, puffing away. None of them looked up as he went past and disappeared inside.

Paige stayed in the shotgun seat, so I climbed behind the wheel. Several minutes went by before I realized I was still clutching the address, crumpled and damp from my sweating hand. I smoothed it out and laid it on the dash. Paige glanced at it, then went back to watching the door through the binoculars. I, in turn, watched her, or a vaguely pornographic version of her. For her transformation was unnervingly entire, right down to the jangling plastic bracelets (where had she found those?) and hair clips. She was sitting that way again, one leg brought up against her chest, only now her legs were bare, her skirt running up her thigh. That I could think like that just then. But it was the last familiar feeling left, the only carryover from that life to this one. Paige was immediate, and all else was finished or to come. Cars flashed past. Lights changed. The city stuck on end-less repeat. I'd broken that cycle. A kid who believed in the impor-tance of nonbelief, the essentialness of inaction. I closed my eyes and was soon engulfed in one of those vague circle-of-life ideas, this one about the far side, where pure selfishness joined its direct opposite, arms locked in mutual disregard for the system at the center. But, no, I was only trying to explain all this away. And you can't explain love.

A red light flashed on the walkie-talkie lying between us. I nudged Paige. She picked it up and pressed the TALK button. "Go ahead," she said softly.

"I'm in an empty storage room on the ground floor," Simon whis-pered. The reception was static-free. His voice was electric. "It's all lights and rigging. Should be safe for now. Any sign?"

"Not yet," Paige said. "I'll let you know."

"Okay."

She put the radio down and resumed her watch, relating what she saw, the smokers coming and going, never more than three or four at a time. Soon, she fell silent. On the sidewalk beside me, well-dressed couples passed with increasing regularity. Dinners were ending, the-aters emptying. The city I'd known.

Keith suddenly seemed like a myth.

I heard Paige say my name, and for a moment it didn't register. But when I turned to her, she was staring at me. "I just . . . I just wanted to let you know," she started, "that I'm really sorry about Julian. I know what it's like to be betrayed by someone you trust. It's the loneliest feeling in the world."

"I guess he was caught in a tough position," I said. But the words had barely escaped before I wished I could take them back. Cressida I could have predicted, but Touché's betrayal had been so stunning and complete that I had, until that moment, refused to accept it as fact. Instead, I'd decided Drudge must have got it wrong, that my "acquain-tance" wasn't ratting me out, but trying somehow to warn me, to save me. But, no, Touché was only saving himself. He'd traveled with me as far as distraction and mild adventure would allow, then run back home to hide. All these years I'd reveled in his soothing self-assurance and celebrated the vague mysteries of his life, as if not knowing him, never *questioning* him, would make us closer. Which is how I'd ended up with a best friend I barely knew. Why had this never bothered me before? Perhaps because it was hardly unique. My world was full of such friendships; it was the basis of the modern urban bargain—that we could flutter in and out of each other's lives like moths, as long, of course, as we kept to the light, the inconsequential, the marginalia. As long, in other words, as we never truly came to know anyone.

I shook off the thought. Beside me, Paige was beginning to fidget. When the walkie-talkie lit up again, she grabbed it impatiently. "Go ahead."

"Anything?" Simon's voice was measured but insistent.

"No."

"You're sure?"

"*Yes.*"

"Maybe they've come and gone."

"Or they're not coming at all," Paige said. "It's almost midnight." She held the radio up, awaiting a response, but none came. "*Simon?*" she whispered tentatively.

"I'm here, I'm here," he said after a moment. "Just had to check the studio, make sure I was alone. I'm going up to the sixth floor to look around. It'll be fine. There won't be anyone up there."

"Well, be careful." Paige put the radio down. She smiled a bit sadly. "Jesus, I sound like my mother."

"No one ever asks how *you're* holding up," I said.

"Not too much, no." She peered through the binoculars again. "Bobby used to."

"Well, *I'm* asking."

Paige brought the lenses to her lap and gazed out the passenger window. Her eyes were wet, but I didn't see the tears until she wiped them away from her upper lip, smudging the layers of gloss she'd applied. "Shit," she said, pulling down the mirrored visor. She dug the lipstick out of her pocket and handed me the binoculars. "Will you watch the building a second?"

I leaned over the center divider, so as to see around the delivery truck. Two new smokers were standing outside the exit door—a man holding a pizza and a woman talking to him. I saw the woman rub her bare arms. The temperature was dropping. The lenses were so powerful that if the man had opened the pizza box, I could have named the toppings. But I couldn't concentrate. Paige was only a few inches away. I could smell the gloss, hear her pursing her lips. I didn't want to move, lest the moment pass. Did she sense it, too? The anxious tug. The sensation of flight. And now her breath, steady and assured. I could feel it on my cheek.

"Aidan," she whispered, her voice a harmony line, searching for accompaniment.

I lowered the lenses, my prop, and turned to her in what seemed like slow motion. What came next? Her hand, light on my arm, I'm sure, though what I remember were her lips, delicate and freshly painted, grazing mine. I kissed her back, her lower lip soft and red as a bull's-eye, lingering between my teeth, below my tongue, our tongues, the moment suspended, a twisted take on that great American tableau: two kids in a parked car, fumbling around in the dark . . .

"*Not now,*" she sighed, pulling away.

"What? Sorry."

"The radio, I mean." The red light was on. Paige picked it up, pressed the button. "Go ahead."

Simon's breathing came through the small speaker. "*We're late,*" he hissed.

"*What?*"

"*The device. It's already here, in the closet.*"

"Is it armed?" Paige asked, her voice suddenly cool again, methodical.

"Looks like it. Hold on." Paige held the walkie-talkie away from her, as if it were suddenly a threat, until Simon's voice returned with a low crackle. "Yeah, it's good to go. Keith didn't color-code the wiring, but I think I can still defuse it."

"Are you sure?"

"Well, it's been a while, but—"

"Leave it then," Paige said. "Leave it and come back down. We'll call the cops."

"No, no, I can do this. But it's too dark in here. I need to move it into the office across the hall."

"*Simon . . .*"

"It's okay, no one's around. Just give me a minute." The radio went dead.

"They've already been there?" I asked, half-stunned, as I tried to add it all up.

Paige nodded. "Keith must have known someone would try to stop him—Simon or me or the Feds. I guess Lindsay snuck inside and planted it while we were still downtown. We must have just missed her. Here, start the car. When Simon's finished, I'll tell him to come down and meet us on the corner of—"

The light came first, a brilliant, blinding flash, all white and burning yellow, followed by the sound, like a deep sonic boom, dull for how close it was. The ground shook, then there was silence—always silence in these things—a second or two that burrowed into me forever. It was shattered by falling glass, then everything was falling, like before, hurtling down from a great height as if the city itself were coming apart. And, of course, it was, everything was—

"Go, go, just drive."

I stepped on the gas and hit the truck in front of us, I remember that much, then Paige was half out the window, looking plaintively up at the gaping hole, the missing chunk of tower, but the smoke was already too thick, and somewhere the sirens were starting, the sirens and the screams, from the building, from the street, and it was all I could do to dodge the detritus, the random debris, and steer us away from the falling world.

PAIGE

· · · ● ● ● ● ● ● ● · · ● ●

FOR A LONG TIME I WAS IN COLUMBUS, OHIO, LIVING ON THE SECOND FLOOR OF a narrow Weinland Park duplex five blocks from OSU. The neighborhood lay like swamp water in the tall shadows of the campus, stagnant and blighted by a profusion of drugs and a lack of anything else. By day, people loitered on stoops or went fitfully about their business—what business they had—no heads raised, no questions asked. By night, booming hip-hop provided a sound track to the drunken howls of students and the panicked cries of victims, to the sirens and occasional gunshots ringing out from what little Section 8 housing the city hadn't yet razed. My block was a fault line between worlds—ivory towers and rotting porches, progress and its opposite, and of course, all the transience and shiftlessness made it the perfect place to hide out, to remain invisible.

I was living as Isabel Clarke and everything was in order—my papers, my backstory, even my appearance (blond now: why not?). My handler was a kid whose parents had spent time in prison for their revolutionary sins. That he was young (twenty-five?), male, and in obvious awe of recent events was initially worrying, but he was sweet and sincere. And he appeared trustworthy. Anyway, I could hardly send him back. I took my chances and settled down to work.

What I started writing—three months ago now—was an explanation for my actions. What it threatened to become was something else entirely. Because *I* had become someone else. And I don't mean Isabel Clarke. I mean that I had changed, evolved, on the *inside,* and fleshing out the events of my recent life began to help me understand exactly how. Everything had happened so quickly—a single year bookended by death—and I needed time. Aidan, I believed, and *still* believe, was writing his own story, and that made a seemingly futile exercise—for who will read these words unless something goes horribly wrong or wonderfully right?—potently worthwhile. There we were, two kids from disparate backgrounds, sifting through the rubble of our culture for hints on how to live, how to survive, what to give in to, and what to fight for. Because the American playbook had been thrown out. This, anyway, is what I envisioned, an examination of the self, a journey with, if not a happy ending, then at least a kind of moral conclusion. Something to point to. Unfortunately, as must be obvious by now, I never got that far. Such were my circumstances: I couldn't even write about a life interrupted without getting interrupted writing.

So what happened? I'd been feeling safe enough to start venturing out to the bookstores and coffee shops on nearby High Street, places thick with oblivious students, their strange collective force enshrouding me. One afternoon, on my way home, I spotted my handler walking with another guy, a postgrad type, half a block ahead of me. That's fine, I thought; the kid has a life. Still, I followed them as they turned left on Chittenden, then right onto my street. They walked two blocks south and stopped within sight of my apartment. That's when my handler pointed. It was subtle but unmistakable: he pointed right at my bedroom window. And his friend? He nodded slowly, as if this solved some kind of mystery. What was going on? Only one explanation made sense: I was about to be handed off to someone new.

The next morning, I walked to the Internet café I'd begun frequenting and found an open computer near the back. I was working there because the secondhand laptop I'd been given had died and my handler had yet to bring me a new one. It was a risk, I knew, but I couldn't just sit home doing nothing. Anyway, I'd come to enjoy the machinations of the writing life—coffee, smoking breaks, *time* . . . the idea of measurable progress, if only on-screen. I wrote in Word, saving each day's work onto a removable flash drive and deleting any evidence on the computer itself. It wasn't a perfect system, as there'd still be traces of what I'd written on the hard drive. But unless someone knew where—and how—to look, he or she wouldn't find anything.

The café was a little way off the main drag, so it was never too crowded. Even better, the computers in the rear offered not just privacy, but an unobstructed view through the front window. And that's where I was gazing as I pondered a critical part of the narrative—my confrontation with Aidan on Weehawken Street—when I suddenly saw him again, my handler's friend. He was standing on the sidewalk directly outside the shop, studying the awning, then peering down at a notepad, as if confirming an address. He looked like a typical student, in Abercrombie and loose jeans, but something wasn't right. He looked *too* typical, *too* forced—like a Mormon dressing hip for Halloween. Did he walk inside? I don't know: I was already out the back door. Two sightings in two days were quite enough for me.

I should say something about the Movement, which is no longer a movement at all (if it ever was one). It has no unified goal. It's not *moving* toward anything, really. Yet, it is real, and effective, and has already saved my life several times. Who are they? They are the end of an ideal. I'm talking about a few hundred people—activists and yuppies, boomers and students, black and white. They are extremely tuned-in and pleasantly tuned-out. They are not whom you'd expect.

What they have in common is each other. If they once charged barricades, they now work covertly, tending to the more daring among us, those willing to act. They feed us and clothe us and move us around. They solve impossible problems. When the bomb exploded that night at N3, something clicked, something deep and instinctive. I knew where we had to go, and that we'd be taken care of when we got there. We were in shock, of course—not the ringing shock of close-quarters detonation (we were far enough away to avoid that), but the deeper, more searing shock of sudden, life-altering loss. Simon was gone. Parts of three floors had been decimated, and Aidan drove through the burning debris as if he'd once driven through war zones for a living. Neither one of us turned to look at what remained. Instead, we pressed on, plan in place, down the West Side Highway, not speaking, not yet. I checked my makeup in the mirror as Aidan dipped back into the city to drop me off at the Ninth Street PATH Station (the Christopher Street stop was too close to his old apartment). When he pulled up to the curb, he kept looking straight ahead. I opened the door and got out, the city that far south still blissfully ignorant of the carnage uptown.

Journal Square in half an hour, I said.

Journal Square, Aidan repeated.

Hey. I leaned back in through the open door. We'll be okay.

Aidan turned to me then, and I saw in his eyes that he wasn't scared. He'd be there on the other side of the river.

The Movement took care of us. In Bernardsville and then Trenton. A colonial mansion on Philadelphia's Main Line, and an apartment near the Warhol Museum in Pittsburgh. We traveled at night, like desert Bedouins, like fleeing slaves. Many were old friends of Simon's, men and women who'd once stood by his side while attempting the impossible, and they fought their ingrained reluctance to ask questions with a very human need to understand what had happened to their former comrade. They wanted some kind of closure. Aidan and I accommodated them as best we could. In the press, we were—and still are—the only suspects, but these people knew the real story. For they knew about Keith. They'd been his believers and benefactors. Now, though, they called him a traitor, an egotist, even a nihilist, and he was all of these things. But in the end he was a genius, too, and this was also grudgingly acknowledged. Facts were facts: despite the contents of the N3 bomb, Simon had been the only casualty. He'd been the only person in the vicinity of the explosion, and had he not disrupted the natural course of events, Keith's plan would have worked to perfection. Would have worked . . . and *has* worked. Just look at N3 now, as post-attack sympathy has turned, in the wake of the network's heavy-handed reaction, to a broad-based condemnation of the company—their bias, their tone, their agenda—and the broader industry as a whole. Just like Indigo.

But at what price? Simon is dead. A man as good as any I've known. And what has he left behind? The heartbreak of a woman outside Woodstock. The aspirations of a Movement outside time. And Aidan.

He's left Aidan.

As far as I knew, this was the first great loss of his life, and I watched him carefully in the long days that followed—days of chaos and constant anxiety. It was overwhelming for him. Julian and then Simon. Deceit and then death. We were all to blame. And we were all innocent. The world held no absolutes—I'd learned that the hard way—and those who believed otherwise were fooling themselves. Yes, a man was dead, *only* one man, and still the loss was horrific. My brother had been one man, too. One death can mean so much.

I think about it all the time, the moment good intentions become something else, something less. Aidan and I were separated after Pittsburgh. It was the only way. We were all over the news, and traveling together had become impossible. We said good-bye at a truck stop—there is symmetry in life—just a few moments alone in a parking lot, one last embrace. We were aiming for stoicism and almost got there. Then it was time to move. Always, it was time to move.

I snuck out of that café in Columbus and never turned around. For weeks, I stayed in lodging houses and roadside motels. I took Greyhound buses and commuter trains, sleeping, when I slept, at an angle, away from the aisle. Paducah. Memphis. Fort Smith. I was riding the American backbone vaguely west, as if pulled, like countless millions before me, toward some mythical promised land. I had coded phone numbers in my pocket, lifelines I'd been given here and there, but after Ohio I felt safer on my own. Still, I knew it was only a matter of time. My face was everywhere, and I was cold and tired and broke.

One shivering morning, in Joplin, Missouri, I walked out of a foul, stinking YWCA and called a number in Chicago.

Another booth in another diner, this one just west of Gary, Indiana. He recognized me with unsettling ease. He was, I'd been told, one of the original Weathermen, and as I slid in across from him, I could tell right away that he'd known Simon. We ordered coffee. He called me Isabel, and for a few minutes we caught each other up on relatives we didn't have. When he was satisfied I hadn't been followed, he left a tip on the table and we walked out to his car. I half-expected him to tell me it was over, that I should turn myself in—as he once surely had—and hope for the best. Instead, he said I had options. There were other cities, other countries. We drove to his home in the southwestern suburbs of Chicago, and I took a shower and cleaned up. I told him a night of solid rest would be enough. Anything more, considering who he was, would be too dangerous. He said he understood.

We reconvened in his modest living room, over pasta and beer. I was wary, at first, of talking about what had happened, but I shouldn't have been. He had more than a passing knowledge of recent events. He knew about Simon's network, and the details of the Actions they'd carried out. He even knew about Columbus.

The man you saw outside the coffee shop was a Federal agent acting on a tip, my new friend said, but he somehow convinced your young handler that he was one of *us*—a member of the Movement sent by higher-ups to look after you.

You're kidding, I said, momentarily shocked at how right my instincts had been.

I wish I were. But you, more than anyone, should know that we're never safe. Our beliefs, our mistakes . . . they stay with us when all the rest fades away. Look at me. He raised his arms—exhibiting the extent of his small apartment, his compromised life, everything reduced by his past—and shook his head. Simon Krauss was the only person I've met who succeeded so thoroughly at being someone else, he said.

And there it was: Simon. The subject that could no longer be ignored. The awful irony of his death: the work of a laced bomb, like the town house forty years before. Wires crossed. Lines crossed.

I asked my host where Aidan was.

I have no idea, he said.

Is he all right?

And even if I did, I couldn't talk about it.

Please. I need to know.

The man sighed and changed the subject.

We should get you to the West Coast, he said. We have people in place out there. And you need time to regroup. You've been through a lot.

He grabbed a napkin and jotted down the name of a town, along with some contact information. I'd never heard of the place. What about San Francisco? I asked.

Too risky.

He was right, I knew. Yet I so badly needed to be around people. The thought of being sequestered somewhere remote was crushing.

I asked then if he might get word to my parents. Let them know I was okay. That I loved them. That I was sorry. He said he would, and I could tell he meant it.

In the morning, he drove me to the Greyhound station in Joliet, and soon I was on the road again. Through Illinois and Iowa, then an ice storm in Lincoln, Nebraska. The duffel bag at my feet said TEXAS IS GOD'S COUNTRY, but surely this was, this rolling world outside the window. Still, I couldn't take my mind off Aidan. I should never have gone to Weehawken Street. I should have said no a thousand times. What was he was writing? I wondered. An indictment, surely, a denunciation—of me. For I'd ruined his life. I stared out at a dark, starless night, the journey dragging endlessly on, mocking the memories of our days and nights together, of things I should have said and didn't. Somewhere near North Platte, I finally fell asleep, my forehead hard against the frosted glass.

When I woke, it was light outside, or almost light, and I dug around in my bag until I found my notebook and a pen. It had been weeks since I'd done any writing, and as I wondered if I should pick up where I'd left off—those first hours in his apartment—I realized, again, what an incredible chance Aidan had taken. He was a man brave enough, in this doctrinaire world, to change his thinking, to walk away from everything he knew for everything he didn't. Now, he was out there somewhere, enduring a life he'd never asked for. I wondered then about the chapters to come, mine and his, the unfolding annals of America, grand proclamations giving way to intimate emotion, loss ceding to love.

Because that's what I feel. I know it now.

If only I'd had a chance to make it right, find him as he'd found me, and save him the same way. Cheyenne, Laramie, Rock Springs. I wrote all morning, and in the early afternoon I looked outside and saw mountains. White mountains, then a white city. I no longer knew what day it was. I no longer cared. We came in past strange, soulless suburbs, the houses pale as the snow, and not until we'd pulled up to the station did I realize I was in downtown Salt Lake.

We were changing buses. I gazed up at the departure board. There was one leaving for San Francisco. *The place you ended up when you could run no further.* Had I reached that point? Certainly, I was close. But I needed to finish the story—to think and write without the world coming at me.

So I got on a bus heading north instead: I-84 up through Idaho and Oregon. And that's where I am as I write this now, sitting in a window seat watching this sprawling country race endlessly by, away from itself, its history, its wars. Only I'm the one who's moving—or the bus anyway—and it's better that way, to stop dwelling on the past, to head somewhere hopeful. I just pulled the napkin out of my pocket and looked at the contact names. My new handlers, Jim and Carol. I'll call them from a pay phone when I get closer.

ACKNOWLEDGMENTS

MANY THANKS TO NAN GRAHAM, SUSAN MOLDOW, KATIE MONAGHAN, PAUL O'Halloran, Whitney Frick, and Scribner's boy-wonder, Paul Whitlatch, who made this book both possible and infinitely better.

To my talented agent provocateur, Kate Garrick, who answers all my calls, against her better judgment.

To my parents, whose bemused support is much appreciated.

And to my friends/family, thanks for all the wit and wisdom: Roberta Lee Webb, Jami Attenberg, Michael Balser, Joan Bingham, Jodi Bullock, Richard Colantuono, Amanda Cordano, Laura Dave, Brian DeFiore, Jason Dobson, Emily Edson, Leonard Ellis, Marion Ettlinger, Holley Fain, Catherine Foulkrod, David Gates, Ana Mena-Gonçalves, Janie Goodwillie, Steve Goodwillie, Ken Hamm, Amy Hempel, Jason Herrick, Erin Hosier, Bradfield Hughes, Brandon Kennedy, Patrick Knisley, Ginger Knowlton, Brooke Laundon, Catherine Lewis, David Lynn, Kirsten Manges, John Manley, Alex Marvar, Josh Morgan, Lisa Myers, Patrick Nicholson, Sarah Norris, Jack O'Neill, Kevin Raidy, Anna Duke Reach, Leslie Robarge, Stephen Rodrick, Sue Shapiro, Scott Sherman, Zack Sultan, Eliza Swann, Gay Talese, Sofia Talvik, Benjamin Taylor, Larry Templeton, Keleigh Thomas, Moe Tkacik, Danielle Trussoni, the Van Kempens of Dordogne, France, and my friends at Café Loup.